T0104241

# Romantic and Horrific Stories

# Romantic and Horrific Stories

Bram Stoker

MINT EDITIONS

*Romantic and Horrific Stories* features work first published between 1872–1915.

This edition published by Mint Editions 2022.

ISBN 9781513211329 | E-ISBN 9781513210124

Published by Mint Editions®

MINT
EDITIONS

minteditionbooks.com

Publishing Director: Jennifer Newens
Design & Production: Rachel Lopez Metzger
Project Manager: Micaela Clark
Typesetting: Westchester Publishing Services

More in This Series:
Weird and Horrific Stories
Mysterious and Horrific Stories
Fantastic and Horrific Stories
Scientific and Horrific Stories

# TABLE OF CONTENTS

# The Chain of Destiny

## I. A Warning

IT WAS SO LATE IN the evening when I arrived at Scarp that I had but little opportunity of observing the external appearance of the house; but, as far as I could judge in the dim twilight, it was a very stately edifice of seemingly great age, built of white stone. When I passed the porch, however, I could observe its internal beauties much more closely, for a large wood fire burned in the hall and all the rooms and passages were lighted. The hall was almost baronial in its size, and opened on to a staircase of dark oak so wide and so generous in its slope that a carriage might almost have been driven up it. The rooms were large and lofty, with their walls, like those of the staircase, panelled with oak black from age. This sombre material would have made the house intensely gloomy but for the enormous width and height of both rooms and passages. As it was, the effect was a homely combination of size and warmth. The windows were set in deep embrasures, and, on the ground story, reached from quite level with the floor to almost the ceiling. The fireplaces were quite in the old style, large and surrounded with massive oak carvings, representing on each some scene from Biblical history, and at the side of each fireplace rose a pair of massive carved iron fire-dogs. It was altogether just such a house as would have delighted the heart of Washington Irving or Nathaniel Hawthorne.

The house had been lately restored; but in effecting the restoration comfort had not been forgotten, and any modern improvement which tended to increase the homelike appearance of the rooms had been added. The old diamond-paned casements, which had remained probably from the Elizabethan age, had given place to more useful plate glass; and, in like manner, many other changes had taken place. But so judiciously had every change been effected that nothing of the new clashed with the old, but the harmony of all the parts seemed complete.

I thought it no wonder that Mrs. Trevor had fallen in love with Scarp the first time she had seen it. Mrs. Trevor's liking the place was tantamount to her husband's buying it, for he was so wealthy that he could get almost anything money could purchase. He was himself a man of good taste, but still he felt his inferiority to his wife in this respect so much that he never dreamt of differing in opinion from her on any matter of choice or judgment. Mrs. Trevor had, without exception, the best taste of anyone whom I ever knew, and, strange to say, her taste was not confined to any branch of art. She did not write, or paint, or sing; but still her judgment in writing, painting, or music, was unquestioned by her friends. It seemed as if nature had denied to her the power of execution in any separate branch of art, in order to make her perfect in her appreciation of what was beautiful and true in all. She was perfect in the art of harmonising—the art of everyday life. Her husband used to say, with a far-fetched joke, that her star must have been in the House of Libra, because everything which she said and did showed such a nicety of balance.

Mr. and Mrs. Trevor were the most model couple I ever knew—they really seemed not twain, but one. They appeared to have adopted something of the French idea of man and wife—that they should not be the less like friends because they were linked together by indissoluble bonds—that they should share their pleasures as well as their sorrows. The former outbalanced the latter, for both husband and wife were of that happy temperament which can take pleasure from everything, and find consolation even in the chastening rod of affliction.

Still, through their web of peaceful happiness ran a thread of care. One that cropped up in strange places, and disappeared again, but which left a quiet tone over the whole fabric—they had no child.

> *"They had their share of sorrow, for when time was ripe*
> *The still affection of the heart became an outward breathing type,*
> *That into stillness passed again,*
> *But left a want unknown before."*

There was something simple and holy in their patient endurance of their lonely life—for lonely a house must ever be without children to those who love truly. Theirs was not the eager, disappointed longing of those whose union had proved fruitless. It was the simple, patient, hopeless resignation of those who find that a common sorrow draws them more closely together than many common joys. I myself could note the warmth of their hearts and their strong philoprogenitive feeling in their manner towards me.

From the time when I lay sick in college when Mrs. Trevor appeared to my fever-dimmed eyes like an angel of mercy, I felt myself growing in their hearts. Who can imagine my gratitude to the lady who, merely because she heard of my sickness and desolation from a college friend, came and nursed me night and day till the fever left me. When I was sufficiently strong to be moved she had me brought away to the country, where good air, care, and attention soon made me stronger than ever. From that time I became a constant visitor at the Trevors' house; and as month after month rolled by I felt that I was growing in their affections. For four summers I spent my long vacation in their house, and each year I could feel Mr. Trevor's shake of the hand grow heartier, and his wife's kiss on my forehead—for so she always saluted me—grow more tender and motherly.

Their liking for me had now grown so much that in their heart of hearts—and it was a sanctum common to them both—they secretly loved me as a son. Their love was returned manifold by the lonely boy, whose devotion to the kindest friends of his youth and his trouble had increased with his growth into manhood. Even in my own heart I was ashamed to confess how I loved them both—how I worshipped Mrs. Trevor as I adored the mother whom I had lost so young, and whose eyes shone sometimes even then upon me, like stars, in my sleep.

It is strange how timorous we are when our affections are concerned. Merely because I had never told her how I loved her as a mother, because she had never told me how she loved me as a son, I used sometimes to think of her with a sort of lurking suspicion that I was trusting too much to my imagination. Sometimes even I would try to avoid thinking of her altogether, till my yearning would grow too strong to be repelled, and then I would think of her long and silently, and would love her more and more. My life was so lonely that I clung to her as the only thing I had to love. Of course I loved her husband, too, but I never thought about him in the same way; for men are less demonstrative about their affections to each other, and even acknowledge them to themselves less.

Mrs. Trevor was an excellent hostess. She always let her guests see that they were welcome, and, unless in the case of casual visitors, that they were expected. She was, as may be imagined, very popular with all classes; but what is more rare, she was equally popular with both sexes. To be popular with her own sex is the touchstone of a woman's worth. To the houses of the peasantry she came, they said, like an angel, and brought comfort wherever she came. She knew the proper way to deal with the poor; she always helped them materially, but never offended their feelings in so doing. Young people all adored her.

My curiosity had been aroused as to the sort of place Scarp was; for, in order to give me a surprise, they would not tell me anything about it, but said that I must wait and judge it for myself. I had looked forward to my visit with both expectation and curiosity.

When I entered the hall, Mrs. Trevor came out to welcome me and kissed me on the forehead, after her usual manner. Several of the old servants came near, smiling and bowing, and wishing welcome to "Master Frank." I shook hands with several of them, whilst their mistress looked on with a pleased smile.

As we went into a snug parlour, where a table was laid out with the materials for a comfortable supper, Mrs. Trevor said to me:

"I am glad you came so soon, Frank. We have no one here at present, so you will be quite alone with us for a few days; and you will be quite alone with me this evening, for Charley is gone to a dinner-party at Westholm."

I told her that I was glad that there was no one else at Scarp, for that I would rather be with her and her husband than anyone else in the world. She smiled as she said:

"Frank, if anyone else said that, I would put it down as a mere compliment; but I know you always speak the truth. It is all very well to be alone with an old couple like Charley and me for two or three days; but just you wait till Thursday, and you will look on the intervening days as quite wasted."

"Why?" I inquired.

"Because, Frank, there is a girl coming to stay with me then, with whom I intend you to fall in love."

I answered jocosely:

"Oh, thank you, Mrs. Trevor, very much for your kind intentions—but suppose for a moment that they should be impracticable. 'One man may lead a horse to the pond's brink.' 'The best laid schemes o' mice an' men.' Eh?"

"Frank, don't be silly. I do not want to make you fall in love against your inclination; but I hope and I believe that you will."

"Well, I'm sure I hope you won't be disappointed; but I never yet heard a person praised that I did not experience a disappointment when I came to know him or her."

"Frank, did I praise anyone?"

"Well, I am vain enough to think that your saying that you knew I would fall in love with her was a sort of indirect praise."

"Dear, me, Frank, how modest you have grown. 'A sort of indirect praise!' Your humility is quite touching."

"May I ask who the lady is, as I am supposed to be an interested party?"

"I do not know that I ought to tell you on account of your having expressed any doubt as to her merits. Besides, I might weaken the effect of the introduction. If I stimulate your curiosity it will be a point in my favour."

"Oh, very well; I suppose I must only wait?"

"Ah, well, Frank, I will tell you. It is not fair to keep you waiting. She is a Miss Fothering."

"Fothering? Fothering? I think I know that name. I remember hearing it somewhere, a long time ago, if I do not mistake. Where does she come from?"

"Her father is a clergyman in Norfolk, but he belongs to the Warwickshire family. I met her at Winthrop, Sir Harry Blount's place, a few months ago, and took a great liking for her, which she returned, and so we became fast friends. I made her promise to pay me a visit this summer, so she and her sister are coming here on Thursday to stay for sometime."

"And, may I be bold enough to inquire what she is like?"

"You may inquire if you like, Frank; but you won't get an answer. I shall not try to describe her. You must wait and judge for yourself."

"Wait," said I, "three whole days? How can I do that? Do, tell me."

She remained firm to her determination. I tried several times in the course of the evening to find out something more about Miss Fothering, for my curiosity was roused; but all the answer I could get on the subject was—"Wait, Frank; wait, and judge for yourself."

When I was bidding her goodnight, Mrs. Trevor said to me—

"By-the-bye, Frank, you will have to give up the room which you will sleep in tonight, after tomorrow. I will have such a full house that I cannot let you have a doubled-bedded room all to yourself; so I will give that room to the Miss Fotherings, and move you up to the second floor. I just want you to see the room, as it has a romantic look about it, and has all the old furniture that was in it when we came here. There are several pictures in it worth looking at."

My bedroom was a large chamber—immense for a bedroom—with two windows opening level with the floor, like those of the parlours and drawing rooms. The furniture was old-fashioned, but not old enough to be curious, and on the walls hung many pictures—portraits—the house was full of portraits—and landscapes. I just glanced at these, intending to examine them in the morning, and went to bed. There was a fire in the room, and I lay awake for sometime looking dreamily at the shadows of the furniture flitting over the walls and ceiling as the flames of the wood fire leaped and fell, and the red embers dropped whitening on the hearth. I tried to give the rein to my thoughts, but they kept constantly to the one subject—the mysterious Miss Fothering, with whom I was to fall in love. I was sure that I had heard her name somewhere, and I had at times lazy recollections of a child's face. At such times I would start awake from my growing drowsiness, but before I could collect my scattered thoughts the idea had eluded me. I could remember neither when nor where I had heard the name, nor could I recall even the expression of the child's face. It must have been long, long ago, when I was young. When I was young my mother was alive. My mother—mother—mother. I found myself half awakening, and repeating the word over and over again. At last I fell asleep.

I thought that I awoke suddenly to that peculiar feeling which we sometimes have on starting from sleep, as if someone had been speaking in the room, and the voice is still echoing through it. All was quite silent, and the fire had gone out. I looked out of the window that lay straight opposite the foot of the bed, and observed a light outside, which gradually grew brighter till the room was almost as light as by day. The window looked like a picture in the framework formed by the cornice over the foot of the bed, and the massive pillars shrouded in curtains which supported it.

With the new accession of light I looked round the room, but nothing was changed. All was as before, except that some of the objects of furniture and ornament were shown in stronger relief than hitherto. Amongst these, those most in relief were the other bed, which was placed across the room, and an old picture that hung on the wall at its foot. As the bed was merely the counterpart of the one in which I lay, my attention became fixed on the picture. I observed it closely and with great interest. It seemed old, and was the portrait of a young girl, whose face, though kindly and merry, bore signs of thought and a capacity for deep feeling—almost for passion. At some moments, as I looked at it, it called up before my mind a vision of Shakespeare's Beatrice, and once I thought of Beatrice Cenci. But this was probably caused by the association of ideas suggested by the similarity of names.

The light in the room continued to grow even brighter, so I looked again out of the window to seek its source, and saw there a lovely sight. It seemed as if there were grouped without the window three lovely children, who seemed to float in mid-air. The light seemed to spring from a point far behind them, and by their side was something dark and shadowy, which served to set off their radiance.

The children seemed to be smiling in upon something in the room, and, following their glances, I saw that their eyes rested upon the other bed. There, strange to say, the head which I had lately seen in the picture rested upon the pillow. I looked at the wall, but the frame was empty, the picture was gone. Then I looked at the bed again, and saw the young girl asleep, with the expression of her face constantly changing, as though she were dreaming.

As I was observing her, a sudden look of terror spread over her face, and she sat up like a sleep-walker, with her eyes wide open, staring out of the window.

Again turning to the window, my gaze became fixed, for a great and weird change had taken place. The figures were still there, but their features and expressions had become woefully different. Instead of the happy innocent look of childhood was one of malignity. With the change the children had grown old, and now three hags, decrepit and deformed, like typical witches, were before me.

But a thousand times worse than this transformation was the change in the dark mass that was near them. From a cloud, misty and undefined, it became a sort of shadow with a form. This gradually, as I looked, grew darker and fuller, till at length it made me shudder. There stood before me the phantom of the Fiend.

There was a long period of dead silence, in which I could hear the beating of my heart; but at length the phantom spoke to the others. His words seemed to issue from his lips mechanically, and without expression—"Tomorrow, and tomorrow, and tomorrow. The fairest and the best." He looked so awful that the question arose in my mind— "Would I dare to face him without the window—would anyone dare to go amongst those fiends?" A harsh, strident, diabolical laugh from without seemed to answer my unasked question in the negative.

But as well as the laugh I heard another sound—the tones of a sweet sad voice in despair coming across the room.

"Oh, alone, alone! is there no human thing near me? No hope—no hope. I shall go mad—or die."

The last words were spoken with a gasp.

I tried to jump out of bed, but could not stir, my limbs were bound in sleep. The young girl's head fell suddenly back upon the pillow, and the limp-hanging jaw and wide-open, purposeless mouth spoke but too plainly of what had happened.

Again I heard from without the fierce, diabolical laughter, which swelled louder and louder, till at last it grew so strong that in very horror I shook aside my sleep and sat up in bed, listened and heard a knocking at the door, but in another moment I became more awake, and knew that the sound came from the hall. It was, no doubt, Mr. Trevor returning from his party.

The hall-door was opened and shut, and then came a subdued sound of tramping and voices, but this soon died away, and there was silence throughout the house.

I lay awake for long thinking, and looking across the room at the picture and at the empty bed; for the moon now shone brightly, and the night was rendered still brighter by occasional flashes of summer lightning. At times the silence was broken by an owl screeching outside.

As I lay awake, pondering, I was very much troubled by what I had seen; but at length, putting several things together, I came to the conclusion that I had had a dream of a kind that might have been expected. The lightning, the knocking at the hall-door, the screeching of the owl, the empty bed, and the face in the picture, when grouped together, supplied materials for the main facts of the vision. The rest was, of course, the offspring of pure fancy, and the natural consequence of the component elements mentioned acting with each other in the mind.

I got up and looked out of the window, but saw nothing but the broad belt of moonlight glittering on the bosom of the lake, which extended miles and miles away, till its farther shore was lost in the night haze, and the green sward, dotted with shrubs and tall grasses, which lay between the lake and the house.

The vision had utterly faded. However, the dream—for so, I suppose, I should call it—was very powerful, and I slept no more till the sunlight was streaming broadly in at the window, and then I fell into a doze.

## II. More Links

LATE IN THE MORNING I was awakened by Parks, Mr. Trevor's man, who always used to attend on me when I visited my friends. He brought me hot water and the local news; and, chatting with him, I forgot for a time my alarm of the night.

Parks was staid and elderly, and a type of a class now rapidly disappearing—the class of old family servants who are as proud of their hereditary loyalty to their masters, as those masters are of name and rank. Like all old servants he had a great loving for all sorts of traditions. He believed them, and feared them, and had the most profound reverence for anything which had a story.

I asked him if he knew anything of the legendary history of Scarp. He answered with an air of doubt and hesitation, as of one carefully delivering an opinion which was still incomplete.

"Well, you see, Master Frank, that Scarp is so old that it must have any number of legends; but it is so long since it was inhabited that no one in the village remembers them. The place seems to have become in a kind of way forgotten, and died out of people's thoughts, and so I am very much afraid, sir, that all the genuine history is lost."

"What do you mean by the genuine history?" I inquired.

"Well, sir, I mean the true tradition, and not the inventions of the village folk. I heard the sexton tell some stories, but I am quite sure that they were not true, for I could see, Master Frank, that he did not believe them himself, but was only trying to frighten us."

"And could you not hear of any story that appeared to you to be true?"

"No, sir, and I tried very hard. You see, Master Frank, that there is a sort of club held every week in the tavern down in the village, composed of very respectable men, sir—very respectable men, indeed—and they asked me to be their chairman. I spoke to the master about it, and he gave me leave to accept their proposal. I accepted it as they made a point of it; and from my position I have of course a fine opportunity of making inquiries. It was at the club, sir, that I was, last night, so that I was not here to attend on you, which I hope that you will excuse."

Parks's air of mingled pride and condescension, as he made the announcement of the club, was very fine, and the effect was heightened by the confiding frankness with which he spoke. I asked him if he could find no clue to any of the legends which must have existed about such an old place. He answered with a very slight reluctance—

"Well, sir, there was one woman in the village who was awfully old and doting, and she evidently knew something about Scarp, for when she heard the name she mumbled out something about 'awful stories,' and 'times of horror,' and such like things, but I couldn't make her understand what it was I wanted to know, or keep her up to the point."

"And have you tried often, Parks? Why do you not try again?"

"She is dead, sir!"

I had felt inclined to laugh at Parks when he was telling me of the old woman. The way in which he gloated over the words "awful stories," and "times of horror," was beyond the power of description; it should have been heard and seen to have been properly appreciated. His voice became deep and mysterious, and he almost smacked his lips at the thought of so much pabulum for nightmares. But when he calmly told me that the woman was dead, a sense of blankness, mingled with awe, came upon me. Here, the last link between myself and the mysterious past was broken, never to be mended. All the rich stores of legend and tradition that had arisen from strange conjunctures of circumstances, and from the belief and imagination of long lines of villagers, loyal to their suzerain lord, were lost forever. I felt quite sad and disappointed; and no attempt was made either by Parks or myself to continue the conversation. Mr. Trevor came presently into my room, and having greeted each other warmly we went together to breakfast.

At breakfast Mrs. Trevor asked me what I thought of the girl's portrait in my bedroom. We had often had discussions as to characters in faces for we were both physiognomists, and she asked the question as if she were really curious to hear my opinion. I told her that I had only seen it for a short time, and so would rather not attempt to give a final opinion without a more careful study; but from what I had seen of it I had been favourably impressed.

"Well, Frank, after breakfast go and look at it again carefully, and then tell me exactly what you think about it."

After breakfast I did as directed and returned to the breakfast room, where Mrs. Trevor was still sitting.

"Well, Frank, what is your opinion-mind, correctly. I want it for a particular reason."

I told her what I thought of the girl's character; which, if there be any truth in physiognomy, must have been a very fine one.

"Then you like the face?"

I answered—

"It is a great pity that we have none such now-a-days. They seem to have died out with Sir Joshua and Greuze. If I could meet such a girl as I believe the prototype of that portrait to have been I would never be happy till I had made her my wife."

To my intense astonishment my hostess jumped up and clapped her hands. I asked her why she did it, and she laughed as she replied in a mocking tone imitating my own voice—

"But suppose for a moment that your kind intentions should be frustrated. 'One man may lead a horse to the pond's brink.' 'The best laid schemes o' mice an' men.' Eh?"

"Well," said I, "there may be some point in the observation. I suppose there must be since you have made it. But for my part I don't see it."

"Oh, I forgot to tell you, Frank, that that portrait might have been painted for Diana Fothering."

I felt a blush stealing over my face. She observed it and took my hand between hers as we sat down on the sofa, and said to me tenderly—

"Frank, my dear boy, I intend to jest with you no more on the subject. I have a conviction that you will like Diana, which has been strengthened by your admiration for her portrait, and from what I know of human nature I am sure that she will like you. Charley and I both wish to see you married, and we would not think of a wife for you who was not in every way eligible. I have never in my life met a girl like Di; and if you and she fancy each other it will be Charley's pleasure and my own to enable you to marry—as far as means are concerned. Now, don't speak. You must know perfectly well how much we both love you. We have always regarded you as our son, and we intend to treat you as our only child when it pleases God to separate us. There now, think the matter over, after you have seen Diana. But, mind me, unless you love each other well and truly, we would far rather not see you married. At all events, whatever may happen you have our best wishes and prayers for your happiness. God bless you, Frank, my dear, dear boy."

There were tears in her eyes as she spoke. When she had finished she leaned over, drew down my head and kissed my forehead very, very tenderly, and then got up softly and left the room. I felt inclined to cry myself. Her words to me were tender, and sensible, and womanly, but I cannot attempt to describe the infinite tenderness and gentleness of her voice and manner. I prayed for every blessing on her in my secret heart, and the swelling of my throat did not prevent my prayers finding voice. There may have been women in the world like Mrs. Trevor, but if there had been I had never met any of them, except herself.

As may be imagined, I was most anxious to see Miss Fothering, and or the remainder of the day she was constantly in my thoughts. That evening a letter came from the younger Miss Fothering apologising for her not being able to keep her promise with reference to her visit, on account of the unexpected arrival of her aunt, with whom she was obliged to go to Paris for some months. That night I slept in my new room, and had neither dream nor vision. I awoke in the morning half ashamed of having ever paid any attention to such a silly circumstance as a strange dream in my first night in an old house.

After breakfast next morning, as I was going along the corridor, I saw the door of my old bedroom open, and went in to have another look at the portrait. Whilst I was looking at it I began to wonder how it could be that it was so like Miss Fothering as Mrs. Trevor said it was. The more I thought of this the more it puzzled me, till suddenly the dream came back—the face in the picture, and the figure in the bed, the phantoms out in the night, and the ominous words—"The fairest and the best." As I thought of these things all the possibilities of the lost legends of the old house thronged so quickly into my mind that I began to feel a buzzing in my ears and my head began to swim, so that I was obliged to sit down.

"Could it be possible," I asked myself, "that some old curse hangs over the race that once dwelt within these walls, and can she be of that race? Such things have been before now!"

The idea was a terrible one for me, for it made to me a reality that which I had come to look upon as merely the dream of a distempered imagination. If the thought had come to me in the darkness and stillness of the night it would have been awful. How happy I was that it had come by daylight, when the sun was shining brightly, and the air was cheerful with the trilling of the song birds, and the lively, strident cawing from the old rookery.

I stayed in the room for some little time longer, thinking over the scene, and, as is natural, when I had got over the remnants of my fear, my reason began to question the genuineness-vraisemblance of the dream. I began to look for the internal evidence of the untruth to facts; but, after thinking earnestly for sometime the only fact that seemed to me of any importance was the confirmatory one of the younger Miss Fothering's apology. In the dream the frightened girl had been alone, and the mere fact of two girls coming on a visit had seemed a sort of disproof of its truth. But, just as if things were conspiring to force on the truth of the dream, one of the sisters was not to come, and the other was she who resembled the portrait whose prototype I had seen sleeping in a vision. I could hardly imagine that I had only dreamt.

I determined to ask Mrs. Trevor if she could explain in anyway Miss Fothering's resemblance to the portrait, and so went at once to seek her.

I found her in the large drawing room alone, and, after a few casual remarks, I broached the subject on which I had come to seek for information. She had not said anything further to me about marrying since our conversation on the previous day, but when I mentioned Miss Fothering's name I could see a glad look on her face which gave me great pleasure. She made none of those vulgar commonplace remarks which many women find it necessary to make when talking to a man about a girl for whom he is supposed to have an affection, but by her manner she put me entirely at my ease, as I sat fidgeting on the sofa, pulling purposelessly the woolly tufts of an antimacassar, painfully conscious that my cheeks were red, and my voice slightly forced and unnatural.

She merely said, "Of course, Frank, I am ready if you want to talk about Miss Fothering, or any other subject." She then put a marker in her book and laid it aside, and, folding her arms, looked at me with a grave, kind, expectant smile.

I asked her if she knew anything about the family history of Miss Fothering. She answered—

"Not further than I have already told you. Her father's is a fine old family, although reduced in circumstances."

"Has it ever been connected with any family in this county? With the former owners of Scarp, for instance?"

"Not that I know of. Why do you ask?"

"I want to find out how she comes to be so like that portrait."

"I never thought of that. It may be that there was some remote connection between her family and the Kirks who formerly owned Scarp. I will ask her when she comes. Or stay. Let us go and look if there is any old book or tree in the library that will throw a light upon the subject. We have rather a good library now, Frank, for we have all our own books, and all those which belonged to the Scarp library also. They are in great disorder, for we have been waiting till you came to arrange them, for we knew that you delighted in such work."

"There is nothing I should enjoy more than arranging all these splendid books. What a magnificent library. It is almost a pity to keep it in a private house."

We proceeded to look for some of those old books of family history which are occasionally to be found in old county houses. The library of Scarp, I saw, was very valuable, and as we prosecuted our search I came across many splendid and rare volumes which I determined to examine at my leisure, for I had come to Scarp for a long visit.

We searched first in the old folio shelves, and, after some few disappointments, found at length a large volume, magnificently printed and bound, which contained views and plans of the house, illuminations of the armorial bearings of the family of Kirk, and all the families with whom it was connected, and having the history of all these families carefully set forth. It was called on the title-page "The Book of Kirk," and was full of anecdotes and legends, and contained a large stock of family tradition. As this was exactly the book which we required, we searched no further, but, having carefully dusted the volume, bore it to Mrs. Trevor's boudoir where we could look over it quite undisturbed.

On looking in the index, we found the name of Fothering mentioned, and on turning to the page specified, found the arms of Kirk quartered on those of Fothering. From the text we learned that one of the daughters of Kirk had, in the year 1573, married the brother of Fothering against the united wills of her father and brother, and that after a bitter feud of some ten or twelve years, the latter, then master of Scarp, had met the brother of Fothering in a duel and had killed him. Upon receiving the news Fothering had sworn a great oath to revenge his brother, invoking the most fearful curses upon himself and his race if he should fail to cut off the hand that had slain his brother, and to nail it over the gate of Fothering. The feud then became so bitter that Kirk seems to have gone quite mad on the subject. When he heard of Fothering's oath he knew that he had but little chance of escape, since his enemy was his master at every weapon; so he determined upon a mode of revenge which, although costing him his own life, he fondly hoped would accomplish the eternal destruction of his brother-in-law through his violated oath. He sent Fothering a letter cursing him and his race, and praying for the consummation of his own curse invoked in case of failure. He concluded his missive by a prayer for the complete destruction, soul, mind, and body, of the first Fothering who should enter the gate of Scarp, who he hoped would be the fairest and best of the race. Having despatched this letter he cut off his right hand and threw it into the centre of a roaring fire, which he had made for the purpose. When it was entirely consumed he threw himself upon his sword, and so died.

A cold shiver went through me when I read the words "fairest and best." All my dream came back in a moment, and I seemed to hear in my ears again the echo of the fiendish laughter. I looked up at Mrs. Trevor, and saw that she had become very grave. Her face had a half-frightened look, as if some wild thought had struck her. I was more frightened than ever, for nothing increases our alarms so much as the sympathy of others with regard to them; however, I tried to conceal my fear. We sat silent for some minutes, and then Mrs. Trevor rose up saying:

"Come with me, and let us look at the portrait."

I remember her saying the and not that portrait, as if some concealed thought of it had been occupying her mind. The same dread had assailed her from a coincidence as had grown in me from a vision. Surely—surely I had good grounds for fear!

We went to the bedroom and stood before the picture, which seemed to gaze upon us with an expression which reflected our own fears. My companion said to me in slightly excited tones: "Frank, lift down the picture till we see its back." I did so, and we found written in strange old writing on the grimy canvas a name and a date, which, after a great deal of trouble, we made out to be "Margaret Kirk, 1572." It was the name of the lady in the book.

Mrs. Trevor turned round and faced me slowly, with a look of horror on her face.

"Frank, I don't like this at all. There is something very strange here."

I had it on my tongue to tell her my dream, but was ashamed to do so. Besides, I feared that it might frighten her too much, as she was already alarmed.

I continued to look at the picture as a relief from my embarrassment, and was struck with the excessive griminess of the back in comparison to the freshness of the front. I mentioned my difficulty to my companion, who thought for a moment, and then suddenly said—

"I see how it is. It has been turned with its face to the wall."

I said no word but hung up the picture again; and we went back to the boudoir.

On the way I began to think that my fears were too wildly improbable to bear to be spoken about. It was so hard to believe in the horrors of darkness when the sunlight was falling brightly around me. The same idea seemed to have struck Mrs. Trevor, for she said, when we entered the room:

"Frank, it strikes me that we are both rather silly to let our imaginations carry us away so. The story is merely a tradition, and we know how report distorts even the most innocent facts. It is true that the Fothering family was formerly connected with the Kirks, and that the picture is that of the Miss Kirk who married against her father's will; it is likely that he quarrelled with her for so doing, and had her picture turned to the wall—a common trick of angry fathers at all times—but that is all. There can be nothing beyond that. Let us not think anymore upon the subject, as it is one likely to lead us into absurdities. However, the picture is a really beautiful one-independent of its being such a likeness of Diana, and I will have it placed in the dining-room."

The change was effected that afternoon, but she did not again allude to the subject. She appeared, when talking to me, to be a little constrained in manner—a very unusual thing with her, and seemed to fear that I would renew the forbidden topic. I think that she did not wish to let her imagination lead her astray, and was distrustful of herself. However, the feeling of constraint wore off before night—but she did not renew the subject.

I slept well that night, without dreams of any kind; and next morning—the third tomorrow promised in the dream—when I came down to breakfast, I was told that I would see Miss Fothering before that evening.

I could not help blushing, and stammered out some commonplace remark, and then glancing up, feeling very sheepish, I saw my hostess looking at me with her kindly smile intensified. She said:

"Do you know, Frank, I felt quite frightened yesterday when we were looking at the picture; but I have been thinking the matter over since, and have come to the conclusion that my folly was perfectly unfounded. I am sure you agree with me. In fact, I look now upon our fright as a good joke, and will tell it to Diana when she arrives."

Once again I was about to tell my dream; but again was restrained by shame. I knew, of course, that Mrs. Trevor would not laugh at me or even think little of me for my fears, for she was too well-bred, and kind-hearted, and sympathetic to do anything of the kind, and, besides, the fear was one which we had shared in common.

But how could I confess my fright at what might appear to others to be a ridiculous dream, when she had conquered the fear that had been common to us both, and which had arisen from a really strange conjuncture of facts. She appeared to look on the matter so lightly that I could not do otherwise. And I did it honestly for the time.

## III. The Third Tomorrow

IN THE AFTERNOON I WAS out in the garden lying in the shadow of an immense beech, when I saw Mrs. Trevor approaching. I had been reading Shelley's "Stanzas Written in Dejection," and my heart was full of melancholy and a vague yearning after human sympathy. I had thought of Mrs. Trevor's love for me, but even that did not seem sufficient. I wanted the love of someone more nearly of my own level, some equal spirit, for I looked on her, of course, as I would have regarded my mother. Somehow my thoughts kept returning to Miss Fothering till I could almost see her before me in my memory of the portrait. I had begun to ask myself the question: "Are you in love?" when I heard the voice of my hostess as she drew near.

"Ha! Frank, I thought I would find you here. I want you to come to my boudoir."

"What for?" I inquired, as I rose from the grass and picked up my volume of Shelley.

"Di has come ever so long ago; and I want to introduce you and have a chat before dinner," said she, as we went towards the house.

"But won't you let me change my dress? I am not in correct costume for the afternoon."

I felt somewhat afraid of the unknown beauty when the introduction was imminent. Perhaps it was because I had come to believe too firmly in Mrs. Trevor's prediction.

"Nonsense, Frank, just as if any woman worth thinking about cares how a man is dressed."

We entered the boudoir and found a young lady seated by a window that overlooked the croquet-ground. She turned round as we came in, so Mrs. Trevor introduced us, and we were soon engaged in a lively conversation. I observed her, as may be supposed, with more than curiosity, and shortly found that she was worth looking at. She was very beautiful, and her beauty lay not only in her features but in her expression. At first her appearance did not seem to me so perfect as it afterwards did, on account of her wonderful resemblance to the portrait with whose beauty I was already acquainted. But it was not long before I came to experience the difference between the portrait and the reality. No matter how well it may be painted a picture falls far short of its prototype. There is something in a real face which cannot exist on canvas—some difference far greater than that contained in the contrast between the one expression, however beautiful of the picture, and the moving features and varying expression of the reality. There is something living and lovable in a real face that no art can represent.

When we had been talking for a while in the usual conventional style, Mrs. Trevor said, "Di, my love, I want to tell you of a discovery Frank and I have made. You must know that I always call Mr. Stanford, Frank—he is more like my own son than my friend, and that I am very fond of him."

She then put her arms round Miss Fothering's waist, as they sat on the sofa together, and kissed her, and then, turning towards me, said, "I don't approve of kissing girls in the presence of gentlemen, but you know that Frank is not supposed to be here. This is my sanctum, and who invades it must take the consequences. But I must tell you about the discovery."

She then proceeded to tell the legend, and about her finding the name of Margaret Kirk on the back of the picture.

Miss Fothering laughed gleefully as she heard the story, and then said, suddenly,

"Oh, I had forgotten to tell you, dear Mrs. Trevor, that I had such a fright the other day. I thought I was going to be prevented coming here. Aunt Deborah came to us last week for a few days, and when she heard that I was about to go on a visit to Scarp she seemed quite frightened, and went straight off to papa and asked him to forbid me to go. Papa asked her why she made the request, so she told a long family legend about any of us coming to Scarp—just the same story that you have been telling me. She said she was sure that some misfortune would happen if I came; so you see that the tradition exists in our branch of the family too. Oh, you can't fancy the scene there was between papa and Aunt Deborah. I must laugh whenever I think of it, although I did not laugh then, for I was greatly afraid that aunty would prevent me coming. Papa got very grave, and aunty thought she had carried her point when he said, in his dear, old, pompous manner;

"'Deborah, Diana has promised to pay Mrs. Trevor, of Scarp, a visit, and, of course, must keep her engagement. And if it were for no other reason than the one you have just alleged, I would strain a point of convenience to have her go to Scarp. I have always educated my children in such a manner that they ought not to be influenced by such vain superstitions; and with my will their practice shall never be at variance with the precepts which I have instilled into them.'

"Poor aunty was quite overcome. She seemed almost speechless for a time at the thought that her wishes had been neglected, for you know that Aunt Deborah's wishes are commands to all our family."

Mrs. Trevor said—

"I hope Mrs. Howard was not offended?"

"Oh, no. Papa talked to her seriously, and at length—with a great deal of difficulty I must say—succeeded in convincing her that her fears were groundless—at least, he forced her to confess that such things as she was afraid of could not be."

I thought of the couplet—

*"A man convinced against his will*
*Is of the same opinion still,"*

but said nothing.

Miss Fothering finished her story by saying—

"Aunty ended by hoping that I might enjoy myself, which I am sure, my dear Mrs. Trevor, that I will do."

"I hope you will, my love."

I had been struck during the above conversation by the mention of Mrs. Howard. I was trying to think of where I had heard the name, Deborah Howard, when suddenly it all came back to me. Mrs. Howard had been Miss Fothering, and was an old friend of my mother's. It was thus that I had been accustomed to her name when I was a child. I remembered now that once she had brought a nice little girl, almost a baby, with her to visit. The child was her niece, and it was thus that I now accounted for my half-recollection of the name and the circumstance on the first night of my arrival at Scarp. The thought of my dream here recalled me to Mrs. Trevor's object in bringing Miss Fothering to her boudoir, so I said to the latter—

"Do you believe these legends?"

"Indeed I do not, Mr. Stanford; I do not believe in anything half so silly."

"Then you do not believe in ghosts or visions?"

"Most certainly not."

How could I tell my dream to a girl who had such profound disbelief? And yet I felt something whispering to me that I ought to tell it to her. It was, no doubt, foolish of me to have this fear of a dream, but I could not help it. I was just going to risk being laughed at, and unburden my mind, when Mrs. Trevor started up, after looking at her watch, saying—

"Dear me, I never thought it was so late. I must go and see if any others have come. It will not do for me to neglect my guests."

We all left the boudoir, and as we did so the gong sounded for dressing for dinner, and so we each sought our rooms.

When I came down to the drawing room I found assembled a number of persons who had arrived during the course of the afternoon. I was introduced to them all, and chatted with them till dinner was announced. I was given Miss Fothering to take into dinner, and when it was over I found that we had improved our acquaintance very much. She was a delightful girl, and as I looked at her I thought with a glow of pleasure of Mrs. Trevor's prediction. Occasionally I saw our hostess observing us, and as she saw us chatting pleasantly together as though we enjoyed it a more than happy look came into her face. It was one of her most fascinating points that in the midst of gaiety, while she never neglected anyone, she specially remembered her particular friends. No matter what position she might be placed in she would still remember that there were some persons who would treasure up her recognition at such moments.

After dinner, as I did not feel inclined to enter the drawing room with the other gentlemen, I strolled out into the garden by myself, and thought over things in general, and Miss Fothering in particular. The subject was such a pleasant one that I quite lost myself in it, and strayed off farther than I had intended. Suddenly I remembered myself and looked around. I was far away from the house, and in the midst of a dark, gloomy walk between old yew trees. I could not see through them on either side on account of their thickness, and as the walk was curved I could see but a short distance either before or behind me. I looked up and saw a yellowish, luminous sky with heavy clouds passing sluggishly across it. The moon had not yet risen, and the general gloom reminded me forcibly of some of the weird pictures which William Blake so loved to paint. There was a sort of vague melancholy and ghostliness in the place that made me shiver, and I hurried on.

At length the walk opened and I came out on a large sloping lawn, dotted here and there with yew trees and tufts of pampass grass of immense height, whose stalks were crowned with large flowers. To the right lay the house, grim and gigantic in the gloom, and to the left the lake which stretched away so far that it was lost in the evening shadow. The lawn sloped from the terrace round the house down to the water's edge, and was only broken by the walk which continued to run on round the house in a wide sweep.

As I came near the house a light appeared in one of the windows which lay before me, and as I looked into the room I saw that it was the chamber of my dream.

Unconsciously I approached nearer and ascended the terrace from the top of which I could see across the deep trench which surrounded the house, and looked earnestly into the room. I shivered as I looked. My spirits had been damped by the gloom and desolation of the yew walk, and now the dream and all the subsequent revelations came before my mind with such vividness that the horror of the thing again seized me, but more forcibly than before. I looked at the sleeping arrangements, and groaned as I saw that the bed where the dying woman had seemed to lie was alone prepared, while the other bed, that in which I had slept, had its curtains drawn all round. This was but another link in the chain of doom. Whilst I stood looking, the servant who was in the room came and pulled down one of the blinds, but, as she was about to do the same with the other, Miss Fothering entered the room, and, seeing what she was about, evidently gave her contrary directions, for she let go the window string, and then went and pulled up again the blind which she had let down. Having done so she followed her mistress out of the room. So wrapped up was I in all that took place with reference to that chamber, that it never even struck me that I was guilty of any impropriety in watching what took place.

I stayed there for some little time longer purposeless and terrified. The horror grew so great to me as I thought of the events of the last few days, that I determined to tell Miss Fothering of my dream, in order that she might not be frightened in case she should see anything like it, or at least that she might be prepared for anything that might happen. As soon as I had come to this determination the inevitable question "when?" presented itself. The means of making the communication was a subject most disagreeable to contemplate, but as I had made up my mind to do it, I thought that there was no time like the present. Accordingly I was determined to seek the drawing room, where I knew I should find Miss Fothering and Mrs. Trevor, for, of course, I had determined to take the latter into our confidence. As I was really afraid to go through the awful yew walk again, I completed the half circle of the house and entered the backdoor, from which I easily found my way to the drawing room.

When I entered Mrs. Trevor, who was sitting near the door, said to me, "Good gracious, Frank, where have you been to make you look so pale? One would think you had seen a ghost!"

I answered that I had been strolling in the garden, but made no other remark, as I did not wish to say anything about my dream before the persons to whom she was talking, as they were strangers to me. I waited for sometime for an opportunity of speaking to her alone, but her duties, as hostess, kept her so constantly occupied that I waited in vain. Accordingly I determined to tell Miss Fothering at all events, at once, and then to tell Mrs. Trevor as soon as an opportunity for doing so presented itself.

With a good deal of difficulty—for I did not wish to do anything marked—I succeeded in getting Miss Fothering away from the persons by whom she was surrounded, and took her to one of the embrasures, under the pretence of looking out at the night view. Here we were quite removed from observation, as the heavy window curtains completely covered the recess, and almost isolated us from the rest of the company as perfectly as if we were in a separate chamber. I proceeded at once to broach the subject for which I had sought the interview; for I feared lest contact with the lively company of the drawing room would do away with my present fears, and so breakdown the only barrier that stood between her and Fate.

"Miss Fothering, do you ever dream?"

"Oh, yes, often. But I generally find that my dreams are most ridiculous."

"How so?"

"Well, you see, that no matter whether they are good or bad they appear real and coherent whilst I am dreaming them; but when I wake I find them unreal and incoherent, when I remember them at all. They are, in fact, mere disconnected nonsense."

"Are you fond of dreams?"

"Of course I am. I delight in them, for whether they are sense or gibberish when you wake, they are real whilst you are asleep."

"Do you believe in dreams?"

"Indeed, Mr. Stanford, I do not."

"Do you like hearing them told?"

"I do, very much, when they are worth telling. Have you been dreaming anything? If you have, do tell it to me."

"I will be glad to do so. It is about a dream which I had that concerns you, that I came here to tell you."

"About me. Oh, how nice. Do, go on."

I told her all my dream, after calling her attention to our conversation in the boudoir as a means of introducing the subject. I did not attempt to heighten the effect in anyway or to draw any inferences. I tried to suppress my own emotion and merely to let the facts speak for themselves. She listened with great eagerness, but, as far as I could see, without a particle of either fear or belief in the dream as a warning. When I had finished she laughed a quiet, soft laugh, and said—

"That is delicious. And was I really the girl that you saw afraid of ghosts? If papa heard of such a thing as that even in a dream what a lecture he would give me! I wish I could dream anything like that."

"Take care," said I, "you might find it too awful. It might indeed prove the fulfilling of the ban which we saw in the legend in the old book, and which you heard from your aunt."

She laughed musically again, and shook her head at me wisely and warningly.

"Oh, pray do not talk nonsense and try to frighten me—for I warn you that you will not succeed."

"I assure you on my honour, Miss Fothering, that I was never more in earnest in my whole life."

"Do you not think that we had better go into the room?" said she, after a few moment's pause.

"Stay just a moment, I entreat you," said I. "What I say is true. I am really in earnest."

"Oh, pray forgive me if what I said led you to believe that I doubted your word. It was merely your inference which I disagreed with. I thought you had been jesting to try and frighten me."

"Miss Fothering, I would not presume to take such a liberty. But I am glad that you trust me. May I venture to ask you a favour? Will you promise me one thing?"

Her answer was characteristic—

"No. What is it?"

"That you will not be frightened at anything which may take place tonight?"

She laughed softly again.

"I do not intend to be. But is that all?"

"Yes, Miss Fothering, that is all; but I want to be assured that you will not be alarmed—that you will be prepared for anything which may happen. I have a horrid foreboding of evil—some evil that I dread to think of—and it will be a great comfort to me if you will do one thing."

"Oh, nonsense. Oh, well, if you really wish it I will tell you if I will do it when I hear what it is."

Her levity was all gone when she saw how terribly in earnest I was. She looked at me boldly and fearlessly, but with a tender, half-pitying glance as if conscious of the possession of strength superior to mine. Her fearlessness was in her free, independent attitude, but her pity was in her eyes. I went on—

"Miss Fothering, the worst part of my dream was seeing the look of agony on the face of the girl when she looked round and found herself alone. Will you take some token and keep it with you till morning to remind you, in case anything should happen, that you are not alone—that there is one thinking of you, and one human intelligence awake for you, though all the rest of the world should be asleep or dead?"

In my excitement I spoke with fervour, for the possibility of her enduring the horror which had assailed me seemed to be growing more and more each instant. At times since that awful night I had disbelieved the existence of the warning, but when I thought of it by night I could not but believe, for the very air in the darkness seemed to be peopled by phantoms to my fevered imagination. My belief had been perfected tonight by the horror of the yew walk, and all the sombre, ghostly thoughts that had arisen amid its gloom.

There was a short pause. Miss Fothering leaned on the edge of the window, looking out at the dark, moonless sky. At length she turned and said to me, with some hesitation, "But really, Mr. Stanford, I do not like doing anything from fear of supernatural things, or from a belief in them. What you want me to do is so simple a thing in itself that I would not hesitate a moment to do it, but that papa has always taught me to believe that such occurrences as you seem to dread are quite impossible, and I know that he would be very much displeased if any act of mine showed a belief in them."

"Miss Fothering, I honestly think that there is not a man living who would wish less than I would to see you or anyone else disobeying a father either in word or spirit, and more particularly when that father is a clergyman; but I entreat you to gratify me on this one point. It cannot do you any harm; and I assure you that if you do not I will be inexpressibly miserable. I have endured the greatest tortures of suspense for the last three days, and tonight I feel a nervous horror of which words can give you no conception. I know that I have not the smallest right to make the request, and no reason for doing it except that I was fortunate, or unfortunate, enough to get the warning. I apologise most sincerely for the great liberty which I have taken, but believe me that I act with the best intentions."

My excitement was so great that my knees were trembling, and the large drops of perspiration rolling down my face.

There was a long pause, and I had almost made up my mind for a refusal of my request when my companion spoke again.

"Mr. Stanford, on that plea alone I will grant your request. I can see that for some reason which I cannot quite comprehend you are deeply moved; and that I may be the means of saving pain to anyone, I will do what you ask. Just please to state what you wish me to do."

I thought from her manner that she was offended with me; however I explained my purpose:

"I want you to keep about you, when you go to bed, some token which will remind you in an instant of what has passed between us, so that you may not feel lonely or frightened—no matter what may happen."

"I will do it. What shall I take?"

She had her handkerchief in her hand as she spoke. So I put my hand upon it and blessed it in the name of the Father, Son, and Holy Ghost. I did this to fix its existence in her memory by awing her slightly about it. "This," said I, "shall be a token that you are not alone." My object in blessing the handkerchief was fully achieved, for she did seem somewhat awed, but still she thanked me with a sweet smile. "I feel that you act from your heart," said she, "and my heart thanks you." She gave me her hand as she spoke, in an honest, straightforward manner, with more the independence of a man than the timorousness of a woman. As I grasped it I felt the blood rushing to my face, but before I let it go an impulse seized me and I bent down and touched it with my lips. She drew it quickly away, and said more coldly than she had yet spoken: "I did not mean you to do that."

"Believe me I did not mean to take a liberty—it was merely the natural expression of my gratitude. I feel as if you had done me some great personal service. You do not know how much lighter my heart is now than it was an hour ago, or you would forgive me for having so offended."

As I made my apologetic excuse, I looked at her wistfully. She returned my glance fearlessly, but with a bright, forgiving smile. She then shook her head slightly, as if to banish the subject.

There was a short pause, and then she said:

"I am glad to be of any service to you; but if there be any possibility of what you fear happening it is I who will be benefited. But mind, I will depend upon you not to say a word of this to anybody. I am afraid that we are both very foolish."

"No, no, Miss Fothering. I may be foolish, but you are acting nobly in doing what seems to you to be foolish in order that you may save me from pain. But may I not even tell Mrs. Trevor?"

"No, not even her. I should be ashamed of myself if I thought that anyone except ourselves knew about it."

"You may depend upon me. I will keep it secret if you wish."

"Do so, until morning at all events. Mind, if I laugh at you then I will expect you to join in my laugh."

"I will," said I. "I will be only too glad to be able to laugh at it." And we joined the rest of the company.

When I retired to my bedroom that night I was too much excited to sleep—even had my promise not forbidden me to do so. I paced up and down the room for sometime, thinking and doubting. I could not believe completely in what I expected to happen, and yet my heart was filled with a vague dread. I thought over the events of the evening—particularly my stroll after dinner through that awful yew walk and my looking into the bedroom where I had dreamed. From these my thoughts wandered to the deep embrasure of the window where I had given Miss Fothering the token. I could hardly realise that whole interview as a fact. I knew that it had taken place, but that was all. It was so strange to recall a scene that, now that it was enacted, seemed half comedy and half tragedy, and to remember that it was played in this practical nineteenth century, in secret, within earshot of a room full of people, and only hidden from them by a curtain, I felt myself blushing, half from excitement, half from shame, when I thought of it. But then my thoughts turned to the way in which Miss Fothering had acceded to my request, strange as it was; and as I thought of her my blundering shame changed to a deeper glow of hope. I remembered Mrs. Trevor's prediction—"from what I know of human nature I think that she will like you"—and as I did so I felt how dear to me Miss Fothering was already becoming. But my joy was turned to anger on thinking what she might be called on to endure; and the thought of her suffering pain or fright caused me greater distress than any suffered myself. Again my thoughts flew back to the time of my own fright and my dream, with all the subsequent revelations concerning it, rushed across my mind. I felt again the feeling of extreme terror—as if something was about to happen—as if the tragedy was approaching its climax. Naturally I thought of the time of night and so I looked at my watch. It was within a few minutes of one o'clock. I remembered that the clock had struck twelve after Mr. Trevor had come home on the night of my dream. There was a large clock at Scarp which tolled the hours so loudly that for a long way round the estate the country people all regulated their affairs by it. The next few minutes passed so slowly that each moment seemed an age.

I was standing, with my watch in my hand, counting the moments when suddenly a light came into the room that made the candle on the table appear quite dim, and my shadow was reflected on the wall by some brilliant light which streamed in through the window. My heart for an instant ceased to beat, and then the blood rushed so violently to my temples that my eyes grew dim and my brain began to reel. However, I shortly became more composed, and then went to the window expecting to see my dream again repeated.

The light was there as formerly, but there were no figures of children, or witches, or fiends. The moon had just risen, and I could see its reflection upon the far end of the lake. I turned my head in trembling expectation to the ground below where I had seen the children and the hags, but saw merely the dark yew trees and tall crested pampass tufts gently moving in the night wind. The light caught the edges of the flowers of the grass, and made them most conspicuous.

As I looked a sudden thought flashed like a flame of fire through my brain. I saw in one second of time all the folly of my wild fancies. The moonlight and its reflection on the water shining into the room was the light of my dream, or phantasm as I now understood it to be. Those three tufts of pampass grass clumped together were in turn the fair young children and the withered leaves and the dark foliage of the yew beside them gave substance to the semblance of the fiend. For the rest, the empty bed and the face of the picture, my half recollection of the name of Fothering, and the long-forgotten legend of the curse. Oh, fool! fool that I had been! How I had been the victim of circumstances, and of my own wild imagination! Then came the bitter reflection of the agony of mind which Miss Fothering might be compelled to suffer. Might not the recital of my dream, and my strange request regarding the token, combined with the natural causes of night and scene, produce the very effect which I so dreaded? It was only at that bitter, bitter moment that I realised how foolish I had been. But what was my anguish of mind to hers? For an instant I conceived the idea of rousing Mrs. Trevor and telling her all the facts of the case so that she might go to Miss Fothering and tell her not to be alarmed. But I had no time to act upon my thought. As I was hastening to the door the clock struck one and a moment later I heard from the room below me a sharp scream—a cry of surprise rather than fear. Miss Fothering had no doubt been awakened by the striking of the clock, and had seen outside the window the very figures which I had described to her.

I rushed madly down the stairs and arrived at the door of her bedroom, which was directly under the one which I now occupied. As I was about to rush in I was instinctively restrained from so doing by the thoughts of propriety; and so for a few moments I stood silent, trembling, with my hand upon the door-handle.

Within I heard a voice—her voice—exclaiming, in tones of stupefied surprise—

"Has it come then? Am I alone?" She then continued joyously, "No, I am not alone. His token! Oh, thank God for that. Thank God for that."

Through my heart at her words came a rush of wild delight. I felt my bosom swell and the tears of gladness spring to my eyes. In that moment I knew that I had strength and courage to face the world, alone, for her sake. But before my hopes had well time to manifest themselves they were destroyed, for again the voice came wailing from the room of blank despair that made me cold from head to foot.

"Ah-h-h! still there? Oh! God, preserve my reason. Oh! for some human thing near me." Then her voice changed slightly to a tone of entreaty: "You will not leave me alone? Your token. Remember your token. Help me. Help me now." Then her voice became more wild, and rose to an inarticulate, wailing scream of horror.

As I heard that agonised cry, I realised the idea that it was madness to delay—that I had hesitated too long already—I must cast aside the shackles of conventionality if I wished to repair my fatal error. Nothing could save her from some serious injury—perhaps madness—perhaps death; save a shock which would break the spell which was over her from fear and her excited imagination. I flung open the door and rushed in, shouting loudly:

"Courage, courage. You are not alone. I am here. Remember the token."

She grasped the handkerchief instinctively, but she hardly comprehended my words, and did not seem to heed my presence. She was sitting up in bed, her face being distorted with terror, and was gazing out upon the scene. I heard from without the hooting of an owl as it flew across the border of the lake. She heard it also, and screamed—

"The laugh, too! Oh, there is no hope. Even he will not dare to go amongst them."

Then she gave vent to a scream, so wild, so appalling that, as I heard it, I trembled, and the hair on the back of my head bristled up. Throughout the house I could hear screams of affright, and the ringing of bells, and the banging of doors, and the rush of hurried feet; but the poor sufferer comprehended not these sounds; she still continued gazing out of the window awaiting the consummation of the dream.

I saw that the time for action and self-sacrifice was come. There was but one way now to repair my fatal error. To burst through the window and try by the shock to wake her from her trance of fear.

I said no word but rushed across the room and hurled myself, back foremost, against the massive plate glass. As I turned I saw Mrs. Trevor rushing into the room, her face wild with excitement. She was calling out—

"Diana, Diana, what is it?"

The glass crashed and shivered into a thousand pieces, and I could feel its sharp edges cutting me like so many knives. But I heeded not the pain, for above the rushing of feet and crashing of glass and the shouting both within and without the room I heard her voice ring forth in a joyous, fervent cry, "Saved. He has dared," as she sank down in the arms of Mrs. Trevor, who had thrown herself upon the bed.

Then I felt a mighty shock, and all the universe seemed filled with sparks of fire that whirled around me with lightning speed, till I seemed to be in the centre of a world of flame, and then came in my ears the rushing of a mighty wind, swelling ever louder, and then came a blackness over all things and a deadness of sound as if all the earth had passed away, and I remembered no more.

## IV. Afterwards

When I next became conscious I was lying in bed in a dark room. I wondered what this was for, and tried to look around me, but could hardly stir my head. I attempted to speak, but my voice was without power—it was like a whisper from another world. The effort to speak made me feel faint, and again I felt a darkness gathering round me.

I BECAME GRADUALLY CONSCIOUS OF something cool on my forehead. I wondered what it was. All sorts of things I conjectured, but could not fix my mind on any of them. I lay thus for sometime, and at length opened my eyes and saw my mother bending over me—it was her hand which was so deliciously cool on my brow. I felt amazed somehow. I expected to see her; and yet I was surprised, for I had not seen her for a long time—a long, long time. I knew that she was dead—could I be dead, too? I looked at her again more carefully, and as I looked, the old features died away, but the expression remained the same. And then the dear, well-known face of Mrs. Trevor grew slowly before me. She smiled as she saw the look of recognition in my eyes, and, bending down, kissed me very tenderly. As she drew back her head something warm fell on my face. I wondered what this could be, and after thinking for a long time, to do which I closed my eyes, I came to the conclusion that it was a tear. After some more thinking I opened my eyes to see why she was crying; but she was gone, and I could see that although the window-blinds were pulled up the room was almost dark. I felt much more awake and much stronger than I had been before, and tried to call Mrs. Trevor. A woman got up from a chair behind the bed-curtains and went to the door, said something, and came back and settled my pillows.

"Where is Mrs. Trevor?" I asked, feebly. "She was here just now."

The woman smiled at me cheerfully, and answered:

"She will be here in a moment. Dear heart! but she will be glad to see you so strong and sensible."

After a few minutes she came into the room, and, bending over me, asked me how I felt. I said that I was all right—and then a thought struck me, so I asked,

"What was the matter with me?"

I was told that I had been ill, very ill, but that I was now much better. Something, I know not what, suddenly recalled to my memory all the scene of the bedroom, and the fright which my folly had caused, and I grew quite dizzy with the rush of blood to my head. But Mrs. Trevor's arm supported me, and after a time the faintness passed away, and my memory was completely restored. I started violently from the arm that held me up, and called out:

"Is she all right? I heard her say, 'saved.' Is she all right?"

"Hush, dear boy, hush—she is all right. Do not excite yourself."

"Are you deceiving me?" I inquired. "Tell me all—I can bear it. Is she well or no?"

"She has been very ill, but she is now getting strong and well, thank God."

I began to cry, half from weakness and half from joy, and Mrs. Trevor seeing this, and knowing with the sweet instinct of womanhood that I would rather be alone, quickly left the room, after making a sign to the nurse, who sank again to her old place behind the bed-curtain.

I thought for long; and all the time from my first coming to Scarp to the moment of unconsciousness after I sprung through the window came back to me as in a dream. Gradually the room became darker and darker, and my thoughts began to give semblance to the objects around me, till at length the visible world passed away from my wearied eyes, and in my dreams I continued to think of all that had been. I have a hazy recollection of taking some food and then relapsing into sleep; but remember no more distinctly until I woke fully in the morning and found Mrs. Trevor again in the room. She came over to my bedside, and sitting down said gaily—

"Ah, Frank, you look bright and strong this morning, dear boy. You will soon be well now I trust."

Her cool deft fingers settled my pillow and brushed back the hair from my forehead. I took her hand and kissed it, and the doing so made me very happy. By and-by I asked her how was Miss Fothering.

"Better, much better this morning. She has been asking after you ever since she has been able; and today when I told her how much better you were she brightened up at once."

I felt a flush painfully strong rushing over my face as she spoke, but she went on—

"She has asked me to let her see you as soon as both of you are able. She wants to thank you for your conduct on that awful night. But there, I won't tell anymore tales—let her tell you what she likes herself."

"To thank me—me—for what? For having brought her to the verge of madness or perhaps death through my silly fears and imagination. Oh, Mrs. Trevor, I know that you never mock anyone—but to me that sounds like mockery."

She leaned over me as she sat on my bedside and said, oh, so sweetly, yet so firmly that a sense of the truth of her words came at once upon me—

"If I had a son I would wish him to think as you have thought, and to act as you have acted. I would pray for it night and day and if he suffered as you have done, I would lean over him as I lean over you now and feel glad, as I feel now, that he had thought and acted as a true-hearted man should think and act. I would rejoice that God had given me such a son; and if he should die—as I feared at first that you should—I would be a prouder and happier woman kneeling by his dead body than I would in clasping a different son, living, in my arms."

Oh, how my weak fluttering heart did beat as she spoke. With pity for her blighted maternal instincts, with gladness that a true-hearted woman had approved of my conduct toward a woman whom I loved, and with joy for the deep love for myself. There was no mistaking the honesty of her words—her face was perfectly radiant as she spoke them.

I put up my arms—it took all my strength to do it—round her neck, and whispered softly in her ear one word, "mother."

She did not expect it, for it seemed to startle her; but her arms tightened around me convulsively. I could feel a perfect rain of tears falling on my upturned face as I looked into her eyes, full of love and long-sought joy. As I looked I felt stronger and better; my sympathy for her joy did much to restore my strength.

For some little time she was silent, and then she spoke as if to herself—"God has given me a son at last. I thank thee, O Father; forgive me if I have at anytime repined. The son I prayed for might have been different from what I would wish. Thou doest best in all things."

For sometime after this she stayed quite silent, still supporting me in her arms. I felt inexpressibly happy. There was an atmosphere of love around me, for which I had longed all my life. The love of a mother, for which I had pined since my orphan childhood, I had got at last, and the love of a woman to become far dearer to me than a mother I felt was close at hand.

At length I began to feel tired, and Mrs. Trevor laid me back on my pillow. It pleased me inexpressibly to observe her kind motherly manner with me now. The ice between us had at last been broken, we had declared our mutual love, and the white-haired woman was as happy in the declaration as the young man.

The next day I felt a shade stronger, and a similar improvement was manifested on the next. Mrs. Trevor always attended me herself, and

BRAM STOKER

her good reports of Miss Fothering's progress helped to cheer me not a little. And so the days wore on, and many passed away before I was allowed to rise from bed.

One day Mrs. Trevor came into the room in a state of suppressed delight. By this time I had been allowed to sit up a little while each day, and was beginning to get strong, or rather less weak, for I was still very helpless.

"Frank, the doctor says that you may be moved into another room tomorrow for a change, and that you may see Di."

As may be supposed I was anxious to see Miss Fothering. Whilst I had been able to think during my illness, I had thought about her all day long, and sometimes all night long. I had been in love with her even before that fatal night. My heart told me that secret whilst I was waiting to hear the clock strike, and saw all my folly about the dream; but now I not only loved the woman but I almost worshipped my own bright ideal which was merged in her. The constant series of kind messages that passed between us tended not a little to increase my attachment, and now I eagerly looked forward to a meeting with her face to face.

I awoke earlier than usual next morning, and grew rather feverish as the time for our interview approached. However, I soon cooled down upon a vague threat being held out, that if I did not become more composed I must defer my visit.

The expected time at length arrived, and I was wheeled in my chair into Mrs. Trevor's boudoir. As I entered the door I looked eagerly round and saw, seated in another chair near one of the windows, a girl, who, turning her head round languidly, disclosed the features of Miss Fothering. She was very pale and ethereal looking, and seemed extremely delicate; but in my opinion this only heightened her natural beauty. As she caught sight of me a beautiful blush rushed over her poor, pale face, and even tinged her alabaster forehead. This passed quickly, and she became calm again, and paler than before. My chair was wheeled over to her, and Mrs. Trevor said, as she bent over and kissed her, after soothing the pillow in her chair—

"Di, my love, I have brought Frank to see you. You may talk together for a little while; but, mind, the doctor's orders are very strict, and if either of you excite yourselves about anything I must forbid you to meet again until you are both much stronger."

She said the last words as she was leaving the room.

I felt red and pale, hot and cold by turns. I looked at Miss Fothering and faltered. However, in a moment or two I summoned up courage to address her.

"Miss Fothering, I hope you forgive me for the pain and danger I caused you by that foolish fear of mine. I assure you that nothing I ever did"—

Here she interrupted me.

"Mr. Stanford, I beg you will not talk like that. I must thank you for the care you thought me worthy of. I will not say how proud I feel of it, and for the generous courage and wisdom you displayed in rescuing me from the terror of that awful scene."

She grew pale, even paler than she had been before, as she spoke the last words, and trembled all over. I feared for her, and said as cheerfully as I could:

"Don't be alarmed. Do calm yourself. That is all over now and past. Don't let its horror disturb you ever again."

My speaking, although it calmed her somewhat, was not sufficient to banish her fear, and, seeing that she was really excited, I called to Mrs. Trevor, who came in from the next room and talked to us for a little while. She gradually did away with Miss Fothering's fear by her pleasant cheery conversation. She, poor girl, had received a sad shock, and the thought that I had been the cause of it gave me great anguish. After a little quiet chat, however, I grew more cheerful, but presently feeling faintish, was wheeled back to my own room and put to bed.

For many long days I continued very weak, and hardly made any advance. I saw Miss Fothering everyday, and each day I loved her more and more. She got stronger as the days advanced, and after a few weeks was comparatively in good health, but still I continued weak. Her illness had been merely the result of the fright she had sustained on that unhappy night; but mine was the nervous prostration consequent on the long period of anxiety between the dream and its seeming fulfilment, united with the physical weakness resulting from my wounds caused by jumping through the window. During all this time of weakness Mrs. Trevor was, indeed, a mother to me. She watched me day and night, and as far as a woman could, made my life a dream of happiness. But the crowning glory of that time was the thought that sometimes forced itself upon me—that Diana cared for me. She continued to remain at Scarp by Mrs. Trevor's request, as her father had gone to the Continent for the winter, and with my adopted mother she shared the attendance on me. Day after day her care for my every want grew greater, till I came to fancy her like a guardian angel keeping watch over me. With the peculiar delicate sense that accompanies extreme physical prostration I could see that the growth of her pity kept pace with the growth of her strength. My love kept pace with both. I often wondered if it could be sympathy and not pity that so forestalled my wants and wishes; or if it could be love that answered in her heart when mine beat for her. She only showed pity and tenderness in her acts and words, but still I hoped and longed for something more.

Those days of my long-continued weakness were to me sweet, sweet days. I used to watch her for hours as she sat opposite to me reading or working, and my eyes would fill with tears as I thought how hard it would be to die and leave her behind me. So strong was the flame of my love that I believed, in spite of my religious teaching, that, should I die, I would leave the better part of my being behind me. I used to think in a vague imaginative way, that was no less powerful because it was undefined, of what speeches I would make to her—if I were well. How I would talk to her in nobler language than that in which I would now allow my thoughts to mould themselves. How, as I talked, my passion, and honesty, and purity would make me so eloquent that she would love to hear me speak. How I would wander with her through the sunny-gladed woods that stretched away before me through the open window, and sit by her feet on a mossy bank beside some purling brook that rippled gaily over the stones, gazing into the depths of her eyes, where my future life was pictured in one long sheen of light. How I would whisper in her ear sweet words that would make me tremble to speak them, and her tremble to hear. How she would bend to me and show me her love by letting me tell her mine without reproof. And then would come, like the shadow of a sudden rain-cloud over an April landscape, the bitter, bitter thought that all this longing was but a dream, and that when the time had come when such things might have been, I would, most likely, be sleeping under the green turf. And she might, perhaps, be weeping in the silence of her chamber sad, sad tears for her blighted love and for me. Then my thoughts would become less selfish, and I would try to imagine the bitter blow of my death—if she loved me—for I knew that a woman loves not by the value of what she loves, but by the strength of her affection and admiration for her own ideal, which she thinks she sees bodied forth in some man. But these thoughts had always the proviso that the dreams of happiness were prophetic. Alas! I had altogether lost faith in dreams. Still, I could not but feel that even if I had never frightened Miss Fothering by telling my vision, she might, nevertheless, have been terrified by the effect of the moonlight upon the flowers of the pampass tufts, and that, under Providence, I was the instrument of saving her from a shock even greater than that which she did experience, for help might not have come to her so soon. This thought always gave me hope. Whenever I thought of her sorrow for my death, I would find my eyes filled with a sudden rush of tears which would shut out from my waking vision the object of my thoughts and fears. Then she would come over to me and place her cool hand on my forehead, and whisper sweet words of comfort and hope in my ears. As I would feel her warm breath upon my cheek and wafting my hair from my brow, I would lose all sense of pain and sorrow and care, and live only in the brightness of the present. At such times I would cry silently from very happiness, for I was sadly weak, and even trifling things touched me deeply. Many a stray memory of some tender word heard or some gentle deed done, or of some sorrow or distress, would set me thinking for hours and stir all the tender feelings of my nature.

Slowly—very slowly—I began to get stronger, but for many days more I was almost completely helpless. With returning strength came the strengthening of my passion—for passion my love for Diana had become. She had been so woven into my thoughts that my love for her was a part of my being, and I felt that away from her my future life would be but a bare existence and no more. But strange to say, with increasing strength and passion came increasing diffidence. I felt in her presence so bashful and timorous that I hardly dared to look at her, and could not speak save to answer an occasional question. I had ceased to dream entirely, for such day-dreams as I used to have seemed now wild and almost sacrilegious to my sur-excited imagination. But when she was not looking at me I would be happy in merely seeing her or hearing her speak. I could tell the moment she left the house or entered it, and her footfall was the music sweetest to my ears—except her voice. Sometimes she would catch sight of my bashful looks at her, and then, at my conscious blushing, a bright smile would flit over her face. It was sweet and womanly, but sometimes I would think that it was no more than her pity finding expression. She was always in my thoughts and these doubts and fears constantly assailed me, so that I could feel that the brooding over the subject—a matter which I was powerless to prevent—was doing me an injury; perhaps seriously retarding my recovery.

One day I felt very sad. There had a bitter sense of loneliness come over me which was unusual. It was a good sign of returning health, for it was like the waking from a dream to a world of fact, with all its troubles and cares. There was a sense of coldness and loneliness in the world, and I felt that I had lost something without gaining anything in return—I had, in fact, lost somewhat of my sense of dependence, which is a consequence of prostration, but had not yet regained my strength. I sat opposite a window itself in shade, but looking over a garden that in the summer had been bright with flowers, and sweet with their odours, but which, now, was lit up only in patches by the quiet mellow gleams of the autumn sun, and brightened by a few stray flowers that had survived the first frosts.

As I sat I could not help thinking of what my future would be. I felt that I was getting strong, and the possibilities of my life seemed very real to me. How I longed for courage to ask Diana to be my wife! Any certainty would be better than the suspense I now constantly endured. I had but little hope that she would accept me, for she seemed to care less for me now than in the early days of my illness. As I grew stronger she seemed to hold somewhat aloof from me; and as my fears and doubts grew more and more, I could hardly bear to think of my joy should she accept me, or of my despair should she refuse. Either emotion seemed too great to be borne.

Today when she entered the room my fears were vastly increased. She seemed much stronger than usual, for a glow, as of health, ruddied her cheeks, and she seemed so lovely that I could not conceive that such a woman would ever condescend to be my wife. There was an unusual constraint in her manner as she came and spoke to me, and flitted round me, doing in her own graceful way all the thousand little offices that only a woman's hand can do for an invalid. She turned to me two or three times, as if she was about to speak; but turned away again, each time silent, and with a blush. I could see that her heart was beating violently. At length she spoke.

"Frank."

Oh! what a wild throb went through me as I heard my name from her lips for the first time. The blood rushed to my head, so that for a moment I was quite faint. Her cool hand on my forehead revived me.

"Frank, will you let me speak to you for a few minutes as honestly as I would wish to speak, and as freely?"

"Go on."

"You will promise me not to think me unwomanly or forward, for indeed I act from the best motives—promise me?"

This was said slowly with much hesitation, and a convulsive heaving of the chest.

"I promise."

"We can see that you are not getting as strong as you ought, and the doctor says that there is some idea too much in your mind—that you brood over it, and that it is retarding your recovery. Mrs. Trevor and I have been talking about it. We have been comparing notes, and I think we have found out what your idea is. Now, Frank, you must not pale and red like that, or I will have to leave off."

"I will be calm—indeed, I will. Go on."

"We both thought that it might do you good to talk to you freely, and we want to know if our idea is correct. Mrs. Trevor thought it better that I should speak to you than she should."

"What is the idea?"

Hitherto, although she had manifested considerable emotion, her voice had been full and clear, but she answered this last question very faintly, and with much hesitation.

"You are attached to me, and you are afraid I—I don't love you."

Here her voice was checked by a rush of tears, and she turned her head away.

"Diana," said I, "dear Diana," and I held out my arms with what strength I had.

The colour rushed over her face and neck, and then she turned, and with a convulsive sigh laid her head upon my shoulder. One weak arm fell round her waist, and my other hand rested on her head. I said nothing. I could not speak, but I felt the beating of her heart against mine, and thought that if I died then I must be happy forever, if there be memory in the other world.

For a long, long, blissful time she kept her place, and gradually our hearts ceased to beat so violently, and we became calm.

Such was the confession of our love. No plighted faith, no passionate vows, but the silence and the thrill of sympathy through our hearts were sweeter than words could be.

Diana raised her head and looked fearlessly but appealingly into my eyes as she asked me—

"Oh, Frank, did I do right to speak? Could it have been better if I had waited?"

She saw my wishes in my eyes, and bent down her head to me. I kissed her on the forehead and fervently prayed, "Thank God that all was as it has been. May He bless my own darling wife forever and ever." "Amen," said a sweet, tender voice.

We both looked up without shame, for we knew the tones of my second mother. Her face, streaming with tears of joy, was lit up by a sudden ray of sunlight through the casement.

End

# THE CASTLE OF THE KING

When they told the poor Poet that the One he loved best was lying sick in the shadow of danger, he was nigh distraught.

For weeks past he had been alone; she, his Wife, having gone afar to her old home to see an aged grandsire ere he died.

The Poet's heart had for some days been oppressed with a strange sorrow. He did not know the cause of it; he only knew with the deep sympathy which is the poet's gift, that the One he loved was sick. Anxiously had he awaited tidings. When the news came, the shock, although he expected a sad message, was too much for him, and he became nigh distraught.

In his sadness and anxiety he went out into the garden which long years he had cultured for Her. There, amongst the bright flowers, where the old statues stood softly white against the hedges of yew, he lay down in the long uncut summer grass, and wept with his head buried low.

He thought of all the past—of how he had won his Wife and how they loved each other; and to him it seemed a sad and cruel thing that she was afar and in danger, and he not near to comfort her or even to share her pain.

Many many thoughts came back to him, telling the story of the weary years whose gloom and solitude he had forgotten in the brightness of his lovely home.—

How in youth they twain had met and in a moment loved. How his poverty and her greatness had kept them apart. How he had struggled and toiled in the steep and rugged road to fame and fortune.

How all through the weary years he had striven with the single idea of winning such a place in the history of his time, that he should be able to come and to her say, "I love you," and to her proud relations, "I am worthy, for I too have become great."

How amid all this dreaming of a happy time which might come, he had kept silent as to his love. How he had never seen her or heard her voice, or even known her habitation, lest, knowing, he should fail in the purpose of his life.

How time—as it ever does to those who work with honesty and singleness of purpose—crowned the labours and the patience of his life.

How the world had come to know his name and reverence and love it as of one who had helped the weak and weary by his example; who had purified the thoughts of all who listened to his words; and who had swept away baseness before the grandeur and simpleness of his noble thoughts.

How success had followed in the wake of fame.

How at length even to his heart, timorous with the doubt of love, had been borne the thought that he had at last achieved the greatness which justified him in seeking the hand of her he loved.

How he had come back to his native place, and there found her still free.

How when he had dared to tell her of his love she had whispered to him that she, too, had waited all the years, for that she knew that he would come to claim her at the end.

How she had come with him as his bride into the home which he had been making for her all these years. How, there, they had lived happily; and had dared to look into the long years to come for joy and content without a bar.

How he thought that even then, when though somewhat enfeebled in strength by the ceaseless toil of years and the care of hoping, he might look to the happy time to come.

But, alas! for hope; for who knoweth what a day may bring forth? Only a little while ago his Dear One had left him hale, departing in the cause of duty; and now she lay sick and he not nigh to help her.

All the sunshine of his life seemed passing away. All the long years of waiting and the patient continuance in well doing which had crowned their years with love, seemed as but a passing dream, and was all in vain—all, all in vain.

Now with the shadow hovering over his Beloved One, the cloud seemed to be above and around them, and to hold in its dim recesses the doom of them both.

"Why, oh why," asked the poor Poet to the viewless air, "did love come to us? Why came peace and joy and happiness, if the darkening wings of peril shadow the air around her, and leave me to weep alone?"

Thus he moaned, and raved, and wept; and the bitter hours went by him in his solitude.

As he lay in the garden with his face buried in the long grass, they came to him and told him with weeping, that tidings—sad, indeed—had come.

As they spoke he lifted his poor head and gazed at them; and they saw in the great, dark, tender eyes that now he was quite distraught. He smiled at them sadly, as though not quite understanding the import of their words. As tenderly as they could they tried to tell him that the One he loved best was dead.

They said:—

"She has walked in the Valley of the Shadow"; but he seemed to understand them not.

They whispered,

"She has heard the Music of the Spheres," but still he comprehended not.

Then they spoke to him sorrowfully and said:

"She now abides in the Castle of the King."

He looked at them eagerly, as if to ask:

"What castle? What king?"

They bowed their heads; and as they turned away weeping they murmured to him softly—

"The Castle of the King of Death."

He spake no word; so they turned their weeping faces to him again. They found that he had risen and stood with a set purpose on his face. Then he said sweetly:

"I go to find her, that where she abideth, I too may there abide."

They said to him:

"You cannot go. Beyond the Portal she is, and in the Land of Death."

Set purpose shone in the Poet's earnest, loving eyes as he answered them for the last time:

"Where she has gone, there go I too. Through the Valley of the Shadow shall I wend my way. In these ears also shall ring the Music of the Spheres. I shall seek, and I shall find my Beloved in the Halls of the Castle of the King. I shall clasp her close—even before the dread face of the King of Death."

As they heard these words they bowed their heads again and wept, and said:

"Alas! alas!"

The poet turned and left them; and passed away. They fain would have followed; but he motioned them that they should not stir. So, alone, in his grief he went.

As he passed on he turned and waved his hand to them in farewell.

Then for a while with uplifted hand he stood, and turned him slowly all around.

Suddenly his outstretched hand stopped and pointed. His friends looking with him saw, where, away beyond the Portal, the idle wilderness spread. There in the midst of desolation the mist from the marshes hung like a pall of gloom on the far off horizon.

As the Poet pointed there was a gleam of happiness—very very faint it was—in his poor sad eyes, distraught with loss, as if afar he beheld some sign or hope of the Lost One.

SWIFTLY AND SADLY THE POET fared on through the burning day.

The Rest Time came; but on he journeyed. He paused not for shade or rest. Never, even for an instant did he stop to cool his parched lips with an icy draught from the crystal springs.

The weary wayfarers resting in the cool shadows beside the fountains raised their tired heads and looked at him with sleepy eyes as he hurried. He heeded them not; but went ever onward with set purpose in his eyes, as though some gleam of hope bursting through the mists of the distant marshes urged him on.

So he fared on through all the burning day, and all the silent night. In the earliest dawn, when the promise of the still unrisen sun quickened the eastern sky into a pale light, he drew anigh the Portal. The horizon stood out blackly in the cold morning light.

There, as ever, stood the Angels who kept watch and ward, and oh, wondrous! although invisible to human eyes, they were seen of him.

As he drew nigh they gazed at him pityingly and swept their great wings out wide, as if to shelter him. He spake; and from his troubled heart the sad words came sweetly through the pale lips:

"Say, Ye who guard the Land, has my Beloved One passed hither on the journey to the Valley of the Shadow, to hear the Music of the Spheres, and to abide in the Castle of the King?"

The Angels at the Portal bowed their heads in token of assent; and they turned and looked outward from the Land to where, far off in the idle wilderness, the dank mists crept from the lifeless bosom of the marsh.

They knew well that the poor lonely Poet was in quest of his Beloved One; so they hindered him not, neither urged they him to stay. They pitied him much for that much he loved.

They parted wide, that through the Portal he might pass without let.

So, the Poet went onwards into the idle desert to look for his Beloved One in the Castle of the King.

For a time he went through gardens whose beauty was riper than the gardens of the Land. The sweetness of all things stole on the senses like the odours from the Isles of the Blest.

The subtlety of the King of Death, who rules in the Realms of Evil, is great. He has ordered that the way beyond the Portal be made full of charm. Thus those straying from the paths ordained for good see around them such beauty that in its joy the gloom and cruelty and guilt of the desert are forgotten.

But as the Poet passed onwards the beauty began to fade away.

The fair gardens looked as gardens do when the hand of care is taken off, and when the weeds in their hideous luxuriance choke, as they spring up, the choicer life of the flowers.

From cool alleys under spreading branches, and from crisp sward which touched as soft as velvet the Wanderer's aching feet, the way became a rugged stony path, full open to the burning glare. The flowers began to lose their odour, and to dwarf to stunted growth. Tall hemlocks rose on every side, infecting the air with their noisome odour.

Great fungi grew in the dark hollows where the pools of dank water lay. Tall trees, with branches like skeletons, rose-trees which had no leaves, and under whose shadow to pause were to die.

Then huge rocks barred the way. These were only passed by narrow, winding passages, overhung by the ponderous cliffs above, which ever threatened to fall and engulph the Sojourner.

Here the night began to fall; and the dim mist rising from the far-off marshes, took weird shapes of gloom. In the distant fastnesses of the mountains the wild beasts began to roar in their cavern lairs. The air became hideous with the fell sounds of the night season.

But the poor Poet heeded not ill sights or sounds of dread. Onward he went ever—unthinking of the terrors of the night. To him there was no dread of darkness—no fear of death—no consciousness of horror. He sought his Beloved One in the Castle of the King; and in that eager quest all natural terrors were forgot.

So fared he onward through the livelong night. Up the steep defiles he trod. Through the shadows of the huge rocks he passed unscathed. The wild animals came around him roaring fiercely—their great eyes flaming like fiery stars through the blackness of the night.

From the high rocks great pythons crawled and hung to seize their prey. From the crevices of the mountain steeps, and from cavernous rifts in the rocky way poisonous serpents glided and rose to strike.

But close though the noxious things came, they all refrained to attack; for they knew that the lonely Sojourner was bound for the Castle of their King.

Onward still, onward he went—unceasing—pausing not in his course—but pressing ever forward in his quest.

When daylight broke at last, the sun rose on a sorry sight. There toiling on the rocky way, the poor lonely Poet went ever onwards, unheeding of cold or hunger or pain.

His feet were bare, and his footsteps on the rock-strewn way were marked by blood. Around and behind him, and afar off keeping equal pace on the summits of the rocky ridges, came the wild beasts that looked on him as their prey, but that refrained from touching him because he sought the Castle of their King.

In the air wheeled the obscene birds who follow ever on the track of the dying and the lost. Hovered the bare-necked vultures with eager eyes, and hungry beaks. Their great wings flapped lazily in the idle air as they followed in the Wanderer's track. The vulture are a patient folk, and they await the falling of the prey.

From the cavernous recesses in the black mountain gorges crept, with silent speed, the serpents that there lurk. Came the python, with his colossal folds and endless coils, whence looked forth cunningly the small flat head. Came the boa and all his tribe, which seize their prey by force and crush it with the dread strictness of their embrace. Came the hooded snakes and all those which with their venom destroy their prey. Here, too, came those serpents most terrible of all to their quarry—which fascinate with eyes of weird magic and by the slow gracefulness of their approach.

Here came or lay in wait, subtle snakes, which take the colour of herb, or leaf, or dead branch, or slimy pool, amongst which they lurk, and so strike their prey unsuspecting.

Great serpents there were, nimble of body, which hang from rock or branch. These gripping tight to their distant hold, strike downward with the rapidity of light as they hurl their whip-like bodies from afar upon their prey.

Thus came forth all these noxious things to meet the Questing Man, and to assail him. But when they knew he was bound for the dread Castle of their King, and saw how he went onward without fear, they abstained from attack.

The deadly python and the boa towering aloft, with colossal folds, were passive, and for the nonce, became as stone. The hooded serpents drew in again their venomous fangs. The mild, deep earnest eyes of the fascinating snake became lurid with baffled spleen, as he felt his power to charm was without avail. In its deadly descent the hanging snake arrested its course, and hung a limp line from rock or branch.

Many followed the Wanderer onwards into the desert wilds, waiting and hoping for a chance to destroy.

Many other perils also were there for the poor Wanderer in the desert idleness. As he went onward the rocky way got steeper and darker. Lurid fogs and deadly chill mists arose.

Then in this path along the trackless wilderness were strange and terrible things.

Mandrakes—half plant, half man—shrieked at him with despairing cry, as, helpless for evil, they stretched out their ghastly arms in vain.

Giant thorns arose in the path; they pierced his suffering feet and tore his flesh as onward he trod. He felt the pain, but he heeded it not.

In all the long, terrible journey he had but one idea other than his eager search for his Beloved One. He thought that the children of men might learn much from the journey towards the Castle of the King, which began so fair, amidst the odorous gardens and under the cool shadow of the spreading trees. In his heart the Poet spake to the multitude of the children of men; and from his lips the words flowed like music, for he sang of the Golden Gate which the Angels call TRUTH.

> *"Pass not the Portal of the Sunset Land!*
> *Pause where the Angels at their vigil stand.*
> *Be warned! and press not though the gates lie wide,*
> *But rest securely on the hither side.*
> *Though odorous gardens and cool ways invite,*
> *Beyond are darkest valleys of the night.*
> *Rest! Rest contented.—Pause whilst undefiled,*
> *Nor seek the horrors of the desert wild."*

Thus treading down all obstacles with his bleeding feet, passed ever onwards, the poor distraught Poet, to seek his Beloved One in the Castle of the King.

Even as onward he went the life that is of the animals seemed to die away behind him. The jackals and the more cowardly savage animals slunk away. The lions and tigers, and bears, and wolves, and all the braver of the fierce beasts of prey which followed on his track even after the others had stopped, now began to halt in their career.

They growled low and then roared loudly with uplifted heads; the bristles of their mouths quivered with passion, and the great white teeth champed angrily together in baffled rage. They went on a little further; and stopped again roaring and growling as before. Then one by one they ceased, and the poor Poet went on alone.

In the air the vultures wheeled and screamed, pausing and halting in their flight, as did the savage beasts. These too ceased at length to follow in air the Wanderer in his onward course.

Longest of all kept up the snakes. With many a writhe and stealthy onward glide, they followed hard upon the footsteps of the Questing Man. In the blood marks of his feet upon the flinty rocks they found a joy and hope, and they followed ever.

But time came when the awful aspect of the places where the Poet passed checked even the serpents in their track—the gloomy defiles whence issue the poisonous winds that sweep with desolation even the dens of the beasts of prey—the sterile fastnesses which march upon the valleys of desolation. Here even the stealthy serpents paused in their course; and they too fell away. They glided back, smiling with deadliest rancour, to their obscene clefts.

Then came places where plants and verdure began to cease. The very weeds became more and more stunted and inane. Farther on they declined into the sterility of lifeless rock. Then the most noxious herbs that grew in ghastly shapes of gloom and terror lost even the power to harm, which outlives their living growth. Dwarfed and stunted even of evil, they were compact of the dead rock. Here even the deadly Upas tree could strike no root into the pestiferous earth.

Then came places where, in the entrance to the Valley of the Shadow, even solid things lost their substance, and melted in the dank and cold mists which swept along.

As he passed, the distraught Poet could feel not solid earth under his bleeding feet. On shadows he walked, and amid them, onward through the Valley of the Shadow to seek his Beloved One in the Castle of the King.

The Valley of the Shadow seemed of endless expanse. Circled by the teeming mist, no eye could pierce to where rose the great mountains between which the Valley lay.

Yet they stood there—Mount Despair on the one hand, and the Hill of Fear upon the other.

Hitherto the poor bewildered brain of the Poet had taken no note of all the dangers, and horrors, and pains which surrounded him—save only for the lesson which they taught. But now, lost as he was in the shrouding vapour of the Valley of the Shadow, he could not but think of the terrors of the way. He was surrounded by grisly phantoms that ever and anon arose silent in the mist, and were lost again before he could catch to the full their dread import.

Then there flashed across his soul a terrible thought—

Could it be possible that hither his Beloved One had travelled? Had there come to her the pains which shook his own form with agony? Was it indeed necessary that she should have been appalled by all these surrounding horrors?

At the thought of her, his Beloved One, suffering such pain and dread, he gave forth one bitter cry that rang through the solitude—that cleft the vapour of the Valley, and echoed in the caverns of the mountains of Despair and Fear.

The wild cry prolonged with the agony of the Poet's soul rang through the Valley, till the shadows that peopled it woke for the moment into life-in-death. They flitted dimly along, now melting away and anon springing again into life—till all the Valley of the Shadow was for once peopled with quickened ghosts.

Oh, in that hour there was agony to the poor distraught Poet's soul.

But presently there came a calm. When the rush of his first agony passed, the Poet knew that to the Dead came not the horrors of the journey that he undertook. To the Quick alone is the horror of the passage to the Castle of the King. With the thought came to him such peace that even there—in the dark Valley of the Shadow—stole soft music that sounded in the desert gloom like the Music of the Spheres.

Then the poor Poet remembered what they had told him; that his Beloved One had walked through the Valley of the Shadow, that she had known the Music of the Spheres, and that she abode in the Castle of the King. So he thought that as he was now in the Valley of the Shadow, and as he heard the Music of the Spheres, that soon he should see the Castle of the King where his Beloved One abode. Thus he went on in hope.

But alas! that very hope was a new pain that ere this he wot not of.

Hitherto he had gone on blindly, recking not of where he went or what came a-nigh him, so long as he pressed onward on his quest; but now the darkness and the peril of the way had new terrors, for he thought of how they might arrest his course. Such thoughts made the way long indeed, for the moments seemed an age with hoping. Eagerly he sought for the end to come, when, beyond the Valley of the Shadow through which he fared, he should see rising the turrets of the Castle of the King.

Despair seemed to grow upon him; and as it grew there rang out, ever louder, the Music of the Spheres.

Onward, ever onward, hurried in mad haste the poor distraught Poet. The dim shadows that peopled the mist shrank back as he passed, extending towards him warning hands with long gloomy fingers of deadly cold. In the bitter silence of the moment, they seemed to say:

"Go back! Go back!"

Louder and louder rang now the Music of the Spheres. Faster and faster in mad, feverish haste rushed the Poet, amid the shrinking Shadows of the gloomy valley. The peopling shadows as they faded away before him, seemed to wail in sorrowful warning:

"Go back! Go back!"

Still in his ears rang ever the swelling tumult of the music.

Faster and faster he rushed onward; till, at last, wearied nature gave way and he fell prone to earth, senseless, bleeding, and alone.

After a time—how long he could not even guess—he awoke from his swoon.

For awhile he could not think where he was; and his scattered senses could not help him.

All was gloom and cold and sadness. A solitude reigned around him, more deadly than aught he had ever dreamt of. No breeze was in the air; no movement of a passing cloud. No voice or stir of living thing in earth, or water, or air. No rustle of leaf or sway of branch—all was silent, dead, and deserted. Amid the eternal hills of gloom around, lay the valley devoid of aught that lived or grew.

The sweeping mists with their multitude of peopling shadows had gone by. The fearsome terrors of the desert even were not there. The Poet, as he gazed around him, in his utter loneliness, longed for the sweep of the storm or the roar of the avalanche to break the dread horror of the silent gloom.

Then the Poet knew that through the Valley of the Shadow had he come; that scared and maddened though he had been, he had heard the Music of the Spheres. He thought that now hard by the desolate Kingdom of Death he trod.

He gazed all around him, fearing lest he should see anywhere the dread Castle of the King, where his Beloved One abode; and he groaned as the fear of his heart found voice:

"Not here! oh not here, amid this awful solitude."

Then amid the silence around, upon distant hills his words echoed:

"Not here! oh not here," till with the echoing and re-echoing rock, the idle wilderness was peopled with voices.

Suddenly the echo voices ceased.

From the lurid sky broke the terrible sound of the thunder peal. Along the distant skies it rolled. Far away over the endless ring of the grey horizon it swept—going and returning—pealing—swelling—dying away. It traversed the aether, muttering now in ominous sound as of threats, and anon crashing with the voice of dread command.

In its roar came a sound as of a word:

"Onward."

To his knees the Poet sank and welcomed with tears of joy the sound of the thunder. It swept away as a Power from Above the silent desolation of the wilderness. It told him that in and above the Valley of the Shadow rolled the mighty tones of Heaven's command.

Then the Poet rose to his feet, and with new heart went onwards into the wilderness.

As he went the roll of the thunder died away, and again the silence of desolation reigned alone.

So TIME WORE ON; BUT never came rest to the weary feet. Onwards, still onwards he went, with but one memory to cheer him—the echo of the thunder roll in his ears, as it pealed out in the Valley of Desolation:

"Onward! Onward!"

Now the road became less and less rocky, as on his way he passed. The great cliffs sank and dwindled away, and the ooze of the fens crept upward to the mountain's feet.

At length the hills and hollows of the mountain fastnesses disappeared. The Wanderer took his way amid mere trackless wastes, where was nothing but quaking marsh and slime.

On, on he wandered; stumbling blindly with weary feet on the endless road.

Over his soul crept ever closer the blackness of despair. Whilst amid the mountain gorges he had been wandering, some small cheer came from the hope that at any moment some turn in the path might show him his journey's end. Some entry from a dark defile might expose to him, looming great in the distance—or even anigh him— the dread Castle of the King. But now with the flat desolation of the silent marsh around him, he knew that the Castle could not exist without his seeing it.

He stood for awhile erect, and turned him slowly round, so that the complete circuit of the horizon was swept by his eager eyes. Alas! never a sight did he see. Nought was there but the black line of the horizon, where the sad earth lay against the level sky. All, all was compact of a silent gloom.

Still on he tottered. His breath came fast and laboured. His weary limbs quivered as they bore him feebly up. His strength—his life—was ebbing fast.

On, on, he hurried, ever on, with one idea desperately fixed in his poor distraught mind—that in the Castle of the King he should find his Beloved One.

He stumbled and fell. There was no obstacle to arrest his feet; only from his own weakness he declined.

Quickly he arose and went onward with flying feet. He dreaded that should he fall he might not be able to arise again.

Again he fell. Again he rose and went on his way desperately, with blind purpose.

So for a while went he onwards, stumbling and falling; but arising ever and pausing not on his way. His quest he followed, of his Beloved One abiding in the Castle of the King.

At last so weak he grew that when he sank he was unable to rise again.

Feebler and feebler he grew as he lay prone; and over his eager eyes came the film of death.

But even then came comfort; for he knew that his race was run, and that soon he would meet his Beloved One in the Halls of the Castle of the King.

To the wilderness his thoughts he spoke. His voice came forth with a feeble sound, like the moaning before a storm of the wind as it passes through reeds in the grey autumn:

"A little longer. Soon I shall meet her in the Halls of the King; and we shall part no more. For this it is worth to pass through the Valley of the Shadow and to listen to the Music of the Spheres with their painful hope. What boots it though the Castle be afar? Quickly speed the feet of the dead. To the fleeting spirit all distance is but a span. I fear not now to see the Castle of the King; for there, within its chiefest Hall, soon shall I meet my Beloved—to part no more."

Even as he spoke he felt that the end was nigh.

Forth from the marsh before him crept a still, spreading mist. It rose silently, higher-higher-enveloping the wilderness for far around. It took deeper and darker shades as it arose. It was as though the Spirit of Gloom were hid within, and grew mightier with the spreading vapour.

To the eyes of the dying Poet the creeping mist was as a shadowy castle. Arose the tall turrets and the frowning keep. The gateway with its cavernous recesses and its beetling towers took shape as a skull. The distant battlements towered aloft into the silent air. From the very ground whereon the stricken Poet lay, grew, dim and dark, a vast causeway leading into the gloom of the Castle gate.

The dying Poet raised his head and looked. His fast failing eyes, quickened by the love and hope of his spirit, pierced through the dark walls of the keep and the gloomy terrors of the gateway.

There, within the great Hall where the grim King of Terrors himself holds his court, he saw her whom he sought. She was standing in the ranks of those who wait in patience for their Beloved to follow them into the Land of Death.

The Poet knew that he had but a little while to wait, and he was patient-stricken though he lay, amongst the Eternal Solitudes.

Afar off, beyond the distant horizon, came a faint light as of the dawn of a coming day.

As it grew brighter the Castle stood out more and more clearly; till in the quickening dawn it stood revealed in all its cold expanse.

The dying Poet knew that the end was at hand. With a last effort he raised himself to his feet, that standing erect and bold, as is the right of manhood, he might so meet face to face the grim King of Death before the eyes of his Beloved One.

The distant sun of the coming day rose over the horizon's edge.

A ray of light shot upward.

As it struck the summit of the Castle keep the Poet's Spirit in an instant of time swept along the causeway. Through the ghostly portal of the Castle it swept, and met with joy the kindred Spirit that it loved before the very face of the King of Death.

Quicker then than the lightning's flash the whole Castle melted into nothingness; and the sun of the coming day shone calmly down upon the Eternal Solitudes.

In the Land within the Portal rose the sun of the coming day. It shone calmly and brightly on a fair garden, where, among the long summer grass lay the Poet, colder than the marble statues around him.

# Buried Treasures

## Chapter I—The Old Wreck

Mr. Stedman spoke.

"I do not wish to be too hard on you; but I will not, I cannot consent to Ellen's marrying you till you have sufficient means to keep her in comfort. I know too well what poverty is. I saw her poor mother droop and pine away till she died, and all from poverty. No, no, Ellen must be spared that sorrow at all events."

"But, sir, we are young. You say you have always earned your living. I can do the same and I thought"—this with a flush—"I thought that if I might be so happy as to win Ellen's love that you might help us."

"And so I would, my dear boy; but what help could I give? I find it hard to keep the pot boiling as it is, and there is only Ellen and myself to feed. No, no, I must have some certainty for Ellen before I let her leave me. Just suppose anything should happen to me"—

"Then, sir, what could be better than to have someone to look after Ellen—someone with a heart to love her as she should be loved, and a pair of hands to be worked to the bone for her sake."

"True, boy; true. But still it cannot be. I must be certain of Ellen's future before I trust her out of my own care. Come now, let me see you with a hundred pounds of your own, and I shall not refuse to let you speak to her. But mind, I shall trust to your honour not to forestall that time."

"It is cruel, sir, although you mean it in kindness. I could as easily learn to fly as raise a hundred pounds with my present opportunities. Just think of my circumstances, sir. If my poor father had lived all would have been different; but you know that sad story."

"No, I do not. Tell it to me."

"He left the Gold Coast after spending half his life there toiling for my poor mother and me. We knew from his letter that he was about to start for home, and that he was coming in a small sailing vessel, taking all his savings with him. But from that time to this he has never been heard of."

"Did you make inquiries?"

"We tried every means, or rather poor mother did, for I was too young, and we could find out nothing."

"Poor boy. From my heart I pity you; still I cannot change my opinion. I have always hoped that Ellen would marry happily. I have worked for her, early and late, since she was born, and it would be mistaken kindness to let her marry without sufficient provisions for her welfare."

Robert Hamilton left Mr. Stedman's cottage in great dejection. He had entered it with much misgiving, but with a hope so strong that it brightened the prospect of success. He went slowly along the streets till he got to his office, and when once there he had so much work to do that little time was left him for reflection until his work for the day was over. That night he lay awake, trying with all the intentness of his nature to conceive some plan by which he might make the necessary sum to entitle him to seek the hand of Ellen Stedman: but all in vain. Scheme after scheme rose up before him, but each one, though born of hope, quickly perished in succession. Gradually his imagination grew in force as the real world seemed to fade away; he built bright castles in the air and installed Ellen as their queen. He thought of all the vast sums of money made each year by chances, of old treasures found after centuries, new treasures dug from mines, and turned from mills and commerce. But all these required capital—except the old treasures—and this source of wealth being a possibility, to it his thoughts clung as a man lost in mid-ocean clings to a spar—clung as he often conceived that his poor father had clung when lost with all his treasure far at sea.

"Vigo Bay, the Schelde, already giving up their long-buried spoil," so thought he. "All round our coasts lie millions lost, hidden but for a time. Other men have benefited by them—why should not I have a chance also?" And then, as he sunk to sleep the possibility seemed to become reality, and as he slept he found treasure after treasure, and all was real to him, for he knew not that he dreamt.

He had many dreams. Most of them connected with the finding of treasures, and in all of them Ellen took a prominent place. He seemed in his dreams to renew his first acquaintance with the girl he loved, and when he thought of the accident that brought them together, it might be expected that the seashore was the scene of many of his dreams. The meeting was in this wise: One holiday, some three years before, he had been walking on the flat shore of the 'Bull,' when he noticed at some distance off a very beautiful young girl, and set to longing for some means of making her acquaintance. The means came even as he wished. The wind was blowing freely, and the girl's hat blew off and hurried seawards over the flat shore. He ran after it and brought it back: and from that hour the two had, after their casual acquaintance had been sanctioned by her father, became fast friends.

Most of his dreams of the night had faded against morning, but one he remembered.

He seemed to be in a wide stretch of sand near the hulk of a great vessel. Beside him lay a large iron-bound box of great weight, which he tried in vain to lift. He had by a lever just forced it through a hole in the side of the ship, and it had fallen on the sand and was sinking. Despite all he could do, it still continued to go down into the sand, but by slow degrees. The mist was getting round him, shutting out the moonlight, and from far he could hear a dull echoing roar muffled by the fog, and the air seemed laden with the clang of distant bells. Then the air became instinct with the forms of life, and amid them floated the form of Ellen, and with her presence the gloom and fog and darkness were dispelled, and the sun rose brightly on the instant, and all was fair and happy.

Next day was Sunday, and so after prayers he went for a walk with his friend, Tom Harrison.

They directed their steps towards Dollymount, and passing across the bridge, over Crab Lake, found themselves on the North Bull. The tide was "black" out, and when they crossed the line of low bent-covered sand-hills, or dunnes, as they are called in Holland, a wide stretch of sand intersected with shallow tidal streams lay before them, out towards the mouth of the bay. As they looked, Robert's dream of the night before flashed into his memory, and he expected to see before him the hulk of the old ship.

Presently Tom remarked:

"I do not think I ever saw the tide so far out before. What an immense stretch of sand there is. It is a wonder there is no rock or anything of the kind all along this shore."

"There is one," said Robert, pointing to where, on the very edge of the water, rose a little mound, seemingly a couple of feet at most, over the level of the sand.

"Let us go out to it," said Tom, and accordingly they both took off their boots and stockings, and walked over the wet sand, and forded the shallow streams till they got within a hundred yards of the mound. Suddenly Tom called out: "It is not a rock at all; it is a ship, bottom upwards, with the end towards us, and sunk in the sand."

Robert's heart stood still for an instant.

What if this should be a treasure-ship, and his dream prove prophetic? In an instant more he shook aside the fancy and hurried on.

They found that Tom had not been mistaken. There lay the hulk of an old ship, with just its bottom over the sand. Close round it the ebb and flow of the tide had worn a hole like the moat round an old castle; and in this pool small fishes darted about, and lazy crabs sidled into the sand.

Tom jumped the narrow moat, and stood balanced on the keel, and a hard task he had to keep his footing on the slippery seaweed. He tapped the timbers with his stick, and they gave back a hollow sound. "The inside is not yet choked up," he remarked.

Robert joined him, and walked all over the bottom of the ship, noticing how some of the planks, half rotten with long exposure, were sinking inwards.

After a few minutes Tom spoke—

"I say, Bob, suppose that this old ship was full of money, and that you and I could get it out."

"I have just been thinking the same."

"Suppose we try," said Tom, and he commenced to endeavour to prize up the end of a broken timber with his stick. Robert watched him for some minutes, and when he had given up the attempt in despair, spoke—

"Suppose we do try, Tom. I have a very strange idea. I had a curious dream last night, and this old ship reminds me of it."

Tom asked Robert to tell the dream. He did so, and when he had finished, and had also confided his difficulty about the hundred pounds, Tom remarked—

"We'll try the hulk, at any rate. Let us come some night and cut a hole in her and look. It might be worth our while; it will be a lark at any rate."

He seemed so interested in the matter that Robert asked him the reason.

"Well, I will tell you," he said. "You know Tomlinson. Well, he told me the other day that he was going to ask Miss Stedman to marry him. He is well off—comparatively, and unless you get your chance soon you may be too late. Don't be offended at me for telling you. I wanted to get an opportunity."

"Thanks, old boy," was Robert's answer, as he squeezed his hand. No more was spoken for a time. Both men examined the hulk carefully, and then came away, and sat again on a sand hill.

Presently a coastguard came along, with his telescope under his arm. Tom entered into conversation with him about the wreck.

"Well, sir," he said, "that was afore my time here. I've been here only about a year, and that's there a matter o' fifteen year or thereabouts. She came ashore here in the great storm when the 'Mallard' was lost in the Scillies. I've heerd tell"—

Robert interrupted him to ask—

"Did anyone ever try what was in her?"

"Well, sir, there I'm out. By rights there should, but I've bin told that about then there was a lawsuit on as to who the shore belonged to. The ship lay in the line between the Ballast Board ground and the Manor ground, or whatever it is, and so nothin' could be done till the suit was ended, and when it was there weren't much use lookin' for anything, for she was settled nigh as low as she is now, and if there ever was anything worth havin' in her the salt water had ruined it long ago."

"Then she was never examined?" said Tom.

"Most like not, sir; they don't never examine little ships like her—if she was a big one we might," and the coastguard departed.

When he was gone Tom said, "By Jove, he forgot to say on whose ground she is," and he ran after him to ask the question. When he came back he said, "It's all right; it belongs to Sir Arthur Forres."

After watching for sometime in silence Robert said, "Tom, I have very strange thoughts about this. Let us get leave from Sir Arthur—he is, I believe, a very generous man—and regularly explore."

"Done," said Tom, and, it being now late, they returned to town.

Chapter II—Wind and Tide

ROBERT AND TOM NEXT DAY wrote a letter to Sir Arthur Forres asking him to let them explore the ship, and by return of post got a kind answer, not only granting the required permission, but making over the whole ship to them to do what they pleased with. Accordingly they held a consultation as to the best means of proceeding, and agreed to commence operations as soon as possible, as it was now well on in December, and every advance of winter would throw new obstacles in their way. Next day they bought some tools, and brought them home in great glee. It often occurred to both of them that they were setting out on the wildest of wild-goose chases, but the novelty and excitement of the whole affair always overcame their scruples. The first moonlight night that came they took their tools, and sallied out to Dollymount to make the first effort on their treasure ship. So intent were they on their object that their immediate surroundings did not excite their attention. It was not, therefore, till they arrived at the summit of the sand hill, from which they had first seen the hulk, that they discovered that the tide was coming in, and had advanced about half way. The knowledge was like a cold bath to each of them, for here were all their hopes dashed to the ground, for an indefinite time at least. It might be far into the winter time—perhaps months—before they could get a union of tide, moonlight, and fair weather, such as alone could make their scheme practicable. They had already tried to get leave from office, but so great was the press of business that their employer told them that unless they had special business, which they could name, he could not dispense with their services. To name their object would be to excite ridicule, and as the whole affair was but based on a chimera they were of course silent.

They went home sadder than they had left it, and next day, by a careful study of the almanac, made out a list of the nights which might suit their purpose—if moon and weather proved favourable. From the fact of their living in their employer's house their time was further curtailed, for it was an inflexible rule that by twelve o'clock everyone should be home. Therefore, the only nights which could suit were those from the 11th to the 15th December, on which there would be low water between the hours of seven and eleven. This would give them on each night about one hour in which to work, for that length of time only was the wreck exposed between the ebbing and flowing tides.

They waited in anxiety for the 11th December, the weather continued beautifully fine, and nearly every night the two friends walked to view the scene of their future operations. Robert was debarred from visiting Ellen by her father's direction, and so was glad to have some object of interest to occupy his thoughts whilst away from her.

As the time wore on, the weather began to change, and Robert and Tom grew anxious. The wind began to blow in short sharp gusts, which whirled the sodden dead leaves angrily about exposed corners, and on the seaboard sent the waves shorewards topped with angry crests. Misty clouds came drifting hurriedly over the sea, and at times the fog became so thick that it was hardly possible to see more than a few yards ahead, still the young men continued to visit their treasure every night. At first, the coastguards had a watchful eye on them, noticing which they unfolded their purpose and showed Sir Arthur's letter making the ship over to their hands.

The sailors treated the whole affair as a good joke, but still promised to do what they could to help them, in the good-humoured way which is their special charm. A certain fear had for sometime haunted the two friends—a fear which neither of them had ever spoken out. From brooding so much as they did on their adventure, they came to think, or rather to feel, that the ship which for fifteen years had been unnoticed and untouched in the sand, had suddenly acquired as great an interest in the eyes of all the world as of themselves. Accordingly, they thought that some evil-designing person might try to cut them out of their adventure by forestalling them in searching the wreck. Their fear was dispelled by the kindly promise of the coastguards not to let anyone meddle with the vessel without their permission. As the weather continued to get more and more broken, the very disappointment of their hopes, which the break threatened served to enlarge those hopes, and when on the night of the tenth they heard a wild storm howling round the chimneys, as they lay in bed, each was assured in his secret heart that the old wreck contained such a treasure as the world had seldom seen.

Seven o'clock next night saw them on the shore of the Bull looking out into the pitchy darkness. The wind was blowing so strongly inshore that the waves were driven high beyond their accustomed line at the same state of the tide, and the channels were running like mill-dams. As each wave came down over the flat shore it was broke up into a mass of foam and spray, and the wind swept away the spume until on shore it fell like rain. Far along the sandy shore was heard the roaring of the waves, hoarsely bellowing, so that hearing the sound we could well imagine how the district got its quaint name.

On such a night it would have been impossible to have worked at the wreck, even could the treasure-seekers have reached it, or could they have even found it in the pitchy darkness. They waited sometime, but seeing that it was in vain, they sadly departed homeward, hoping fondly that the next evening would prove more propitious.

Vain were their hopes. The storm continued for two whole days, for not one moment of which, except between the pauses of the rushing or receding waves, was the wreck exposed. Seven o'clock each night saw the two young men looking over the sand-hills, waiting in the vain hope of a chance of visiting the vessel, hoping against hope that a sudden calm would give the opportunity they wished. When the storm began to abate their hopes were proportionally raised, and on the morning of the 14th when they awoke and could not hear the wind whistling through the chimneys next their attic, they grew again sanguine of success. That night they went to the Bull in hope, and came home filled with despair. Although the storm had ceased, the sea was still rough. Great, heavy, sullen waves, sprayless, but crested ominously, from ridges of foam, came rolling into the bay, swelling onward with great speed and resistless force, and bursting over the shallow waste of sand so violently that even any attempt to reach the wreck was out of the question. As Robert and Tom hurried homeward—they had waited to the latest moment on the Bull, and feared being late—they felt spiritless and dejected. But one more evening remained on which they might possibly visit the wreck, and they feared that even should wind and tide be suitable one hour would not do to explore it. However, youth is never without hope, and next morning they both had that sanguine feeling which is the outcome of despair—the feeling that the tide of fortune must sometime turn, and that the loser as well as the winner has his time. As they neared the Bull that night their hearts beat so loud that they could almost hear them. They felt that there was ground for hope. All the way from town they could see the great flats opposite Clontarf lying black in the moonlight, and they thought that over the sands the same calm must surely rest. But, alas, they did not allow for the fact that two great breakwaters protect the harbour, but that the sands of the Bull are open to all the storms that blow—that the great Atlantic billows, broken up on the northern and southern coasts, yet still strong enough to be feared, sweep up and down the Channel, and beat with every tide into the harbours and bays along the coast. Accordingly, on reaching the sand-hills, they saw what dashed their hopes at once.

The moon rose straight before them beyond the Bailey Lighthouse, and the broad belt of light which stretched from it passed over the treasure-ship. The waves, now black, save where the light caught the sloping sides, lay blank, but ever and anon as they passed on far over their usual range, the black hull rose among the gleams of light. There was not a chance that the wreck could be attempted, and so they went sadly home—remembering the fact that the night of the 24th December was the earliest time at which they could again renew their effort.

# Chapter III—The Iron Chest

THE DAYS THAT INTERVENED WERE long to both men.

To Robert they were endless; even the nepenthe of continued hard work could not quiet his mind. Distracted on one side by his forbidden love for Ellen, and on the other by the expected fortune by which he might win her, he could hardly sleep at night. When he did sleep he always dreamed, and in his dreams Ellen and the wreck were always associated. At one time his dream would be of unqualified good fortune—a vast treasure found and shared with his love; at another, all would be gloom, and in the search for the treasure he would endanger his life, or, what was far greater pain, forfeit her love.

However, it is one consolation, that, whatever else may happen in the world, time wears on without ceasing, and the day longest expected comes at last.

On the evening of the 24th December, Tom and Robert took their way to Dollymount in breathless excitement.

As they passed through town, and saw the vast concourse of people all intent on one common object—the preparation for the greatest of all Christian festivals—the greatest festival, which is kept all over the world, wherever the True Light has fallen, they could not but feel a certain regret that they, too, could not join in the throng. Robert's temper was somewhat ruffled by seeing Ellen leaning on the arm of Tomlinson, looking into a brilliantly-lighted shop window, so intently, that she did not notice him passing. When they had left the town, and the crowds, and the overflowing stalls, and brilliant holly-decked shops, they did not so much mind, but hurried on.

So long as they were within city bounds, and even whilst there were brightly-lit shop windows, all seemed light enough. When, however, they were so far from town as to lose the glamour of the lamplight in the sky overhead, they began to fear that the night would indeed be too dark for work.

They were prepared for such an emergency, and when they stood on the slope of sand, below the dunnes, they lit a dark lantern and prepared to cross the sands. After a few moments they found that the lantern was a mistake. They saw the ground immediately before them so far as the sharp triangle of light, whose apex was the bulls-eye, extended, but beyond this the darkness rose like a solid black wall. They closed the lantern, but this was even worse, for after leaving the light, small though it was, their eyes were useless in the complete darkness. It took them nearly an hour to reach the wreck.

At last they got to work, and with hammer and chisel and saw commenced to open the treasure ship.

The want of light told sorely against them, and their work progressed slowly despite their exertions. All things have an end, however, and in time they had removed several planks so as to form a hole some four feet wide, by six long—one of the timbers crossed this; but as it was not in the middle, and left a hole large enough to descend by, it did not matter.

It was with beating hearts that the two young men slanted the lantern so as to turn the light in through the aperture. All within was black, and not four feet below them was a calm glassy pool of water that seemed like ink. Even as they looked this began slowly to rise, and they saw that the tide had turned, and that but a few minutes more remained. They reached down as far as they could, plunging their arms up to their shoulders in the water, but could find nothing. Robert stood up and began to undress.

"What are you going to do?" said Tom.

"Going to dive—it is the only chance we have."

Tom did not hinder him, but got the piece of rope they had brought with them and fastened it under Robert's shoulders and grasped the other end firmly. Robert arranged the lamp so as to throw the light as much downwards as possible, and then, with a silent prayer, let himself down through the aperture and hung on by the beam. The water was deadly cold—so cold, that, despite the fever heat to which he was brought through excitement, he felt chilled. Nevertheless he did not hesitate, but, letting go the beam, dropped into the black water.

"For Ellen," he said, as he disappeared.

In a quarter of a minute he appeared again, gasping, and with a convulsive effort climbed the short rope, and stood beside his friend.

"Well?" asked Tom, excitedly.

"Oh-h-h-h! good heavens, I am chilled to the heart. I went down about six feet, and then touched a hard substance. I felt round it, and so far as I can tell it is a barrel. Next to it was a square corner of a box, and further still something square made of iron."

"How do you know it is iron?"

"By the rust. Hold the rope again, there is no time to lose; the tide is rising every minute, and we will soon have to go."

Again he went into the black water and this time stayed longer. Tom began to be frightened at the delay, and shook the rope for him to ascend. The instant after he appeared with face almost black with suffused blood. Tom hauled at the rope, and once more he stood on the bottom of the vessel. This time he did not complain of the cold. He seemed quivering with a great excitement that overcame the cold. When he had recovered his breath he almost shouted out—

"There's something there. I know it—I feel it."

"Anything strange?" asked Tom, in fierce excitement.

"Yes, the iron box is heavy—so heavy that I could not stir it. I could easily lift the end of the cask, and two or three other boxes, but I could not stir it."

Whilst he was speaking, both heard a queer kind of hissing noise, and looking down in alarm saw the water running into the pool around the vessel. A few minutes more and they would be cut off from shore by some of the tidal streams. Tom cried out:

"Quick, quick! or we shall be late. We must put down the beams before the tide rises or it will wash the hold full of sand."

Without waiting even to dress, Robert assisted him and they placed the planks on their original position and secured them with a few strong nails. Then they rushed away for shore. When they had reached the sand-hill, Robert, despite his exertions, was so chilled that he was unable to put on his clothes.

To bathe and stay naked for half an hour on a December night is no joke.

Tom drew his clothes on him as well as he could, and after adding his overcoat and giving him a pull from the flask, he was something better. They hurried away, and what with exercise, excitement, and hope were glowing when they reached home.

Before going to bed they held a consultation as to what was best to be done. Both wished to renew their attempt as they could begin at half-past seven o'clock; for although the morrow was Christmas Day, they knew that any attempt to rescue goods from the wreck should be made at once. There were now two dangers to be avoided—rough weather and the drifting of the sand—and so they decided that not a moment was to be lost.

At the daybreak they were up, and the first moment that saw the wreck approachable found them wading out towards it. This time they were prepared for wet and cold. They had left their clothes on the beach and put on old ones, which, even if wet, would still keep off the wind, for a strong, fitful breeze was now blowing in eddies, and the waves were beginning to rise ominously. With beating hearts they examined the closed-up gap; and, as they looked, their hopes fell. One of the timbers had been lifted off by the tide, and from the deposit of sand in the crevices, they feared that much must have found its way in. They had brought several strong pieces of rope with them, for their effort today was to be to lift out the iron chest, which both fancied contained a treasure.

Robert prepared himself to descend again. He tied one rope round his waist, as before, and took the other in his hands. Tom waited breathlessly till he returned. He was a long time coming up, and rose with his teeth chattering, but had the rope no longer with him. He told Tom that he had succeeded in putting it under the chest. Then he went down again with the other rope, and when he rose the second time, said that he had put it under also, but crossing the first. He was so chilled that he was unable to go down a third time. Indeed, he was hardly able to stand so cold did he seem; and it was with much shrinking of spirit that his friend prepared to descend to make the ropes fast, for he knew that should anything happen to him Robert could not help him up. This did not lighten his task or serve to cheer his spirits as he went down for the first time into the black water. He took two pieces of rope; his intention being to tie Robert's ropes round the chest, and then bring the spare ends up. When he rose he told Robert that he had tied one of the ropes round the box, but had not time to tie the others. He was so chilled that he could not venture to go down again, and so both men hurriedly closed the gap as well as they could, and went on shore to change their clothes. When they had dressed, and got tolerably warm, the tide had begun to turn, and so they went home, longing for the evening to come, when they might make the final effort.

Chapter IV—Lost and Found

Tom was to dine with some relatives where he was living. When he was leaving Robert he said to him, "Well, Bob, seven o'clock, sharp."

"Tom, do not forget or be late. Mind, I trust you."

"Never fear, old boy. Nothing short of death shall keep me away; but if I should happen not to turn up do not wait for me. I will be with you in spirit if I cannot be in the flesh."

"Tom, don't talk that way. I don't know what I should do if you didn't come. It may be all a phantom we're after, but I do not like to think so. It seems so much to me."

"All right, old man," said Tom, cheerily, "I shan't fail—seven o'clock," and he was gone.

Robert was in a fever all day. He went to the church where he knew he would see Ellen, and get a smile from her in passing. He did get a smile, and a glance from her lovely dark eyes which said as plainly as if she had spoken the words with her sweet lips, "How long you have been away; you never come to see me now." This set Robert's heart bounding, but it increased his fever. "How would it be," he thought, "if the wreck turned out a failure, and the iron box a deception? If I cannot get £100 those dark eyes will have to look sweet things to someother man; that beautiful mouth to whisper in the ears of someone who would not—could not—love her half so well as I do."

He could not bear to meet her, so when service was over he hurried away. When she came out her eyes were beaming, for she expected to see Robert waiting for her. She looked anxiously, but could only see Mr. Tomlinson, who did not rise in her favour for appearing just then.

Robert had to force himself to eat his dinner. Every morsel almost choked him, but he knew that strength was necessary for his undertaking, and so compelled himself to eat. As the hour of seven approached he began to get fidgety. He went often to the window, but could see no sign of Tom. Seven o'clock struck, but no Tom came. He began to be alarmed. Tom's words seemed to ring in his ears, "nothing short of death shall keep me away." He waited a little while in terrible anxiety, but then bethought him of his companion's other words, "if I should not happen to turn up do not wait for me," and knowing that whether he waited or no the tide would still come in all the same, and his chance of getting out the box would pass away, determined to set out alone. His determination was strengthened by the fact that the gusty wind of the morning had much increased, and sometimes swept along laden with heavy clinging mist that bespoke a great fog bank somewhere behind the wind.

Till he had reached the very shore of the "Bull" he did not give up hopes of Tom, for he thought it just possible that he might have been delayed, and instead of increasing the delay by going home, had come on straight to the scene of operation.

There was, however, no help for it; as Tom had not come he should work alone. With misgivings he prepared himself. He left his clothes on the top of a sand-hill, put on the old ones he had brought with him, took his tools, ropes, and lantern, and set out. There was cause for alarm. The wind was rising, and it whistled in his ears as the gusts swept past. Far away in the darkness the sea was beginning to roar on the edge of the flats, and the mist came driving inland in sheets like the spume from a cataract. The water in the tidal streams as he waded across them beat against his legs and seemed cold as ice. Although now experienced in the road, he had some difficulty in finding the wreck, but at length reached it and commenced operations.

He had taken the precaution of bringing with him a second suit of old clothes and an oilskin coat. His first care was to fix the lamp where the wind could not harm it; his second, to raise the planks, and expose the interior of the wreck. Then he prepared his ropes, and, having undressed once again, went beneath the water to fasten the second rope. This he accomplished safely, and let the knot of it be on the opposite side to where the first rope was tied. He then ascended and dressed himself in all his clothes to keep him warm. He then cut off a portion in another plank, so as to expose a second one of the ship's timbers. Round this he tied one of the ropes, keeping it as taut as he could. He took a turn of the other rope round the other beam and commenced to pull. Little by little he raised the great chest from its position, and when he had raised it all he could he made that rope fast and went to the other.

By attacking the ropes alternately he raised the chest, so that he could feel from its situation that it hung suspended in the water. Then he began to shake the ropes till the chest swung like a pendulum. He held firmly both ropes, having a turn of each round its beam, and each time the weight swung he gained a little rope. So he worked on little by little, till at last, to his infinite joy, he saw the top of the box rise above the water. His excitement then changed to frenzy. His strength redoubled, and, as faster and faster the box swung, he gained more and more rope, and raised it higher and higher, till at last it ceased to rise, and he found he had reached the maximum height attainable by this means. As, however, it was now nearly up he detached a long timber, and using it as a lever, slowly, after repeated failures, prized up the chest through the gap till it reached the bottom of the ship, and then, toppling over, fell with a dull thud upon the sand.

With a cry of joy Robert jumped down after it, but in jumping lit on the edge of it and wrenched his ankle so severely that when he rose up and attempted to stand on it it gave way under him, and he fell again. He managed, however, to crawl out of the hulk, and reached his lantern. The wind by this time was blowing louder and louder, and the mist was gathering in white masses, and sweeping by, mingled with sleet. In endeavouring to guard the lantern from the wind he slipped once more on the wet timbers, and fell down, striking his leg against the sharp edge of the chest. So severe was the pain that for a few moments he became almost insensible, and when he recovered his senses found he was quite unable to stir.

The lantern had fallen in a pool of water, and had of course gone out. It was a terrible situation, and Robert's heart sank within him, as well it might, as he thought of what was to come. The wind was rapidly rising to a storm, and swept by him, laden with the deadly mist in fierce gusts. The roaring of the tide grew nearer and nearer, and louder and louder. Overhead was a pall of darkness, save when in the leaden winter sky some white pillar of mist swept onward like an embodied spirit of the storm. All the past began to crowd Robert's memory, and more especially the recent past. He thought of his friend's words— "Nothing short of death shall keep me away," and so full of dismal shadows, and forms of horror was all the air, that he could well fancy that Tom was dead, and that his spirit was circling round him, wailing through the night. Then again, arose the memory of his dream, and his very heart stood still, as he thought of how awfully it had been fulfilled. There he now lay; not in a dream, but in reality, beside a ship on a waste of desert sand. Beside him lay a chest such as he had seen in his dreams, and, as before, death seemed flapping his giant wings over his head. Strange horrors seemed to gather round him, borne on the wings of the blast. His father, whom he had never seen, he felt to be now beside him. All the dead that he had ever known circled round him in a weird dance. As the stormy gusts swept by, he heard amid their screams the lugubrious tolling of bells; bells seemed to be all around him; whichever way he turned he heard his knell. All forms were gathered there, as in his dreams—all save Ellen. But hark! even as the thought flashed across his brain; his ears seemed to hear her voice as one hears in a dream. He tried to cry out, but was so overcome by cold, that he could barely hear his own voice. He tried to rise, but in vain, and then, overcome by pain and excitement, and disappointed hope, he became insensible.

Was his treasure-hunting to end thus?

As Mr. Stedman and Ellen was sitting down to tea that evening, Arthur Tomlinson being the only other guest, a hurried knock came to the cottage door. The little servant came into the room a moment after, looking quite scared, and holding a letter in her hand. She came over to Ellen and faltered out, "Oh, please, miss, there's a man from the hospital, and he says as how you're to open the letter and to come at once; it's a matter of life and death."

Ellen grew white as a sheet, and stood up quickly, trembling as she opened the letter. Mr. Stedman rose up, too. Arthur Tomlinson sat still, and glared at the young servant till, thinking she had done something wrong, she began to cry. The letter was from the doctor of the hospital, written for Tom, and praying her to come at once, as the latter had something to tell her of the greatest import to one for whom he was sure she would do much. She immediately ran and put on her cloak, and asked her father to come with her.

"Surely you won't go?" said Tomlinson.

"What else should I do?" she asked, scornfully; "I must apologise for leaving you, unless you will come with us."

"No, thank you; I am not a philanthropist."

In half an hour they had reached the hospital, and had heard Tom's story. Poor fellow, when hurrying home to Robert, he had been knocked down by a car and had his leg broken. As soon as he could he had sent word to Ellen, for he feared for Robert being out alone at the wreck, knowing how chilled he had been on the previous night, and he thought that if anyone would send him aid Ellen would.

No sooner had the story been told, and Ellen had understood the danger Robert was in, than with her father she hurried off to the "Bull."

They got a car with some difficulty, and drove as fast as the horse could go, and arriving at the "Bull," called to the coastguard-station. None of the coastguards had seen Robert that evening, but on learning of his possible danger all that were in the station at once turned out. They wrapped Ellen and her father in oilskins, and, taking lanterns and ropes, set out for the wreck. They all knew its position, and went as straight for it as they could, and, as they crossed the sandhills, found Robert's clothes. At this they grew very grave. They wanted to leave Ellen on the shore, but she refused point blank. By this time the storm was blowing wildly, and the roaring of the sea being borne on the storm was frightful to hear. The tidal streams were running deeper than usual, and there was some difficulty in crossing to the wreck.

In the mist the men lost their way a little, and could not tell exactly how far to go. They shouted as loudly as they could, but there was no reply. Ellen's terror grew into despair. She too, shouted, although fearing that to shout in the teeth of such a wind her woman's voice would be of no avail. However, her clear soprano rang out louder than the hoarse shouts of the sturdy sailors, and cleft the storm like a wedge. Twice or thrice she cried, "Robert, Robert, Robert," but still there was no reply. Suddenly she stopped, and, bending her head, cried joyfully, "He is there, he is there; I hear his voice," and commenced running as fast as she could through the darkness towards the raging sea. The coastguards called out to her to mind where she was going, and followed her with the lanterns as fast as they could run.

When they came up with her they found her sitting on an iron chest close to the wreck, with Robert resting on her knees, and his head pillowed on her breast. He had opened his eyes, and was faintly whispering, "Ellen, my love, my love. It was to win you I risked my life."

She bent and kissed him, even there among rough sailors, and then, amid the storm, she whispered softly, "It was not risked in vain."

# The Crystal Cup

## I. The Dream-Birth

THE BLUE WATERS TOUCH THE walls of the palace; I can hear their soft, lapping wash against the marble whenever I listen. Far out at sea I can see the waves glancing in the sunlight, ever-smiling, ever-glancing, ever-sunny. Happy waves!—happy in your gladness, thrice happy that ye are free!

I rise from my work and spring up the wall till I reach the embrasure. I grasp the corner of the stonework and draw myself up till I crouch in the wide window. Sea, sea, out away as far as my vision extends. There I gaze till my eyes grow dim; and in the dimness of my eyes my spirit finds its sight. My soul flies on the wings of memory away beyond the blue, smiling sea—away beyond the glancing waves and the gleaming sails, to the land I call my home. As the minutes roll by, my actual eyesight seems to be restored, and I look round me in my old birth-house. The rude simplicity of the dwelling comes back to me as something new. There I see my old books and manuscripts and pictures, and there, away on their old shelves, high up above the door, I see my first rude efforts in art.

How poor they seem to me now! And yet, were I free, I would not give the smallest of them for all I now possess. Possess? How I dream.

The dream calls me back to waking life. I spring down from my window-seat and work away frantically, for every line I draw on paper, every new form that springs on the plaster, brings me nearer freedom. I will make a vase whose beauty will put to shame the glorious works of Greece in her golden prime! Surely a love like mine and a hope like mine must in time make some form of beauty spring to life! When He beholds it he will exclaim with rapture, and will order my instant freedom. I can forget my hate, and the deep debt of revenge which I owe him when I think of liberty—even from his hands. Ah! then on the wings of the morning shall I fly beyond the sea to my home—her home—and clasp her to my arms, never more to be separated!

But, oh Spirit of Day! if she should be—No, no, I cannot think of it, or I shall go mad. Oh Time, Time! maker and destroyer of men's fortunes, why hasten so fast for others whilst thou laggest so slowly for me? Even now my home may have become desolate, and she—my bride of an hour—may sleep calmly in the cold earth. Oh this suspense will drive me mad! Work, work! Freedom is before me; Aurora is the reward of my labour!

So I rush to my work; but to my brain and hand, heated alike, no fire or no strength descends. Half mad with despair, I beat myself against the walls of my prison, and then climb into the embrasure, and once more gaze upon the ocean, but find there no hope. And so I stay till night, casting its pall of blackness over nature, puts the possibility of effort away from me for yet another day.

So my days go on, and grow to weeks and months. So will they grow to years, should life so long remain an unwelcome guest within me; for what is man without hope? and is not hope nigh dead within this weary breast?

Last night, in my dreams, there came, like an inspiration from the Day-Spirit, a design for my vase.

All day my yearning for freedom—for Aurora, or news of her—had increased tenfold, and my heart and brain were on fire. Madly I beat myself, like a caged bird, against my prison-bars. Madly I leaped to my window-seat, and gazed with bursting eyeballs out on the free, open sea. And there I sat till my passion had worn itself out; and then I slept, and dreamed of thee, Aurora—of thee and freedom. In my ears I heard again the old song we used to sing together, when as children we wandered on the beach; when, as lovers, we saw the sun sink in the ocean, and I would see its glory doubled as it shone in thine eyes, and was mellowed against thy cheek; and when, as my bride, you clung to me as my arms went round you on that desert tongue of land whence rushed that band of sea-robbers that tore me away. Oh! how my heart curses those men—not men, but fiends! But one solitary gleam of joy remains from that dread encounter,—that my struggle stayed those hell-hounds, and that, ere I was stricken down, this right hand sent one of them to his home. My spirit rises as I think of that blow that saved thee from a life worse than death. With the thought I feel my cheeks burning, and my forehead swelling with mighty veins. My eyes burn, and I rush wildly round my prison-house, "Oh! for one of my enemies, that I might dash out his brains against these marble walls, and trample his heart out as he lay before me!" These walls would spare him not. They are pitiless, alas! I know too well. "Oh, cruel mockery of kindness, to make a palace a prison, and to taunt a captive's aching heart with forms of beauty and sculptured marble!" Wondrous, indeed, are these sculptured walls! Men call them passing fair; but oh, Aurora! with thy beauty ever before my eyes, what form that men call lovely can be fair to me? Like him who gazes sun-wards, and then sees no light on earth, from the glory that dyes his iris, so thy beauty or its memory has turned the fairest things of earth to blackness and deformity.

In my dream last night, when in my ears came softly, like music stealing across the waters from afar, the old song we used to sing together, then to my brain, like a ray of light, came an idea whose grandeur for a moment struck me dumb. Before my eyes grew a vase of such beauty that I knew my hope was born to life, and that the Great Spirit had placed my foot on the ladder that leads from this my palace—dungeon to freedom and to thee. Today I have got a block of crystal—for only in such pellucid substance can I body forth my dream—and have commenced my work.

I found at first that my hand had lost its cunning, and I was beginning to despair, when, like the memory of a dream, there came back in my ears the strains of the old song. I sang it softly to myself, and as I did so I grew calmer; but oh! how differently the song sounded to me when thy voice, Aurora, rose not in unison with my own! But what avails pining? To work! To work! Every touch of my chisel will bring me nearer thee.

My vase is daily growing nearer to completion. I sing as I work, and my constant song is the one I love so well. I can hear the echo of my voice in the vase; and as I end, the wailing song note is prolonged in sweet, sad music in the crystal cup. I listen, ear down, and sometimes I weep as I listen, so sadly comes the echo to my song. Imperfect though it be, my voice makes sweet music, and its echo in the cup guides my hand towards perfection as I work. Would that thy voice rose and fell with mine, Aurora, and then the world would behold a vase of such beauty as never before woke up the slumbering fires of mans love for what is fair; for if I do such work in sadness, imperfect as I am in my solitude and sorrow, what would I do in joy, perfect when with thee? I know that my work is good as an artist, and I feel that it is as a man; and the cup itself, as it daily grows in beauty, gives back a clearer echo. Oh! if I worked in joy how gladly would it give back our voices! Then would we hear an echo and music such as mortals seldom hear; but now the echo, like my song, seems imperfect. I grow daily weaker; but still I work on—work with my whole soul—for am I not working for freedom and for thee?

My work is nearly done. Day by day, hour by hour, the vase grows more finished. Ever clearer comes the echo whilst I sing; ever softer, ever more sad and heart-rending comes the echo of the wail at the end of the song. Day by day I grow weaker and weaker; still I work on with all my soul. At night the thought comes to me, whilst I think of thee, that I will never see thee more—that I breathe out my life into the crystal cup, and that it will last there when I am gone.

So beautiful has it become, so much do I love it, that I could gladly die to be maker of such a work, were it not for thee—for my love for thee, and my hope of thee, and my fear for thee, and my anguish for thy grief when thou knowest I am gone.

My work requires but few more touches. My life is slowly ebbing away, and I feel that with my last touch my life will pass out forever into the cup. Till that touch is given I must not die—I will not die. My hate has passed away. So great are my wrongs that revenge of mine would be too small a compensation for my woe. I leave revenge to a juster and a mightier than I. Thee, oh Aurora, I will await in the land of flowers, where thou and I will wander, never more to part, never more! Ah, never more! Farewell, Aurora—Aurora—Aurora!

## II. The Feast of Beauty

The Feast of Beauty approaches rapidly, yet hardly so fast as my royal master wishes. He seems to have no other thought than to have this feast greater and better than any ever held before. Five summers ago his Feast of Beauty was nobler than all held in his sires reign together; yet scarcely was it over, and the rewards given to the victors, when he conceived the giant project whose success is to be tested when the moon reaches her full. It was boldly chosen and boldly done; chosen and done as boldly as the project of a monarch should be. But still I cannot think that it will end well. This yearning after completeness must be unsatisfied in the end—this desire that makes a monarch fling his kingly justice to the winds, and strive to reach his Mecca over a desert of blighted hopes and lost lives. But hush! I must not dare to think ill of my master or his deeds; and besides, walls have ears. I must leave alone these dangerous topics, and confine my thoughts within proper bounds.

The moon is waxing quickly, and with its fulness comes the Feast of Beauty, whose success as a whole rests almost solely on my watchfulness and care; for if the ruler of the feast should fail in his duty, who could fill the void? Let me see what arts are represented, and what works compete. All the arts will have trophies: poetry in its various forms, and prose-writing; sculpture with carving in various metals, and glass, and wood, and ivory, and engraving gems, and setting jewels; painting on canvas, and glass, and wood, and stone and metal; music, vocal and instrumental; and dancing. If that woman will but sing, we will have a real triumph of music; but she appears sickly too. All our best artists either get ill or die, although we promise them freedom or rewards or both if they succeed.

Surely never yet was a Feast of Beauty so fair or so richly dowered as this which the full moon shall behold and hear; but ah! the crowning glory of the feast will be the crystal cup. Never yet have these eyes beheld such a form of beauty, such a wondrous mingling of substance and light. Surely some magic power must have helped to draw such loveliness from a cold block of crystal. I must be careful that no harm happens the vase. Today when I touched it, it gave forth such a ringing sound that my heart jumped with fear lest it should sustain any injury. Henceforth, till I deliver it up to my master, no hand but my own shall touch it lest any harm should happen to it.

Strange story has that cup. Born to life in the cell of a captive torn from his artist home beyond the sea, to enhance the splendour of a feast by his labour—seen at work by spies, and traced and followed till a chance—cruel chance for him—gave him into the hands of the emissaries of my master. He too, poor moth, fluttered about the flame: the name of freedom spurred him on to exertion till he wore away his life. The beauty of that cup was dearly bought for him. Many a man would forget his captivity whilst he worked at such a piece of loveliness; but he appeared to have some sorrow at his heart, some sorrow so great that it quenched his pride.

How he used to rave at first! How he used to rush about his chamber, and then climb into the embrasure of his window, and gaze out away over the sea! Poor captive! perhaps over the sea someone waited for his coming who was dearer to him than many cups, even many cups as beautiful as this, if such could be on earth. . . Well, well, we must all die soon or late, and who dies first escapes the more sorrow, perhaps, who knows? How, when he had commenced the cup, he used to sing all day long, from the moment the sun shot its first fiery arrow into the retreating hosts of night-clouds, till the shades of evening advancing drove the lingering sunbeams into the west—and always the same song!

How he used to sing, all alone! Yet sometimes I could almost imagine I heard not one voice from his chamber, but two. . . No more will it echo again from the wall of a dungeon, or from a hillside in free air. No more will his eyes behold the beauty of his crystal cup.

It was well he lived to finish it. Often and often have I trembled to think of his death, as I saw him day by day grow weaker as he worked at the unfinished vase. Must his eyes never more behold the beauty that was born of his soul? Oh, never more! Oh Death, grim King of Terrors, how mighty is thy sceptre! All-powerful is the wave of thy hand that summons us in turn to thy kingdom away beyond the poles!

Would that thou, poor captive, hadst lived to behold thy triumph, for victory will be thine at the Feast of Beauty such as man never before achieved. Then thou mightst have heard the shout that hails the victor in the contest, and the plaudits that greet him as he passes out, a free man, through the palace gates. But now thy cup will come to light amid the smiles of beauty and rank and power, whilst thou liest there in thy lonely chamber, cold as the marble of its walls.

And, after all, the feast will be imperfect, since the victors cannot all be crowned. I must ask my master's direction as to how a blank place of a competitor, should he prove a victor, is to be filled up. So late? I must see him ere the noontide hour of rest be past.

GREAT SPIRIT! HOW I TREMBLED as my master answered my question!

I found him in his chamber, as usual in the noontide. He was lying on his couch disrobed, half-sleeping; and the drowsy zephyr, scented with rich odours from the garden, wafted through the windows at either side by the fans, lulled him to complete repose. The darkened chamber was cool and silent. From the vestibule came the murmuring of many fountains, and the pleasant splash of falling waters. "Oh, happy," said I, in my heart, "oh, happy great King, that has such pleasures to enjoy!" The breeze from the fans swept over the strings of the AEolian harps, and a sweet, confused, happy melody arose like the murmuring of children's voices singing afar off in the valleys, and floating on the wind.

As I entered the chamber softly, with muffled foot-fall and pent-in breath, I felt a kind of awe stealing over me. To me who was born and have dwelt all my life within the precincts of the court—to me who talk daily with my royal master, and take his minutest directions as to the coming feast—to me who had all my life looked up to my king as to a spirit, and had venerated him as more than mortal—came a feeling of almost horror; for my master looked then, in his quiet chamber, half-sleeping amid the drowsy music of the harps and fountains, more like a common man than a God. As the thought came to me I shuddered in affright, for it seemed to me that I had been guilty of sacrilege. So much had my veneration for my royal master become a part of my nature, that but to think of him as another man seemed like the anarchy of my own soul.

I came beside the couch, and watched him in silence. He seemed to be half-listening to the fitful music; and as the melody swelled and died away his chest rose and fell as he breathed in unison with the sound.

After a moment or two he appeared to become conscious of the presence of someone in the room, although by no motion of his face could I see that he heard any sound, and his eyes were shut. He opened his eyes, and, seeing me, asked, "Was all right about the Feast of Beauty?" for that is the subject ever nearest to his thoughts. I answered that all was well, but that I had come to ask his royal pleasure as to how a vacant place amongst the competitors was to be filled up. He asked, "How vacant?" and on my telling him, "from death," he asked again, quickly, "Was the work finished?" When I told him that it was, he lay back again on his couch with a sigh of relief, for he had half arisen in his anxiety as he asked the question. Then he said, after a minute, "All the competitors must be present at the feast." "All?" said I. "All," he answered again, "alive or dead; for the old custom must be preserved, and the victors crowned." He stayed still for a minute more, and then said, slowly, "Victors or martyrs." And I could see that the kingly spirit was coming back to him.

Again he went on. "This will be my last Feast of Beauty; and all the captives shall be set free. Too much sorrow has sprung already from my ambition. Too much injustice has soiled the name of king."

He said no more, but lay still and closed his eyes. I could see by the working of his hands and the heaving of his chest that some violent emotion troubled him, and the thought arose, "He is a man, but he is yet a king; and, though a king as he is, still happiness is not for him.

Great Spirit of Justice! thou metest out his pleasures and his woes to man, to king and slave alike! Thou lovest best to whom thou givest peace!"

Gradually my master grew more calm, and at length sunk into a gentle slumber; but even in his sleep he breathed in unison with the swelling murmur of the harps.

"To each is given," said I gently, "something in common with the world of actual things. Thy life, oh King, is bound by chains of sympathy to the voice of Truth, which is Music! Tremble, lest in the presence of a master-strain thou shouldst feel thy littleness, and die!" and I softly left the room.


### III. The Story of the Moonbeam

SLOWLY I CREEP ALONG THE bosom of the waters.

Sometimes I look back as I rise upon a billow, and see behind me many of my kin sitting each upon a wave-summit as upon a throne. So I go on for long, a power that I wist not forcing me onward, without will or purpose of mine.

At length, as I rise upon a mimic wave, I see afar a hazy light that springs from a vast palace, through whose countless windows flame lamps and torches. But at the first view, as if my coming had been the signal, the lights disappear in an instant.

Impatiently I await what may happen; and as I rise with each heart-beat of the sea, I look forward to where the torches had gleamed. Can it be a deed of darkness that shuns the light?

THE TIME HAS COME WHEN I can behold the palace without waiting to mount upon the waves. It is built of white marble, and rises steep from the brine. Its sea-front is glorious with columns and statues; and from the portals the marble steps sweep down, broad and wide to the waters, and below them, down as deep as I can see.

No sound is heard, no light is seen. A solemn silence abounds, a perfect calm.

Slowly I climb the palace walls, my brethren following as soldiers up a breach. I slide along the roofs, and as I look behind me walls and roofs are glistening as with silver. At length I meet with something smooth and hard and translucent; but through it I pass and enter a vast hall, where for an instant I hang in mid-air and wonder.

My coming has been the signal for such a burst of harmony as brings back to my memory the music of the spheres as they rush through space; and in the full-swelling anthem of welcome I feel that I am indeed a sun-spirit, a child of light, and that this is homage to my master.

I look upon the face of a great monarch, who sits at the head of a banquet-table. He has turned his head upwards and backwards, and looks as if he had been awaiting my approach. He rises and fronts me with the ringing out of the welcome-song, and all the others in the great hall turn towards me as well. I can see their eyes gleaming. Down along the immense table, laden with plate and glass and flowers, they stand holding each a cup of ruby wine, with which they pledge the monarch when the song is ended, as they drink success to him and to the "Feast of Beauty."

I survey the hall. An immense chamber, with marble walls covered with bas-reliefs and frescoes and sculptured figures, and panelled by great columns that rise along the surface and support a dome-ceiling painted wondrously; in its centre the glass lantern by which I entered.

On the walls are hung pictures of various forms and sizes, and down the centre of the table stretches a raised platform on which are placed works of art of various kinds.

At one side of the hall is a dais on which sit persons of both sexes with noble faces and lordly brows, but all wearing the same expression—care tempered by hope. All these hold scrolls in their hands.

At the other side of the hall is a similar dais, on which sit others fairer to earthly view, less spiritual and more marked by surface-passion. They hold music-scores. All these look more joyous than those on the other platform, all save one, a woman, who sits with downcast face and dejected mien, as of one without hope. As my light falls at her feet she looks up, and I feel happy. The sympathy between us has called a faint gleam of hope to cheer that poor pale face.

Many are the forms of art that rise above the banquet-table, and all are lovely to behold. I look on all with pleasure one by one, till I see the last of them at the end of the table away from the monarch, and then all the others seem as nothing to me. What is this that makes other forms of beauty seem as nought when compared with it, when brought within the radius of its lustre? A crystal cup, wrought with such wondrous skill that light seems to lose its individual glory as it shines upon it and is merged in its beauty. "Oh Universal Mother, let me enter there. Let my life be merged in its beauty, and no more will I regret my sun-strength hidden deep in the chasms of my moon-mother. Let me live there and perish there, and I will be joyous whilst it lasts, and content to pass into the great vortex of nothingness to be born again when the glory of the cup has fled."

Can it be that my wish is granted, that I have entered the cup and become a part of its beauty? "Great Mother, I thank thee."

Has the cup life? or is it merely its wondrous perfectness that makes it tremble, like a beating heart, in unison with the ebb and flow, the great wave-pulse of nature? To me it feels as if it had life.

I look through the crystal walls and see at the end of the table, isolated from all others, the figure of a man seated. Are those cords that bind his limbs? How suits that crown of laurel those wide, dim eyes, and that pallid hue? It is passing strange. This Feast of Beauty holds some dread secrets, and sees some wondrous sights.

I hear a voice of strange, rich sweetness, yet wavering—the voice of one almost a king by nature. He is standing up; I see him through my palace-wall. He calls a name and sits down again.

Again I hear a voice from the platform of scrolls, the Throne of Brows; and again I look and behold a man who stands trembling yet flushed, as though the morning light shone bright upon his soul. He reads in cadenced measure a song in praise of my moon-mother, the Feast of Beauty, and the king. As he speaks, he trembles no more, but seems inspired, and his voice rises to a tone of power and grandeur, and rings back from walls and dome. I hear his words distinctly, though saddened in tone, in the echo from my crystal home. He concludes and sits down, half-fainting, amid a whirlwind of applause, every note, every beat of which is echoed as the words had been.

Again the monarch rises and calls "Aurora," that she may sing for freedom. The name echoes in the cup with a sweet, sad sound. So sad, so despairing seems the echo, that the hall seems to darken and the scene to grow dim.

"Can a sun-spirit mourn, or a crystal vessel weep?"

She, the dejected one, rises from her seat on the Throne of Sound, and all eyes turn upon her save those of the pale one, laurel-crowned. Thrice she essays to begin, and thrice nought comes from her lips but a dry, husky sigh, till an old man who has been moving round the hall settling all things, cries out, in fear lest she should fail, "Freedom!"

The word is re-echoed from the cup. She hears the sound, turns towards it and begins.

Oh, the melody of that voice! And yet it is not perfect alone; for after the first note comes an echo from the cup that swells in unison with the voice, and the two sounds together, seem as if one strain came ringing sweet from the lips of the All-Father himself. So sweet it is, that all throughout the hall sit spell-bound, and scarcely dare to breathe.

In the pause after the first verses of the song, I hear the voice of the old man speaking to a comrade, but his words are unheard by any other, "Look at the king. His spirit seems lost in a trance of melody. Ah! I fear me some evil: the nearer the music approaches to perfection the more rapt he becomes. I dread lest a perfect note shall prove his death-call." His voice dies away as the singer commences the last verse.

Sad and plaintive is the song; full of feeling and tender love, but love overshadowed by grief and despair. As it goes on the voice of the singer grows sweeter and more thrilling, more real; and the cup, my crystal time-home, vibrates more and more as it gives back the echo. The monarch looks like one entranced, and no movement is within the hall. . . The song dies away in a wild wail that seems to tear the heart of the singer in twain; and the cup vibrates still more as it gives back the echo. As the note, long-swelling, reaches its highest, the cup, the Crystal Cup, my wondrous home, the gift of the All-Father, shivers into millions of atoms, and passes away.

Ere I am lost in the great vortex I see the singer throw up her arms and fall, freed at last, and the King sitting, glory-faced, but pallid with the hue of Death.

End

# The Secret of the Growing Gold

When Margaret Delandre went to live at Brent's Rock the whole neighbourhood awoke to the pleasure of an entirely new scandal. Scandals in connection with either the Delandre family or the Brents of Brent's Rock, were not few; and if the secret history of the county had been written in full both names would have been found well represented. It is true that the status of each was so different that they might have belonged to different continents—or to different worlds for the matter of that—for hitherto their orbits had never crossed. The Brents were accorded by the whole section of the country an unique social dominance, and had ever held themselves as high above the yeoman class to which Margaret Delandre belonged, as a blue-blooded Spanish hidalgo out-tops his peasant tenantry.

The Delandres had an ancient record and were proud of it in their way as the Brents were of theirs. But the family had never risen above yeomanry; and although they had been once well-to-do in the good old times of foreign wars and protection, their fortunes had withered under the scorching of the free trade sun and the "piping times of peace." They had, as the elder members used to assert, "stuck to the land," with the result that they had taken root in it, body and soul. In fact, they, having chosen the life of vegetables, had flourished as vegetation does—blossomed and thrived in the good season and suffered in the bad. Their holding, Dander's Croft, seemed to have been worked out, and to be typical of the family which had inhabited it. The latter had declined generation after generation, sending out now and again some abortive shoot of unsatisfied energy in the shape of a soldier or sailor, who had worked his way to the minor grades of the services and had there stopped, cut short either from unheeding gallantry in action or from that destroying cause to men without breeding or youthful care—the recognition of a position above them which they feel unfitted to fill. So, little by little, the family dropped lower and lower, the men brooding and dissatisfied, and drinking themselves into the grave, the women drudging at home, or marrying beneath them—or worse. In process of time all disappeared, leaving only two in the Croft, Wykham Delandre and his sister Margaret. The man and woman seemed to have inherited in masculine and feminine form respectively the evil tendency of their race, sharing in common the principles, though manifesting them in different ways, of sullen passion, voluptuousness and recklessness.

The history of the Brents had been something similar, but showing the causes of decadence in their aristocratic and not their plebeian forms. They, too, had sent their shoots to the wars; but their positions had been different, and they had often attained honour—for without flaw they were gallant, and brave deeds were done by them before the selfish dissipation which marked them had sapped their vigour.

The present head of the family—if family it could now be called when one remained of the direct line—was Geoffrey Brent. He was almost a type of a worn-out race, manifesting in some ways its most brilliant qualities, and in others its utter degradation. He might be fairly compared with some of those antique Italian nobles whom the painters have preserved to us with their courage, their unscrupulousness, their refinement of lust and cruelty—the voluptuary actual with the fiend potential. He was certainly handsome, with that dark, aquiline, commanding beauty which women so generally recognise as dominant. With men he was distant and cold; but such a bearing never deters womankind. The inscrutable laws of sex have so arranged that even a timid woman is not afraid of a fierce and haughty man. And so it was that there was hardly a woman of any kind or degree, who lived within view of Brent's Rock, who did not cherish some form of secret admiration for the handsome wastrel. The category was a wide one, for Brent's Rock rose up steeply from the midst of a level region and for a circuit of a hundred miles it lay on the horizon, with its high old towers and steep roofs cutting the level edge of wood and hamlet, and far-scattered mansions.

So long as Geoffrey Brent confined his dissipations to London and Paris and Vienna—anywhere out of sight and sound of his home—opinion was silent. It is easy to listen to far off echoes unmoved, and we can treat them with disbelief, or scorn, or disdain, or whatever attitude of coldness may suit our purpose. But when the scandal came close to home it was another matter; and the feelings of independence and integrity which is in people of every community which is not utterly spoiled, asserted itself and demanded that condemnation should be expressed. Still there was a certain reticence in all, and no more notice was taken of the existing facts than was absolutely necessary. Margaret Delandre bore herself so fearlessly and so openly—she accepted her position as the justified companion of Geoffrey Brent so naturally that people came to believe that she was secretly married to him, and therefore thought it wiser to hold their tongues lest time should justify her and also make her an active enemy.

The one person who, by his interference, could have settled all doubts was debarred by circumstances from interfering in the matter. Wykham Delandre had quarrelled with his sister—or perhaps it was that she had quarrelled with him—and they were on terms not merely of armed neutrality but of bitter hatred. The quarrel had been antecedent to Margaret going to Brent's Rock. She and Wykham had almost come to blows. There had certainly been threats on one side and on the other; and in the end Wykham overcome with passion, had ordered his sister to leave his house. She had risen straightway, and, without waiting to pack up even her own personal belongings, had walked out of the house. On the threshold she had paused for a moment to hurl a bitter threat at Wykham that he would rue in shame and despair to the last hour of his life his act of that day. Some weeks had since passed; and it was understood in the neighbourhood that Margaret had gone to London, when she suddenly appeared driving out with Geoffrey Brent, and the entire neighbourhood knew before nightfall that she had taken up her abode at the Rock. It was no subject of surprise that Brent had come back unexpectedly, for such was his usual custom. Even his own servants never knew when to expect him, for there was a private door, of which he alone had the key, by which he sometimes entered without anyone in the house being aware of his coming. This was his usual method of appearing after a long absence.

Wykham Delandre was furious at the news. He vowed vengeance—and to keep his mind level with his passion drank deeper than ever. He tried several times to see his sister, but she contemptuously refused to meet him. He tried to have an interview with Brent and was refused by him also. Then he tried to stop him in the road, but without avail, for Geoffrey was not a man to be stopped against his will. Several actual encounters took place between the two men, and many more were threatened and avoided. At last Wykham Delandre settled down to a morose, vengeful acceptance of the situation.

Neither Margaret nor Geoffrey was of a pacific temperament, and it was not long before there began to be quarrels between them. One thing would lead to another, and wine flowed freely at Brent's Rock. Now and again the quarrels would assume a bitter aspect, and threats would be exchanged in uncompromising language that fairly awed the listening servants. But such quarrels generally ended where domestic altercations do, in reconciliation, and in a mutual respect for the fighting qualities proportionate to their manifestation. Fighting for its own sake is found by a certain class of persons, all the world over, to be a matter of absorbing interest, and there is no reason to believe that domestic conditions minimise its potency. Geoffrey and Margaret made occasional absences from Brent's Rock, and on each of these occasions Wykham Delandre also absented himself; but as he generally heard of the absence too late to be of any service, he returned home each time in a more bitter and discontented frame of mind than before.

At last there came a time when the absence from Brent's Rock became longer than before. Only a few days earlier there had been a quarrel, exceeding in bitterness anything which had gone before; but this, too, had been made up, and a trip on the Continent had been mentioned before the servants. After a few days Wykham Delandre also went away, and it was some weeks before he returned. It was noticed that he was full of some new importance—satisfaction, exaltation— they hardly knew how to call it. He went straightway to Brent's Rock, and demanded to see Geoffrey Brent, and on being told that he had not yet returned, said, with a grim decision which the servants noted:

"I shall come again. My news is solid—it can wait!" and turned away. Week after week went by, and month after month; and then there came a rumour, certified later on, that an accident had occurred in the Zermatt valley. Whilst crossing a dangerous pass the carriage containing an English lady and the driver had fallen over a precipice, the gentleman of the party, Mr. Geoffrey Brent, having been fortunately saved as he had been walking up the hill to ease the horses. He gave information, and search was made. The broken rail, the excoriated roadway, the marks where the horses had struggled on the decline before finally pitching over into the torrent—all told the sad tale. It was a wet season, and there had been much snow in the winter, so that the river was swollen beyond its usual volume, and the eddies of the stream were packed with ice. All search was made, and finally the wreck of the carriage and the body of one horse were found in an eddy of the river. Later on the body of the driver was found on the sandy, torrent-swept waste near Tasch; but the body of the lady, like that of the other horse, had quite disappeared, and was—what was left of it by that time—whirling amongst the eddies of the Rhone on its way down to the Lake of Geneva.

Wykham Delandre made all the enquiries possible, but could not find any trace of the missing woman. He found, however, in the books of the various hotels the name of "Mr. and Mrs. Geoffrey Brent." And he had a stone erected at Zermatt to his sister's memory, under her married name, and a tablet put up in the church at Bretten, the parish in which both Brent's Rock and Dander's Croft were situated.

There was a lapse of nearly a year, after the excitement of the matter had worn away, and the whole neighbourhood had gone on its accustomed way. Brent was still absent, and Delandre more drunken, more morose, and more revengeful than before.

Then there was a new excitement. Brent's Rock was being made ready for a new mistress. It was officially announced by Geoffrey himself in a letter to the Vicar, that he had been married some months before to an Italian lady, and that they were then on their way home. Then a small army of workmen invaded the house; and hammer and plane sounded, and a general air of size and paint pervaded the atmosphere. One wing of the old house, the south, was entirely re-done; and then the great body of the workmen departed, leaving only materials for the doing of the old hall when Geoffrey Brent should have returned, for he had directed that the decoration was only to be done under his own eyes. He had brought with him accurate drawings of a hall in the house of his bride's father, for he wished to reproduce for her the place to which she had been accustomed. As the moulding had all to be re-done, some scaffolding poles and boards were brought in and laid on one side of the great hall, and also a great wooden tank or box for mixing the lime, which was laid in bags beside it.

When the new mistress of Brent's Rock arrived the bells of the church rang out, and there was a general jubilation. She was a beautiful creature, full of the poetry and fire and passion of the South; and the few English words which she had learned were spoken in such a sweet and pretty broken way that she won the hearts of the people almost as much by the music of her voice as by the melting beauty of her dark eyes.

Geoffrey Brent seemed more happy than he had ever before appeared; but there was a dark, anxious look on his face that was new to those who knew him of old, and he started at times as though at some noise that was unheard by others.

And so months passed and the whisper grew that at last Brent's Rock was to have an heir. Geoffrey was very tender to his wife, and the new bond between them seemed to soften him. He took more interest in his tenants and their needs than he had ever done; and works of charity on his part as well as on his sweet young wife's were not lacking.

He seemed to have set all his hopes on the child that was coming, and as he looked deeper into the future the dark shadow that had come over his face seemed to die gradually away.

All the time Wykham Delandre nursed his revenge. Deep in his heart had grown up a purpose of vengeance which only waited an opportunity to crystallise and take a definite shape. His vague idea was somehow centred in the wife of Brent, for he knew that he could strike him best through those he loved, and the coming time seemed to hold in its womb the opportunity for which he longed. One night he sat alone in the living-room of his house. It had once been a handsome room in its way, but time and neglect had done their work and it was now little better than a ruin, without dignity or picturesqueness of any kind. He had been drinking heavily for sometime and was more than half stupefied. He thought he heard a noise as of someone at the door and looked up. Then he called half savagely to come in; but there was no response. With a muttered blasphemy he renewed his potations. Presently he forgot all around him, sank into a daze, but suddenly awoke to see standing before him someone or something like a battered, ghostly edition of his sister. For a few moments there came upon him a sort of fear. The woman before him, with distorted features and burning eyes seemed hardly human, and the only thing that seemed a reality of his sister, as she had been, was her wealth of golden hair, and this was now streaked with grey. She eyed her brother with a long, cold stare; and he, too, as he looked and began to realise the actuality of her presence, found the hatred of her which he had had, once again surging up in his heart. All the brooding passion of the past year seemed to find a voice at once as he asked her:—

"Why are you here? You're dead and buried."

"I am here, Wykham Delandre, for no love of you, but because I hate another even more than I do you!" A great passion blazed in her eyes.

"Him?" he asked, in so fierce a whisper that even the woman was for an instant startled till she regained her calm.

"Yes, him!" she answered. "But make no mistake, my revenge is my own; and I merely use you to help me to it." Wykham asked suddenly:

"Did he marry you?"

The woman's distorted face broadened out in a ghastly attempt at a smile. It was a hideous mockery, for the broken features and seamed scars took strange shapes and strange colours, and queer lines of white showed out as the straining muscles pressed on the old cicatrices.

"So you would like to know! It would please your pride to feel that your sister was truly married! Well, you shall not know. That was my revenge on you, and I do not mean to change it by a hair's breadth. I have come here tonight simply to let you know that I am alive, so that if any violence be done me where I am going there may be a witness."

"Where are you going?" demanded her brother.

"That is my affair! and I have not the least intention of letting you know!" Wykham stood up, but the drink was on him and he reeled and fell. As he lay on the floor he announced his intention of following his sister; and with an outburst of splenetic humour told her that he would follow her through the darkness by the light of her hair, and of her beauty. At this she turned on him, and said that there were others beside him that would rue her hair and her beauty too. "As he will," she hissed; "for the hair remains though the beauty be gone. When he withdrew the lynch-pin and sent us over the precipice into the torrent, he had little thought of my beauty. Perhaps his beauty would be scarred like mine were he whirled, as I was, among the rocks of the Visp, and frozen on the ice pack in the drift of the river. But let him beware! His time is coming!" and with a fierce gesture she flung open the door and passed out into the night.

LATER ON THAT NIGHT, MRS. BRENT, who was but half-asleep, became suddenly awake and spoke to her husband:

"Geoffrey, was not that the click of a lock somewhere below our window?"

But Geoffrey—though she thought that he, too, had started at the noise—seemed sound asleep, and breathed heavily. Again Mrs. Brent dozed; but this time awoke to the fact that her husband had arisen and was partially dressed. He was deadly pale, and when the light of the lamp which he had in his hand fell on his face, she was frightened at the look in his eyes.

"What is it, Geoffrey? What dost thou?" she asked.

"Hush! little one," he answered, in a strange, hoarse voice. "Go to sleep. I am restless, and wish to finish some work I left undone."

"Bring it here, my husband," she said; "I am lonely and I fear when thou art away."

For reply he merely kissed her and went out, closing the door behind him. She lay awake for awhile, and then nature asserted itself, and she slept.

Suddenly she started broad awake with the memory in her ears of a smothered cry from somewhere not far off. She jumped up and ran to the door and listened, but there was no sound. She grew alarmed for her husband, and called out: "Geoffrey! Geoffrey!"

After a few moments the door of the great hall opened, and Geoffrey appeared at it, but without his lamp.

"Hush!" he said, in a sort of whisper, and his voice was harsh and stern. "Hush! Get to bed! I am working, and must not be disturbed. Go to sleep, and do not wake the house!"

With a chill in her heart—for the harshness of her husband's voice was new to her—she crept back to bed and lay there trembling, too frightened to cry, and listened to every sound. There was a long pause of silence, and then the sound of some iron implement striking muffled blows! Then there came a clang of a heavy stone falling, followed by a muffled curse. Then a dragging sound, and then more noise of stone on stone. She lay all the while in an agony of fear, and her heart beat dreadfully. She heard a curious sort of scraping sound; and then there was silence. Presently the door opened gently, and Geoffrey appeared. His wife pretended to be asleep; but through her eyelashes she saw him wash from his hands something white that looked like lime.

In the morning he made no allusion to the previous night, and she was afraid to ask any question.

From that day there seemed come shadow over Geoffrey Brent. He neither ate nor slept as he had been accustomed, and his former habit of turning suddenly as though someone were speaking from behind him revived. The old hall seemed to have some kind of fascination for him. He used to go there many times in the day, but grew impatient if anyone, even his wife, entered it. When the builder's foreman came to inquire about continuing his work Geoffrey was out driving; the man went into the hall, and when Geoffrey returned the servant told him of his arrival and where he was. With a frightful oath he pushed the servant aside and hurried up to the old hall. The workman met him almost at the door; and as Geoffrey burst into the room he ran against him. The man apologised:

"Beg pardon, sir, but I was just going out to make some enquiries. I directed twelve sacks of lime to be sent here, but I see there are only ten."

"Damn the ten sacks and the twelve too!" was the ungracious and incomprehensible rejoinder.

The workman looked surprised, and tried to turn the conversation.

"I see, sir, there is a little matter which our people must have done; but the governor will of course see it set right at his own cost."

"What do you mean?"

"That 'ere 'arth-stone, sir: Some idiot must have put a scaffold pole on it and cracked it right down the middle, and it's thick enough you'd think to stand hanythink." Geoffrey was silent for quite a minute, and then said in a constrained voice and with much gentler manner:

"Tell your people that I am not going on with the work in the hall at present. I want to leave it as it is for a while longer."

"All right sir. I'll send up a few of our chaps to take away these poles and lime bags and tidy the place up a bit."

"No! No!" said Geoffrey, "leave them where they are. I shall send and tell you when you are to get on with the work." So the foreman went away, and his comment to his master was:

"I'd send in the bill, sir, for the work already done. 'Pears to me that money's a little shaky in that quarter."

Once or twice Delandre tried to stop Brent on the road, and, at last, finding that he could not attain his object rode after the carriage, calling out:

"What has become of my sister, your wife?" Geoffrey lashed his horses into a gallop, and the other, seeing from his white face and from his wife's collapse almost into a faint that this object was attained, rode away with a scowl and a laugh.

That night when Geoffrey went into the hall he passed over to the great fireplace, and all at once started back with a smothered cry. Then with an effort he pulled himself together and went away, returning with a light. He bent down over the broken hearth-stone to see if the moonlight falling through the storied window had in anyway deceived him. Then with a groan of anguish he sank to his knees.

There, sure enough, through the crack in the broken stone were protruding a multitude of threads of golden hair just tinged with grey!

He was disturbed by a noise at the door, and looking round, saw his wife standing in the doorway. In the desperation of the moment he took action to prevent discovery, and lighting a match at the lamp, stooped down and burned away the hair that rose through the broken stone. Then rising nonchalantly as he could, he pretended surprise at seeing his wife beside him.

For the next week he lived in an agony; for, whether by accident or design, he could not find himself alone in the hall for any length of time.

At each visit the hair had grown afresh through the crack, and he had to watch it carefully lest his terrible secret should be discovered. He tried to find a receptacle for the body of the murdered woman outside the house, but someone always interrupted him; and once, when he was coming out of the private doorway, he was met by his wife, who began to question him about it, and manifested surprise that she should not have before noticed the key which he now reluctantly showed her. Geoffrey dearly and passionately loved his wife, so that any possibility of her discovering his dread secrets, or even of doubting him, filled him with anguish; and after a couple of days had passed, he could not help coming to the conclusion that, at least, she suspected something.

That very evening she came into the hall after her drive and found him there sitting moodily by the deserted fireplace. She spoke to him directly.

"Geoffrey, I have been spoken to by that fellow Delandre, and he says horrible things. He tells to me that a week ago his sister returned to his house, the wreck and ruin of her former self, with only her golden hair as of old, and announced some fell intention. He asked me where she is—and oh, Geoffrey, she is dead, she is dead! So how can she have returned? Oh! I am in dread, and I know not where to turn!"

For answer, Geoffrey burst into a torrent of blasphemy which made her shudder. He cursed Delandre and his sister and all their kind, and in especial he hurled curse after curse on her golden hair.

"Oh, hush! hush!" she said, and was then silent, for she feared her husband when she saw the evil effect of his humour. Geoffrey in the torrent of his anger stood up and moved away from the hearth; but suddenly stopped as he saw a new look of terror in his wife's eyes. He followed their glance, and then he, too, shuddered—for there on the broken hearth-stone lay a golden streak as the points of the hair rose through the crack.

"Look, look!" she shrieked. "It is some ghost of the dead! Come away—come away!" and seizing her husband by the wrist with the frenzy of madness, she pulled him from the room.

That night she was in a raging fever. The doctor of the district attended her at once, and special aid was telegraphed for to London. Geoffrey was in despair, and in his anguish at the danger of his young wife almost forgot his own crime and its consequences. In the evening the doctor had to leave to attend to others; but he left Geoffrey in charge of his wife. His last words were:

"Remember, you must humour her till I come in the morning, or till someother doctor has her case in hand. What you have to dread is another attack of emotion. See that she is kept warm. Nothing more can be done."

Late in the evening, when the rest of the household had retired, Geoffrey's wife got up from her bed and called to her husband.

"Come!" she said. "Come to the old hall! I know where the gold comes from! I want to see it grow!"

Geoffrey would fain have stopped her, but he feared for her life or reason on the one hand, and lest in a paroxysm she should shriek out her terrible suspicion, and seeing that it was useless to try to prevent her, wrapped a warm rug around her and went with her to the old hall. When they entered, she turned and shut the door and locked it.

"We want no strangers amongst us three tonight!" she whispered with a wan smile.

"We three! nay we are but two," said Geoffrey with a shudder; he feared to say more.

"Sit here," said his wife as she put out the light. "Sit here by the hearth and watch the gold growing. The silver moonlight is jealous! See it steals along the floor towards the gold—our gold!" Geoffrey looked with growing horror, and saw that during the hours that had passed the golden hair had protruded further through the broken hearth-stone. He tried to hide it by placing his feet over the broken place; and his wife, drawing her chair beside him, leant over and laid her head on his shoulder.

"Now do not stir, dear," she said; "let us sit still and watch. We shall find the secret of the growing gold!" He passed his arm round her and sat silent; and as the moonlight stole along the floor she sank to sleep.

He feared to wake her; and so sat silent and miserable as the hours stole away.

Before his horror-struck eyes the golden-hair from the broken stone grew and grew; and as it increased, so his heart got colder and colder, till at last he had not power to stir, and sat with eyes full of terror watching his doom.

IN THE MORNING WHEN THE London doctor came, neither Geoffrey nor his wife could be found. Search was made in all the rooms, but without avail. As a last resource the great door of the old hall was broken open, and those who entered saw a grim and sorry sight.

There by the deserted hearth Geoffrey Brent and his young wife sat cold and white and dead. Her face was peaceful, and her eyes were closed in sleep; but his face was a sight that made all who saw it shudder, for there was on it a look of unutterable horror. The eyes were open and stared glassily at his feet, which were twined with tresses of golden hair, streaked with grey, which came through the broken hearth-stone.

End

# The Squaw

Nurnberg at the time was not so much exploited as it has been since then. Irving had not been playing Faust, and the very name of the old town was hardly known to the great bulk of the travelling public. My wife and I being in the second week of our honeymoon, naturally wanted someone else to join our party, so that when the cheery stranger, Elias P. Hutcheson, hailing from Isthmian City, Bleeding Gulch, Maple Tree County, Neb., turned up at the station at Frankfort, and casually remarked that he was going on to see the most all-fired old Methusaleh of a town in Yurrup, and that he guessed that so much travelling alone was enough to send an intelligent, active citizen into the melancholy ward of a daft house, we took the pretty broad hint and suggested that we should join forces. We found, on comparing notes afterwards, that we had each intended to speak with some diffidence or hesitation so as not to appear too eager, such not being a good compliment to the success of our married life; but the effect was entirely marred by our both beginning to speak at the same instant—stopping simultaneously and then going on together again. Anyhow, no matter how, it was done; and Elias P. Hutcheson became one of our party. Straightway Amelia and I found the pleasant benefit; instead of quarrelling, as we had been doing, we found that the restraining influence of a third party was such that we now took every opportunity of spooning in odd corners. Amelia declares that ever since she has, as the result of that experience, advised all her friends to take a friend on the honeymoon. Well, we "did" Nurnberg together, and much enjoyed the racy remarks of our Transatlantic friend, who, from his quaint speech and his wonderful stock of adventures, might have stepped out of a novel. We kept for the last object of interest in the city to be visited the Burg, and on the day appointed for the visit strolled round the outer wall of the city by the eastern side.

The Burg is seated on a rock dominating the town, and an immensely deep fosse guards it on the northern side. Nurnberg has been happy in that it was never sacked; had it been it would certainly not be so spick and span perfect as it is at present. The ditch has not been used for centuries, and now its base is spread with tea-gardens and orchards, of which some of the trees are of quite respectable growth. As we wandered round the wall, dawdling in the hot July sunshine, we often paused to admire the views spread before us, and in especial the great plain covered with towns and villages and bounded with a blue line of hills, like a landscape of Claude Lorrain. From this we always turned with new delight to the city itself, with its myriad of quaint old gables and acre-wide red roofs dotted with dormer windows, tier upon tier. A little to our right rose the towers of the Burg, and nearer still, standing grim, the Torture Tower, which was, and is, perhaps, the most interesting place in the city. For centuries the tradition of the Iron Virgin of Nurnberg has been handed down as an instance of the horrors of cruelty of which man is capable; we had long looked forward to seeing it; and here at last was its home.

In one of our pauses we leaned over the wall of the moat and looked down. The garden seemed quite fifty or sixty feet below us, and the sun pouring into it with an intense, moveless heat like that of an oven. Beyond rose the grey, grim wall seemingly of endless height, and losing itself right and left in the angles of bastion and counterscarp. Trees and bushes crowned the wall, and above again towered the lofty houses on whose massive beauty Time has only set the hand of approval. The sun was hot and we were lazy; time was our own, and we lingered, leaning on the wall. Just below us was a pretty sight—a great black cat lying stretched in the sun, whilst round her gambolled prettily a tiny black kitten. The mother would wave her tail for the kitten to play with, or would raise her feet and push away the little one, as an encouragement to further play. They were just at the foot of the wall, and Elias P. Hutcheson, in order to help the play, stooped and took from the walk a moderate sized pebble.

"See!" he said, "I will drop it near the kitten, and they will both wonder where it came from."

"Oh, be careful," said my wife; "you might hit the dear little thing!"

"Not me, ma'am," said Elias P. "Why, I'm as tender as a Maine cherry-tree. Lor, bless ye, I wouldn't hurt the poor pooty little critter more'n I'd scalp a baby. An' you may bet your variegated socks on that! See, I'll drop it fur away on the outside so's not to go near her!" Thus saying, he leaned over and held his arm out at full length and dropped the stone. It may be that there is some attractive force which draws lesser matters to greater; or more probably that the wall was not plumb but sloped to its base—we not noticing the inclination from above; but the stone fell with a sickening thud that came up to us through the hot air, right on the kitten's head, and shattered out its little brains then and there. The black cat cast a swift upward glance, and we saw her eyes like green fire fixed an instant on Elias P. Hutcheson; and then her attention was given to the kitten, which lay still with just a quiver of her tiny limbs, whilst a thin red stream trickled from a gaping wound. With a muffled cry, such as a human being might give, she bent over the kitten, licking its wound and moaning. Suddenly she seemed to realise that it was dead, and again threw her eyes up at us. I shall never forget the sight, for she looked the perfect incarnation of hate. Her green eyes blazed with lurid fire, and the white, sharp teeth seemed to almost shine through the blood which dabbled her mouth and whiskers. She gnashed her teeth, and her claws stood out stark and at full length on every paw. Then she made a wild rush up the wall as if to reach us, but when the momentum ended fell back, and further added to her horrible appearance for she fell on the kitten, and rose with her black fur smeared with its brains and blood. Amelia turned quite faint, and I had to lift her back from the wall. There was a seat close by in shade of a spreading plane-tree, and here I placed her whilst she composed herself. Then I went back to Hutcheson, who stood without moving, looking down on the angry cat below.

As I joined him, he said:

"Wall, I guess that air the savagest beast I ever see—'cept once when an Apache squaw had an edge on a half-breed what they nicknamed 'Splinters' 'cos of the way he fixed up her papoose which he stole on a raid just to show that he appreciated the way they had given his mother the fire torture. She got that kinder look so set on her face that it jest seemed to grow there. She followed Splinters more'n three year till at last the braves got him and handed him over to her. They did say that no man, white or Injun, had ever been so long a-dying under the tortures of the Apaches. The only time I ever see her smile was when I wiped her out. I kem on the camp just in time to see Splinters pass in his checks, and he wasn't sorry to go either. He was a hard citizen, and though I never could shake with him after that papoose business—for it was bitter bad, and he should have been a white man, for he looked like one—I see he had got paid out in full. Durn me, but I took a piece of his hide from one of his skinnin' posts an' had it made into a pocket-book. It's here now!" and he slapped the breast pocket of his coat.

Whilst he was speaking the cat was continuing her frantic efforts to get up the wall. She would take a run back and then charge up, sometimes reaching an incredible height. She did not seem to mind the heavy fall which she got each time but started with renewed vigour;

and at every tumble her appearance became more horrible. Hutcheson was a kind-hearted man—my wife and I had both noticed little acts of kindness to animals as well as to persons—and he seemed concerned at the state of fury to which the cat had wrought herself.

"Wall, now!" he said, "I du declare that that poor critter seems quite desperate. There! there! poor thing, it was all an accident—though that won't bring back your little one to you. Say! I wouldn't have had such a thing happen for a thousand! Just shows what a clumsy fool of a man can do when he tries to play! Seems I'm too darned slipperhanded to even play with a cat. Say Colonel!" it was a pleasant way he had to bestow titles freely—"I hope your wife don't hold no grudge against me on account of this unpleasantness? Why, I wouldn't have had it occur on no account."

He came over to Amelia and apologised profusely, and she with her usual kindness of heart hastened to assure him that she quite understood that it was an accident. Then we all went again to the wall and looked over.

The cat missing Hutcheson's face had drawn back across the moat, and was sitting on her haunches as though ready to spring. Indeed, the very instant she saw him she did spring, and with a blind unreasoning fury, which would have been grotesque, only that it was so frightfully real. She did not try to run up the wall, but simply launched herself at him as though hate and fury could lend her wings to pass straight through the great distance between them. Amelia, womanlike, got quite concerned, and said to Elias P. in a warning voice:

"Oh! you must be very careful. That animal would try to kill you if she were here; her eyes look like positive murder."

He laughed out jovially. "Excuse me, ma'am," he said, "but I can't help laughin'. Fancy a man that has fought grizzlies an' Injuns bein' careful of bein' murdered by a cat!"

When the cat heard him laugh, her whole demeanour seemed to change. She no longer tried to jump or run up the wall, but went quietly over, and sitting again beside the dead kitten began to lick and fondle it as though it were alive.

"See!" said I, "the effect of a really strong man. Even that animal in the midst of her fury recognises the voice of a master, and bows to him!"

"Like a squaw!" was the only comment of Elias P. Hutcheson, as we moved on our way round the city fosse. Every now and then we looked over the wall and each time saw the cat following us. At first she had kept going back to the dead kitten, and then as the distance grew greater took it in her mouth and so followed. After a while, however, she abandoned this, for we saw her following all alone; she had evidently hidden the body somewhere. Amelia's alarm grew at the cat's persistence, and more than once she repeated her warning; but the American always laughed with amusement, till finally, seeing that she was beginning to be worried, he said:

"I say, ma'am, you needn't be skeered over that cat. I go heeled, I du!" Here he slapped his pistol pocket at the back of his lumbar region. "Why sooner'n have you worried, I'll shoot the critter, right here, an' risk the police interferin' with a citizen of the United States for carryin' arms contrairy to reg'lations!" As he spoke he looked over the wall, but the cat, on seeing him, retreated, with a growl, into a bed of tall flowers, and was hidden. He went on: "Blest if that ar critter ain't got more sense of what's good for her than most Christians. I guess we've seen the last of her! You bet, she'll go back now to that busted kitten and have a private funeral of it, all to herself!"

Amelia did not like to say more, lest he might, in mistaken kindness to her, fulfil his threat of shooting the cat: and so we went on and crossed the little wooden bridge leading to the gateway whence ran the steep paved roadway between the Burg and the pentagonal Torture Tower. As we crossed the bridge we saw the cat again down below us. When she saw us her fury seemed to return, and she made frantic efforts to get up the steep wall. Hutcheson laughed as he looked down at her, and said:

"Goodbye, old girl. Sorry I injured your feelin's, but you'll get over it in time! So long!" And then we passed through the long, dim archway and came to the gate of the Burg.

When we came out again after our survey of this most beautiful old place which not even the well-intentioned efforts of the Gothic restorers of forty years ago have been able to spoil—though their restoration was then glaring white—we seemed to have quite forgotten the unpleasant episode of the morning. The old lime tree with its great trunk gnarled with the passing of nearly nine centuries, the deep well cut through the heart of the rock by those captives of old, and the lovely view from the city wall whence we heard, spread over almost a full quarter of an hour, the multitudinous chimes of the city, had all helped to wipe out from our minds the incident of the slain kitten.

We were the only visitors who had entered the Torture Tower that morning—so at least said the old custodian—and as we had the place all to ourselves were able to make a minute and more satisfactory survey than would have otherwise been possible. The custodian, looking to us as the sole source of his gains for the day, was willing to meet our wishes in anyway. The Torture Tower is truly a grim place, even now when many thousands of visitors have sent a stream of life, and the joy that follows life, into the place; but at the time I mention it wore its grimmest and most gruesome aspect. The dust of ages seemed to have settled on it, and the darkness and the horror of its memories seem to have become sentient in a way that would have satisfied the Pantheistic souls of Philo or Spinoza. The lower chamber where we entered was seemingly, in its normal state, filled with incarnate darkness; even the hot sunlight streaming in through the door seemed to be lost in the vast thickness of the walls, and only showed the masonry rough as when the builder's scaffolding had come down, but coated with dust and marked here and there with patches of dark stain which, if walls could speak, could have given their own dread memories of fear and pain. We were glad to pass up the dusty wooden staircase, the custodian leaving the outer door open to light us somewhat on our way; for to our eyes the one long-wick'd, evil-smelling candle stuck in a sconce on the wall gave an inadequate light. When we came up through the open trap in the corner of the chamber overhead, Amelia held on to me so tightly that I could actually feel her heart beat. I must say for my own part that I was not surprised at her fear, for this room was even more gruesome than that below. Here there was certainly more light, but only just sufficient to realise the horrible surroundings of the place. The builders of the tower had evidently intended that only they who should gain the top should have any of the joys of light and prospect. There, as we had noticed from below, were ranges of windows, albeit of mediaeval smallness, but elsewhere in the tower were only a very few narrow slits such as were habitual in places of mediaeval defence. A few of these only lit the chamber, and these so high up in the wall that from no part could the sky be seen through the thickness of the walls. In racks, and leaning in disorder against the walls, were a number of headsmen's swords, great double-handed weapons with broad blade and keen edge. Hard by were several blocks whereon the necks of the victims had lain, with here and there deep notches where the steel had bitten through the guard of flesh and shored into the wood. Round the chamber, placed in all sorts of irregular ways, were many implements of torture which made one's heart ache to see—chairs full of spikes which gave instant and excruciating pain; chairs and couches with dull knobs whose torture was seemingly less, but which, though slower, were equally efficacious; racks, belts, boots, gloves, collars, all made for compressing at will; steel baskets in which the head could be slowly crushed into a pulp if necessary; watchmen's hooks with long handle and knife that cut at resistance—this a specialty of the old Nurnberg police system; and many, many other devices for man's injury to man. Amelia grew quite pale with the horror of the things, but fortunately did not faint, for being a little overcome she sat down on a torture chair, but jumped up again with a shriek, all tendency to faint gone. We both pretended that it was the injury done to her dress by the dust of the chair, and the rusty spikes which had upset her, and Mr. Hutcheson acquiesced in accepting the explanation with a kind-hearted laugh.

But the central object in the whole of this chamber of horrors was the engine known as the Iron Virgin, which stood near the centre of the room. It was a rudely-shaped figure of a woman, something of the bell order, or, to make a closer comparison, of the figure of Mrs. Noah in the children's Ark, but without that slimness of waist and perfect rondeur of hip which marks the aesthetic type of the Noah family. One would hardly have recognised it as intended for a human figure at all had not the founder shaped on the forehead a rude semblance of a woman's face. This machine was coated with rust without, and covered with dust; a rope was fastened to a ring in the front of the figure, about where the waist should have been, and was drawn through a pulley, fastened on the wooden pillar which sustained the flooring above. The custodian pulling this rope showed that a section of the front was hinged like a door at one side; we then saw that the engine was of considerable thickness, leaving just room enough inside for a man to be placed. The door was of equal thickness and of great weight, for it took the custodian all his strength, aided though he was by the contrivance of the pulley, to open it. This weight was partly due to the fact that the door was of manifest purpose hung so as to throw its weight downwards, so that it might shut of its own accord when the strain was released. The inside was honeycombed with rust-nay more, the rust alone that comes through time would hardly have eaten so deep into the iron walls; the rust of the cruel stains was deep indeed! It was only, however, when we came to look at the inside of the door that the diabolical intention was manifest to the full. Here were several long spikes, square and massive, broad at the base and sharp at the points, placed in such a position that when the door should close the upper ones would pierce the eyes of the victim, and the lower ones his heart and vitals. The sight was too much for poor Amelia, and this time she fainted dead off, and I had to carry her down the stairs, and place her on a bench outside till she recovered. That she felt it to the quick was afterwards shown by the fact that my eldest son bears to this day a rude birthmark on his breast, which has, by family consent, been accepted as representing the Nurnberg Virgin.

When we got back to the chamber we found Hutcheson still opposite the Iron Virgin; he had been evidently philosophising, and now gave us the benefit of his thought in the shape of a sort of exordium.

"Wall, I guess I've been learnin' somethin' here while madam has been gettin' over her faint. 'Pears to me that we're a long way behind the times on our side of the big drink. We uster think out on the plains that the Injun could give us points in tryin' to make a man oncomfortable; but I guess your old mediaeval law-and-order party could raise him everytime. Splinters was pretty good in his bluff on the squaw, but this here young miss held a straight flush all high on him. The points of them spikes air sharp enough still, though even the edges air eaten out by what uster be on them. It'd be a good thing for our Indian section to get some specimens of this here play-toy to send round to the Reservations jest to knock the stuffin' out of the bucks, and the squaws too, by showing them as how old civilisation lays over them at their best. Guess but I'll get in that box a minute jest to see how it feels!"

"Oh no! no!" said Amelia. "It is too terrible!"

"Guess, ma'am, nothin's too terrible to the explorin' mind. I've been in some queer places in my time. Spent a night inside a dead horse while a prairie fire swept over me in Montana Territory—an' another time slept inside a dead buffler when the Comanches was on the war path an' I didn't keer to leave my kyard on them. I've been two days in a caved-in tunnel in the Billy Broncho gold mine in New Mexico, an' was one of the four shut up for three parts of a day in the caisson what slid over on her side when we was settin' the foundations of the Buffalo Bridge. I've not funked an odd experience yet, an' I don't propose to begin now!"

We saw that he was set on the experiment, so I said: "Well, hurry up, old man, and get through it quick?"

"All right, General," said he, "but I calculate we ain't quite ready yet. The gentlemen, my predecessors, what stood in that thar canister, didn't volunteer for the office—not much! And I guess there was some ornamental tyin' up before the big stroke was made. I want to go into this thing fair and square, so I must get fixed up proper first. I dare say this old galoot can rise some string and tie me up accordin' to sample?"

This was said interrogatively to the old custodian, but the latter, who understood the drift of his speech, though perhaps not appreciating to the full the niceties of dialect and imagery, shook his head. His protest was, however, only formal and made to be overcome. The American thrust a gold piece into his hand, saying, "Take it, pard! it's your pot; and don't be skeer'd. This ain't no necktie party that you're asked to assist in!" He produced some thin frayed rope and proceeded to bind our companion with sufficient strictness for the purpose. When the upper part of his body was bound, Hutcheson said:

"Hold on a moment, Judge. Guess I'm too heavy for you to tote into the canister. You jest let me walk in, and then you can wash up regardin' my legs!"

Whilst speaking he had backed himself into the opening which was just enough to hold him. It was a close fit and no mistake. Amelia looked on with fear in her eyes, but she evidently did not like to say anything. Then the custodian completed his task by tying the American's feet together so that he was now absolutely helpless and fixed in his voluntary prison. He seemed to really enjoy it, and the incipient smile which was habitual to his face blossomed into actuality as he said:

"Guess this here Eve was made out of the rib of a dwarf! There ain't much room for a full-grown citizen of the United States to hustle. We uster make our coffins more roomier in Idaho territory. Now, Judge, you jest begin to let this door down, slow, on to me. I want to feel the same pleasure as the other jays had when those spikes began to move toward their eyes!"

"Oh no! no! no!" broke in Amelia hysterically. "It is too terrible! I can't bear to see it!—I can't! I can't!"

But the American was obdurate. "Say, Colonel," said he, "Why not take Madame for a little promenade? I wouldn't hurt her feelin's for the world; but now that I am here, havin' kem eight thousand miles, wouldn't it be too hard to give up the very experience I've been pinin' an' pantin' fur? A man can't get to feel like canned goods everytime! Me and the Judge here'll fix up this thing in no time, an' then you'll come back, an' we'll all laugh together!"

Once more the resolution that is born of curiosity triumphed, and Amelia stayed holding tight to my arm and shivering whilst the custodian began to slacken slowly inch by inch the rope that held back the iron door. Hutcheson's face was positively radiant as his eyes followed the first movement of the spikes.

"Wall!" he said, "I guess I've not had enjoyment like this since I left Noo York. Bar a scrap with a French sailor at Wapping—an' that warn't much of a picnic neither—I've not had a show fur real pleasure in this dod-rotted Continent, where there ain't no b'ars nor no Injuns, an' wheer nary man goes heeled. Slow there, Judge! Don't you rush this business! I want a show for my money this game—I du!"

The custodian must have had in him some of the blood of his predecessors in that ghastly tower, for he worked the engine with a deliberate and excruciating slowness which after five minutes, in which the outer edge of the door had not moved half as many inches, began to overcome Amelia. I saw her lips whiten, and felt her hold upon my arm relax. I looked around an instant for a place whereon to lay her, and when I looked at her again found that her eye had become fixed on the side of the Virgin. Following its direction I saw the black cat crouching out of sight. Her green eyes shone like danger lamps in the gloom of the place, and their colour was heightened by the blood which still smeared her coat and reddened her mouth. I cried out:

"The cat! look out for the cat!" for even then she sprang out before the engine. At this moment she looked like a triumphant demon. Her eyes blazed with ferocity, her hair bristled out till she seemed twice her normal size, and her tail lashed about as does a tiger's when the quarry is before it. Elias P. Hutcheson when he saw her was amused, and his eyes positively sparkled with fun as he said:

"Darned if the squaw hain't got on all her war paint! Jest give her a shove off if she comes any of her tricks on me, for I'm so fixed everlastingly by the boss, that durn my skin if I can keep my eyes from her if she wants them! Easy there, Judge! don't you slack that ar rope or I'm euchered!"

At this moment Amelia completed her faint, and I had to clutch hold of her round the waist or she would have fallen to the floor. Whilst attending to her I saw the black cat crouching for a spring, and jumped up to turn the creature out.

But at that instant, with a sort of hellish scream, she hurled herself, not as we expected at Hutcheson, but straight at the face of the custodian. Her claws seemed to be tearing wildly as one sees in the Chinese drawings of the dragon rampant, and as I looked I saw one of them light on the poor man's eye, and actually tear through it and down his cheek, leaving a wide band of red where the blood seemed to spurt from every vein.

With a yell of sheer terror which came quicker than even his sense of pain, the man leaped back, dropping as he did so the rope which held back the iron door. I jumped for it, but was too late, for the cord ran like lightning through the pulley-block, and the heavy mass fell forward from its own weight.

As the door closed I caught a glimpse of our poor companion's face. He seemed frozen with terror. His eyes stared with a horrible anguish as if dazed, and no sound came from his lips.

And then the spikes did their work. Happily the end was quick, for when I wrenched open the door they had pierced so deep that they had locked in the bones of the skull through which they had crushed, and actually tore him-it-out of his iron prison till, bound as he was, he fell at full length with a sickly thud upon the floor, the face turning upward as he fell.

I rushed to my wife, lifted her up and carried her out, for I feared for her very reason if she should wake from her faint to such a scene. I laid her on the bench outside and ran back. Leaning against the wooden column was the custodian moaning in pain whilst he held his reddening handkerchief to his eyes. And sitting on the head of the poor American was the cat, purring loudly as she licked the blood which trickled through the gashed socket of his eyes.

I think no one will call me cruel because I seized one of the old executioner's swords and shore her in two as she sat.

End

# When The Sky Rains Gold

T he earliest recollection of Victor Paterson was of a stern and unbending father to whom all around him paid almost extravagant homage, and who frowned when any of his children had the hardihood to appear in his presence. Indeed, he felt from the tears and kisses of his mother on such occasions that some kindly and protective power had exercised on his behalf. Whilst he was yet—as it seemed to him afterwards—a very baby he had been conscious of a stern, loud voice raised in menace and a soft, appealing one in reply from the mother to whose heart he was clasped; and he felt, rather than remembered, that to what had passed at that interview was due any kindness shown later on to him or to either of his younger brothers. This feeling was partly due to an interview several years later when he was a great, brawny boy. His father had sent for him to his library, and when he had entered and stood almost trembling before him, said:—

"I have sent for you, sir, because you are now of an age to understand your position in life, and to realise what I have arranged concerning the future of yourself and your brothers."

Here Victor tried to mumble out some sort of thanks, but his father, holding up a warning hand, went on: "I want no thanks—no recognition of any kind. I have no desire whatsoever to have sons to make my own life worried to the extent that children can disarrange settled plans. Candidly, I wish that none of you had ever been born; but since you are here and the law does not give me power of life and death over you, I have yielded to your mother's wishes that you should be in some way placed in an independent position. I have acquiesced in this the more freely since I shall thus be able to secure through your absence a larger measure of quite for myself. I have therefore arranged that you are to have an estate of your own; and in order that you may not be closer to me than necessary, I have chosen your abode the Island of Skye. You may be aware that my means are vast; let me add to your informational this item; that they are absolutely and entirely at my own disposal. What I do for you now is final, and you need never expect during my life, or at my death, any addition to your fortune from this source. As your mother has urged on me that you, as her eldest son, should have even better provision than your brothers I have settled on you an estates which is of larger area, and which carries with it some territorial influence, for it makes you a Laird. It will under all ordinary circumstances be adequate for your requirement; but be careful with it and husband your resources, for if anything should happen adversely you will find yourself in a very different position, and will never, under any circumstances whatever, get any help from me. Your brothers I have taken care of in a proportionate degree. As I daresay you have gathered from the peculiar bent of his education, Hobson will take his place in the Royal Navy. My influence can secure that for him, and also that he will be kept on the Australian station—certainly at first, and afterwards by his own wish, for the liberal provision which I make for him is contingent on his remaining in distant waters. Aide will be a mining engineer, and for his future is secured a large mining tract at the upper waters of the Amazon. Thus he, too, will remain far from me, and I shall thus be able to maintain my purposes unaltered, and my self-possession unimparied. Today, therefore, you may all take farewell of your mother. As for me, I desire no farewells. I am creditably rid of you all, and shall henceforth forget that you have ever existed. You may, if you wish, look on yourself as the head of a new family and act accordingly. You will now please to make your brothers acquainted with my wishes and with the separate arrangements for their future made for them, as I have no wish to undergo a similar interview of this sort."

So saying he touched the bell of his table and resumed his work. Victor, without a word, bowed, and withdrew.

He straightaway called his brothers to him and told them exactly the messages which he had to deliver. Then, having taken an affectionate leave of his mother, he started that evening for Skye, as the journey had been arranged for him.

At Skye he was all-powerful, and as he was of a nature at once masterful and kindly he soon became a sort of beneficient despot among his tenants. The estate which had been given him was of vast extent, and though much of the ground was poor and there were many mountains absolutely sterile, sufficient remained of more generous nature to make him rich even for a territorial magnate. For nearly ten years he had been enjoyment of his fortune, and had grown almost to forget the loneliness and disappointment of his early years. The Island of Skye is not a place where life goes very rapidly, and the local pleasures are of a somewhat primitive kind, tempered with that spirit of obedience in all things to the chief which is common to feudalism and the semi-barbaric method of clanship.

He had but lately started on a sailing trip in his little yacht *The Eagle*, when one afternoon, leaving his yacht outside the rocks and islands to the north, he had pulled his punt in shorewards to enjoy the view of Quairang from the seaside. The day was hot and all around him was calm, and so coming as near shore as he could without losing, under the shadow of the cliffs, sight of the mountain top, he pulled in his cars and lay down lazily, letting the boat rock on the swell whilst the set of the tide drifted him along shore. The rocking motion and the heat made him drowsy, and for awhile the whole scene around him faded away into the darkness of dreamless sleep.

He awoke with the sound of a distant cry ringing in his ears, and instinctivel sitting up and grasping the cars, listened for a repetition. It came quickly, and seeking within his eyes the direction of the sound, he saw on a cliff, near which the boat had drifted, a woman wildly waving a scarf with one hand whilst with the other she pointed down the cliff, all while screaming. Victor Paterson saw that there was some danger afoot, and being a man of action turned his boat's head to the scene, and exerting his strength drove her through the water with powerful strokes. A very short time brought him near enough to realize the cause of the screaming and the danger to which it attracted. Another woman was struggling in the water at the foot of the cliff, which was here some thirty or forty feet high. The air in her clothes had hitherto buoyed her up, but those were becoming saturated and she was beginning to sink, when driving his boat alongside her, he grasped her hand and drew her to the boat. The swell under the cliff was strong, and the little boat rocked about so much that he saw there would be some difficulty in taking aboard the woman, who was of a large and heavy pattern. So, stopping over the stern, he fastened the end of the painter round her waist and made it fast.

"Now," he said, "hold on to the boat and I will row ashore; it will be much safer than trying to get you into the boat with such a swell on."

The woman in the water hasped as she answered as pluckily as he could:

"Go on as quickly as you can! I'll do my best."

She was neither too young nor too well favoured, and the tumble from the cliff into the sea had played sad havoc with her toilet; but Victory saw easily that she was a lady. Speech, and thought, and manner are above all accidents of flood and field. He pulled out a little way, so that he might see the coast and judge the nearest point where landing would be possible, and as he did so he opened to his vision to the top of the cliff. The other woman who had been waving with her scarf was there still, but had now realised the situation at a glance, and was running to and fro, and peering over the rocks in search of an opening where the boat might land.

She ran along the cliff to the most northerly point where the land was highest, and at once turned and signalled the boat, shouting at the same time with a strong, clear voice to attract Victor's attention in case he had not kept eyes on her. As she pointed north Victor turned the boat's bend that way, and made to round the outmost point of rock. A few strokes too him to it, and just inside he saw a tiny strip of yello beach at the bottom of a gully running down between the cliffs. Towards this he pulled, and within a couple of minutes succeeded in beaching the boating. He then jumped out, and, untying the rope from the lady's waist, carried her ashore. As he did so he felt her head fall over, and her weight to seemingly increase. She had fainted.

He laid her on the beach, and, as he did, so caught sight of the other lady coming down the gully at breakneck speed, jumping from rock to rock, or plunging among the edge and bog which marked the course of the tiny stream. As he carried the lady up the beach to where the tumbling stream had formed a tiny basin among the rocks, the new comer reached him, and helped to lift her from his shoulder; she gasped out, as she did so—

"She is not dead?"

"No! No! She has only fainted—and that only after we got to land. She will be alright in a few moments."

She threw herself on her knees beside her friend, and dipping her handkerchief in the bright water, bathed the face and smoothed the grey hair back, and generally adjusted the dishevelled clothing. It was evident that the invalid was recovering, so she simply waited. Victor waited too, and during his wait was able to take stock of the newcomer.

She was a young girl of not much more than twenty years, with a well-made figure of the slim order, and radiantly beautiful. Her features were good, and ger brown skin was so clear that the rosy hue of health, heightened by her mental disturbance, and the warmth of her charge down the hill side, seemed to shine through it from within. Brown hair, brown eyes full of a fire that took yellow colour when the sunshine met them, a mouth like pearl and ruby where the white teeth shone through the parted lips, looked in perfect keeping with the snowy frock of ducked faced with a falling drapery of some sort of ganzy stuff of fairy green over the breasts, and fastened with a brooch composed of a single flashing ruby. Victor Paterson felt a thrill go through him as he realised the feeling of Geraint of old:

"Here by God's grace is the one maid for me!"

It was a genuine case on his part of love at first sight, and the natural instinct of his race prompted him forthwith to so bear himself, that all things might be ordered to the accomplishment of his aim. Therefore, like a wise man, he simply waited.

When the elderly lady opened her eyes and saw the sweet young face bending over her she seemed at once to realise her position, and drawing down the face to hers kissed it and murmured:

"Thank God, Riddy, it was not you who fell over the cliff—your father would have never forgiven me."

"Oh hush Aunt Joe!" said the girl, "Hush, hush! You musn't say things like that or I shall never forgive you. Ah, Aunty dear; thank God you are safe. I have been in such dreadful fear. Thank you, sir! Oh! Thank you for saving my dear aunt!" And before he knew what she intended she seized his hand and kissed it, as women sometimes do under sudden semi-hysterical emotion. Victor, taken aback by the suddenness of the act, was equal to the occasion, and withdrew his hand gently, but with a firmness which acknowledged no resistance.

"No!" he said, and with a grave commanding dignity which went straight to the girl's heart, "No! You must not do that, I am not worthy of it!" Then seeing a certain embarrassment in both ladies he went on quickly:

"And now what is to be done? Have you a carriage here?"

The young lady shook her head and the elder answered:

"We walked over from Quairang, intending to spending the afternoon on the cliffs, and the carriage was to come out and wait for us on the road beyond at eight o'clock, so that we might drive back to Portree by moonlight."

As she spoke Victor's mind was made up, and he said, so authoritatively that his words did not admit of any disputing:

"Then it is quite simple. You must not run the risk of remaining in your wet clothes. You must come on my yacht, and there you can make yourselves comfortable, and I shall sail you back to Portree!" As he spoke he took from the boat's locker a revolver and fired one shot, and then three in rapid succession.

"The boat will soon be here," he added. He then ran to the top of the cliff, and a few minutes later they could see him waving his arms as he directed the approaching boat. It seemed to both ladies like magic, but in what seemed a few moments they were seated in a good-sized whale boat, which was driven through the water at great speed by four red-haired, big-bearded, brawny giants who spoke in Gaelic. Victor took the helm himself, the steerman having been left to find the carriage and bring it back to Portree.

Victor Paterson had hitherto been proud of his beautiful little yacht, but as he helped the ladies aboard he wished that she were more worthy of her visitors and that the accommodations were better. He ran down to his cabin and threw a bundle of flannels on the bunk, and then coming up, said to Aunt Joe:

"You must take off your wet clothes at once. You can either go to bed till they are dry or put on what you find. We have, of course, no women on board, so perhaps your niece will be your lady's maid. My men are capital hands at washing and drying, and all sorts of things, so you will not have to wait long."

The ladies retired below, and it seemed an incredibly short time till the clothes which the girl brought out of the cabin were brought back dry and actually ironed!—Surely there is no one so absolutely handy as a sailor.—In the meantime an early dinner had been prepared, and when the ladies emerged in spick and span order they were greeted by the welcome sight of a most appetising, if plain, meal. With her restored toilet, Aunt Joe had on her best manner and at once made the introductions:

"I am Mrs. Bates, and this is my niece, Miss Dans. And neither she nor I know adequately how to thank you for the vital help you gave me today, and for the courtesy and hospitality which you have shown us since."

To which he replied with equal formality:

"I am Victor Paterson, of Uiskorchie; they call me laird in my own parts. I am more proud and happy than I can say to be of any service to any ladies. There is too great a reward for any effort of mine in that you are the ladies whom I have been privileged to assist."

To his surprise the elder lady spoke out:

"Victor Paterson! Why Riddy's great-grandfather had the same name. It would be strange if the accident of today should bring us a new relative or connection."

Riddy said in fun:

"'Us,' Aunt Joe? Mr. Paterson—the other Mr. Paterson—and you cannot be very near relatives."

"Nonsense, my dear Riddy. In great families all relationships are near enough and far enough, just as we like to make them. Old Mr. Paterson would be in close relationship with me in the highlands. Why anyone can follow the connection; aye, and even understand it!"

"What is the exact relationship, Aunt Joe?" she asked, demurely.

"He was my daughter's brother-in-law's father-in-law's father," came the ready answer.

They all laughed, and Mrs. Joe Bates remained mistress of the situation, whilst the badinage helped to put them all upon a familiar footing. They fell upon the dinner, and enjoyed themselves immensely. They then went on deck and found that the sailors had rigged up an awning, under which they sat restfully and enjoyed the contrast of their own shady ease with the fierce glare of the sun. The waste of waters around them was like a sea of diamond and sapphire, whereon the distant islands seemed to rest airily, as a bird however; whiles the shores were dim with the heat haze, and the mountains stood out clear. As she looked, Riddy seemed to realise that Skye was well named, for it was indeed aerial realm.

It was an ideal day for lazy sailing, and none of the party were anxious that the journey should soon come to an end. Victor was in a trance of delight. All the dreams of his young manhood seemed to have been realised at once, and the elements seemed to have lent themselves as though obedient to his wishes. There was just sufficient breeze to fill the sails, and on even keel the pretty, swift winged yacht drifted on to Portree. Presently tea was served on deck and as they sipped it the evening fell, the sun sank lower and lower, till at length great flaming disc was cleft along by the black serrated line of the island. All three stood rapt in speechless delight; for Victor the glory of earth and sea and sky had a new value in which was something of holiness, and with his eyes fixed on Dana's face he waited in silence. In a few minutes the sun had sunk below the horizon's rim and twilight was upon them. The red sky over the island still flared, but it was with a feeble light, which threw into indistinct poetical effect all the noble beauty of the scene. It was the true Scottish "gloamin'" in which is this strange effect: That looking upward there is nothing but light, whilst earthward there is nought but darkness. It took the man-artist many a century to realise what the God-artist learned at a glance—that black is a colour of exceeding value in art. With a sigh of delight Miss Dana turned to her companion and said:

"Oh, Aunt Joe, isn't it just noble? It is worth coming across the Atlantic to see. I wish we could have such twilight at home!"

Victor felt that his stock of knowledge was increased a little—his companions were Americans.

The sail by moonlight was like another sweet dream—the same, but different, as when children drink into their memories the glories of coloured fireworks, and all the various charms which the same scene has when the shells and rockets spread their many-coloured fires. Following the red glare of the sunset and the misty poetry of the twilight came a sort of dawn, where the white, misty light of the moon sailed on after the departing day. Then the moon rose, full and broad, and threw a golden light over the world in such a way that all things denied its direct radiance became of the inky hue. And then the twinkling lights of Portress, and the dim windows of the scattered houses around it began to shine through the night; and the old lady thought sweetly on things that had been, whilst the young people sat in contented silence and had strange imaginings.

But even such an idyllic journey must have an end, and although the shouting from the shore though the darkness—for even moonlight is dark by comparison, when a narrow barbour has to be won through a rushing tide—and the lanterns waving to and fro seemed all fraught with poetry and romance, the prosaic end of parting came. After another hurried thanks which seemed, and was, more formal—for no rugged, lonely nature, but the conventionality of civilisation surrounded them—Victor took his way back to the yacht.

He slept but little that night, for he had a feeling that the morrow had something in store for him. At the dawn he arose and watched the shore which had now a new charm for him, for it was the casket that held his jewel. He knew that he dare not make a call so early, and sat and dreamed as the hour stol away. He heard the warning bell of Glasgow streamer sound, and saw her cast off and cleave her way eastward to Oban. As he looked at her he mused and thought to himself, "There are someone that boat who go to meet those they love, and some who leave the better part of their lives behind them. As for me, either may be in store for me this day." From which one who could have read his thought would have known he had resolved to put in the coming hours his fortune to the touch, "and win or lose it all."

At noon he took his way to the hotel, and there were few feminine eyes but turned on him admiringly, as with free, bold gait he strode up the little street.

But it was not long before he strode down the street again, with gait as free, but with his eager look turned to one of bitterness. The Indies had left by the Glasgow boat, without leaving a word for him, or even their address, or saying whither they were bound.

Victor went to his cabin, and with his soul filled with bitterness tried to fix some plan of action. He felt that Miss Dana was his fate, and there was for him no happiness, no rest, till he had won her. Back to his memory came like the pictures in a diorama every moment of the previous say since he had first seen her; and with each retrospect came a stronger conviction that all that had passed was sincere—that there was in those true eyes no deceit, no guile.

There must then be someother cause for the sudden departure.

There had not been time for them to have even had created a fear of him, or any advance of his. So he made up his mind to make for Oban and try if he could see Miss Dana once more, and at least learn where or how he might meet her again. The order to sail given, the yacht flew over the water to Oban, and Victor had the melancholy satisfaction of seeing as he drew near the port that if he had started but a little earlier he might have got equal with the streamer, if not ahead of her. He did not neglect his chance, however, but tried round the hotels in case the American party had arranged to stay the night. Then he ulvd the railway officials, but so many parties consisting of two ladies had left that it was hopeless to try and discover in which direction those he sought had gone.

Victor Paterson returned to his yacht baffled and despairing, and forthwith sailed away for Portree again, for he felt that at least he might visit the enchanted spot where he had seen her who was henceforth to rule his thoughts. The next day he was sorry he had gone for the place looked and felt so lonely that it made all his adventure seem only like a beautiful dream, from which this was the melancholy awakening.

More than two years had passed, and during all that time Victor treasured in his heart the image of the lovely stranger. He did not know where or how to look, or should he have willingly begun a search through the world, so he did the only thing to be done, waited; possessing his soul in such patience as he might.

At last the Goddess Fortune brought him a clue. He was making a visit to Quairang in the late autumn, and was seated on the table rock, looking seawards to where the one sad, sweet adventure of his life had taken place, when he mechanically picked up a piece of old newspaper—a lunch wrapper left by some previous tourist. In Skye any kind of chance literature is not to be despised and he threw his eye over it. It was not apparently of a very interesting nature—few trade journals are interesting to laymen of the craft; and this one, the *Auctioneers and Valuers' Gazette*, was seemingly no exception to the rule. Mechanically, he read through lists of houses to let, and such similar advertisements, set forth in the most attractive auctioneer English: but at last he came across a paragraph which brought him up sitting all aglow:

"We are glad to learn that the estate of Brassy Tower, near Westernford, on the Stanmore and Watford line, which has been so long in the market, has been at last disposed of through the instrumentality of Messrs. Topping, Son, and Hickson of 32, Budge's-corner, Watford. This noble estate, which is the last of the 'ring-fence' properties left on the northside of the metropolis, makes a departure from its historic traditions, in the walks which the feet of Burke and Steele rendered sacred to lovers of our national glories, the feet of a younger and an alien dynasty will henceforth tread. Where the gleams of sunlight falling through the leafy veils of summer, the brown mantle of autumn, on the 'bare poles' under which the ship of winter sails towards the green islands of spring, traced the long hours in their succession as on nature's own sundial will now be recorded, we trust, happy memories of a childhood spent in the western world. The new owner of this delightful mansion, by whose sale Messrs. Topping, Son, and Hickson have added another bayleaf to their career of commercial well-doing, is Miss E. Dana, the millionaire American heiress, of whom the society papers have of late given certain mysterious hints."

A true lover is a person of limited ideas: whilst the epithet can apply to him his thoughts are limited to one. Thus it was only in accordance with the habit of things that Victor at once found his troubles at an end. There might be more than one American Miss Dana, but of the supposition he took no heed. Here was Miss Dana with a location habitation and a man, and of course it was his Miss Dana—he would be but a poor-spirited lover, indeed, who would admit even to the secret recesses of his soul a single doubt on such a subject. But complete assurance makes its own doubts, and as he turned the scarp of paper over in his hands and sought vainly for further information Victor Paterson began to have fears. What was the date of the paper? It certainly looked old, but examine it how he would he could nowhere find the year. At last he got a clue; in one advertisement allusion was made to Thursday, October 1, and looking at his pocket-book he found that in the current year October 1 had fallen on Sunday: the newspaper was, therefore, of three years before, unless, indeed, it were very much older. It was characteristic of the man's nature that as he carefully folded the precious scrap of paper and place it in his pocket-book, he rose and took his own way towards the cave-like entrance to the table rock of Quairang.

That night he slept at home. The next day he made preparations for departure for an unlimited time: and on the day following he was on the way to Glasgow on the bi-weekly steamer. Whilst there was no clue whatever to his departed object of affection, he was sadly content to wait: but with the least hope his imagination filled the whole dark way before him with a brilliant series of fortunate episodes.

When he got to London he put up at a quiet hotel, and having obtained an Ordnance Map of the county of Middlesex, he began to study the topography of Northern London. It cannot be imagined that he expected to find the Ordnance map in error, so it must have been a tremor arising from someother cause that made his heart bound with a new gladness when he found marked on the map, between Stanmore and Watford, the name "Brassy Towers." Next morning he had taken train to Watford, bringing with him only a small handbag with a sufficient change of toilet for all emergencies. At Watford he had procured a carriage and driven along the road to Stanmore. The driver certainly must have thought him a very inquisitive person, for he insisted on being informed as to the name and ownership of every house along the road; if he did not know, he had to stop the next pedestrian and make inquiry. After a drive of a couple of hours the ground began to rise, and presently the road ran under the shadow of a high red brick wall. Victor had a sort of presentiment that kept him silent; he felt that he would rather that the name of the house they were passing should be given to him than that he should have to ask it. He was not surprised when the driver said:

"That, sir, is Brassy Towers, where the Yankee ladies do shut themselves up."

This gave Victor an opportunity of making inquiries, and within a few minutes he was given all that was known by the gossip of the neighbourhood of the occupants of "The Towers," as the driver said the place was familiarity known. He was told that two ladies, one old and one young, lived there alone; that the young lady was very beautiful, and that they saw no company whatever; that sometimes they drove about the country side, in a fine carriage with fine horses—and that was all. When Victor asked if it was not about time to give the horses a rest the driver replied that there was a capital little inn at hand and that he had hoped that they might rest there for awhile.

The inn at hand seemed to be a most capital little place, for Victor Paterson liked it so well that he then and there determined to remain for at least the night; so he sent his bag up to his bedroom, which looked over the demesne of Brassy Towers, and sat down to lunch. When this was over he went up to his room and sat at the window studying the prospect before him, and trying to imagine what would be at the end of his venture. Hope suggested some such glowing possibility, that all the air seemed charged with music at the very thought; but fear drew in the front of his mind's eye a rugged veil of doubt, through whose rents a waste of dreary darkness appeared. He could get no glimpse of the house, for a great grover of forest trees intervened, but now and then a mist of smoke rising above them, showed its locality.

Victor remained as patient as he could until late in the afternoon, and then, having made his toilet with something of extra care, sallied out to pay his visit to The Towers, and try to see Miss Dana.

And now he felt, for the first time in his life, Victor Paterson of secondary importance. Nevertheless, he held himself at his proudest; his type of man is at its best when fighting at the odds—and what odds are so great as doubt to a lover? At that moment the whole fighting spirit of him—and it was an imperious one—wasn't its best, and any qualms which might have of his ultimate success were relentlessly crushed down by an iron will.

The lodge-keeper would probably have denied him admission had he asked, but as he opened, himself, the wicket beside the great gate and passed on without hesitation, the man seemed to take it for granted that some right or business empowered him to enter, and stayed in his lodge, fully intending to deny any knowledge whatever of his entry if questioned on the subject.

As he walked through the winding avenue amongst, and at times under, the splendid trees, rich in all their summer beauty of foliage, which a dry autumn had aided in retaining till unusually late in the year, he marvelled afresh at the rich beauty around him. Coming from the wild barrenness of Skye,such leafy splendour seemed almost tropical, and it was little wonder that, when a bend in the avenue opened it to his eyes, the beautiful old red brick house with its many angles and gables, its quaint little towers surmounted by miniature cupolas, on which the copper roofing was of a lovely soft green with age, seemed like an enchanted palace which held the fairy queen whom he had come so far to seek. There must be some natural law of compensation which makes the boldest man the most timid and under proper conditions, and *vice versa*, for this young laird, who had come the length of Britain to try to win a girl whom he had seen but once, and who had seemingly run away from him, felt more and more faint-hearted as be approached the hall door. Here again, however, his inner qualm did not show itself in any outward demeanour, for he walked boldly to the door as though the house were his own, and, having rung the bell, at once entered the hall without waiting. It was quite evident, from the manner in which the butler came forward, that visitors at Brassy Towers were neither usual nor expected: for the man seemed at first surprised, and then in a deferential way, indignant.

Before he had time to speak Victor said, "I want to see Miss Dana."

The servant said as respectfully as he could:

"Neither Miss Dana nor Mrs. Bates receives any visitors, sir."

This brought joy to Victor, for now he *knew* what before he had only surmised, that the Miss Danan who lived at Brassy Towers was *his* Miss Dana. Without a word he placed a ten-pound note in the man's hand, and when the butler had swiftly and furtively conveyed it to his pocket, and he knew that the bribe was taken he said.

"You will not get into any trouble. You, being in doubt, did not like to refuse admission to the visitors to your mistress without definite instructions. If you had known of course. You placed the strange gentlemen in the drawing room and came at once to inform your mistress herself; but forgot in the flurry of the moment to ask his name."

The man bowed, and without a word abowed him into the nearest drawing room and departed.

It needed all Victor Pateron's truculence of disposition to sustain him as he paced to and fro, for he could not but be aware that he was very much in the position of a trespasser. But it is not only at the moment of death that the mind had retrospects and inspirations: the *mauvais quart d'heure* has a logic of its own in which there are comforting conclusions. At this painful time Victor felt the compensation of the hurried and ungracious departure of his friends from Skye. He had not been forbidden to call, and was therefore within his conventional rights.

Within five minutes Miss Dana made her appearance radiant in beauty, and with an added charm in a soft, shy blush; she came quickly into the room after the manner of one whose time is precious, and who must act on impulse. As Victor stepped swiftly to meet her and took her hand in his she raised her eyes to his, and said, frankly:

"I am very, very glad to see you." She pronounced the adverbs, "vurry, vurry," but the quaintness seemed to Victor an added pleasure. She went on, "I feared we should never see you again!"

Victor's heart leaped. "Then you did not forget me!" was all he could say, but he still held her hand and she made no effort to withdraw it. And so they stood, seeming to both to stand soul to soul as hand to hand for a few flying moments, which had, however in them the essence of an eternity.

His dream was broken by the time the hurried voice of Mrs. Bates in the hall.

"A what?"

"A gentleman, ma'am."

"What is his name?"

"I do not know, ma'am."

"And you showed in a stranger without permission? I shall see you later."

The butler felt that he was earning his douceur.

As Mrs. Bates entered the room there was no semblance of haste about her, but there certainly was a reality of great haughtiness: even Miss Dana was surprised to see the metamorphosis in her aunt. When, however, Mrs. Bates recognised the visitor her face softened, and she was at once more like the lady whom he had known. Her salutation was hearty, but Victor could not but recognise that there was going on in her mind some duplicate process of thought. It was as though there were in the one person two different individualities, each with its own aims and objects, its own positive and restraining powers. At the sound of her voice the two young people had let go each other's hand, and stood a trifle further apart and in more conventional attitude. Victor still looked somewhat sheepish, as a man always does in moments of disturbed emotions; but, womanlike, Miss Dana retained entirely her ease and self-possession. Mrs.Bates looked from one to the other inquiringly, and seemed to make her mind up pretty quickly, for her face hardened somewhat, and she seemed to take a sort of formal possession of the young man. She sat down and made him sit beside her in the vis-a-vis, and plunged into conversation with a persistence which left no opportunity for her niece.

Victor felt somehow new quite content; his hand-clasp with the young American with the look into each other's eyes which had accompanied it together with the knowledge that these precious moments had become a secret which they shared made him self-confident. This bearing in itself helped to enlighten Mrs. Bates, for as the minutes flew by she became more and more hard in her demeanour, and at last rising up, suddenly said:

"Mr. Paterson, may I have a few words with you in my boudoir? I have something of a business duty to do, and perhaps we had better do it alone. You will pardon me, Eurydice, will you not?"

"Certainly! Aunt Joe," replied Miss Dana, sweetle: and without a word further Victor followed her from the room. Mrs. Bates side-long look was upon him, so he did not venture to turn his head toward Miss Dana; he had to content himself by looking in a mirror, in whose mysterious depths their glances met.

In the boudoir Mrs. Bates mentioned to Victor to be seated, and she sat herself opposite to him, and without preface began her business.

"Mr. Paterson," said Mrs. Bates, "do not think me ungrateful or wanting in any form of sympathy. There is every reason why I should, if I cannot please you, at least cause you as little pain as possible. You saved my life, and, indeed—indeed—I am not ungrateful; but I have a duty to do which I solemnly undertook to perform, and which I have, though not without some pain to myself and much self-denial, carried out heretofore. Now I ask for no confidence from you. I simply want to lay a certain matter before you, and so the first part of my duty will be done. In a word, my niece must not marry! Her father's wishes forbid it imperatively, for the present at all events, and she is herself under a very sacred promise which, until the conditions of it are fulfilled, she must abide by. Now I am old enough to know, and to have known by experience, that a young girl's wishes and her day dreams are more or less dependent on her surroundings, and that what is forbidden is not of necessity a thing to be desired. It is for this reason that I have isolated her here—and condemned myself to share her charming prison. I have been in hopes that as we lived a life of absolute seclusion no disturbing element should come into her life in the shape of a man that she feels could love—"

"Do you believe that such a hope can be realised?"

"You must not ask me that! It is not my belief, but the wishes of another, backed by a very solemn promise from myself and Riddy, that rules the present situation. I can but try—and try my best—to do what I think to be right!"

Victor thought a moment and then asked:

"Is there any valid reason—such a reason as average men of the world would accept as sufficient, why Miss Dana should not marry? I mean anything beyond and outside the will of the person to whom these mysterious promises were given? If there be then I trust that I am man enough to forget my own wishes and do what is best for the lady's—for any lady's—good!"

As he spoke he looked so manly and handsome that the old lady's heart warmed to him: but with a start she pulled herself together and went on:

"You must judge that matter for yourself. I shall do my best to give you materials for judgement. Riddy's father is a very remarkable man, of good extraction but entirely self-made, as the saying is. He left his home for reasons which we need not go into and went out to seek his fortune. After drifting about for awhile he became one of the adventurers to California when the gold fever broke out there. He was one of the 'Forty-niners' as they were called or 'Argonauts,' who crossed the Rockies amid incredible hardships and won fortune—those of them who survived. He was—is still—a man of iron will, and the most material man I ever met. I ought to know, for his brother was married to my daughter, and of course, I saw much of them both. My son-in-law was a masterful man, too, and more than once the brothers actually came to blows; it was a constant dread to me lest one or the other should be killed. My own husband, poor Joe Bates, was a self-willed man himself, and glad I am that he and Riddy's father never met, for if they had, there not being the tie of blood between them to prevent actual murder, I fear one or other must have gone under. Well. Riddy's father soon became the leader of the party which he had joined. He had a saying that; 'any man could rule a crisis if he had sand in him,' and he certainly did come out when occasion called. Whether it was Indians, starvation, or drought, or wolves, or bears, or snow storms, or burning prairies, he was in the front; and it was not long before they gave him a nickname which sticks to him still."

"What is that?" asked Victor, who was getting thoroughly interested.

"'Crisis!' If you were to mention that you knew Crisis Dana today anywhere in California where there is an old man present, it would be as good as a Washinginton introduction. Now and again there were men who rebelled against his ruling, but they say that he was handier than anyone with either gun or bowie, and when the row was over the rest of the party went on quite satisfied. I've heard tell that of all the parties that cross the Rockies in '43 or '49 not one but lost more men all told than Dana's, so that there was sense in his ruling anyhow. Well, he kept his masterful spirit all the time, and the richer he got, and the more powerful, the less and less would he let anyone interfere with him. But he is a good sort at heart, and once in my life, when I went to him in trouble and knelt to him, he took me up and swore to see me through it. I tell you I wasn't sorry then for his masterfulness, for, with his courage, it saved my poor girl's husband."

"Tell me about it," asked Victor. He spoke partly out of interest, and partly because he knew that there is no better way to win an old woman to your side than to listen to her, and let her talk of the past. So Mrs. Bates went on:

"Chris—that was Riddy's father—and my girl's husband had had an awful row, and I fear that Chris wasn't altogether wrong in the matter. Anyhow, they were not on speaking terms, and each had sworn before a host of their friends that they would never speak again. They said that they didn't fight it out and settle the matter there and then because they were brothers, but that henceforth they were strangers, and would treat each other as such. When things were this way, Spud—that was the name they gave my son-in-law—got into some trouble about a sluice that someone else owned. I never quite knew the rights of it, and I didn't want to know, for what I did hear didn't seem all right. The vigilantes took up the matter, and one night my girl came to me nearly dead with fright, and told me that there was a necktie party afoot; that they were after Spud, and that nothing could save him if Chris didn't take it up. I went off without my bonnet, and woke up Chris, and threw myself on my knees before him, and implored him not to let them string up his brother. He was kind to me—more than kind. He heeled himself right away, and swore that no harm should come to his brother, even if he had to waltz into the crowd himself and slice."

Victor could not buy notice that as the old lady got on with her narrative, and as her memory began to realise past moments, she fell into ways of speech habitual to her in those days. Mrs. Bates went on:

"True it was that none but Chris could have reasoned with that crowd. But Chris was a good reasoner in such times, and he generally reasoned with a derringer. I followed him, though he had told me to run home and comfort Ante, and hung on the outskirts of the crowd. Christ got up and made them a speech like this:

"'Boys, you know me! Well, I'm goin' to take a hand in this game!' Then someone called out:

"'Go home Christ. This ain't no place for you. We left ye out o' purpose!'

"'Oh, indeed! So you left me out. Well, I don't generally get left, and I'm going to reason this out with you. But, perhaps, you don't know logic, so I'll give a lesson. There's a major premiss and a minor premiss, and there's a conclusion—you see I didn't go to college for nothing! Well, the major premiss is me and the minor premiss is this—and he drew his gun and faced the crowd. "And the conclusion is that the prisoner is going to be handed over to me, and I'll decide on him right here; and then if you're dissatisfied you are to let him go and tackle me. I'll hold up my hands for you, so help me God!" With that he stepped down from the box he stood on and went over and cut the rope that bound Spud. 'Now,' says he to him, 'this charge may be true or not—I am not going into that—but the punishment is that you either go or stay here. If you go you must never show your face here again, for I undertake to those gentlemen that if you do, I'll shoot you on sight! But if you stay I'll make good the harm done to Halligan's sluice and pay the owners what they ask themselves; and whilst you stay here, I'll be responsible for you, whatever you may do. And if the vigilantes won't deal with me, then I'll put the rope on my own neck! So pards'—and he looked round him—'I think we've either got rid of a nuisance or else we've got one more good citizen amongst up; or if I'm wrong you'll be free before long from both the nuisance and the blasted fool that trusted his own flesh and blood. See!'"

"Well, with that the men all began to cheer, and Spud came up to Crhis and held out his hand, and the two walked away together; and they never had a hard word one for the other till poor Spud followed my girl to her grave twelve years ago."

"Then I say," said Victor, "that Mr. Dana was and is a splendid fellow, and no wonder he has such a daughter!"

"Ah! And there I must go on," said the old lady, sadly. "When Spud died—it was very shortly after Chris's own poor wife had gone—Eurydice was a good soul, and she asked Chris to ask me to come and take care of her baby girl—little Riddy. He made my home as happy as he could: and all that affection and thought could do he did to make us comfortable. Riddy was like a child to me, and I am sure no mother could love her better than I do." Here the old lady's eyes filled with tears—though she smiled through them as Victor muttered—"No wonder!" Then she went on:

"Riddy and I have been together all her life since then, and if she were in reality my own child, I could not be more fond of her. Her father used to come and go, for he owns great mines in all parts of the West; in fact, his friends say that he won't be contented till he has got the earth. But he never interfered with her education, or her bringing up in anyway till she was quite a big girl. Then one day, when he came home after a long absence of nearly six months, he took Riddy by the elbows, and stood her up before him and said:

"'Why, sister, the little girl is becoming a woman!' He said no more then, but I could see his brows knit, and I knew that he was thinking of something serious. When Riddy was gone to bed he took me into his study and made me sit down. He didn't sit himself, but he walked about the room all the time—and you know how trying that is to a woman's nerves—or stood with his back to the fire while he spoke.

"'That little girl is growing into a woman—she'll be up to high-water mark before we know where we are! Now sister, I want you to make a promise.' He stopped there and I felt my heart sink in my breast as I asked him:

"'What is it, Chris?'

"'I want you to promise me that you will not let Riddy marry any man without my leave!' I thought I'd try to keep that matter open, so I tried a little laugh and said to him: 'Why, Chris. How am I to prevent her marrying? Maids like to chose for themselves—at least, they used to do so in my time—and I don't suppose they propose to change the system now.' If I had any sort of idea that I was going to put Chris Dana off his intention by any light word of mine, well, I might have known better. 'Look here, sister,' said he, 'I've got my own plans in life, and I intend to carry them out in my own way. What I want you to do is promise me—aye, and take your oath on it—for though we men don't think much differ between the two, you women are afraid to break an oath, though ye'll lie all over the ranch, swear to me, solemn and true, that you'll not let Riddy marry any man if you can keep her from it!'"

"'No!' said I, 'Chris Dana; you have no right to ask me to take such an oath!' Well, he looked at me full a minute, and then I saw that dark look come up in his face that I heard tell of when he was about to shoot: and, says he, with quiet, cold words, that seemed to drop out one by one from a mouth of steel:

"'When you went down on your knees to me to take that precious Spud out of the hands of the neck-tie party you didn't stop to examine my rights. From that day to this I have never asked for a single favour; what I have had has been yours, and I didn't hear no complaint. Now I ask you to do one thing for me—mind you, a thing that any man has a right to ask about his own daughter—and yet you refuse!' Mr. Paterson, you men have your own rules of honour, and we women have ours, but there are certain matters which are common to us both. I ask you fairly, could I refuse when the duty was put to me in that way?"

"No! A thousand times no!" said Victor, stoutly, so Mrs. Bates went on.

"I took the oath, and then Chris rand the bell, and asked the help to ask Miss Ridy to be good enough to come down for a few minutes—not to mind coming in her dressing gown. So down ran Riddy in a few minutes. When she came in her father said to her:—

"'Riddy, dear, I want you to make me a promise!'

"'What is it, father?'

"'I want you to promise, little girl, that you'll not marry any man without my consent.'

"'But, father, I don't want to marry anyone, consent or no consent!'

"'All right, little girl; but promise me.' Riddy is her father's daughter, and has a mind and a will of her own, so she thought the matter over a minute or two, and then said, suddenly:

"'Why do you want me to promise father?' He admired her for speaking up to him: I could see it in his face as he said—

"'Little girl, isn't it enough that I want it?'

"'Quite, father! But a promise is a very sacred thing, and may bind all one's life. Surely if I'm asked to do that I ought to know the reason!' When Chris heard that he slapped his thigh, and burst out laughing. 'Bully for you, little girl,' said he, 'you're a true chip of the old block. Well, come here, Sissy, and I'll tell you.' So Riddy came and sat on his knee, and put her arms round his neck as she had used to do when she was a baby, and she smiled at her father as he unfolded his reasons:

"'You see, little girl, that this here is just about the hang of it. I've got my own plans and I mean to work them out in my own way. It's all for you, my dear, in the end, but while I'm doin' it I don't want not Board of Inspection coming along an' interfering with me. You're the main shaft of my lode, little girl, and you and me understand each other; but I know well that young people gets fond of each other the woman's will goes into her husbands.'"

"'But, Dad, I've not got a husband, and I don't want one, and if I had one I don't see why my will should leave me.'"

"'That's all right, Sis, but you're young yet, and mayhap some day you'll see some young man waltz along, and his face will shut out all the rest of the sunshine of the world for you. What'll become of your will then? No! You're a good girl and an obedient daughter, and I know that if you promise me you'll keep your word. Then I'll know that I'm not to have anyone comin messin about my property, and figuring up my profits, and wanting to boss the shebang generally! I tell you, little girl, that it needs all the nerve a man has got for big mining, and if I was to be thinkin, 'I'll have to give some explanation of this,' or 'Maybe this won't pan out as well as Mr. Riddy expects,' why, I'd feel as if I was handcuffed all the time—aye, and in leg-irons and a straight jacket. You tumble, little girl?'"

Riddy did tumble, for she held out her hand; and when the old man held out his she put it in and said, imitating his voice:

"'Place it ther! Shake, pard! I promise!'"

"'Bully for you!' said the old man, as he held her from him at arm's length and looked at her admiringly. 'And now, little girl, that's done so handsome that I'll tell you what I'll do. I'll try to take care that temptation don't come in your way. You'll go over to Europe and have a high old time. I'll buy you an estate, and you and Aunt Joe can shut yourselves up in it and have a picnic all to yourselves, without disturbing young men to sign and sling poetry at you and make you feel generally how hard-hearted your old dad is. But just you wait! It won't be long before my pile is made; and then I'll come on! So if you look round and then care to pick out any young man for yourself, darn but I'll buy him for you, even if he's a royal prince!'"

"'I don't want any man that can be bought,' said Riddy, hotly. 'If I ever marry a man—with your consent dad, of course—it will be because he is worth of all love and respect. Now, dad, I've been good, haven't I?'"

"'That you have, Chick, as good as gold.'"

"'And I deserve a reward?'"

"'Yes, little girl; what'll you have?' I could see that Riddy had been thinking and I soon saw why."

"'Dad,' said she, 'you've given me in one way a hard row to hoe. I'm not better than other girls or different from them, I suppose: and now that I'm tied up with a promise I may feel as you would have—handcuffs, leg-bolts, straight jacket and all—and may want to get free. Won't you slack the rope a bit so that it won't cut me everytime?'"

"'How do you mean?' says the father, smiling, but with his brows set. 'Don't make it so hard and fast! Give some little element of chance; some condition that may or may not happen.'"

"'But why should I? Hard and fast it just what I want.'"

"'Yes, father; but the rope my gall. Happiness may be at stake on my side; and your side is only to increase a store of gold!' Right there Chris rose up smiling, and said he:

"'All right, little girl, I'll give you something that may or may not happen; and when it does you may listen to a young man making love to you, and you may marry him without my consent.'"

"'What is it, dear father?' asked Riddy joyously; but my own heart was heavy, for I knew Chris too well to think that he would take any chances on a point he valued. He kissed Riddy lovingly, and moving towards the door said, before he passed out:

"'Well, little girl, I'm going to get gold and silver, so I'll give you, too, a chance on a specific basis! When the earth is silver and the sky rains gold you may marry whom you will, whether I like it or not!'"

"Well Mr. Paterson," went on the old lady, "Christ was as good as his word, and he sent Riddy and me over on a trip, and told us to pick out the estate in all England that we liked the best, and he would buy it. So we came to London, and by chance we heard of Brassy Towers, and Riddy took a fancy to it. Her father bought the place and made it over to her almost by return of post. Here have we remained all by ourselves, and we have made no friends; for we thought it would be easier for Riddy to know no one than to run any chances of—of—of being upset in keeping her promise to her father. A year after we came Riddy was feeling a little under the weather, and the doctor sent us on a trip to

Scotland to brace up. All went well with us, and we kept ourselves to ourselves, so that we did not make a single friend, or even acquaintance, until that unlucky visit to Skye."

Here, Victor cut in:

"I can't endorse that!"

"Ah! My dear, that's all very well for you; but what of us?" Victor smile. There was so much taken for granted by the old lady that he felt that his ground was in one way—and that not the least important to a lover—sure, and he could afford to laugh.

"I'm not so dangerous as I look, I assure you!" was all that he said.

But the old lady was very resolute, and would not be put off. "You see how we are placed," she said, "what with Riddy's promise not to marry without her father's consent, and my promise not to let her do so, we are so tied up that we dare not entertain a proposal from any honourable gentleman, even if Riddy's heart was inclined to him."

Victor had had on his thinking cap all the time, and now it was evident that he wore it with some result, for suddenly he spoke out with the old masterful ring in his voice;

"Was not Riddy's promise that she was not marry without consent?"

"Yes."

"Well then there is no difficulty about her becoming engaged!" In his triumphant selfishness he had no thought except for his own happiness; but the old lady shook her head sadly. "And what of dear Riddy—is that a thing to start in life on?" she said—and, after a pause, added—"even if in all honour such a fine-drawing of a promise were allowable."

Victor answered from the noble side of his nature:

"And Riddy must do what is right, what is most honourable! God forbid that I should make her deflect by a hair's breadth!"

"Well spoken!" said Mrs. Bates, "well spoken! That makes me your friend!" And she held out her hand, which he took impulsively, and held in his. "And now that you know," she went on, "how affairs stand, you must try to help us. I believe that you care for Riddy, and you will not make the dear girl's life harder to bear than need be. She is only a young girl after all, and you are a man, and must help to shield her. Surely it is the duty of love to keep harm away!"

As she spoke she looked at Victor appealingly, and the tears welled over in her eyes, and ran down her cheeks. Victor's noble nature rose to the appeal: he stood up, and taking her hand, bent over and kissed it. "You are right," he said, "It is a hard duty, but I suppose all duty that is worth anything is hard! I promise to help you. I shall go away at once, and wait for a better time. I daresay Riddy will remember me if she thinks I am worth remembering."

"That's good; that's real good! And if I know Riddy Dana—and I think I do—nothing you could ever say or do would go deeper into her heart. And now my dear boy, that you have done your duty as a man, I can perhaps make things easier for toy. As you are to wait and hope, there is not reason why you should not see Riddy. Stay with us here today, and enjoy yourself. I will send to the hotel for your grip-sack, and I don't suppose that when you go away tomorrow—without a word of love to Riddy, or anything that can upset her—you and she will be less to each other, or be able to wait with less heart."

So Victor stay on, and that day never afterwards faded from his memory. Mrs. Bates trusted his honour, and, though she spoke no word of what had taken place to her niece, the two women understood each other completely by some of that subtle language of sympathy which belongs to their sex alone.

Victor and Riddy were together all day, sometimes alone and sometimes with Mrs.Bates. Together they wandered through the shady walks which the trees overhung heavily, being still in all their leafy splendour. The summer had run on unbroken and the sap still ran till the rich tints of autumn's livery were mellowed and deepened. The air was very still, and something of an echo of the hum of summer insects came from the pastures. Under the great beeches and birches and elms the ground, hardened by the drip and shelter of a century, was covered with dark green moss which felt like velvet underfoot.

Though, truth to tell, this sensation was lost on the young people, or, rather, was lost in a less material experience, for they seemed to tread on air. In the gloom under the trees, from whence the tall branches rising in the light beyond seemed like a miniature forest, the two walked, oftener silent than not and oftener, therefore, in more complete sympathy. Somewhere, far away, in the book of Victor's consciousness was the thought that this was the last, as it was the greatest, pleasure of his life. But he resolutely kept the thought in the background and went on his way with full intent to enjoy. As for Riddy, the day seemed like the dawning of a new life. For long she looked on the meeting in Skye as a beautiful dream, and was almost content to so think of it as not clashing with her father's wish or with her promise to him. And now the dream had come true: the "ideal he" had become materalised and took Victor's shape. Aunt Joe, strong in her sense of having done her duty, did not fear to leave the young people together. She had had his bag brought from the tavern and had answered Victor's half-hearted protest, for he thought that she might be doing violence to her feelings in making him so welcome.

"Nonsense! My dear boy. Chris would never forgive me if I were not to show you hospitability. He wouldn't let you out of the house himself if he were here; even if he had to shoot you to keep you there, or if he intended to shoot you next day for being there!"

At sunset the air grew very chill, and as Victor and Riddy stood on the terrace and looked westward the scene was indescribably beautiful. As the red sun sank the trees began to stand out blackly, till the whole mystery of evening was complete. More and more chill came up the misty breath of the valley, and Victor breathed a long sigh as he went indoors, having, as he thought, taken his last look at the beautiful scene which was now forever so deeply graven on his memory. In the dim light of drawing room, where the lamps had not yet been lit, and where the leaping of the flames in the grate threw fitful shadows through the room, there seemed still to rise before him the wondrous colour of the autumn.

Dinner that night was an ethereal function, and the music afterwards was a dream of delight. Miss Dana had one of those pure, sweet voices which, though seemingly having no special excellence, yet go straight to the heart. She sang without effort; and as her songs were all simple, tender little things, like flowers of the garden of sound. It was little wonder that Victor sat entranced. In his waking moments, when the stern reality of his situation came to him like discords in the melody, he did not know whether the brightness of the present or the darkness which must follow it were the stronger. Riddy ranged from Balte to Schubert, and from Schubert to Mozart, and from Mozart to Dvořák and from Dvořák to Grieg: and at each new sweetness her lover's heart grew warmer and his fears more cold.

After a simple goodnight whose after silence was more than speech, and where the gentle lingering pressure of hands, each to each, was an ecstasy, Victor went to his room. Pulling aside the heavy curtains, he looked again at the wide landscape now bathed in the light of a golden moon-mist.

Once again as he looked his heart grew bitter, for he felt that gold and gold alone—gold with its power over a man's heart—stood between him and his hopes.

It may have been his fancy, but the whole universe seemed that night stained with the tiny of gold. The broad moon was burnished as a shield and the mist fell away from it in a golden halo and seemed to have wetted the yellow leaves, till they shone golden too. With a muttered curse he swept the heavy curtain back again and shut out the beautiful, sordid sight. For a long, long time he sat before the fire which he never heeded, for his thoughts were wandering towards Riddy, whom, in his mind's eye, he saw wrapped in gentle sleep. He did not know that she too was sitting awake and dreaming of him in a waking dream where, too, the flickering fire gave a living reality. At last the fire of each died down into a simple glow; and this too faded into dull red and finally went out. Then the lovers shuddered their sad, happy loneliness, and went to bed and lay away thinking each of the other.

In the morning Victor awoke early, and, pulling the curtain aside, looked again on the scene which he now knew so well. The brightness and freshness of the morning were upon his soul and upon his eyes, just as it was on the flower and sward, and an exclamation of happy wonder broke from his lips as he drank in the beauty of the scene.

Before him lay a great open expense of park, sloping away to the west, the sward dotted with great trees, towering, singly, or massed in clumps till they faded in the distance in a vague line. Then, beyond still, lay a great sheet of water shining like a mirror in the morning light; and farther still away the hills that make the bounds of the valley of the Colne ross dimly blue with morning mist. But all the scene did not merely wear its habitual beauty of park and sward and grove. In the night had been one of those heavy still white frosts which usher in winter at the close of late October. The whole ground, so far as the eye could reach, was one mighty sheet of silver, glistening in the light. The trees still wore their full panoply of leaves, but the autumn tints of these had been completed and intensified by the frost of the night; they were now dead—for the sap in them had yielded to the frost which had burst their stems and they only wanted to rigour of the ice itself to lessen in order to fail. The whole scene was a blaze of gold, and each tree was like a miracle of goldsmith's work. Chestnut and maple and elm and birch and beech, each with its own special glory of lear, stood like a wonder of the gnomes in fairy land.

As he looked, something of the old bitterness of last night against the gold and all it wrought crept into Victor's heart. He could not entirely banish the idea that Nature had put forth her picturesque forms surely to cause him pain, and the feelin was intensified when his eyes, hanging over the landscape, lit here and there on the silver birch and the copper beeches which seemed to symbolise the baser forms of bullion. However, such thoughts were but fleeting, and were soon lost in the greater pain of the loss which he now felt to be coming close indeed to him. Victor Paterson was now at the crossing of the ways of his life; he felt that he had a stern duty before him, and one that demanded all the better qualities of his nature. With an effort he braced himself up and proceeded to dress himself. He felt the sting of his cold bath do him good, and it was with resolution manifest in his bearing and his spring stride that he opened the French window of the dining room and stepped out upon the terrace.

The sun was rising higher each moment, but as yet there was no potency in its beams, and the hoar frost sparkled as it crackled under his feet. He cross the lawn and went under the spreading limes where the previous evening he had walked with Riddy, and where he had felt that their hearts spoke in communion through the mystic silence of the evening; and as he walked, there fell upon his soul a great gush of tenderness, till the tears rose in his eyes and trickled down his cheeks. It is a mistake to think men never cry: they do, but differently from women, and they hide it scrupulously. They even try to hide it from themselves. And then and there a noble resolution was completed in Victor's soul, that come what might he spare Riddy all the pain he could; that he would so bear himself that no matter what he might suffer she should rest free from any care that he might be able to avert from her.

So it was in a mood peaceful with the sweetness of self-sacrifice that he took his way again in front of the terrace, and sat on a rustic seat placed in the shelter of a birch tree, which was in its turn overhung by the spreading branches of a gigantic chestnut. The leaves of both trees were of most brilliant yellow, and they did not even quiver in the still aire, so that the idea came once again with renewed force that the scene around him was of the kingdom of gnomes. As he sat under the tree treading on silver frost, and with the shadow of the golden leaves upon him he could see the terrace, and watched eagerly in case the morning beauty should tempt Riddy to come forth.

There is perhaps a sympathy so occult that even those who experience it are note conscious of its magnitude; and it may have been due to such a communion of souls that Riddy, waking early, had looked from her window and, beholding the wondrous beauty of the scene, had hurried out to enjoy it to the full; or it may have been that the two young people who really loved each other were imbued with an equal restlessness, which made them wake early with an equal secret belief that there might be a meeting—by chance—and an equal hope that something might happen before Victor went away. However, be the occult causes what they might, Riddy appeared on the terrace in a dress of snowy white and with a look in her eyes, happy and still yearning, that made Victor's heart leap to see. She did not see him, sheltered as he was by the thick foliage of the tree which drooped around him, but by some divine instinct she took her way towards him across the frosty grass as though he were a magnet and she of iron. For the needle does not turn more truly to the Pole than was the directness of her steps. Seeing her coming he rose impulsively and stepped from under the tree, and that instant Riddy's eyes and his met. Neither knew if the usual salutation of the morning was uttered, for as their hands met there was a greeting which transcended speech. Without either suggesting it they went back and sat together on the rustic seat.

For a while they sat in silence and looked out on the beautiful expanse where the frost-clad sward rolled away below them into the distance of the spreading trees. Then Victor summoned up his courage to speak as conventionally as he could:

"What a beautiful scene, is it not? I do not think that I could ever forget it."

Riddy tried to answer him, but something stuck in her throat, and she was silent. The silence around them was so profound that the mooing of a cow in a distant pasture seemed close at hand, and the rolling of wheels which must have been on the high road sounded as if just behind the house. Victor came gallantly onwards again with another commonplace:

"Is there anything which I can do in Skye or the Highlands for you or your aunt?"

Riddy mastered herself this time, and answered him:

"Nothing, thanks—only sometimes to remember us." There is a limit to the patience of the most self-sacrificing young man, and the fervour of Victor's speech and he answered thrilled through every fibre of Riddy's benign and brought the hot blood mantling up in her cheeks.

"Ah! There won't be any trouble about executing that commission!" Then, seeing he perturbation of his companion, he added, with a forced laugh: "Unless, of course, your command is a limitation!"

Riddy made no answer, but the blush on her cheeks grew brighter.

Then for awhile they sat in silence, and bother were so wrought that neither could tell if the throbbing of the heart which seemed to come though the silence was that of self or companion.

All this while the sun was rising higher, and the potency of its beams was beginning to be felt; the silver of the sward was disappearing, and except in the shadow, the grass was cropping out emerald green after its dew-bath.

Crash! The lovers started, but smiled instantly as they saw that a chestnut had fallen through the leaves of its own high tree, and of the birch under which they sat. Then came another and another; the sun was doing its work in the high branches amongst the frozen stems. And then as the rays became more direct the stems of the leaves on the outside branches overheat became thawed from their icy rigidity, and, twisting and turning as they fell through the silent air, began to sprinkle the ground beneath. They did not notice these at first, for their thoughts were elsewhere; but as the sun grew stronger a perfect shower began falling on them, and making little shadows as they fluttered between them and the sun. The grass, still silver white around them in the shelter of the tree, began to be thickly strewn with the golden leaves.

Suddenly Riddy gave a cry and started up.

"Look, Victor! Oh, look! Look!" she said. "It has come true. The earth is silver, and it is raining gold!" In the sincerity of great love, all such minor qualities as bashfulness disappeared, and, without a word, as though their souls had spoken to each other, Victor opened his arms. She sank into them, and their lips met in a long kiss. Then they sat together gazing into each other's eyes, and seeing nothing there except the perfect love, and that happiness which true love brings.

Their dream was broken by a dark shadow, and, looking up, they saw a big bronzed man with an iron-grey beard gazing at them and heard him say:

"Guess, little girl, you've got the bulge on me this time?"

With a glad cry of "Father, dear father!" Riddy threw herself into his arms, which he opened to receive her. The old man stroked her hair lovingly as he went on:

"And so it's all come true, Riddy, the silver earth and the sky raining gold! Darn! But these trees ought to grow out in the West, and we had our species ready coined. Gold! Silver! Copper! It's all here! Well, little girl, Aunt Joe has told me all—perhaps more than you know—and I've glad you've chosen an honourable man. It doesn't matter anyhow, for I've made my pile and I came to tell you that you might choose for yourself."

Here, he held out a great brown hand to Victor and went on:

"Anyhow, you've chosen your pard—and my little girl's pard is my pard! Shake!"

# The Judge's House

When the time for his examination drew near Malcolm Malcolmson made up his mind to go somewhere to read by himself. He feared the attractions of the seaside, and also he feared completely rural isolation, for of old he knew its charms, and so he determined to find some unpretentious little town where there would be nothing to distract him. He refrained from asking suggestions from any of his friends, for he argued that each would recommend some place of which he had knowledge, and where he had already acquaintances. As Malcolmson wished to avoid friends he had no wish to encumber himself with the attention or friends' friends, and so he determined to look out for a place for himself. He packed a portmanteau with some clothes and all the books he required, and then took ticket for the first name on the local time-table which he did not know.

"When at the end of three hours' journey he alighted at Benchurch, he felt satisfied that he had so far obliterated his tracks as to be sure of having a peaceful opportunity of pursuing his studies. He went straight to the one inn which the sleepy little place contained, and put up for the night. Benchurch was a market town, and once in three weeks was crowded to excess, but for the remainder of the twenty-one days it was as attractive as a desert. Malcolmson looked around the day after his arrival to try to find quarters more isolated than even so quiet an inn as "The Good Traveller" afforded. There was only one place which took his fancy, and it certainly satisfied his wildest ideas regarding quiet; in fact, quiet was not the proper word to apply to it—desolation was the only term conveying any suitable idea of its isolation. It was an old rambling, heavy-built house of the Jacobean style, with heavy gables and windows, unusually small, and set higher than was customary in such houses, and was surrounded with a high brick wall massively built. Indeed, on examination, it looked more like a fortified house than an ordinary dwelling. But all these things pleased Malcolmson. "Here," he thought, "is the very spot I have been looking for, and if I can only get opportunity of using it I shall be happy." His joy was increased when he realised beyond doubt that it was not at present inhabited.

From the post-office he got the name of the agent, who was rarely surprised at the application to rent a part of the old house. Mr. Carnford, the local lawyer and agent, was a genial old gentleman, and frankly confessed his delight at anyone being willing to live in the house.

"To tell you the truth," said he, "I should be only too happy, on behalf of the owners, to let anyone have the house rent free for a term of years if only to accustom the people here to see it inhabited. It has been so long empty that some kind of absurd prejudice has grown up about it, and this can be best put down by its occupation—if only," he added with a sly glance at Malcomson, "by a scholar like yourself, who wants its quiet for a time."

Malcolmson thought it needless to ask the agent about the "absurd prejudice"; he knew he would get more information, if he should require it, on that subject from other quarters. He paid his three months' rent, got a receipt, and the name of an old woman who would probably undertake to "do" for him, and came away with the keys in his pocket. He then went to the landlady of the inn, who was a cheerful and most kindly person, and asked her advice as to such stores and provisions as he would be likely to require. She threw up her hands in amazement when he told her where he was going to settle himself.

"Not in the Judge's House!" she said, and grew pale as she spoke. He explained the locality of the house, saying that he did not know its name. When he had finished she answered:

"Aye, sure enough—sure enough the very place! It is the Judge's House sure enough." He asked her to tell him about the place, why so called, and what there was against it. She told him that it was so called locally because it had been many years before—how long she could not say, as she was herself from another part of the country, but she thought it must have been a hundred years or more—the abode of a judge who was held in great terror on account of his harsh sentences and his hostility to prisoners at Assizes. As to what there was against the house itself she could not tell. She had often asked, but no one could inform her; but there was a general feeling that there was something, and for her own part she would not take all the money in Drinkwater's Bank and stay in the house an hour by herself. Then she apologised to Malcolmson for her disturbing talk.

"It is too bad of me, sir, and you—and a young gentleman, too—if you will pardon me saying it, going to live there all alone. If you were my boy—and you'll excuse me for saying it—you wouldn't sleep there a night, not if I had to go there myself and pull the big alarm bell that's on the roof!" The good creature was so manifestly in earnest, and was so kindly in her intentions, that Malcolmson, although amused, was touched. He told her kindly how much he appreciated her interest in him, and added:

"But, my dear Mrs. Witham, indeed you need not be concerned about me! A man who is reading for the Mathematical Tripos has too much to think of to be disturbed by any of these mysterious 'somethings,' and his work is of too exact and prosaic a kind to allow of his having any corner in his mind for mysteries of any kind. Harmonical Progression, Permutations and Combinations, and Elliptic Functions have sufficient mysteries for me!" Mrs. Witham kindly undertook to see after his commissions, and he went himself to look for the old woman who had been recommended to him. When he returned to the Judge's House with her, after an interval of a couple of hours, he found Mrs. Witham herself waiting with several men and boys carrying parcels, and an upholsterer's man with a bed in a cart, for she said, though tables and chairs might be all very well, a bed that hadn't been aired for mayhap fifty years was not proper for young bones to lie on. She was evidently curious to see the inside of the house; and though manifestly so afraid of the 'somethings' that at the slightest sound she clutched on to Malcolmson, whom she never left for a moment, went over the whole place.

After his examination of the house, Malcolmson decided to take up his abode in the great dining-room, which was big enough to serve for all his requirements; and Mrs. Witham, with the aid of the charwoman, Mrs. Dempster, proceeded to arrange matters. When the hampers were brought in and unpacked, Malcolmson saw that with much kind forethought she had sent from her own kitchen sufficient provisions to last for a few days. Before going she expressed all sorts of kind wishes; and at the door turned and said:

"And perhaps, sir, as the room is big and draughty it might be well to have one of those big screens put round your bed at night—though, truth to tell, I would die myself if I were to be so shut in with all kinds of—of 'things,' that put their heads round the sides, or over the top, and look on me!" The image which she had called up was too much for her nerves, and she fled incontinently.

Mrs. Dempster sniffed in a superior manner as the landlady disappeared, and remarked that for her own part she wasn't afraid of all the bogies in the kingdom.

"I'll tell you what it is, sir," she said; "bogies is all kinds and sorts of things—except bogies! Rats and mice, and beetles; and creaky doors, and loose slates, and broken panes, and stiff drawer handles, that stay out when you pull them and then fall down in the middle of the night. Look at the wainscot of the room! It is old—hundreds of years old! Do you think there's no rats and beetles there! And do you imagine, sir, that you won't see none of them! Rats is bogies, I tell you, and bogies is rats; and don't you get to think anything else!"

"Mrs. Dempster," said Malcolmson gravely, making her a polite bow, "you know more than a Senior Wrangler! And let me say, that, as a mark of esteem for your indubitable soundness of head and heart, I shall, when I go, give you possession of this house, and let you stay here by yourself for the last two months of my tenancy, for four weeks will serve my purpose."

"Thank you kindly, sir!" she answered, "but I couldn't sleep away from home a night. I am in Greenhow's Charity, and if I slept a night away from my rooms I should lose all I have got to live on. The rules is very strict; and there's too many watching for a vacancy for me to run any risks in the matter. Only for that, sir, I'd gladly come here and attend on you altogether during your stay."

"My good woman," said Malcolmson hastily, "I have come here on purpose to obtain solitude; and believe me that I am grateful to the late Greenhow for having so organised his admirable charity—whatever it is—that I am perforce denied the opportunity of suffering from such a form of temptation! Saint Anthony himself could not be more rigid on the point!"

The old woman laughed harshly. "Ah, you young gentlemen," she said, "you don't fear for naught; and belike you'll get all the solitude you want here." She set to work with her cleaning; and by nightfall, when Malcolmson returned from his walk—he always had one of his books to study as he walked—he found the room swept and tidied, a fire burning in the old hearth, the lamp lit, and the table spread for supper with Mrs. Witham's excellent fare. "This is comfort, indeed," he said, as he rubbed his hands.

When he had finished his supper, and lifted the tray to the other end of the great oak dining-table, he got out his books again, put fresh wood on the fire, trimmed his lamp, and set himself down to a spell of real hard work. He went on without pause till about eleven o'clock, when he knocked off for a bit to fix his fire and lamp, and to make himself a cup of tea. He had always been a tea-drinker, and during his college life had sat late at work and had taken tea late. The rest was a great luxury to him, and he enjoyed it with a sense of delicious, voluptuous ease. The renewed fire leaped and sparkled, and threw quaint shadows through the great old room; and as he sipped his hot tea he revelled in the sense of isolation from his kind. Then it was that he began to notice for the first time what a noise the rats were making.

"Surely," he thought, "they cannot have been at it all the time I was reading. Had they been. I must have noticed it!" Presently, when the noise increased, he satisfied himself that it was really new. It was evident that at first the rats had been frightened at the presence of a stranger, and the light of fire and lamp; but that as the time went on they had grown bolder and were now disporting themselves as was their wont.

How busy they were! and hark to the strange noises! Up and down behind the old wainscot, over the ceiling and under the floor they raced, and gnawed, and scratched! Malcolmson smiled to himself as he recalled to mind the saying of Mrs. Dempster, "Bogies is rats, and rats is bogies!" The tea began to have its effect of intellectual and nervous stimulus, he saw with joy another long spell of work to be done before the night was past, and in the sense of security which it gave him, he allowed himself the luxury of a good look round the room. He took his lamp in one hand, and went all around, wondering that so quaint and beautiful an old house had been so long neglected. The carving of the oak on the panels of the wainscot was fine, and on and round the doors and windows it was beautiful and of rare merit. There were some old pictures on the walls, but they were coated so thick with dust and dirt that he could not distinguish any detail of them, though he held his lamp as high as he could over his head. Here and there as he went round he saw some crack or hole blocked for a moment by the face of a rat with its bright eyes glittering in the light, but in an instant it was gone, and a squeak and a scamper followed.

The thing that most struck him, however, was the rope of the great alarm bell on the roof, which hung down in a corner of the room on the right-hand side of the fireplace. He pulled up close to the hearth a great high-backed carved oak chair, and sat down to his last cup of tea. When this was done he made up the fire, and went back to his work, sitting at the corner of the table, having the fire to his left. For a while the rats disturbed him somewhat with their perpetual scampering, but he got accustomed to the noise as one does to the ticking of a clock or to the roar of moving water; and he became so immersed in his work that everything in the world, except the problem which he was trying to solve, passed away from him.

He suddenly looked up, his problem was still unsolved, and there was in the air that sense of the hour before the dawn, which is so dread to doubtful life. The noise of the rats had ceased. Indeed it seemed to him that it must have ceased but lately and that it was the sudden cessation which had disturbed him. The fire had fallen low, but still it threw out a deep red glow. As he looked he started in spite of his sang froid.

There on the great high-backed carved oak chair by the right side of the fireplace sat an enormous rat, steadily glaring at him with baleful eyes. He made a motion to it as though to hunt it away, but it did not stir. Then he made the motion of throwing something. Still it did not stir, but showed its great white teeth angrily, and its cruel eyes shone in the lamplight with an added vindictiveness.

Malcolmson felt amazed, and seizing the poker from the hearth ran at it to kill it. Before, however, he could strike it, the rat, with a squeak that sounded like the concentration of hate, jumped upon the floor, and, running up the rope of the alarm bell, disappeared in the darkness beyond the range of the green-shaded lamp. Instantly, strange to say, the noisy scampering of the rats in the wainscot began again.

By this time Malcolmson's mind was quite off the problem; and as a shrill cock-crow outside told him of the approach of morning, he went to bed and to sleep.

He slept so sound that he was not even waked by Mrs. Dempster coming in to make up his room. It was only when she had tidied up the place and got his breakfast ready and tapped on the screen which closed in his bed that he woke. He was a little tired still after his night's hard work, but a strong cup of tea soon freshened him up, and, taking his book, he went out for his morning walk, bringing with him a few sandwiches lest he should not care to return till dinner time. He found a quiet walk between high elms some way outside the town, and here he spent the greater part of the day studying his Laplace. On his return he looked in to see Mrs. Witham and to thank her for her kindness. When she saw him coming through the diamond-paned bay-window of her sanctum she came out to meet him and asked him in. She looked at him searchingly and shook her head as she said:

"You must not overdo it, sir. You are paler this morning than you should be. Too late hours and too hard work on the brain isn't good for any man! But tell me, sir, how did you pass the night? Well, I hope? But, my heart! sir, I was glad when Mrs. Dempster told me this morning that you were all right and sleeping sound when she went in."

"Oh, I was all right," he answered, smiling, "the 'somethings' didn't worry me, as yet. Only the rats; and they had a circus, I tell you, all over the place. There was one wicked looking old devil that sat up on my own chair by the fire, and wouldn't go till I took the poker to him, and then he ran up the rope of the alarm bell and got to somewhere up the wall or the ceiling—I couldn't see where, it was so dark."

"Mercy on us," said Mrs. Witham, "an old devil, and sitting on a chair by the fireside! Take care, sir! take care! There's many a true word spoken in jest."

"How do you mean? 'Pon my word I don't understand."

"An old devil! The old devil, perhaps. There! sir, you needn't laugh," for Malcolmson had broken into a hearty peal. "You young folks thinks it easy to laugh at things that makes older ones shudder. Never mind, sir! never mind! Please God, you'll laugh all the time. It's what I wish you myself!" and the good lady beamed all over in sympathy with his enjoyment, her fears gone for a moment.

"Oh, forgive me!" said Malcolmson presently. "Don't think me rude; but the idea was too much for me—that the old devil himself was on the chair last night!" And at the thought he laughed again. Then he went home to dinner.

This evening the scampering of the rats began earlier; indeed it had been going on before his arrival, and only ceased whilst his presence by its freshness disturbed them. After dinner he sat by the fire for a while and had a smoke; and then, having cleared his table, began to work as before. Tonight the rats disturbed him more than they had done on the previous night. How they scampered up and down and under and over! How they squeaked, and scratched, and gnawed! How they, getting bolder by degrees, came to the mouths of their holes and to the chinks and cracks and crannies in the wainscoting till their eyes shone like tiny lamps as the firelight rose and fell. But to him, now doubtless accustomed to them, their eyes were not wicked; only their playfulness touched him. Sometimes the boldest of them made sallies out on the floor or along the mouldings of the wainscot. Now and again as they disturbed him Malcolmson made a sound to frighten them, smiting the table with his hand or giving a fierce "Hsh, hsh," so that they fled straightway to their holes.

And so the early part of the night wore on; and despite the noise Malcolmson got more and more immersed in his work.

All at once he stopped, as on the previous night, being overcome by a sudden sense of silence. There was not the faintest sound of gnaw, or scratch, or squeak. The silence was as of the grave. He remembered the odd occurrence of the previous night, and instinctively he looked at the chair standing close by the fireside. And then a very odd sensation thrilled through him.

There, on the great old high-backed carved oak chair beside the fireplace sat the same enormous rat, steadily glaring at him with baleful eyes.

Instinctively he took the nearest thing to his hand, a book of logarithms, and flung it at it. The book was badly aimed and the rat did not stir, so again the poker performance of the previous night was repeated; and again the rat, being closely pursued, fled up the rope of the alarm bell. Strangely too, the departure of this rat was instantly followed by the renewal of the noise made by the general rat community. On this occasion, as on the previous one, Malcolmson could not see at what part of the room the rat disappeared, for the green shade of his lamp left the upper part of the room in darkness, and the fire had burned low.

On looking at his watch he found it was close on midnight; and, not sorry for the divertissement, he made up his fire and made himself his nightly pot of tea. He had got through a good spell of work, and thought himself entitled to a cigarette; and so he sat on the great carved oak chair before the fire and enjoyed it. Whilst smoking he began to think that he would like to know where the rat disappeared to, for he had certain ideas for the morrow not entirely disconnected with a rat-trap. Accordingly he lit another lamp and placed it so that it would shine well into the right-hand corner of the wall by the fireplace. Then he got all the books he had with him, and placed them handy to throw at the vermin. Finally he lifted the rope of the alarm bell and placed the end of it on the table, fixing the extreme end under the lamp. As he handled it he could not help noticing how pliable it was, especially for so strong a rope, and one not in use. "You could hang a man with it," he thought to himself. When his preparations were made he looked around, and said complacently:

"There now, my friend, I think we shall learn something of you this time!" He began his work again, and though as before somewhat disturbed at first by the noise of the rats, soon lost himself in his propositions and problems.

Again he was called to his immediate surroundings suddenly. This time it might not have been the sudden silence only which took his attention; there was a slight movement of the rope, and the lamp moved. Without stirring, he looked to see if his pile of books was within range, and then cast his eye along the rope. As he looked he saw the great rat drop from the rope on the oak armchair and sit there glaring at him. He raised a book in his right hand, and taking careful aim, flung it at the rat. The latter, with a quick movement, sprang aside and dodged the missile. He then took another book, and a third, and flung them one after another at the rat, but each time unsuccessfully. At last, as he stood with a book poised in his hand to throw, the rat squeaked and seemed afraid. This made Malcolmson more than ever eager to strike, and the book flew and struck the rat a resounding blow. It gave a terrified squeak, and turning on its pursuer a look of terrible malevolence, ran up the chair-back and made a great jump to the rope of the alarm bell and ran up it like lightning. The lamp rocked under the sudden strain, but it was a heavy one and did not topple over. Malcolmson kept his eyes on the rat, and saw it by the light of the second lamp leap to a moulding of the wainscot and disappear through a hole in one of the great pictures which hung on the wall, obscured and invisible through its coating of dirt and dust.

"I shall look up my friend's habitation in the morning," said the student, as he went over to collect his books. "The third picture from the fireplace; I shall not forget." He picked up the books one by one, commenting on them as he lifted them. "Conic Sections he does not mind, nor Cycloidal Oscillations, nor the Principia, nor Quaternions, nor Thermodynamics. Now for the book that fetched him!" Malcolmson took it up and looked at it. As he did so he started, and a sudden pallor overspread his face. He looked round uneasily and shivered slightly, as he murmured to himself:

"The Bible my mother gave me! What an odd coincidence." He sat down to work again, and the rats in the wainscot renewed their gambols. They did not disturb him, however; somehow their presence gave him a sense of companionship. But he could not attend to his work, and after striving to master the subject on which he was engaged gave it up in despair, and went to bed as the first streak of dawn stole in through the eastern window.

He slept heavily but uneasily, and dreamed much; and when Mrs. Dempster woke him late in the morning he seemed ill at ease, and for a few minutes did not seem to realise exactly where he was. His first request rather surprised the servant.

"Mrs. Dempster, when I am out today I wish you would get the steps and dust or wash those pictures—specially that one the third from the fireplace—I want to see what they are." Late in the afternoon Malcolmson worked at his books in the shaded walk, and the cheerfulness of the previous day came back to him as the day wore on, and he found that his reading was progressing well. He had worked out to a satisfactory conclusion all the problems which had as yet baffled him, and it was in a state of jubilation that he paid a visit to Mrs. Witham at "The Good Traveller." He found a stranger in the cosy sitting-room with the landlady, who was introduced to him as Dr. Thornhill. She was not quite at ease, and this, combined with the Doctor's plunging at once into a series of questions, made Malcolmson come to the conclusion that his presence was not an accident, so without preliminary he said:

"Dr. Thornhill, I shall with pleasure answer you any question you may choose to ask me if you will answer me one question first."

The Doctor seemed surprised, but he smiled and answered at once. "Done! What is it?" "Did Mrs. Witham ask you to come here and see me and advise me?"

Dr. Thornhill for a moment was taken aback, and Mrs. Witham got fiery red and turned away; but the doctor was a frank and ready man, and he answered at once and openly:

"She did: but she didn't intend you to know it. I suppose it was my clumsy haste that made you suspect. She told me that she did not like the idea of your being in that house all by yourself, and that she thought you took too much strong tea. In fact, she wants me to advise you if possible to give up the tea and the very late hours. I was a keen student in my time, so I suppose I may take the liberty of a college man, and without offence, advise you not quite as a stranger."

Malcolmson with a bright smile held out his hand. "Shake! as they say in America," he said. "I must thank you for your kindness and Mrs. Witham too, and your kindness deserves a return on my part. I promise to take no more strong tea—no tea at all till you let me—and I shall go to bed tonight at one o'clock at latest. Will that do?"

"Capital," said the Doctor. "Now tell us all that you noticed in the old house," and so Malcolmson then and there told in minute detail all that had happened in the last two nights. He was interrupted every now and then by some exclamation from Mrs. Witham, till finally when he told of the episode of the Bible the landlady's pent-up emotions found vent in a shriek; and it was not till a stiff glass of brandy and water had been administered that she grew composed again. Dr. Thornhill listened with a face of growing gravity, and when the narrative was complete and Mrs. Witham had been restored he asked:

"The rat always went up the rope of the alarm bell?"

"Always."

"I suppose you know," said the Doctor after a pause, "what the rope is?"

"No!"

"It is," said the Doctor slowly, "the very rope which the hangman used for all the victims of the Judge's judicial rancour!" Here he was interrupted by another scream from Mrs. Witham, and steps had to be taken for her recovery. Malcolmson having looked at his watch, and found that it was close to his dinner hour, had gone home before her complete recovery.

When Mrs. Witham was herself again she almost assailed the Doctor with angry questions as to what he meant by putting such horrible ideas into the poor young man's mind. "He has quite enough there already to upset him," she added. Dr. Thornhill replied:

"My dear madam, I had a distinct purpose in it! I wanted to draw his attention to the bell rope, and to fix it there. It may be that he is in a highly overwrought state, and has been studying too much, although I am bound to say that he seems as sound and healthy a young man, mentally and bodily, as ever I saw—but then the rats—and that suggestion of the devil." The doctor shook his head and went on. "I would have offered to go and stay the first night with him but that I felt sure it would have been a cause of offence. He may get in the night some strange fright or hallucination; and if he does I want him to pull that rope. All alone as he is it will give us warning, and we may reach him in time to be of service. I shall be sitting up pretty late tonight and shall keep my ears open. Do not be alarmed if Benchurch gets a surprise before morning."

"Oh, Doctor, what do you mean? What do you mean?"

"I mean this; that possibly—nay, more probably—we shall hear the great alarm bell from the Judge's House tonight," and the Doctor made about as effective an exit as could be thought of.

When Malcolmson arrived home he found that it was a little after his usual time, and Mrs. Dempster had gone away—the rules of Greenhow's Charity were not to be neglected. He was glad to see that the place was bright and tidy with a cheerful fire and a well-trimmed lamp. The evening was colder than might have been expected in April, and a heavy wind was blowing with such rapidly-increasing strength that there was every promise of a storm during the night. For a few minutes after his entrance the noise of the rats ceased; but so soon as they became accustomed to his presence they began again. He was glad to hear them, for he felt once more the feeling of companionship in their noise, and his mind ran back to the strange fact that they only ceased to manifest themselves when that other—the great rat with the baleful eyes—came upon the scene. The reading-lamp only was lit and its green shade kept the ceiling and the upper part of the room in darkness, so that the cheerful light from the hearth spreading over the floor and shining on the white cloth laid over the end of the table was warm and cheery. Malcolmson sat down to his dinner with a good appetite and a buoyant spirit. After his dinner and a cigarette he sat steadily down to work, determined not to let anything disturb him, for he remembered his promise to the doctor, and made up his mind to make the best of the time at his disposal.

For an hour or so he worked all right, and then his thoughts began to wander from his books. The actual circumstances around him, the calls on his physical attention, and his nervous susceptibility were not to be denied. By this time the wind had become a gale, and the gale a storm. The old house, solid though it was, seemed to shake to its foundations, and the storm roared and raged through its many chimneys and its queer old gables, producing strange, unearthly sounds in the empty rooms and corridors. Even the great alarm bell on the roof must have felt the force of the wind, for the rope rose and fell slightly, as though the bell were moved a little from time to time, and the limber rope fell on the oak floor with a hard and hollow sound.

As Malcolmson listened to it he bethought himself of the doctor's words, "It is the rope which the hangman used for the victims of the Judge's judicial rancour," and he went over to the corner of the fireplace and took it in his hand to look at it. There seemed a sort of deadly interest in it, and as he stood there he lost himself for a moment in speculation as to who these victims were, and the grim wish of the Judge to have such a ghastly relic ever under his eyes. As he stood there the swaying of the bell on the roof still lifted the rope now and again; but presently there came a new sensation—a sort of tremor in the rope, as though something was moving along it.

Looking up instinctively Malcolmson saw the great rat coming slowly down towards him, glaring at him steadily. He dropped the rope and started back with a muttered curse, and the rat turning ran up the rope again and disappeared, and at the same instant Malcolmson became conscious that the noise of the rats, which had ceased for a while, began again.

All this set him thinking, and it occurred to him that he had not investigated the lair of the rat or looked at the pictures, as he had intended. He lit the other lamp without the shade, and, holding it up, went and stood opposite the third picture from the fireplace on the right-hand side where he had seen the rat disappear on the previous night.

At the first glance he started back so suddenly that he almost dropped the lamp, and a deadly pallor overspread his face. His knees shook, and heavy drops of sweat came on his forehead, and he trembled like an aspen. But he was young and plucky, and pulled himself together, and after the pause of a few seconds stepped forward again, raised the lamp, and examined the picture which had been dusted and washed, and now stood out clearly.

It was of a judge dressed in his robes of scarlet and ermine. His face was strong and merciless, evil, crafty, and vindictive, with a sensual mouth, hooked nose of ruddy colour, and shaped like the beak of a bird of prey. The rest of the face was of a cadaverous colour. The eyes were of peculiar brilliance and with a terribly malignant expression. As he looked at them, Malcolmson grew cold, for he saw there the very counterpart of the eyes of the great rat. The lamp almost fell from his hand, he saw the rat with its baleful eyes peering out through the hole in the corner of the picture, and noted the sudden cessation of the noise of the other rats. However, he pulled himself together, and went on with his examination of the picture. The Judge was seated in a great high-backed carved oak chair, on the right-hand side of a great stone fireplace where, in the corner, a rope hung down from the ceiling, its end lying coiled on the floor. With a feeling of something like horror, Malcolmson recognised the scene of the room as it stood, and gazed around him in an awe-struck manner as though he expected to find some strange presence behind him. Then he looked over to the corner of the fireplace—and with a loud cry he let the lamp fall from his hand.

There, in the Judge's arm-chair, with the rope hanging behind, sat the rat with the Judge's baleful eyes, now intensified and with a fiendish leer. Save for the howling of the storm without there was silence.

The fallen lamp recalled Malcolmson to himself. Fortunately it was of metal, and so the oil was not spilt. However, the practical need of attending to it settled at once his nervous apprehensions. When he had turned it out, he wiped his brow and thought for a moment.

"This will not do," he said to himself. "If I go on like this I shall become a crazy fool. This must stop! I promised the Doctor I would not take tea. Faith, he was pretty right! My nerves must have been getting into a queer state. Funny I did not notice it. I never felt better in my life. However, it is all right now, and I shall not be such a fool again."

Then he mixed himself a good stiff glass of brandy and water and resolutely sat down to his work.

It was nearly an hour when he looked up from his book, disturbed by the sudden stillness. Without, the wind howled and roared louder than ever, and the rain drove in sheets against the windows, beating like hail on the glass; but within there was no sound whatever save the echo of the wind as it roared in the great chimney, and now and then a hiss as a few raindrops found their way down the chimney in a lull of the storm. The fire had fallen low and had ceased to flame, though it threw out a red glow. Malcolmson listened attentively, and presently heard a thin, squeaking noise, very faint. It came from the corner of the room where the rope hung down, and he thought it was the creaking of the rope on the floor as the swaying of the bell raised and lowered it. Looking up, however, he saw in the dim light the great rat clinging to the rope and gnawing it. The rope was already nearly gnawed through—he could see the lighter colour where the strands were laid bare. As he looked the job was completed, and the severed end of the rope fell clattering on the oaken floor, whilst for an instant the great rat remained like a knob or tassel at the end of the rope, which now began to sway to and fro. Malcolmson felt for a moment another pang of terror as he thought that now the possibility of calling the outer world to his assistance was cut off, but an intense anger took its place, and seizing the book he was reading he hurled it at the rat. The blow was well aimed, but before the missile could reach it the rat dropped off and struck the floor with a soft thud. Malcolmson instantly rushed over towards it, but it darted away and disappeared in the darkness of the shadows of the room. Malcolmson felt that his work was over for the night, and determined then and there to vary the monotony of the proceedings by a hunt for the rat, and took off the green shade of the lamp so as to insure a wider spreading light. As he did so the gloom of the upper part of the room was relieved, and in the new flood of light, great by comparison with the previous darkness, the pictures on the wall stood out boldly. From where he stood, Malcolmson saw right opposite to him the third picture on the wall from the right of the fireplace. He rubbed his eyes in surprise, and then a great fear began to come upon him.

In the centre of the picture was a great irregular patch of brown canvas, as fresh as when it was stretched on the frame. The background was as before, with chair and chimney-corner and rope, but the figure of the Judge had disappeared.

Malcolmson, almost in a chill of horror, turned slowly round, and then he began to shake and tremble like a man in a palsy. His strength seemed to have left him, and he was incapable of action or movement, hardly even of thought. He could only see and hear.

There, on the great high-backed carved oak chair sat the Judge in his robes of scarlet and ermine, with his baleful eyes glaring vindictively, and a smile of triumph on the resolute, cruel mouth, as he lifted with his hands a black cap. Malcolmson felt as if the blood was running from his heart, as one does in moments of prolonged suspense. There was a singing in his ears. Without, he could hear the roar and howl of the tempest, and through it, swept on the storm, came the striking of midnight by the great chimes in the market place. He stood for a space of time that seemed to him endless, still as a statue and with wide-open, horror-struck eyes, breathless. As the clock struck, so the smile of triumph on the Judge's face intensified, and at the last stroke of midnight he placed the black cap on his head.

Slowly and deliberately the Judge rose from his chair and picked up the piece of the rope of the alarm bell which lay on the floor, drew it through his hands as if he enjoyed its touch, and then deliberately began to knot one end of it, fashioning it into a noose. This he tightened and tested with his foot, pulling hard at it till he was satisfied and then making a running noose of it, which he held in his hand. Then he began to move along the table on the opposite side to Malcolmson, keeping his eyes on him until he had passed him, when with a quick movement he stood in front of the door. Malcolmson then began to feel that he was trapped, and tried to think of what he should do. There was some fascination in the Judge's eyes, which he never took off him, and he had, perforce, to look. He saw the Judge approach—still keeping between him and the door—and raise the noose and throw it towards him as if to entangle him. With a great effort he made a quick movement to one side, and saw the rope fall beside him, and heard it strike the oaken floor. Again the Judge raised the noose and tried to ensnare him, ever keeping his baleful eyes fixed on him, and each time by a mighty effort the student just managed to evade it. So this went on for many times, the Judge seeming never discouraged nor discomposed at failure, but playing as a cat does with a mouse. At last in despair, which had reached its climax, Malcolmson cast a quick glance round him. The lamp seemed to have blazed up, and there was a fairly good light in the room. At the many rat-holes and in the chinks and crannies of the wainscot he saw the rats' eyes; and this aspect, that was purely physical, gave him a gleam of comfort. He looked around and saw that the rope of the great alarm bell was laden with rats. Every inch of it was covered with them, and more and more were pouring through the small circular hole in the ceiling whence it emerged, so that with their weight the bell was beginning to sway.

Hark! it had swayed till the clapper had touched the bell. The sound was but a tiny one, but the bell was only beginning to sway, and it would increase.

At the sound the Judge, who had been keeping his eyes fixed on Malcolmson, looked up, and a scowl of diabolical anger overspread his face. His eyes fairly glowed like hot coals, and he stamped his foot with a sound that seemed to make the house shake. A dreadful peal of thunder broke overhead as he raised the rope again, whilst the rats kept running up and down the rope as though working against time. This time, instead of throwing it, he drew close to his victim, and held open the noose as he approached. As he came closer there seemed something paralysing in his very presence, and Malcolmson stood rigid as a corpse. He felt the Judge's icy fingers touch his throat as he adjusted the rope. The noose tightened—tightened. Then the Judge, taking the rigid form of the student in his arms, carried him over and placed him standing in the oak chair, and stepping up beside him, put his hand up and caught the end of the swaying rope of the alarm bell. As he raised his hand the rats fled squeaking, and disappeared through the hole in the ceiling. Taking the end of the noose which was round Malcolmson's neck he tied it to the hanging bell-rope, and then descending pulled away the chair.

WHEN THE ALARM BELL OF the Judge's House began to sound a crowd soon assembled. Lights and torches of various kinds appeared, and soon a silent crowd was hurrying to the spot. They knocked loudly at the door, but there was no reply. Then they burst in the door, and poured into the great dining-room, the doctor at the head.

There at the end of the rope of the great alarm bell hung the body of the student, and on the face of the Judge in the picture was a malignant smile.

End

# OUR NEW HOUSE

W e spoke of it as our New House simply because we thought of it as such and not from any claim to the title, for it was just about as old and as ricketty as a house supposed to be habitable could well be. It was only new to us. Indeed with the exception of the house there was nothing new about us. Neither my wife nor myself was, in any sense of the word, old, and we were still, comparatively speaking, new to each other.

It had been my habit, for the few years I had been in Somerset House, to take my holidays at Littlehampton, partly because I liked the place, and partly—and chiefly, because it was cheap. I used to have lodgings in the house of a widow, Mrs. Compton, in a quiet street off the sea frontage. I had this year, on my summer holiday, met there my fate in the person of Mrs. Compton's daughter Mary, just home from school. I returned to London engaged. There was no reason why we should wait, for I had few friends and no near relatives living, and Mary had the consent of her mother. I was told that her father, who was a merchant captain, had gone to sea shortly after her birth, but had never been heard of since, and had consequently been long ago reckoned as "with the majority." I never met any of my new relatives; indeed, there was not the family opportunity afforded by marriage under conventional social conditions. We were married in the early morning at the church at Littlehampton, and, without any formal wedding breakfast, came straight away in the train. As I had to attend to my duties at Somerset House, the preliminaries were all arranged by Mrs. Compton at Littlehampton, and Mary gave the required notice of residency. We were all in a hurry to be off, as we feared missing the train; indeed, whilst Mary was signing the registry I was settling the fees and tipping the verger.

When we began to look about for a house, we settled on one which was vacant in a small street near Sloane Square. There was absolutely nothing to recommend the place except the smallness of the rent—but this was everything to us. The landlord, Mr. Gradder, was the very hardest man I ever came across. He did not even go through the form of civility in his dealing.

"There is the house," he said, "and you can either take it or leave it. I have painted the outside, and you must paint the inside. Or, if you like

BRAM STOKER

it as it is, you can have it so; only you must paint and paper it before you give it up to me again—be it in one year or more."

I was pretty much of a handy man, and felt equal to doing the work myself; so, having looked over the place carefully, we determined to take it. It was, however, in such a terribly neglected condition that I could not help asking my ironclad lessor as to who had been the former tenant, and what kind of person he had been to have been content with such a dwelling.

His answer was vague. "Who he was I don't know. I never knew more than his name. He was a regular oddity. Had this house and another of mine near here, and used to live in them both, and all by himself. Think he was afraid of being murdered or robbed. Never knew which he was in. Dead lately. Had to bury him—worse luck. Expenses swallowed up value of all he'd got."

We signed an agreement to take out a lease, and when, in a few days, I had put in order two rooms and a kitchen, my wife and I moved in. I worked hard every morning before I went to my office, and every evening after I got home, so I got the place in a couple of weeks in a state of comparative order. We had, in fact, arrived so far on our way to perfection that we had seriously begun to consider dispensing with the services of our charwoman and getting a regular servant.

One evening my landlord called on me. It was about nine o'clock, and, as our temporary servant had gone home, I opened the door myself. I was somewhat astonished at recognising my visitor, and not a little alarmed, for he was so brutally simple in dealing with me that I rather dreaded any kind of interview. To my astonishment he began to speak in what he evidently meant for a hearty manner.

"Well, how are you getting on with your touching up?"

"Pretty well," I answered, "but 'touching up' is rather a queer name for it. Why, the place was like an old ash heap. The very walls seemed pulled about."

"Indeed!" he said quickly.

I went on, "It is getting into something like order, however. There is only one more room to do, and then we shall be all right."

"Do you know," he said, "that I have been thinking it is hardly fair that you should have to do all this yourself."

I must say that I was astonished as well as pleased, and found myself forming a resolution not to condemn ever again anyone for hardness until I had come to know something about his real nature. I felt somewhat guilty as I answered, "You are very kind, Mr. Gradder. I shall let you know what it all costs me, and then you can repay me a part as you think fair."

"Oh, I don't mean that at all." This was said very quickly.

"Then what do you mean," I asked.

"That I should do some of it in my own way, at my own cost."

I did not feel at all inclined to have either Mr. Gradder or strange workmen in the house. Moreover, my pride rebelled at the thought that I should be seen by real workmen doing labourers' work—I suppose there is something of the spirit of snobbery in all of us. So I told him I could not think of such a thing; that all was going on very well; and more to the same effect. He seemed more irritated than the occasion warranted. Indeed, it struck me as odd that a man should be annoyed at his generous impulse being thwarted. He tried, with a struggle for calmness, to persuade me, but I did not like the controversy, and stood to my refusal of assistance. He went away in a positive fury of suppressed rage.

The next evening he called in to see me. Mary had, after he had gone, asked me not to allow him to assist, as she did not like him; so when he came in I refused again with what urbanity I could. Mary kept nudging me to be firm, and he could not help noticing it. He said: "Of course, if your wife objects"—and stopped. He spoke the words very rudely, and Mary spoke out:

"She does object, Mr. Gradder. We are all right, thank you, and do not want help from anyone."

For reply Mr. Gradder put on his hat, knocked it down on his head firmly and viciously, and walked out, banging the door behind him.

"There is a nice specimen of a philanthropist," said Mary, and we both laughed.

The next day, while I was in my office, Mr. Gradder called to see me. He was in a very amiable mood, and commenced by apologising for what he called "his unruly exit." "I am afraid you must have thought me rude," he said.

As the nearest approach to mendacity I could allow myself, was the suppressio veri, I was silent.

"You see," he went on, "your wife dislikes me, and that annoys me; so I just called to see you alone, and try if we could arrange this matter— we men alone."

"What matter?" I asked.

"You know—about the doing up those rooms."

I began to get annoyed myself, for there was evidently some underlying motive of advantage to himself in his persistence. Any shadowy belief I had ever entertained as to a benevolent idea had long ago vanished and left not a wrack behind. I told him promptly and briefly that I would not do as he desired, and that I did not care to enter any further upon the matter. He again made an "unruly exit." This time he nearly swept away in his violence a young man who was entering through the swing door, to get some papers stamped. The youth remonstrated with that satirical force which is characteristic of the lawyer's clerk. Mr. Gradder was too enraged to stop to listen, and the young man entered the room grumbling and looking back at him.

"Old brute!" he said. "I know him. Next time I see him I'll advise him to buy some manners with his new fortune."

"His new fortune?" I asked, naturally interested about him. "How do you mean, Wigley?"

"Lucky old brute! I wish I had a share of it. I heard all about it at Doctors Commons yesterday."

"Why, is it anything strange?"

"Strange! Why, it's no name for it. What do you think of an old flint like that having a miser for a tenant who goes and dies and leaves him all he's got—£40,000 or £50,000—in a will, providing a child of his own doesn't turn up to claim it."

"He died recently, then?"

"About three or four weeks ago. Old Gradder only found the will a few days since. He had been finding pots of gold and bundles of notes all over the house, and it was like drawing a tooth from him to make an inventory, as he had to do under a clause of the will. The old thief would have pocketed all the coin without a word, only for the will, and he was afraid he'd risk everything if he did not do it legally."

"You know all about it," I remarked, wishing to hear more.

"I should think I did. I asked Cripps, of Bogg and Snagleys, about it this morning. They're working for him, and Cripps says that if they had not threatened him with the Public Prosecutor, he would not have given even a list of the money he found."

I began now to understand the motive of Mr. Gradder's anxiety to aid in working at my house. I said to Wigley:

"This is very interesting. Do you know that he is my landlord?"

"Your landlord! Well, I wish you joy of him. I must be off now. I have to go down to Doctors Commons before one o'clock. Would you mind getting these stamped for me, and keeping them till I come back?"

"With pleasure," I said, "and look here! Would you mind looking out that will of Gradder's, and make a mem. of it for me, if it isn't too long? I'll go a shilling on it." And I handed him the coin.

Later in the day he came back and handed me a paper.

"It isn't long," he said. "We might put up the shutters if men made wills like that. That is an exact copy. It is duly witnessed, and all regular."

I took the paper and put it in my pocket, for I was very busy at the time.

After supper that evening I got a note from Gradder, saying that he had got an offer from another person who had been in treaty with him before I had taken the, house, wanting to have it, and offering to pay a premium. "He is an old friend," wrote Gradder, "and I would like to oblige him; so if you choose I will take back the lease and hand you over what he offers to pay." This was £25, altered from £20.

I then told Mary of his having called on me at the office, and of the subsequent revelation of the will. She was much impressed.

"Oh, Bob," she said, "it is a real romance."

With a woman's quickness of perception, she guessed at once our landlord's reason for wishing to help us.

"Why, he thinks the old miser has hidden money here, and wants to look for it. Bob," this excitedly, "this house may be full of money; the walls round us may hold a fortune. Let us begin to look at once!"

I was as much excited as she was, but I felt that someone must keep cool, so I said:

"Mary, dear, there may be nothing; but even if there is, it does not belong to us."

"Why not?" she asked.

"Because it is all arranged in the will," I answered; "and, by the bye, I have a mem. of it here," and I took from my pocket the paper which Wigley had given me.

With intense interest we read it together, Mary holding me tightly by the arm. It certainly was short. It ran as follows:

7, Little Butler Street, S.W., London
I hereby leave to my child or children, if I have any living,
all I own, and in default of such everything is to go to John

Gradder, my landlord, who is to make an inventory of all he can find in the two houses occupied by me, this house and 2, Lampeter Street, S.W. London, and to lodge all money and securities in Coutts's Bank. If my children or any of them do not claim in writing by an application before a Justice of the Peace within one calendar month from my decease, they are to forfeit all rights. Ignorance of my death or their relationship to be no reason for noncompliance. Lest there be any doubt of my intentions, I hereby declare that I wish in such default of my natural heirs John Gradder aforesaid to have my property, because he is the hardesthearted man I ever knew, and will not fool it away in charities or otherwise, but keep it together. If any fooling is to be done, it will be by my own.

(Signed) GILES ARMER, Master Mariner,
Formerly of Whitby

When I came near the end, Mary, who had been looking down the paper in advance of my reading, cried out; "Giles Armer! Why, that was my father!"

"Good God!" I cried out, as I jumped to my feet.

"Yes," she said, excitedly; "didn't you see me sign Mary Armer at the registry? We never spoke of the name because he had a quarrel with mother and deserted her, and after seven years she married my step-father, and I was always called by his name."

"And was he from Whitby?" I asked. I was nearly wild with excitement.

"Yes," said Mary. "Mother was married there, and I was born there."

I was reading over the will again. My hands were trembling so that I could hardly read. An awful thought struck me. What day did he die? Perhaps it was too late—it was now the thirtieth of October. However, we were determined to be on the safe side, and then and there Mary and I put on our hats and wraps and went to the nearest police-station.

There we learned the address of a magistrate, after we had explained to the inspector the urgency of the case.

We went to the address given, and after some delay were admitted to an interview.

The Magistrate was at first somewhat crusty at being disturbed at such an hour, for by this time it was pretty late in the evening. However, when we had explained matters to him he was greatly interested, and we went through the necessary formalities. When it was done he ordered in cake and wine, and wished us both luck. "But remember," he said to Mary, "that as yet your possible fortune is a long way off. There may be more Giles Armers than one, and moreover there may be some difficulty in proving legally that the dead man was the same person as your father. Then you will also have to prove, in a formal way, your mother's marriage and your own birth. This will probably involve heavy expenses, for lawyers fight hard when they are well paid. However, I do not wish to discourage you, but only to prevent false hopes; at any rate, you have done well in making your Declaration at once. So far you are on the high road to success." So he sent us away filled with hopes as well as fears.

When we got home we set to work to look for hidden treasures in the unfinished room. I knew too well that there was nothing hidden in the rooms which were finished, for I had done the work myself, and had even stripped the walls and uncovered the floors.

It took us a couple of hours to make an accurate search, but there was absolutely no result. The late Master Mariner had made his treasury in the other house.

Next morning I went to find out from the parish registry the date of the death of Giles Armer, and to my intense relief and joy learned that it had occurred on the 30th of September, so that by our prompt action in going at once to the magistrate's, we had, if not secured a fortune, at least, not forfeited our rights or allowed them to lapse.

The incident was a sort of good omen, and cheered us up; and we needed a little cheering, for, despite the possible good fortune, we feared we might have to contest a lawsuit, a luxury which we could not afford.

We determined to keep our own counsel for a little, and did not mention the matter to a soul.

That evening Mr. Gradder called again, and renewed his offer of taking the house off my hands. I still refused, for I did not wish him to see any difference in my demeanour. He evidently came determined to effect a surrender of the lease, and kept bidding higher and higher, till at last I thought it best to let him have his way; and so we agreed for no less a sum than a hundred pounds that I should give him immediate possession and cancel the agreement. I told him we would clear out within one hour after the money was handed to me.

Next morning at half-past nine o'clock he came with the money. I had all our effects—they were not many—packed up and taken to a new lodging, and before ten o'clock Mr. Gradder was in possession of the premises.

Whilst he was tearing down my new wall papers, and pulling out the grates, and sticking his head up the chimneys and down the water tanks in the search for more treasures, Mary and I were consulting the eminent solicitor, Mr. George, as to our method of procedure. He said he would not lose an hour, but go by the first train to Littlehampton himself to examine Mrs. Compton as to dates and places.

Mary and I went with him. In the course of the next twenty-four hours he had, by various documents and the recollections of my mother-in-law, made out a clear case, the details of which only wanted formal verification.

We all came back to London jubilant, and were engaged on a high tea when there came a loud knocking at the door. There was a noise and scuffle in the passage, and into the room rushed Mr. Gradder, covered with soot and lime dust, with hair dishevelled and eyes wild with anger, and haggard with want of sleep. He burst out at me in a torrent of invective.

"Give me back my money, you thief! You ransacked the house yourself, and have taken it all away! My money, do you hear? my money!" He grew positively speechless with rage, and almost foamed at the mouth.

I took Mary by the hand and led her up to him.

"Mr. Gradder," I said, "let us both thank you. Only for your hurry and persistency we might have let the time lapse, and have omitted the declaration which, on the evening before last, we, or rather, she, made."

He started as though struck.

"What declaration? What do you mean?"

"The declaration made by my wife, only daughter of Giles Armer, Master Mariner, late of Whitby."

# The Watter's Mou'

## Chapter I

It threatened to be a wild night. All day banks of sea-fog had
come and gone, sweeping on shore with the south-east wind, which is
so fatal at Cruden Bay, and indeed all along the coast of Aberdeenshire,
and losing themselves in the breezy expanses of the high uplands beyond.
As yet the wind only came in puffs, followed by intervals of ominous
calm; but the barometer had been falling for days, and the sky had on
the previous night been streaked with great "mare's-tails" running in
the direction of the dangerous wind. Up to early morning the wind
had been south-westerly, but had then "backed" to south-east; and the
sudden change, no less than the backing, was ominous indeed. From
the waste of sea came a ceaseless muffled roar, which seemed loudest
and most full of dangerous import when it came through the mystery
of the driving fog. Whenever the fog-belts would lift or disperse, or
disappear inland before the gusts of wind, the sea would look as though
swept with growing anger; for though there were neither big waves as
during a storm, nor a great swell as after one, all the surface of the water
as far as the eye could reach was covered with little waves tipped with
white. Closer together grew these waves as the day wore on, the angrier
ever the curl of the white water where they broke. In the North Sea it
does not take long for the waves to rise; and all along the eastern edge
of Buchan it was taken for granted that there would be wild work on
the coast before the night was over.

In the little look-out house on the top of the cliff over the tiny
harbour of Port Erroll the coastguard on duty was pacing rapidly to and
fro. Every now and again he would pause, and lifting a field-glass from
the desk, sweep the horizon from Girdleness at the south of Aberdeen,
when the lifting of the mist would let him see beyond the Scaurs,
away to the north, where the high cranes of the Blackman quarries
at Murdoch Head seemed to cleave the sky like gigantic gallows-trees.

He was manifestly in high spirits, and from the manner in which,
one after another, he looked again and again at the Martini-Henry rifle
in the rack, the navy revolver stuck muzzle down on a spike, and the
cutlass in its sheath hanging on the wall, it was easy to see that his
interest arose from something connected with his work as a coastguard.

On the desk lay an open telegram smoothed down by his hard hands, with the brown envelope lying beside it. It gave some sort of clue to his excitement, although it did not go into detail. "Keep careful watch tonight; run expected; spare no efforts; most important."

William Barrow, popularly known as Sailor Willy, was a very young man to be a chief boatman in the preventive service, albeit that his station was one of the smallest on the coast. He had been allowed, as a reward for saving the life of his lieutenant, to join the coast service, and had been promoted to chief boatman as a further reward for a clever capture of smugglers, wherein he had shown not only great bravery, but much ability and power of rapid organisation.

The Aberdeen coast is an important one in the way of guarding on account of the vast number of fishing-smacks which, during the season, work from Peterhead up and down the coast, and away on the North Sea right to the shores of Germany and Holland. This vast coming and going affords endless opportunities for smuggling; and, despite of all vigilance, a considerable amount of "stuff" finds its way to the consumers without the formality of the Custom House. The fish traffic is a quick traffic, and its returns come all at once, so that a truly enormous staff would be requisite to examine adequately the thousand fish-smacks which use the harbour of Peterhead, and on Sundays pack its basins with a solid mass of boats. The coast-line for some forty miles south is favourable for this illicit traffic. The gneiss and granite formations broken up by every convulsion of nature, and worn by the strain and toil of ages into every conceivable form of rocky beauty, offers an endless variety of narrow creeks and bays where the daring, to whom the rocks and the currents and the tides are known, may find secret entrance and speedy exit for their craft. This season the smuggling had been chiefly of an overt kind—that is, the goods had been brought into the harbour amongst the fish and nets, and had been taken through the streets under the eyes of the unsuspecting Customs officers. Some of these takes were so large, that the authorities had made up their minds that there must be a great amount of smuggling going on. The secret agents in the German, Dutch, Flemish, and French ports were asked to make extra exertions in discovering the amount of the illicit trade, and their later reports were of an almost alarming nature. They said that really vast amounts of tobacco, brandy, rum, silks, laces, and all sorts of excisable commodities were being secretly shipped in the British fishing-fleet; and as only a very small proportion of this was discovered, it was manifest that smuggling to a large extent was once more to the fore. Accordingly precautions were doubled all along the east coast frequented by the fishing-fleets. Not only were the coastguards warned of the danger and cautioned against devices which might keep them from their work at critical times, but they were apprised of every new shipment as reported from abroad. Furthermore, the detectives of the service were sent about to parts where the men were suspected of laxity—or worse.

Thus it was that Sailor Willy, with the experience of two promotions for cause, and with the sense of responsibility which belonged to his office, felt in every way elated at the possibility of some daring work before him. He knew, of course, that a similar telegram had been received at every station on the coast, and that the chance of an attempt being made in Cruden Bay or its surroundings was a small one; but he was young and brave and hopeful, and with an adamantine sense of integrity to support him in his work. It was unfortunate that his comrade was absent, ill in the hospital at Aberdeen, and that the strain at present on the service, together with the men away on annual training and in the naval manoeuvres, did not permit of a substitute being sent to him. However, he felt strong enough to undertake any amount of duty—he was strong enough and handsome enough to have a good opinion of himself, and too brave and too sensible to let his head be turned by vanity.

As he walked to and fro there was in the distance of his mind—in that dim background against which in a man's mind a woman's form finds suitable projection—some sort of vague hope that a wild dream of rising in the world might be sometime realised. He knew that every precaution in his power had been already taken, and felt that he could indulge in fancies without detriment to his work. He had signalled the coastguard at Whinnyfold on the south side of the Bay, and they had exchanged ideas by means of the signal language. His appliances for further signalling by day or night were in perfect order, and he had been right over his whole boundary since he had received the telegram seeing that all things were in order. Willy Barrow was not one to leave things to chance where duty was concerned.

His day-dreams were not all selfish. They were at least so far unselfish that the results were to be shared with another; for Willy Barrow was engaged to be married. Maggie MacWhirter was the daughter of an old fisherman who had seen days more prosperous than the present.

He had once on a time owned a fishing-smack, but by degrees he had been compelled to borrow on her, till now, when, although he was nominal owner, the boat was so heavily mortgaged that at any moment he might lose his entire possession. That such an event was not unlikely was manifest, for the mortgagee was no other than Solomon Mendoza of Hamburg and Aberdeen, who had changed in like manner the ownership of a hundred boats, and who had the reputation of being as remorseless as he was rich. MacWhirter had long been a widower, and Maggie since a little girl had kept house for her father and her two brothers, Andrew and Niel. Andrew was twenty-seven—six years older than Maggie—and Niel had just turned twenty. The elder brother was a quiet, self-contained, hard-working man, who now and again manifested great determination, though generally at unexpected times; the younger was rash, impetuous, and passionate, and though in his moments of quiescence more tender to those he cared for than was usual with men of his class, he was a never-ending source of anxiety to his father and his sister. Andrew, or Sandy as he was always called, took him with consistent quietness.

The present year, although a good one in the main, had been but poor for MacWhirter's boat. Never once had he had a good take of fish—not one-half the number of crans of the best boat; and the season was so far advanced, and the supply had been so plentiful, that a few days before, the notice had been up at Peterhead that after the following week the buyers would not take anymore herring.

This notice naturally caused much excitement, and the whole fishing industry determined to make every effort to improve the shining hours left to them. Exertions were on all sides redoubled, and on sea and shore there was little idleness. Naturally the smuggling interest bestirred itself too; its chance for the year was in the rush and bustle and hurry of the coming and going fleet, and anything held over for a chance had to be ventured now or left over for a year—which might mean indefinitely. Great ventures were therefore taken by some of the boats; and from their daring the authorities concluded that either heavy bribes were given, or else that the goods were provided by others than the fishermen who undertook to run them. A few important seizures, however, made the men wary; and it was understood from the less frequent but greater importance of the seizures, that the price for "running" had greatly gone up. There was much passionate excitement amongst those who were found out and their friends, and a general wish to discover the informers.

Some of the smuggling fishermen at first refused to pay the fines until they were told who had informed. This position being unsupportable, they had instead paid the fines and cherished hatred in their hearts. Some of the more reckless and turbulent spirits had declared their intention of avenging themselves on the informers when they should be known. It was only natural that this feeling of rage should extend to the Customs officers and men of the preventive service, who stood between the unscrupulous adventurers and their harvest; and altogether matters had become somewhat strained between the fishermen and the authorities.

The Port Erroll boats, like those from Collieston, were all up at Peterhead, and of course amongst them MacWhirter's boat the Sea Gull with her skipper and his two sons. It was now Friday night, and the boats had been out for several days, so that it was pretty certain that there would be a full harbor at Peterhead on the Saturday. A marriage had been arranged to take place this evening between Thomas Keith of Boddam and Alice MacDonald, whose father kept the public-house The Jamie Fleeman on the northern edge of the Erroll estate. Though the occasion was to be a grand one, the notice of it had been short indeed. It was said by the bride's friends that it had been fixed so hurriedly because the notice of the closing of the fishing season had been so suddenly given out at Peterhead. Truth to tell, some sort of explanation was necessary, for it was only on Wednesday morning that word had been sent to the guests, and as these came from all sorts of places between Peterhead and Collieston, and taking a sweep of some ten miles inland, there was need of some preparation. The affair was to top all that had ever been seen at Port Erroll, and as The Jamie Fleeman was but a tiny place—nothing, in fact, but a wayside public-house—it was arranged that it was to take place in the new barn and storehouses Matthew Beagrie had just built on the inner side of the sandhills, where they came close to the Water of Cruden.

Throughout all the east side of Buchan there had for sometime existed a wonder amongst the quiet-going people as to the strange prosperity of MacDonald. His public-house had, of course, a practical monopoly; for as there was not a licensed house on the Erroll estate, and as his was the nearest house of call to the port, he naturally got what custom there was going. The fishermen all along the coast for some seven or eight miles went to him either to drink or to get their liquor for drinking elsewhere; and not a few of the Collieston men on their Saturday journey home from Peterhead and their Sunday journey out there again made a detour to have a glass and a chat and a pipe, if time permitted, with "Tammas Mac"—for such was his sobriquet. To the authorities he and his house were also sources of interest; for there was some kind of suspicion that some of the excellent brandy and cigars which he dispensed had arrived by a simpler road than that through the Custom House. It was at this house, in the good old days of smuggling, that the coastguards used to be entertained when a run was on foot, and where they slept off their drunkenness whilst the cargoes were being hidden or taken inland in the ready carts. Of course all this state of things had been altered, and there was as improved a decorum amongst the smugglers as there was a sterner rule and discipline amongst the coastguards. It was many a long year since Philip Kennedy met his death at Kirkton at the hands of the exciseman Anderson. Comparatively innocent deception was now the smugglers' only wile.

Tonight the whole country-side was to be at the wedding, and the dance which was to follow it; and for this occasion the lion was to lie down with the lamb, for the coastguards were bidden to the feast with the rest. Sailor Willy had looked forward to the dance with delight, for Maggie was to be there, and on the Billy Ruffian, which had been his last ship, he had been looked on as the best dancer before the mast. If there be any man who shuns a dance in which he knows he can shine, and at which his own particular girl is to be present, that man is not to be found in the Royal Naval Marine, even amongst those of them who have joined in the preventive service. Maggie was no less delighted, although she had a source of grief which for the present she had kept all to herself. Her father had of late been much disturbed about affairs. He had not spoken of them to her, and she did not dare to mention the matter to him; for old MacWhirter was a closemouthed man, and did not exchange many confidences even with his own children. But Maggie guessed at the cause of the sadness—of the down-bent head when none were looking; the sleepless nights and the deep smothered groans which now and again marked his heavy sleep told the tale loudly enough to reach the daughter's ears. For the last few weeks, whenever her father was at home, Maggie had herself lain awake listening, listening, in increasing agony of spirit, for one of these half moans or for the sound of the tossing of the restless man. He was as gentle and kind to his daughter as ever; but on his leaving the last time there had been an omission on his part which troubled her to the quick. For the first time in his life he had not kissed her as he went away.

On the previous day Sailor Willy had said he would come to the wedding and the dance if his duties should permit him; and, when asked if he could spare a few rockets for the occasion, promised that he would let off three Board of Trade rockets, which he could now deal with as it was three months since he had used any. He was delighted at the opportunity of meeting the fisherfolk and his neighbours; for his officers had impressed on him the need of being on good terms with all around him, both for the possibility which it would always afford him of knowing how things were going on, and for the benefit of the rocket-service whenever there might be need of willing hands and hearts to work with him, for in the Board of Trade rocket-service much depends on voluntary aid. That very afternoon he had fixed the rockets on the wall of the barn with staples, so that he could fire them from below with a slow match, which he fixed ready. When he had got the telegram he had called in to Maggie and told her if he did not come to fetch her she was to go on to the wedding by herself, and that he would try to join her later. She had appeared a little startled when he told her he might not be present; but after a pause smiled, and said she would go, and that he was not to lose anytime coming when he was free. Now that every arrangement was complete, and as he had between puffs of the sea-fog got a clean sweep of the horizon and saw that there was no sail of any kind within sight, he thought he might have a look through the village and keep in evidence so as not to create any suspicion in the minds of the people. As he went through the street he noticed that nearly every house door was closed—all the women were at the new barn. It was now eight o'clock, and the darkness, which is slow of coming in the North, was closing in. Down by the barn there were quite a number of carts, and the horses had not been taken out, though the wedding was not to be till nine o'clock, or perhaps even later; for Mrs. MacDonald had taken care to tell her friends that Keith might not get over from Boddam till late. Willy looked at the carts carefully—some idea seemed to have struck him. Their lettering shewed them to be from all parts round, and the names mostly of those who had not the best reputation. When his brief survey was finished he looked round and then went swiftly behind the barn so that no one might see him. As he went he muttered reflectively:

"Too many light carts and fast horses—too much silence in the barn—too little liquor going, to be all safe. There's something up here tonight." He was under the lee of the barn and looked up where he had fixed the rockets ready to fire. This gave him a new idea.

"I fixed them low so as to go over the sandhills and not be noticeable at Collieston or beyond. They are now placed up straight and will be seen for fifty miles if the weather be clear."

It was too dark to see very clearly, and he would not climb up to examine them lest he should be noticed and his purpose of acquiring information frustrated; but then and there he made up his mind that Port Erroll or its neighbourhood had been the spot chosen for the running of the smuggled goods. He determined to find out more, and straightaway went round to the front and entered the room.

## Chapter II

As soon as Sailor Willy was seen to enter, a large part of the gathering looked relieved, and at once began to chat and gabble in marked contrast to their previous gloom and silence. Port Erroll was well represented by its womankind, and by such of its men as were not away at the fishing; for it was the intention to mask the smuggling scheme by an assemblage at which all the respectability would be present. There appeared to be little rivalry between the two shoemakers, MacPherson and Beagrie, who chatted together in a corner, the former telling his companion how he had just been down to the lifeboat-house to see, as one of the Committee, that it was all ready in case it should be wanted before the night was over. Lang John and Lang Jim, the policemen of the place, looked sprucer even than usual, and their buttons shone in the light of the many paraffin lamps as if they had been newly burnished. Mitchell and his companions of the salmon fishery were grouped in another corner, and Andrew Mason was telling Mackay, the new flesher, whose shed was erected on the edge of the burn opposite John Reid's shop, of a great crab which he had taken that morning in a pot opposite the Twa Een.

But these and nearly all the other Port Erroll folk present were quiet, and their talk was of local interest; the main clack of tongues came from the many strange men who stood in groups near the centre of the room and talked loudly. In the midst of them was the bridegroom, more joyous than any, though in the midst of his laughter he kept constantly turning to look at the door. The minister from Peterhead sat in a corner with the bride and her mother and father—the latter of whom, despite his constant laughter, had an anxious look on his face. Sailor Willy was greeted joyously, and the giver of the feast and the bridegroom each rose, and, taking a bottle and glass, offered him a drink.

"To the bride," said he; but seeing that no one else was drinking, he tapped the bridegroom on the shoulder, "Come, drink this with me, my lad!" he added. The latter paused an instant and then helped himself from MacDonald's bottle. Willy did not fail to notice the act, and holding out his glass said:

"Come, my lad, you drink with me! Change glasses in old style!" An odd pallor passed quickly across the bridegroom's face, but MacDonald spoke quickly:

"Tak it, mon, tak it!" So he took the glass, crying "No heel-taps," threw back his head, and raised the glass. Willy threw back his head too, and tossed off his liquor, but, as he did so, took care to keep a sharp eye on the other, and saw him, instead of swallowing his liquor, pour it into his thick beard. His mind was quite made up now. They meant to keep him out of the way by fair means or foul.

Just then two persons entered the room, one of them, James Cruickshank of the Kilmarnock Arms, who was showing the way to the other, an elderly man with a bald head, keen eyes, a ragged grey beard, a hooked nose, and an evil smile. As he entered MacDonald jumped up and came over to greet him.

"Oh! Mr. Mendoza, this is braw! We hopit tae see ye the nicht, but we were that feared that ye wadna come."

"Mein Gott, but why shall I not come—on this occasion of all— the occasion of the marriage of the daughter of mein goot frient, Tam Smack? And moreovers when I bring these as I haf promise. For you, mein frient Keith, this cheque, which one week you cash, and for you, my tear Miss Alice, these so bright necklace, which you will wear, ant which will sell if so you choose."

As he spoke he handed his gifts to the groom and bride. He then walked to the corner where Mrs. Mac sat, exchanging a keen look with his host as he did so. The latter seemed to have taken his cue and spoke out at once.

"And now, reverend sir, we may proceed—all is ready." As he spoke the bridal pair stood up, and the friends crowded round. Sailor Willy moved towards the door, and just as the parson opened his book, began to pass out. Tammas Mac immediately spoke to him:

"Ye're no gangin', Sailor Willy? Sure ye'll wait and see Tam Keith marrit on my lass?"

He instantly replied: "I must go for a while. I have somethings to do, and then I want to try to bring Maggie down for the dance!" and before anything could be said, he was gone.

The instant he left the door he slipped round to the back of the barn, and running across the sandhills to the left, crossed the wooden bridge, and hurrying up the roadway by the cottage on the cliff gained the watch-house. He knew that none of the company in the barn could leave till the service was over, with the minister's eye on them, without giving cause for after suspicion; and he knew, too, that as there were no windows on the south side of the barn, nothing could be seen from that side. Without a moment's delay he arranged his signals for the call for aid; and as the rockets whizzed aloft, sending a white glare far into the sky, he felt that the struggle had entered on its second stage.

The night had now set in with a darkness unusual in August. The swaithes of sea-mist whirled in by the wind came fewer and fainter, and at times a sudden rift through the driving clouds showed that there was starlight somewhere between the driving masses of mist and gloom. Willy Barrow once more tried all his weapons and saw that all his signals were in order. Then he strapped the revolver and the cutlass in his belt, and lit a dark lantern so that it might be ready in case of need. This done, he left the watch-house, locking the door behind him, and, after looking steadily across the Bay to the Skaurs beyond, turned and walked northward towards the Watter's Mou'. Between the cliff on the edge of this and the watch-house there was a crane used for raising the granite boulders quarried below, and when he drew near this he stopped instinctively and called out, "Who is there?" for he felt, rather than saw, some presence. "It is only me, Willy," came a soft voice, and a woman drew a step nearer through the darkness from behind the shaft of the crane.

"Maggie! Why, darling, what brings you here? I thought you were going to the wedding!"

"I knew ye wadna be there, and I wanted to speak wi' ye"—this was said in a very low voice.

"How did you know I wouldn't be there?—I was to join you if I could."

"I saw Bella Cruickshank hand ye the telegram as ye went by the Post Office, and—and I knew there would be something to keep ye. O Willy, Willy! why do ye draw awa frae me?" for Sailor Willy had instinctively loosened his arms which were round her and had drawn back—in the instant his love and his business seemed as though antagonistic. He answered with blunt truthfulness:

"I was thinking, Maggie, that I had no cause to be making love here and now. I've got work, mayhap, tonight!"

"I feared so, Willy—I feared so!" Willy was touched, for it seemed to him that she was anxious for him, and answered tenderly:

"All right, dear! All right! There's no danger—why, if need be, I am armed," and he slipped his hand on the butt of the revolver in his belt. To his surprise Maggie uttered a deep low groan, and turning away sat on the turf bank beside her, as though her strength was failing her. Willy did not know what to say, so there was a space of silence. Then Maggie went on hurriedly:

"Oh my God! it is a dreadfu' thing to lift yer han' in sic a deadly manner against yer neighbours, and ye not knowing what woe ye mau cause." Willy could answer this time:

"Ah, lass! it's hard indeed, and that's the truth. But that's the very reason that men like me are put here that can and will do their duty no matter how hard it may be."

Another pause, and then Maggie spoke again. Willy could not see her face, but she seemed to speak between gasps for breath.

"Ye're lookin' for hard wark the nicht?"

"I am!—I fear so."

"I can guess that that telegram tellt ye that some boats would try to rin in somewhere the nicht."

"Mayhap, lass. But the telegrams are secret, and I must not speak of what's in them."

After a long pause Maggie spoke again, but in a voice so low that he could hardly hear her amid the roar of the breaking waves which came in on the wind:

"Willy, ye're not a cruel man!—ye wadna, if ye could help it, dae harm to them that loved ye, or work woe to their belongin's?"

"My lass! that I wouldn't." As he answered he felt a horrible sinking of the heart. What did all this mean? Was it possible that Maggie, too, had any interest in the smuggling? No, no! a thousand times no! Ashamed of his suspicion he drew closer and again put his arm around her in a protecting way. The unexpected tenderness overcame her, and, bursting into tears, she threw herself on Willy's neck and whispered to him between her sobs:

"O Willy, Willy! I'm in sic sair trouble, and there's nane that I can speak to. Nae! not ane in the wide warld."

"Tell me, darling; you know you'll soon be my wife, and then I'll have a right to know all!"

"Oh, I canna! I canna! I canna!" she said, and taking her arms from around his neck she beat her hands wildly together. Willy was something frightened, for a woman's distress touches a strong man in direct ratio to his manliness. He tried to soothe her as though she were a frightened child, and held her tight to him.

"There! there! my darling. Don't cry. I'm here with you, and you can tell me all your trouble." She shook her head; he felt the movement on his breast, and he went on:

"Don't be frightened, Maggie; tell me all. Tell me quietly, and mayhap I can help ye out over the difficult places." Then he remained silent, and her sobs grew less violent; at last she raised her head and dashed away her tears fiercely with her hand. She dragged herself away from him: he tried to stop her, but she said:

"Nae, nae, Willy dear; let me speak it in my ain way. If I canna trust ye, wha can I trust? My trouble is not for mysel." She paused, and he asked:

"Who, then, is it for?"

"My father and my brothers." Then she went on hurriedly, fearing to stop lest her courage should fail her, and he listened in dead silence, with a growing pain in his heart.

"Ye ken that for several seasons back our boat has had bad luck—we took less fish and lost mair nets than any of the boats; even on the land everything went wrong. Our coo died, and the shed was blawn doon, and then the blight touched the potatoes in our field. Father could dae naething, and had to borrow money on the boat to go on with his wark; and the debt grew and grew, till now he only owns her in name, and we never ken when we may be sold up. And the man that has the mortgage isn't like to let us off or gie time!"

"Who is he? His name?" said Willy hoarsely.

"Mendoza—the man frae Hamburg wha lends to the boats at Peterhead."

Willy groaned. Before his eyes rose the vision of that hard, cruel, white face that he had seen only a few minutes ago, and again he saw him hand over the presents with which he had bought the man and woman to help in his wicked scheme. When Maggie heard the groan her courage and her hope arose. If her lover could take the matter so much to heart all might yet be well, and in the moment all the womanhood in her awoke to the call. Her fear had broken down the barriers that had kept back her passion, and now the passion came with all the force of a virgin nature. She drew Willy close to her—closer still—and whispered to him in a low sweet voice, that thrilled with emotion:

"Willy, Willy, darlin'; ye wouldna see harm come to my father—my father, my father!" and in a wave of tumultuous, voluptuous passion she kissed him full in the mouth. Willy felt for the moment half dazed. Love has its opiates that soothe and stun even in the midst of their activity. He clasped Maggie close in his arms, and for a moment their hearts beat together and their mouths breathed the same air. Then Willy drew back, but Maggie hung limp in his arms. The silence which hung in the midst of nature's tumult broke its own spell. Willy realised what and where he was: with the waves dashing below his feet and the night wind laden with drifting mist wreathing around him in the darkness, and whistling amongst the rocks and screaming sadly through the ropes and stays of the flagstaff on the cliff. There was a wild fear in his heart and a burning desire to know all that was in his sweetheart's mind.

"Go on, Maggie! go on!" he said. Maggie roused herself and again took up the thread of her story—this time in feverish haste. The moment of passion had disquieted and disturbed her. She seemed to herself to be two people, one of whom was new to her, and whom she feared, but woman-like, she felt that as she had begun so much she go on; and thus her woman's courage sustained her.

"Some weeks ago, father began to get letters frae Mr. Mendoza, and they aye upset him. He wrote answers and sent them away at once. Then Mr. Mendoza sent him a telegram frae Hamburg, and he sent a reply—and a month ago father got a telegram telling him to meet him at Peterhead. He was very angry at first and very low-spirited after; but he went to Peterhead, and when he cam back he was very still and quite pale. He would eat naething, and went to bed although it was only seven o'clock. Then there were more letters and telegrams, but father answered nane o' them—sae far as I ken—and then Mr. Mendoza cam to our hoose. Father got as pale as a sheet when he saw him, and then he got red and angry, and I thocht he was going to strike him; but Mr. Mendoza said not to frichten his daughter, and father got quiet and sent me oot on a message to the Nether Mill. And when I cam back

Mr. Mendoza had gone, and father was sitting with his face in his hands, and he didna hear me come in. When I spoke, he started up and he was as white as a sheet, and then he mumbled something and went into his room. And ever since then he hardly spoke to anyone, and seemed to avoid me a'thegither. When he went away the last time he never even kissed me. And so, Willy—so, I fear that that awfu' Mr. Mendoza has made him dae something that he didna want to dae, and it's all breaking my heart!" and again she laid her head on her lover's breast and sobbed. Willy breathed more freely; but he could not be content to remain in doubt, and his courage was never harder tried than when he asked his next question.

"Then, Maggie, you don't know anything for certain?"

"Naething, Willy—but I fear."

"But there may be nothing, after all!" Maggie's hopes rose again, for there was something in her lover's voice which told her that he was willing to cling to any straw, and once again her woman's nature took advantage of her sense of right and wrong. "Please God, Willy, there may be naething! but I fear much that it may be so; but we must act as if we didna fear. It wadna dae to suspect poor father without some cause. You know, Willy, the Earl has promised to mak him the new harbourmaster. Old Forgie is bedridden now, and when winter comes he'll no even be able to pretend to work, so the Earl is to pension him, and father will get the post and hae the hoose by the harbour, and you know that everyone's sae glad, for they a' respect father."

"Ay, lass," interrupted Willy, "that's true; and why, then, should we—you and me, Maggie—think he would do ill to please that damned scoundrel, Mendoza?"

"Indeed, I'm thinkin' that it's just because that he is respeckit that Mendoza wants him to help him. He kens weel that nane would suspeck father, and—" here she clipped her lover close in her arms once again, and her breath came hot in his face till it made him half drunk with a voluptuous intoxication—"he kens that father, my father, would never be harmt by my lover!"

Even then, at the moment when the tragedy of his life seemed to be accomplished, when the woman he loved and honoured seemed to be urging him to some breach of duty, Willy Barrow could not but feel that some responsibility for her action rested on him. That first passionate kiss, which had seemed to unlock the very gates of her soul—in which she had yielded herself to him—had some mysterious bond or virtue like that which abides in the wedding ring. The Maggie who thus acted was his Maggie, and in all that came of it he had a part. But his mind was made up; nothing—not Maggie's kisses or Maggie's fears—would turn him from his path of duty, and strong in this resolution he could afford to be silent to the woman in his arms. Maggie instinctively knew that silence could now be her best weapon, and said no word as they walked towards the guard-house, Willy casting keen looks seawards, and up and down the coast as they went. When they were so close that in its shelter the roar of the surf seemed muffled, Maggie again nestled close to her lover, and whispered in his ear as he looked out over Cruden Bay:

"The Sea Gull comes hame the nicht!" Willy quivered, but said nothing for a time that seemed to be endless. Then he answered—"They'll find it hard to make the Port tonight. Look! the waves are rolling high and the wind is getting up. It would be madness to try it." Again she whispered to him:

"Couldna she rin in somewhere else—there are other openings besides Port Erroll in Buchan!" Willy laughed the laugh of a strong man who knew well what he said:

"Other openings! Ay, lass, there are other openings; but the coble isn't built that can run them this night. With a south-east gale, who would dare to try? The Bullers, or Robies Haven, or Dunbuy, or Twa Havens, or Lang Haven, or The Watter's Mou'—why, lass, they'd be in matches on the rocks before they could turn their tiller or slack a sail."

She interrupted him, speaking with a despairing voice:

"Then ye'll no hae to watch nane o' them the nicht?"

"Nay, Maggie. Port Erroll is my watch tonight; and from it I won't budge."

"And the Watter's Mou'?" she asked, "it that no safe wi'oot watch? it's no far frae the Port." Again Willy laughed his arrogant, masculine laugh, which made Maggie, despite her trouble, admire him more than ever, and he answered:

"The Watter's Mou'? To try to get in there in this wind would be to court sudden death. Why, lass, it would take a man all he knew to get out from there, let alone get in, in this weather! And then the chances would be ten to one that he'd be dashed to pieces on the rocks beyond," and he pointed to where a line of sharp rocks rose between the billows on the south side of the inlet. Truly it was a fearful-looking place to be dashed on, for the great waves broke on the rocks with a loud roaring, and even in the semi-darkness they could see the white lines as the waters poured down to leeward in the wake of the heaving wave. The white cluster of rocks looked like a ghostly mouth opened to swallow whatever might come in touch. Maggie shuddered; but some sudden idea seemed to strike her, and she drew away from her lover for a moment, and looked towards the black cleft in the rocks of which they could just see the top from where they stood—the entrance to the Watter's Mou'.

And then with one long, wild, appealing glance skyward, as though looking a prayer which she dared not utter even in her heart, Maggie turned towards her lover once more. Again she drew close to him, and hung around his neck, and said with many gasps and pauses between her words:

"If the Sea Gull should come in to the Port the nicht, and if ony attempt that ye feared should tak you away to Whinnyfold or to Dunbuy so that you might be a bit—only a wee bit—late to search when the boat cam in—"

She stopped affrighted, for Willy put her from him to arm's length, not too gently either, and said to her so sternly that each word seemed to smite her like the lash of a whip, till she shrunk and quivered and cowered away from him:

"Maggie, lass! What's this you're saying to me? It isn't fit for you to speak or me to hear! It's bad enough to be a smuggler, but what is it that you would make of me? Not only a smuggler, but a perjurer and a traitor too. God! am I mistaken? Is it you, Maggie, that would make this of me? Of me! Maggie MacWhirter, if this be your counsel, then God help us both! you are no fit wife for me!" In an instant the whole truth dawned on Maggie of what a thing she would make of the man she loved, whom she had loved at the first because he was strong and brave and true. In the sudden revulsion of her feelings she flung herself on her knees beside him, and took his hand and held it hard, and despite his efforts to withdraw it, kissed it wildly in the humility of her self-abasement, and poured out to him a passionate outburst of pleading for his forgiveness, of justification of herself, and of appeals to his mercy for her father.

"Oh Willy, Willy! dinna turn frae me this nicht! My heart is sae fu' o' trouble that I am nigh mad! I dinna ken what to dae nor where to look for help! I think, and think, and think, and everywhere there is nought but dark before me, just as there is blackness oot ower the sea, when I look for my father. And noo when I want ye to help me—ye that are all I hae, and the only ane on earth that I can look tae in my wae and trouble—I can dae nae mair than turn ye frae me! Ye that I love! oh, love more than my life or my soul! I must dishonour and mak ye hate me! Oh, what shall I dae? What shall I dae? What shall I dae?" and again she beat the palms of her hands together in a paroxysm of wild despair, whilst Willy looked on with his heart full of pain and pity, though his resolution never flinched. And then through the completeness of her self-abasement came the pleading of her soul from a depth of her nature even deeper than despair. Despair has its own bravery, but hope can sap the strongest resolution. And the pleadings of love came from the depths of that Pandora's box which we call human nature.

"O Willy, Willy! forgie me—forgie me! I was daft to say what I did! I was daft to think that ye would be so base!—daft to think that I would like you to so betray yoursel! Forgie me, Willy, forgie me, and tak my wild words as spoken not to ye but to the storm that maks me fear sae for my father! Let me tak it a' back, Willy darlin'—Willy, my Willy; and dinna leave me desolate here with this new shadow ower me!" Here, as she kissed his hand again, her lover stooped and raised her in his strong arms and held her to him. And then, when she felt herself in a position of security, the same hysterical emotion came sweeping up in her brain and her blood—the same self-abandonment to her lover overcame her—and the current of her thought once again turned to win from him something by the force of her woman's wile and her woman's contact with the man.

"Willy," she whispered, as she kissed him on the mouth and then kissed his head on the side of his neck, "Willy, ye have forgien me, I ken—and I ken that ye'll harm father nae mair than ye can help—but if—"

What more she was going to say she hardly knew herself. As for Willy, he felt that something better left unsaid was coming, and unconsciously his muscles stiffened till he held her from him rather than to him. She, too, felt the change, and held him closer—closer still, with the tenacity induced by a sense of coming danger. Their difficulty was solved for them, for just on the instant when the suggestion of treachery to his duty was hanging on her lips, there came from the village below, in a pause between the gusts of wind, the fierce roar of a flying rocket. Up and up and up, as though it would never stop—up it rose with its prolonged screech, increasing in sound at the first till it began to die away in the aerial heights above, so that when the explosion came it seemed to startle a quietude around it. Up in the air a thousand feet over their heads the fierce glitter of the falling fires of red and blue made a blaze of light which lit up the coast-line from the Scaurs to Dunbuy, and with an instinctive intelligence Willy Barrow took in all he saw, including the many men at the little port below, sheltering under the sea-wall from the sweeping of the waves as they looked out seawards. Instinctively also he counted the seconds till the next rocket should be fired—one, two, three; and then another roar and another blaze of coloured lights. And then another pause, of six seconds this time! and then the third rocket sped aloft with its fiery message. And then the darkness seemed blacker than ever, and the mysterious booming of the sea to grow louder and louder as though it came through silence. By this time the man and the woman were apart no less in spirit than physically. Willy, intent on his work, was standing outside the window of the guard-house, whence he could see all around the Bay and up and down the coast, and at the same time command the whole of the harbour. His feet were planted wide apart, for on the exposed rock the sweep of the wind was strong, and as he raised his arm with his field-glass to search the horizon the wind drove back his jacket and showed the butt of his revolver and the hilt of his cutlass. Maggie stood a little behind him, gazing seawards, with no less eager eyes, for she too expected what would follow. Her heart seemed to stand still though her breath came in quick gasps, and she did not dare to make a sound or to encroach on the business-like earnestness of the man. For full a minute they waited thus, and then far off at sea, away to the south, they saw a faint blue light, and then another and another, till at the last three lights were burning in a row. Instantly from the town a single rocket went up—not this time a great Board of Trade rocket, laden with coloured fire, but one which left a plain white track of light behind it. Willy gazed seawards, but there was no more sign from the far-off ship at sea; the signal, whatever it was, was complete. The coastguard was uncertain as to the meaning, but to Maggie no explanation was necessary. There, away at sea, tossed on the stormy waters, was her father. There was danger round him, but a greater danger on the shore— every way of entrance was barred by the storm—save the one where, through his fatal cargo, dishonour lay in wait for him. She seemed to see her duty clear before her, and come what might she meant to do it: her father must be warned. It was with a faint voice indeed that she now spoke to her lover:

"Willy!"

His heart was melted at the faltering voice, but he feared she was trying some new temptation, so, coldly and hardly enough, he answered:

"What is it, lass?"

"Willy, ye wadna see poor father injured?"

"No, Maggie, not if I could help it. But I'd have to do my duty all the same."

"And we should a' dae oor duty—whatever it might be—at a' costs?"

"Ay, lass—at all costs!" His voice was firm enough now, and there was no mistaking the truth of its ring. Maggie's hope died away. From the stern task which seemed to rise before her over the waste of the black sea she must not shrink. There was but one more yielding to the weakness of her fear, and she said, so timidly that Willy was startled, the voice and manner were so different from those he had ever known:

"And if—mind I say 'if', Willy—I had a duty to dae and it was fu' o' fear and danger, and ye could save me frae it, wad ye?" As she waited for his reply, her heart beat so fast and so heavily that Willy could hear it: her very life, she felt, lay in his answer. He did not quite understand the full import of her words and all that they implied, but he knew that she was in deadly earnest, and he felt that some vague terror lay in his answer; but the manhood in him rose to the occasion—Willy Barrow was of the stuff of which heroes are made—and he replied:

"Maggie, as God is above us, I have no other answer to give! I don't know what you mean, but I have a shadow of fear! I must do my duty whatever comes of it!" There was a long pause, and then Maggie spoke again, but this time in so different a voice that her lover's heart went out to her in tenfold love and passion, with never a shadow of doubt or fear.

"Willy, tak me in your arms—I am not unworthy, dear, though for a moment I did falter!" He clasped her to him, and whispered when their lips had met:

"Maggie, my darling, I never loved you like now. I would die for you if I could do you good."

"Hush, dear, I ken it weel. But your duty is not only for yoursel, and it must be done! I too hae a duty to dae—a grave and stern ane!"

"What is it? Tell me, Maggie dear!"

"Ye maunna ask me! Ye maun never ken! Kiss me once again, Willy, before I go—for oh, my love, my love! it may be the last!"

Her words were lost in the passionate embrace which followed. Then, when he least expected it, she suddenly tore herself away and fled through the darkness across the field which lay between them and her home, whilst he stood doggedly at his watch looking out for another signal between sea and shore.

## Chapter III

WHEN SHE GOT TO THE far side of the field, Maggie, instead of turning to the left, which would have brought her home, went down the sloping track to the right, which led to the rustic bridge crossing the Back Burn near the Pigeon Tower. Thence turning to the right she scrambled down the bank beside the ruined barley-mill, so as to reach the little plots of sea-grass—islands, except at low tide—between which the tide rises to meet the waters of the stream.

The whole situation of Cruden is peculiar. The main stream, the Water of Cruden, runs in a south-easterly direction, skirts the sandhills, and, swirling under the stone bridge, partly built with the ruins of the old church which Malcolm erected to celebrate his victory over Sueno, turns suddenly to the right and runs to sea over a stony bottom. The estuary has in its wash some dangerous outcropping granite rocks, nearly covered at high tide, and the mouth opens between the most northerly end of the sandhills and the village street, whose houses mark the slope of the detritus from the rocks. Formerly the Water of Cruden, instead of taking this last turn, used to flow straight on till it joined the lesser stream known as the Back Dunn, and together the streams ran seawards. Even in comparatively recent years, in times of flood or freshet, the spate broke down or swept over the intervening tongue of land, and the Water of Cruden took its old course seaward. This course is what is known as the Watter's Mou'. It is a natural cleft—formed by primeval fire or earthquake or some sort of natural convulsion—which runs through the vast mass of red granite which forms a promontory running due south. Water has done its work as well as fire in the formation of the gully as it now is, for the drip and flow and rush of water that mark the seasons for countless ages have completed the work of the pristine fire. As one sees this natural mouth of the stream in the rocky face of the cliff, it is hard to realise that Nature alone has done the work.

At first the cleft runs from west to east, and broadens out into a wide bay of which on one side a steep grassy slope leads towards the new castle of Slains, and on the other rises a sheer bank, with tufts of the thick grass growing on the ledges, where the earth has been blown. From this the cleft opens again between towering rocks like what in America is called a canon and tends seaward to the south between precipices two hundred feet high, and over a bottom of great boulders exposed at low water towards the northern end. The precipice to the left or eastward side is twice rent with great openings, through which, in time of storm, the spray and spume of the easterly gale piling the great waves into the Castle Bay are swept. These openings are, however, so guarded with masses of rock that the force of the wildest wave is broken before it can leap up the piles of boulders which rise from their sandy floors. At the very mouth the cleft opens away to the west, where the cliff falls back, and seaward of which rise great masses of black frowning rock, most of which only show their presence at high water by the angry patches of foam which even in calm weather mark them—for the current here runs fast. The eastern portal is composed of a giant mass of red granite, which, from its overhanging shape, is known as "the Ship's Starn." It lies somewhat lower than the cliff of which it is a part, being attached to it by a great sloping shelf of granite, over which, when the storm is easterly, the torrent of spray sent up by the dashing waves rolls down to join the foamy waves in the Watter's Mou'.

Maggie knew that close to the Barley Mill, safe from the onset of the waves—for the wildest waves that ever rise lose their force fretting and churning on the stony sides and bottom of the Watter's Mou'—was kept a light boat belonging to her brother, which he sometimes used when the weather was fine and he wanted to utilise his spare time in line fishing. Her mind was made up that it was her duty to give her father warning of what awaited him on landing—if she could. She was afraid to think of the danger, of the myriad chances against her success; but, woman-like, when once the idea was fixed in her mind she went straight on to its realisation. Truly, thought of any kind would have been an absolute barrier to action in such a case, for anyone of the difficulties ahead would have seemed sufficient. To leave the shore at all on such a night, and in such a frail craft, with none but a girl to manage it; then to find a way, despite storm and current, out to the boat so far off at sea; and finally, to find the boat she wanted at all in the fret of such a stormy sea—a wilderness of driving mist—in such a night, when never a star even was to be seen: the prospect might well appal the bravest.

But to think was to hesitate, and to hesitate was to fail. Keeping her thoughts on the danger to her father, and seeing through the blackness of the stormy night his white, woe-laden face before her, and hearing through the tumult of the tempest his sobs as on that night when her fear for him began to be acute, she set about her work with desperate energy. The boat was moored on the northern side of the largest of the little islands of sea-grass, and so far in shelter that she could get all in readiness. She set the oars in their places, stepped the mast, and rigged the sail ready to haul up. Then she took a small spar of broken wood and knotted to it a piece of rope, fastening the other end of the rope, some five yards long, just under the thwarts near the centre of the boat, and just a little forward on the port side. The spar she put carefully ready to throw out of the boat when the sweep of the wind should take her sail—for without some such strain as it would afford, the boat would probably heel over. Then she guided the boat in the shallow water round the little island till it was stern on to the sea side. It was rough work, for the rush and recoil of the waves beat the boat back on the sandy bank or left her now and again dry till a new wave lifted her.

All this time she took something of inspiration from the darkness and the roar of the storm around her. She was not yet face to face with danger, and did not realise, or try to realise, its magnitude. In such a mystery of darkness as lay before, above, and around her, her own personality seemed as nought. Truly there is an instinct of one's own littleness which becomes consciously manifest in the times when Nature puts forth her might. The wind swept up the channel of the Watter's Mou' in great gusts, till the open bay where she stood became the centre of an intermittent whirlwind. The storm came not only from the Mouth itself, but through the great gaps in the eastern wall. It drove across the gully till high amongst the rocks overhead on both sides it seemed now and again to scream as a living thing in pain or anger. Great sheets of mist appeared out of the inky darkness beyond, coming suddenly as though like the great sails of ships driving up before the wind. With gladness Maggie saw that the sheets of fog were becoming fewer and thinner, and realised that so far her dreadful task was becoming possible. She was getting more inspired by the sound and elemental fury around her. There was in her blood, as in the blood of all the hardy children of the northern seas, some strain of those study Berserkers who knew no fear, and rode the very tempest on its wings with supreme bravery. Such natures rise with the occasion, and now, when the call had come, Maggie's brave nature answered it. It was with a strong, almost an eager, heart that she jumped into the boat, and seizing the oars, set out on her perilous course. The start was difficult, for the boat was bumping savagely on the sand; but, taking advantage of a big wave, two or three powerful strokes took her out into deeper water. Here, too, there was shelter, for the cliffs rose steeply; and when she had entered the elbow of the gully and saw before her the whole length of the Watter's Mou', the drift of the wind took it over her head, and she was able to row in comparative calmness under the shadow of the cliffs. A few minutes took her to the first of the openings in the eastern cliff, and here she began to feel the full fury of the storm. The opening itself was sheer on each side, but in the gap between was piled a mass of giant boulders, the work of the sea at its wildest during the centuries of stress. On the farther side of these the waves broke, and sent up a white cloud of spume that drove instantly into the darkness beyond. Maggie knew that here her first great effort had to be made, and lending her strength pulled the boat through the turmoil of wind and wave. As she passed the cleft, driven somewhat more out into the middle of the channel, she caught, in a pause between the rush of the waves, a glimpse of the lighted windows of the castle on the cliff. The sight for an instant unnerved her, for it brought into opposition her own dreadful situation, mental and physical, with the happy faces of those clustered round the comforting light. But the reaction was helpful, for the little jealousy which was at the base of the idea was blotted out by the thought of that stem and paramount duty which she had undertaken. Not seldom in days gone by had women like her, in times of test and torment, taken their way over the red-hot ploughshares under somewhat similar stress of mind.

She was now under the shelter of the cliff, and gaining the second and last opening in the rocky wall: as the boat advanced the force of the waves became greater, for every yard up the Watter's Mou' the fretting of the rocky bottom and sides had broken their force. This was brought home to her roughly when the breaking of a coming wave threw a sheet of water over her as she bent to her oars. Chop! chop! went the boat into the trough of each succeeding wave, till it became necessary to bale out the boat or she might never even get started on her way. This done she rowed on, and now came to the second opening in the cliff. This was much wilder than the first, for outside of it, to the east, the waves of the North Sea broke in all their violence, and with the breaking of each a great sheet of water came drifting over the wall of piled up boulders. Again Maggie kept out in the channel, and, pulling with all her might, passed again into the shelter of the cliff. Here the water was stiller, for the waves were breaking directly behind the sheltering cliff, and the sound of them was heard high overhead in the rushing wind.

Maggie drew close to the rock, and, hugging it, crept on her outward way. There was now only one danger to come, before her final effort. The great shelf of rock inside the Ship's Starn was only saved from exposure by its rise on the outer side; but here, happily, the waves did not break, they swept under the overhanging slope on the outer side, and then passed on their way; the vast depth of the water outside was their protection within. Now and then a wave broke on the edge of the Ship's Starn, and then a great wall of green water rose and rushed down the steep slope, but in the pause between Maggie passed along; and now the boat nestled on the black water, under the shelter of the very outermost wall of rock. The Ship's Starn was now her last refuge. As she hurriedly began to get the sail ready she could hear the whistling of the wind round the outer side of the rock and overhead. The black water underneath her rose and fell, but in some mysterious eddy or backwater of Nature's forces she rested in comparative calm on the very edge of the maelstrom. By contrast with the darkness of the Watter's Mou' between the towering walls of rock, the sea had some mysterious light of its own, and just outside the opening on the western side she could see the white water pouring over the sunken rocks as the passing waves exposed them, till once more they looked like teeth in the jaws of the hungry sea.

And now came the final struggle in her effort to get out to open water. The moment she should pass beyond the shelter of the Ship's Starn the easterly gale would in all probability drive her straight upon the outer reef of rocks amongst those angry jaws, where the white teeth would in an instant grind her and her boat to nothingness. But if she should pass this last danger she should be out in the open sea and might make her way to save her father. She held in her mind the spot whence she had seen the answering signal to the rockets, and felt a blind trust that God would help her in her difficulty. Was not God pleased with self-sacrifice? What could be better for a maid than to save her father from accomplished sin and the discovery which made sin so bitter to bear? "Greater love hath no man than this, that a man lay down his life for his friend." Besides there was Sailor Willy! Had not he—even he—doubted her; and might she not by this wild night's work win back her old place in his heart and his faith? Strong in this new hope, she made careful preparation for her great effort. She threw overboard the spar and got ready the tiller. Then having put the sheet round the thwart on the starboard side, and laid the loose end where she could grasp it whilst holding the tiller, she hoisted the sail and belayed the rope that held it. In the eddy of the storm behind the sheltered rock the sail hung idly for a few seconds, and in this time she jumped to the stern and held the tiller with one hand and with the other drew the sheet of the sail taut and belayed it. An instant after, the sail caught a gust of wind and the boat sprang, as though a living thing, out toward the channel. The instant the shelter was past the sail caught the full sweep of the easterly gale, and the boat would have turned over only for the strain from the floating spar line, which now did its part well. The bow was thrown round towards the wind, and the boat began rushing through the water at a terrific pace. Maggie felt the coldness of death in her heart; but in that wild moment the bravery of her nature came out. She shut her teeth and jammed the tiller down hard, keeping it in place against her thigh, with the other leg pressed like a pillar against the side of the boat. The little craft seemed sweeping right down on the outer rocks; already she could see the white wall of water, articulated into white lines like giant hairs, rushing after the retreating waves, and a great despair swept over her. But at that moment the rocks on the western side of the Watter's Mou' opened so far that she caught a glimpse of Sailor Willy's lamp reflected through the window of the coastguard hut. This gave her new hope, and with a mighty effort she pressed the tiller harder. The boat sank in the trough of the waves, rose again, the spar caught the rush of the receding wave and pulled the boat's head a point round, and then the outer rock was passed, and the boat, actually touching the rock so that the limpets scraped her side, ran free in the stormy waves beyond.

Maggie breathed a prayer as with trembling hand she unloosed the rope of the floating spar; then, having loosened the sheet, she turned the boat's head south, and, tacking, ran out in the direction where she had seen the signal light of her father's boat.

By contrast with the terrible turmoil amid the rocks, the great waves of the open sea were safety itself. No one to whom the sea is an occupation ever fears it in the open; and this fisher's daughter, with the Viking blood in her veins, actually rejoiced as the cockleshell of a boat, dipping and jerking like an angry horse, drove up and down the swell of the waves. She was a good way out now, and the whole coast-line east and west was opening up to her. The mist had gone by, or, if it lasted, hung amid the rocks inshore; and through the great blackness round she saw the lights in the windows of the castle, the glimmering lights of the village of Cruden, and far off the powerful light at Girdleness blazing out at intervals. But there was one light on which her eyes lingered fixedly—the dim window of the coastguard's shelter, where she knew that her lover kept his grim watch. Her heart was filled with gladness as she thought that by what she was doing she would keep pain and trouble from him. She knew now, what she had all along in her heart believed, that Sailor Willy would not flinch from any duty however stern and pain-laden to him it might be; and she knew, too, that neither her rugged father nor her passionate young brother would ever forgive him for that duty. But now she would not, could not, think of failing, but gripped the tiller hard, and with set teeth and fixed eyes held on her perilous way.

Time went by hour by hour, but so great was her anxiety that she never noted how it went, but held on her course, tacking again and again as she tried to beat her way to her father through the storm. The eyes of sea folk are not ordinary eyes—they can pierce the darkness wherein the vision of land folk becomes lost or arrested; and the sea and the sky over it, and the coastline, however black and dim—however low-lying or distant—have lessons of their own. Maggie began by some mysterious instinct to find her way where she wanted to go, till little by little the coast line, save for the distant lights of Girdleness and Boddam, faded out of sight. Lying as she was on the very surface of the water, she had the horizon rising as it were around her, and there is nearly always some slight sign of light somewhere on the horizon's rim. There came now and again rents in the thick clouding of the stormy sky, and at such moments here and there came patches of lesser darkness like oases of light in the desert of the ebon sea. At one such moment she saw far off to the port side the outline of a vessel well known on the coast, the revenue cutter which was the seaward arm of the preventive service. And then a great fear came over poor Maggie's heart; the sea was no longer the open sea, for her father was held in the toils of his enemies, and escape seaward became difficult or would be almost impossible, when the coming morn would reveal all the mysteries that the darkness hid. Despair, however, has its own courage, and Maggie was too far in her venture now to dread for more than a passing moment anything which might follow. She knew that the Sea Gull lay still to the front, and with a beating heart and a brain that throbbed with the eagerness of hope and fear she held on her course. The break in the sky which had shown her the revenue cutter was only momentary, and all was again swallowed up in the darkness; but she feared that somether such rent in the cloudy night might expose her father to his enemies. Every moment, therefore, became precious, and steeling her heart and drawing the sheet of her sail as tight as she dared, she sped on into the darkness—on for a time that seemed interminable agony. Suddenly something black loomed up ahead of her, thrown out against the light of the horizon's rim, and her heart gave a great jump, for something told her that the Powers which aid the good wishes of daughters had sent her father out of that wilderness of stormy sea. With her sea-trained eyes she knew in a few moments that the boat pitching so heavily was indeed the Sea Gull. At the same moment someone on the boat's deck saw her sail, and a hoarse muffled murmur of voices came to her over the waves in the gale. The coble's head was thrown round to the wind, and in that stress of storm and chopping sea she beat and buffeted, and like magic her way stopped, and she lay tossing. Maggie realised the intention of the manoeuvre, and deftly swung her boat round till she came under the starboard quarter of the fishing-boat, and in the shadow of her greater bulk and vaster sail, reefed though it was, found a comparative calm. Then she called out:

"Father! It's me—Maggie! Dinna show a licht, but try to throw me a rope."

With a shout in which were mingled many strong feelings, her father leaned over the bulwark, and, with seaman's instinct of instant action, threw her a rope. She deftly caught it, and, making it fast to the bows of her boat, dropped her sail. Then someone threw her another rope, which she fastened round her waist. She threw herself into the sea, and, holding tight to the rope, was shortly pulled breathless on board the Sea Gull.

She was instantly the centre of a ring of men. Not only were her father and two brothers on board, but there were no less than six men, seemingly foreigners, in the group.

"Maggie!" said her father, "in God's name, lass, hoo cam ye oot here? Were ye ovrta'en by the storm? God be thankit that ye met us, for this is a wild nicht to be oot on the North Sea by yer lanes."

"Father!" said she, in a hurried whisper in his ear. "I must speak wi' ye alane. There isna a moment to lose!"

"Speak on, lass."

"No' before these strangers, father. I must speak alane!" Without a word, MacWhirter took his daughter aside, and, amid a muttered dissatisfaction of the strange men, signed to her to proceed. Then, as briefly as she could, Maggie told her father that it was known that a cargo was to be run that night, that the coastguard all along Buchan had been warned, and that she had come out to tell him of his danger.

As she spoke the old man groaned, and after a pause said: "I maun tell the rest. I'm no' the maister here the noo. Mendoza has me in his grip, an' his men rule here!"

"But, father, the boat is yours, and the risk is yours. It is you'll be punished if there is a discovery!"

"That may be, lass, but I'm no' free."

"I feared it was true, father, but I thocht it my duty to come!" Doubtless the old man knew that Maggie would understand fully what he meant, but the only recognition he made of her act of heroism was to lay his hand heavily on her shoulder. Then stepping forward he called the men round him, and in his own rough way told them of the danger. The strangers muttered and scowled; but Andrew and Neil drew close to their sister, and the younger man put his arm around her and pressed her to him. Maggie felt the comfort of the kindness, and laying her head on her brother's shoulder, cried quietly in the darkness. It was a relief to her pent-up feelings to be able to give way if only so far. When MacWhirter brought his tale to a close, and asked: "And now, lads, what's to be done?" one of the strangers, a brawny, heavily-built man, spoke out harshly:

"But for why this? Was it not that this woman's lover was of the guard? In this affair the women must do their best too. This lover of the guard—" He was hotly interrupted by Neil:

"Tisna the part of Maggie to tak a hand in this at a'."

"But I say it is the part of all. When Mendoza bought this man he bought all—unless there be traitors in his housed!" This roused Maggie, who spoke out quickly, for she feared her brother's passion might brew trouble:

"I hae nae part in this dreadfu' affair. It's no' by ma wish or ma aid that father has embarked in this—this enterprise. I hae naught to dae wi't o' ony kind."

"Then for why are you here?" asked the burly man, with a coarse laugh.

"Because ma father and ma brithers are in danger, danger into which they hae been led, or been forced, by ye and the like o' ye. Do you think it was for pleasure, or, O my God! for profit either, that I cam oot this nicht—an' in that?" and as she spoke she pointed to where the little boat strained madly at the rope which held her. Then MacWhirter spoke out fiercely, so fiercely that the lesser spirits who opposed him were cowed:

"Leave the lass alane, I say! Yon's nane o' her doin'; and if ye be men ye'd honour her that cam oot in sic a tempest for the sake o' the likes o' me—o' us!"

But when the strangers were silent, Neil, whose passion had been aroused, could not be quietened, and spoke out with a growing fury which seemed to choke him:

"So Sailor Willy told ye the danger and then let ye come oot in this nicht! He'll hae to reckon wi' me for that when we get in."

"He telt me naething. I saw Bella Cruickshank gie him the telegram, and I guessed. He doesna ken I'm here—and he maun never ken. Nane must ever ken that a warning cam the nicht to father!"

"But they'll watch for us comin' in."

"We maun rin back to Cuxhaven," said the quiet voice of Andrew, who had not yet spoken."

"But ye canna," said Maggie; "the revenue cutter is on the watch, and when the mornin' comes will follow ye; and besides, hoo can ye get to Cuxhaven in this wind?"

"Then what are we to do, lass?" said her father.

"Dae, father? Dae what ye should dae—throw a' this poisonous stuff that has brought this ruin owerboard. Lichten yer boat as ye will lighten yer conscience, and come hame as ye went oot!"

The bruly ran swore a great oath.

"Nothing overboard shall be thrown. These belongs not to you but to Mendoza. If they be touched he closes on your boat and ruin it is for you!" Maggie saw her father hesitate, and feared that other counsels might prevail, so she spoke out as by an inspiration. There, amid the surges of the perilous seas, the daughter's heroic devotion and her passionate earnestness made a new calm in her father's life:

"Father, dinna be deceived. Wi' this wind on shore, an' the revenue cutter ootside an' the dawn no' far off ye canna escape. Noo in the darkness ye can get rid o' the danger. Dinna lose a moment. The storm is somewhat lesser just enoo. Throw a' owerboard and come back to yer old self! What if we be ruined? We can work; and shall a' be happy yet!"

Something seemed to rise in the old man's heart and give him strength. Without pause he said with a grand simplicity:

"Ye're reet, lass, ye're reet! Haud up the casks, men, and stave them in!"

Andrew and Neil rushed to his bedding. Mendoza's men protested, but were afraid to intervene, and one after another bales and casks were lifted on deck. The bales were tossed overboard and the heads of the casks stove in till the scuppers were alternately drenched with brandy and washed with the seas.

In the midst of this, Maggie, knowing that if all were to be of any use she must be found at home in the morning, quietly pulled her boat as close as she dared, and slipping down the rope managed to clamber into it. Then she loosed the painter; and the wind and waves took her each instant farther and farther away. The sky over the horizon was brightening every instant, and there was a wild fear in her heart which not even the dull thud of the hammers as the casks were staved in could allay. She felt that it was a race against time, and her overexcited imagination multiplied her natural fear; her boat's head was to home, steering for where she guessed was the dim light on the cliff, towards which her heart yearned. She hauled the sheets close—as close as she dared, for now speed was everything if she was to get back unseen. Well she knew that Sailor Willy on his lonely vigil would be true to his trust, and that his eagle eye could not fail to note her entry when once the day had broken. In a fever of anxiety she kept her eye on the Girdleness light by which she had to steer, and with the rise and fall of every wave as she swept by them, threw the boat's head a point to the wind and let it fall away again.

The storm had nearly spent itself, but there were still angry moments when the mist was swept in masses before fresh gusts. These, however, were fewer and fewer, and in a little while she ceased to heed them or even to look for them, and at last her eager eye began to discern through the storm the flickering lights of the little port. There came a moment when the tempest poured out the lees of its wrath in one final burst of energy, which wrapped the flying boat in a wraith of mist.

And then the tempest swept onward, shoreward, with the broken mist showing white in the springing dawn like the wings of some messenger of coming peace.

# Chapter IV

MATTERS LOOKED SERIOUS ENOUGH ON the Sea Gull when the
time came in which rather the darkness began to disappear than the
light to appear. Night and day have their own mysteries, and their
nascence is as distant and as mysterious as the origin of life. The sky and
the waters still seemed black, and the circle in which the little craft lived
was as narrow as ever; but here and there in sky and on sea were faint
streaks perceptible rather than distinguishable, as though swept thither
by the trumpet blast of the messenger of the dawn. Mendoza's men
did not stint their curses nor their threats, and Neil with passionate
violence so assailed them in return that both MacWhirter and Andrew
had to exercise their powers of restraint. But blood is hot, and the lives
of lawless men are prone to make violence a habit; the two elder men
were anxious that there should be no extension of the present bitter
bickering. As for MacWhirter, his mind was in a whirl and tumult of
mixed emotions. First came his anxiety for Maggie when she had set
forth alone on the stormy sea with such inadequate equipment. Well the
old fisherman knew the perils that lay before her in her effort to win the
shore, and his heart was postively sick with anxiety when every effort of
thought or imagination concerning her ended in something like despair.
In one way he was happier than he had been for many months; the
impending blow had fallen, and though he was ruined it had come
in such a time that his criminal intent had not been accomplished.
Here again his anxiety regarding Maggie became intensified, for was
it not to save him that she had set forth on her desperate enterprise.
He groaned aloud as he thought of the price that he might yet have to
pay—that he might have paid already, though he knew it not as yet—for
the service which had saved him from the after-consequences of his sin.
He dared not think more on the subject, for it would, he feared, madden
him, and he must have other work to engross his thoughts. Thus it was
that the danger of collision between Neil and Mendoza's men became an
anodyne to his pain. He knew that a quarrel among seamen and under
such conditions would be no idle thing, for they had all their knives, and
with such hot blood on all sides none would hesitate to use them. The
whole of the smuggled goods had by now been thrown overboard, the
tobacco having gone the last, the bales having been broken up. So heavy
had been the cargo that there was a new danger in that the boat was too
much lightened. As Mendoza had intended that force as well as fraud

was to aid this venture he had not stuck at trifles. There was no pretence of concealment and even the ballast had made way for cask and box and bale. The Sea Gull had been only partially loaded at Hamburg, but when out of sight of port her cargo had been completed from other boats which had followed, till, when she started for Buchan, she was almost a solid mass of contraband goods. Mendoza's men felt desperate at this hopeless failure of the venture; and as Neil, too, was desperate, in a different way, there was a grim possibility of trouble on board at any minute.

The coming of the dawn was therefore a welcome relief, for it united—if only for a time—all on board to try to avert a common danger.

Lighter and lighter grew the expanse of sea and sky, until over the universe seemed to spread a cool, pearly grey, against which every object seemed to stand starkly out. The smugglers were keenly on the watch, and they saw, growing more clearly each instant out of the darkness, the black, low-lying hull, short funnel, and tapering spars of the revenue cutter about three or four miles off the starboard quarter. The preventive men seemed to see them at the same time, for there was a manifest stir on board, and the cutter's head was changed. Then MacWhirter knew it was necessary to take some bold course of action, for the Sea Gull lay between two fires, and he made up his mind to run then and there for Port Erroll.

As the Sea Gull drew nearer in to shore the waves became more turbulent, for there is ever a more orderly succession in deep waters than where the onward rush is broken by the undulations of the shore. Minute by minute the dawn was growing brighter, and the shore was opening up. The Sea Gull, lightened of her load, could not with safety be thrown across the wind, and so the difficulty of her tacks was increased. The dawn was just shooting its first rays over the eastern sea when the final effort to win the little port came to be made.

The harbour of Port Erroll is a tiny haven of refuge won from the jagged rocks that bound the eastern side of Cruden Bay. It is sheltered on the northern side by the cliff which runs as far as the Watter's Mou', and separated from the mouth of the Water of Cruden, with its waste of shifting sands, by a high wall of concrete. The harbour faces east, and its first basin is the smaller of the two, the larger opening sharply to the left a little way in. At the best of times it is not an easy matter to gain the harbour, for only when the tide has fairly risen is it available at all, and the rapid tide which runs up from the Scaurs makes in itself a difficulty at such times. The tide was now at three-quarters flood, so that in as far as water was concerned there was no difficulty; but the fierceness of the waves which sent up a wall of white water all along the cliffs looked ominous indeed.

As the Sea Gull drew nearer to the shore, considerable commotion was caused on both sea and land. The revenue cutter dared not approach so close to the shore, studded as it was with sunken rocks, as did the lighter draughted coble; but her commander evidently did not mean to let this be to the advantage of the smuggler. A gun was fired to attract the authorities on shore, and signals were got ready to hoist.

The crowd of strangers who thronged the little port had instinctively hidden themselves behind rock and wall and boat, as the revelation of the dawn came upon them, so that the whole place presented the appearance of a warren when the rabbits are beginning to emerge after a temporary scare. There were not wanting, however, many who stood out in the open, affecting, with what nonchalance they could, a simple business interest at the little port. Sailor Willy was on the cliff between the guard-house and the Watter's Mou', where he had kept his vigil all the night long. As soon as possible after he had sent out his appeal for help the lieutenant had come over from Collieston with a boatman and three men, and these were now down on the quay waiting for the coming of the Sea Gull. When he had arrived, and had learned the state of things, the lieutenant, who knew of Willy Barrow's relations with the daughter of the suspected man, had kindly ordered him to watch the cliff, whilst he himself with the men would look after the port. When he had first given the order in the presence of the other coastguards, Willy had instinctively drawn himself up as though he felt that he, too, had come under suspicion, so the lieutenant took the earliest opportunity when they were alone of saying to Willy:

"Barrow, I have arranged your duties as I have done, not by any means because I suspect that you would be drawn by your sympathies into any neglect of duty—I know you too well for that—but simply because I want to spare you pain in case things may be as we suspect!"

Willy saluted and thanked him with his eyes as he turned away, for he feared that the fullness of his heart might betray him. The poor fellow was much overwrought. All night long he had paced the cliffs in the dull routine of his duty, with his heart feeling like a lump of lead, and his brain on fire with fear. He knew from the wildness of Maggie's rush away from him that she was bent on some desperate enterprise, and as he had no clue to her definite intentions he could only imagine. He thought and thought until his brain almost began to reel with the intensity of his mental effort; and as he was so placed, tied to the stake of his duty, that he could speak with no one on the subject, he had to endure alone, and in doubt, the darkness of his soul, tortured alike by hopes and fears, through all the long night. At last, however, the pain exhausted itself, and doubt became its own anodyne. Despair has its calms—the backwaters of fears—where the tired imagination may rest awhile before the strife begins anew.

With joy he saw that the storm was slackening with the coming of the dawn; and when the last fierce gust had swept by him, screaming through the rigging of the flagstaff overhead, and sweeping inland the broken fragments of the mist, he turned to the sea, now of a cool grey with the light of the coming dawn, and swept it far and wide with his glass. With gladness—and yet with an ache in his heart which he could not understand—he realised that there was in sight only one coble—the Sea Gull—he knew her well—running for the port, and farther out the hull and smoke, the light spars and swift lines of the revenue cutter, which was evidently following her. He strolled with the appearance of leisureliness, though his heart was throbbing, towards the cliff right over the little harbour, so that he could look down and see from close quarters all that went on. He could not but note the many strangers dispersed about, all within easy distance of a rush to the quay when the boat should land, or the way in which the lieutenant and his men seemed to keep guard over the whole place. As first the figures, the walls of the port, the cranes, the boats, and the distant headlands were silhouetted in black against the background of grey sea and grey sky; but as the dawn came closer each object began to stand out in its natural proportions. All kept growing clearer and yet clearer and more and more thoroughly outlined, till the moment came when the sun, shooting over the horizon, set every living thing whose eyes had been regulated to the strain of the darkness and the twilight blinking and winking in the glory of the full light of day.

Eagerly he searched the faces of the crowd with his glass for Maggie, but he could not see her anywhere, and his heart seemed to sink within him, for well he knew that it must be no ordinary cause which kept Maggie from being one of the earliest on the look-out for her father. Closer and closer came the Sea Gull, running for the port with a speed and recklessness that set both the smugglers and the preventive men all agog. Such haste and such indifference to danger sprang, they felt, from no common cause, and they all came to the conclusion that the boat, delayed by the storm, discovered by the daylight, and cut off by the revenue cutter, was making a desperate push for success in her hazard. And so all, watchers and watched, braced themselves for what might come about. Amongst the groups moved the tall figure of Mendoza, whispering and pointing, but keeping carefully hidden from the sight of the coastguards. He was evidently inciting them to some course from which they held back.

Closer and closer came the Sea Gull, lying down to the scuppers as she tacked; lightened as she was she made more leeway than was usual to so crank a boat. At last she got her head in the right direction for a run in, and, to the amazement of all who saw her, came full tilt into the outer basin, and, turning sharply round, ran into the inner basin under bare poles. There was not one present, smuggler or coastguard, who did not set down the daring attempt as simply suicidal. In a few seconds the boat stuck on the sandbank accumulated at the western end of the basin and stopped, her bows almost touching the side of the pier. The coastguards had not expected any such manoeuvre, and had taken their place on either side of the entrance to the inner basin, so that it took them a few seconds to run the length of the pier and come opposite the boat. The crowd of the smugglers and the smugglers' friends was so great that just as Neil and his brother began to shove out a plank from the bows to step ashore there was so thick a cluster round the spot that the lieutenant as he came could not see what was going on. Some little opposition was made to his passing through the mass of people, which was getting closer every instant, but his men closed up behind, and together they forced a way to the front before anyone from the Sea Gull could spring on shore. A sort of angry murmur— that deep undertone which marks the passion of a mass—arose, and the lieutenant, recognising its import, faced round like lightning, his revolver pointed straight in the faces of the crowd, whilst the men with him drew their cutlasses.

To Sailor Willy this appearance of action gave a relief from almost intolerable pain. He was in feverish anxiety about Maggie, but he could do nothing—nothing; and to an active and resolute man this feeling is in itself the worst of pain. His heart was simply breaking with suspense, and so it was that the sight of drawn weapons, in whatever cause, came like an anodyne to his tortured imagination. The flash of the cutlasses woke in him the instinct of action, and with a leaping heart he sprang down the narrow winding path that led to the quay.

Before the lieutenant's pistol the crowd fell back. It was not that they were afraid—for cowardice is pretty well unknown in Buchan—but authority, and especially in arms, has a special force with law-breakers. But the smugglers did not mean going back altogether now that their booty was so close to them, and the two bodies stood facing each other when Sailor Willy came upon the scene and stood beside the officers. Things were looking pretty serious when the resonant voice of MacWhirter was heard:

"What d'ye mean, men, crowdin' on the officers. Stand back, there, and let the coastguards come aboard an they will. There's naught here that they mayn't see."

The lieutenant turned and stepped on the plank—which Neil had by this time shoved on shore—and went on board, followed by two of his men, the other remaining with the boatman and Willy Barrow on the quay. Neil went straight to the officer, and said:

"I want to go ashore at once! Search me an ye will!" He spoke so rudely that the officer was angered, and said to one of the men beside him:

"Put your hands over him and let him go," adding, sotto voce, "He wants a lesson in manners!" The man lightly passed his hands over him to see that he had nothing contraband about him, and, being satisfied on the point, stood back and nodded to his officer, and Neil sprang ashore, and hurried off towards the village.

Willy had, by this time, a certain feeling of relief, for he had been thinking, and he knew that MacWhirter would not have been so ready to bring the coastguards on board if he had any contraband with him. Hope did for him what despair could not, for as he instinctively turned his eyes over the waste of angry sea, for an instant he did not know if it were the blood in his eyes or, in reality, the red of the dawn which had shot up over the eastern horizon.

Mendoza's men, having been carefully searched by one of the coastguards, came sullenly on shore and went to the back of the crowd, where their master, scowling and white-faced, began eagerly to talk with them in whispers. MacWhirter and his elder son busied themselves with apparent nonchalance in the needful matters of the landing, and the crowd seemed holding back for a spring. The suspense of all was broken by the incoming of a boat sent off from the revenue cutter, which, driven by four sturdy oarsmen, and steered by the commander himself, swept into the outer basin of the harbour, tossing amongst the broken waves. In the comparative shelter of the wall it turned, and driving into the inner basin pulled up on the slip beyond where the Sea Gull lay. The instant the boat touched, six bluejackets sprang ashore, followed by the commander, and all seven men marched quietly but resolutely to the quay opposite the Sea Gull's bow. The oarsmen followed, when they had hauled their boat up on the slip. The crowd now abandoned whatever had been its intention, and fell back looking and muttering thunder.

By this time the lieutenant was satisfied that the coble contained nothing that was contraband, and, telling its master so, stepped on shore just as Neil, with his face white as a sheet, and his eyes blazing, rushed back at full speed. He immediately attacked Sailor Willy:

"What hae ye dune wi' ma sister Maggie?"

He answered as quietly as he could, although there shot through his heart a new pain, a new anxiety:

"I know naught of her. I haven't seen her since last night, when Alice MacDonald was being married. Is she not at home?"

"Dinna ye ken damned weel that she's no'. Why did ye send her oot?" And he looked at him with the menace of murder in his eyes. The lieutenant saw from the looks of the two men that something was wrong, and asked Neil shortly:

"Where did you see her last?" Neil was going to make some angry reply, but in an instant Mendoza stepped forward, and in a loud voice gave instruction to one of his men who had been on board the Sea Gull to take charge of her, as she was his under a bill of sale. This gave Neil time to think, and his answer came sullenly:

"Nane o' ye're business—mind yer ain affairs!" MacWhirter, when he had seen Neil come running back, had realised the worst, and leaned on the taffrail of the boat, groaning. Mendoza's man sprang on board, and, taking him roughly by the shoulder, said:

"Come, clear out here. This boat is to Mendoza; get away!" The old man was so overcome with his feelings regarding Maggie that he made no reply, but quietly, with bent form, stepped on the plank and gained the quay. Willy Barrow rushed forward and took him by the hand and whispered to him:

"What does he mean?"

"He means," said the old man in a low, strained voice, "that for me an' him, an' to warn us she cam oot last nicht in the storm in a wee bit boat, an' that she is no' to her hame!" and he groaned. Willy was smitten with horror. This, then, was Maggie's high and desperate purpose when she left him. He knew now the meaning of those despairing words, and the darkness of the grave seemed to close over his soul. He moaned out to the old man: "She did not tell me she was going. I never knew it. O my God!" The old man, with the protective instinct of the old to the young, laid his hand on his shoulder, as he said to him in a broken voice:

"A ken it, lad! A ken it weel! She tell't me sae hersel! The sin is a' wi' me, though you, puir lad, must e'en bear yer share o' the pain!" The commander said quietly to the lieutenant:

"Looks queer, don't it—the coastguard and the smuggler whispering?"

"All right," came the answer, "I know Barrow; he is as true as steel, but he's engaged to the old man's daughter. But I gather there's something queer going on this morning about her. I'll find out. Barrow," he added, calling Willy to him, "what is it about MacWhirter's daughter?"

"I don't know for certain, sir, but I fear she was out at sea last night."

"At sea," broke in the commander; "at sea last night—how?"

"She was in a bit fishin'-boat," broke in MacWhirter. "Neighbours, hae ony o' ye seen her this mornin'? 'Twas ma son Andra's boat, that he keeps i' the Downans!"—another name for the Watter's Mou'. A sad silence that left the angry roar of the waves as they broke on the rocks and on the long strand in full possession was the only reply.

"Is the boat back in the Watter's Mou'?" asked the lieutenant sharply.

"No." said a fisherman. "A cam up jist noo past the Barley Mill, an' there's nae boat there."

"Then God help her, an' God forgie me," said MacWhirter, tearing off his cap and holding up his hands, "for A've killed her—her that sae loved her auld father, that she went oot alane in a bit boat i' the storm i' the nicht to save him frae the consequence o' his sin." Willy Barrow groaned, and the lieutenant turned to him: "Heart, man, heart! God won't let a brave girl like that be lost. That's the lass for a sailor's wife. 'Twill be all right—you'll be proud of her yet!"

But Sailor Willy only groaned despite the approval of his conscience; his words of last night came back to him. "Ye're no fit wife for me!" Now the commander spoke out to MacWhirter:

"When did you see her last?"

"Aboot twa o'clock i' the mornin'."

"Where?"

"Aboot twenty miles off the Scaurs."

"How did she come to leave you?"

"She pulled the boat that she cam in alongside the coble, an' got in by hersel—the last I saw o' her she had hoisted her sail an' was running nor'west. . . But A'll see her nae mair—a's ower wi' the puir, brave lass—an' wi' me, tae, that killed her—a's ower the noo—a's ower!" and he covered his face with his hands and sobbed. The commander said kindly enough, but with a stern gravity that there was no mistaking:

"Do I take it rightly that the girl went out in the storm to warn you?"

"Ay! Puir lass—'twas an ill day that made me put sic a task on her—God forgie me!" and there and then he told them all of her gallant deed.

The commander turned to the lieutenant, and spoke in the quick, resolute, masterful accent of habitual command:

"I shall leave you the bluejackets to help—send your men all out, and scour every nook and inlet from Kirkton to Boddam. Out with all the lifeboats on the coast! And you, men!" he turned to the crowd, "turn out, all of you, to help! Show that there's some man's blood in you, to atone if you can for the wrong that sent this young girl out in a storm to save her father from you and your like!" Here he turned again to the lieutenant, "Keep a sharp eye on that man—Mendoza, and all his belongings. We'll attend to him later on: I'll be back before night."

"Where are you off to, Commander?"

"I'm going to scour the sea in the track of the storm where that gallant lass went last night. A brave girl that dared what she did for her father's sake is not to be lost without an effort; and, by God, she shan't lack it whilst I hold Her Majesty's command! Boatswain, signal the cutter full steam up—no, you! We mustn't lose time, and the boatswain comes with me. To your oars, men!"

The seamen gave a quick, sharp "Hurrah!" as they sprang to their places, whilst the man of the shore party to whom the order had been given climbed the sea-wall and telegraphed the needful orders; the crowd seemed to catch the enthusiasm of the moment, and scattered right and left to make search along the shore. In a few seconds the revenue boat was tossing on the waves outside the harbour, the men laying to their work as they drove her along, their bending oars keeping time to the swaying body of the commander, who had himself taken the tiller. The lieutenant said to Willy with thoughtful kindness:

"Where would you like to work on the search? Choose which part you will!" Willy instinctively touched his cap as he answered sadly:

"I should like to watch here, sir, if I may. She would make straight for the Watter's Mou'!"

## Chapter V

THE SEARCH FOR THE MISSING girl was begun vigorously, and carried on thoroughly and with untiring energy. The Port Erroll lifeboat was got out and proceeded up coast, and a telegram was sent to Kirkton to get out the lifeboat there, and follow up the shore to Port Erroll. From either place a body of men with ropes followed on shore keeping pace with the boat's progress. In the meantime the men of each village and hamlet all along the shore of Buchan from Kirkton to Boddam began a systematic exploration of all the openings on the coast. Of course there were some places where no search could at present be made. The Bullers, for instance, was well justifying its name with the wild turmoil of waters that fretted and churned between its rocky walls, and the neighbourhood of the Twa Een was like a seething caldron. At Dunbuy, a great sheet of foam, perpetually renewed by the rush and recoil of the waves among the rocks, lay like a great white blanket over the inlet, and effectually hid any flotsam or jetsam that might have been driven thither. But on the high cliffs around these places, on every coign of vantage, sat women and children, who kept keen watch for aught that might develop. Every now and again a shrill cry would bring a rush to the place and eager eyes would follow the pointing hand of the watcher who had seen some floating matter; but in every case a few seconds and a little dispersing of the shrouding foam put an end to expectation. Throughout that day the ardour of the searchers never abated. Morning had come rosy and smiling over the waste of heaving waters, and the sun rose and rose till its noonday rays beat down oppressively. But Willy Barrow never ceased from his lonely vigil on the cliff. At dinner-time a good-hearted woman brought him some food, and in kindly sympathy sat by him in silence, whilst he ate it. At first it seemed to him that to eat at all was some sort of wrong to Maggie, and he felt that to attempt it would choke him. But after a few mouthfuls the human need in him responded to the occasion, and he realised how much he wanted food. The kindly neighbour then tried to cheer him with a few words of hope, and a many words of Maggie's worth, and left him, if not cheered, at least sustained for what he had to endure.

All day long his glass ranged the sea in endless, ever-baffled hope. He saw the revenue boat strike away at first towards Girdleness, and then turn and go out to where Maggie had left the Sea Gull; and then under full steam churn her way north-west through the fretted seas. Now and again he saw boats, far and near, pass on their way; and as they went through that wide belt of sea where Maggie's body might be drifting with the wreckage of her boat, his heart leaped and fell again under stress of hope and despair. The tide fell lower and ever lower, till the waves piling into the estuary roared among the rocks that paved the Watter's Mou'. Again and again he peered down from every rocky point in fear of seeing amid the turmoil—what, he feared to think. There was ever before his eyes the figure of the woman he loved, spread out rising and falling with the heaving waves, her long hair tossing wide and making an aureole round the upturned white face. Turn where he would, in sea or land, or in the white clouds of the summer sky, that image was ever before him, as though it had in some way burned into his iris.

Later in the afternoon, as he stood beside the crane, where he had met Maggie the night before, he saw Neil coming towards him, and instinctively moved from the place, for he felt that he would not like to meet on that spot, forever to be hallowed in his mind, Maggie's brother with hatred in his heart. So he moved slowly to meet him, and when he had got close to the flagstaff waited till he should come up, and swept once again the wide horizon with his glass—in vain. Neil, too, had begun to slow his steps as he drew nearer. Slower and slower he came, and at last stood close to the man whom in the morning he had spoken to with hatred and murder in his heart.

All the morning Neil had worked with a restless, feverish actively, which was the wonder of all. He had not stayed with the searching party with whom he had set out; their exhaustive method was too slow for him, and he soon distanced them, and alone scoured the whole coast as far as Murdoch Head. Then in almost complete despair, for his mind was satisfied that Maggie's body had never reached that part of the shore, he had retraced his steps almost at a run, and, skirting the sands of Cruden Bay, on whose wide expanse the beakers still rolled heavily and roared loudly, he glanced among the jagged rocks that lay around Whinnyfold and stretched under the water away to the Scaurs. Then he came back again, and the sense of desolation complete upon him moved his passionate heart to sympathy and pity. It is when the soul within us feels the narrow environments of our selfishness that she really begins to spread her wings.

Neil walked over the sandhills along Cruden Bay like a man in a dream. With a sailor's habit he watched the sea, and now and again had his attention attracted by the drifting masses of seaweed torn from its rocky bed by the storm. In such tossing black masses he sometimes thought Maggie's body might lie, but his instinct of the sea was too true to be long deceived. And then he began to take himself to task. Hitherto he had been too blindly passionate to be able to think of anything but his own trouble; but now, despite what he could do, the woe-stricken face of Sailor Willy would rise before his inner eye like the embodiment or the wraith of a troubled conscience. When once this train of argument had been started, the remorseless logic which is the mechanism of the spirit of conscience went on its way unerringly. Well he knew it was the ill-doing of which he had a share, and not the duty that Willy owed, that took his sister out alone on the stormy sea. He knew from her own lips that Willy had neither sent her nor even knew of her going, and the habit of fair play which belonged to his life began to exert an influence. The first sign of his change of mind was the tear which welled up in his eye and rolled down his cheek. "Poor Maggie! Poor Willy!" he murmured to himself, half unconsciously, "A'll gang to him an' tak it a' back!" With this impulse on him he quickened his steps, and never paused till he saw Willy Barrow before him, spy-glass to eye, searching the sea for any sign of his lost love. Then his fears, and the awkwardness which a man feels at such a moment, no matter how poignant may be the grief which underlies it, began to trip him up. When he stood beside Willy Barrow, he said, with what bravery he could:

"I tak it a' back, Sailor Willy! Ye werena to blame! It was oor daein'! Will ye forgie me?" Willy turned and impulsively grasped the hand extended to him. In the midst of his overwhelming pain this was some little gleam of sunshine. He had himself just sufficient remorse to make the assurance of his innocence by another grateful. He knew well that if he had chosen to sacrifice his duty Maggie would never have gone out to sea, and though it did not even occur to him to repent of doing his duty, the mere temptation—the mere struggle against it, made a sort of foothold where flying remorse might for a moment rest. When the eyes of the two men met, Willy felt a new duty rise within his. He had always loved Neil, who was younger than himself, and was Maggie's brother, and he could not but see the look of anguish in the eyes that were so like Maggie's. He saw there something which in one way transcended his own pain, and made him glad that he had not on his soul the guilt of treachery to his duty. Not for the wide world would he have gazed into Maggie's eyes with such a look as that in his own. And yet—and yet—there came back to him with an over-powering flood of anguish the thought that, though the darkness had mercifully hidden it, Maggie's face, after she had tempted him, had had in it something of the same expression. It is a part of the penalty of being human that we cannot forbid the coming of thoughts, but it is a glory of humanity that we can wrestle with them and overcome them. Quick on the harrowing memory of Maggie's shame came the thought of Maggie's heroic self-devotion: her true spirit had found a way out of shame and difficulty, and the tribute of the lieutenant, "That's the lass for a sailor's wife!" seemed to ring in Willy's ears. As far as death was concerned, Willy Barrow did not fear it for himself, and how could he feel the fear for another. Such semblance of fear as had been in his distress was based on the selfishness which is a part of man's love, and in this wild hour of pain and distress became a thing of naught. All this reasoning, all this sequence of emotions, passed in a few seconds, and, as it seemed to him all at once, Willy Barrow broke out crying with the abandon which marks strong men when spiritual pain breaks down the barriers of their pride. Men of Willy's class seldom give way to their emotions. The prose of life is too continuous to allow of any habit of prolonged emotional indulgence; the pendulum swings back from fact to fact and things go on as before. So it was with Sailor Willy. His spasmodic grief was quick as well as fierce, like an April shower; and in a few seconds he had regained his calm. But the break, though but momentary, had relieved his pent-up feelings, and his heart beat more calmly for it. Then some of the love which he had for Maggie went out to her brother, and as he saw that the pain in his face did not lessen, a great pity overcame him and he tried to comfort Neil.

"Don't grieve, man. Don't grieve. I know well you'd give your heart's blood for Maggie"—he faltered as he spoke her name, but with a great gulp went on bravely: "There's your father—her father, we must try and comfort him. Maggie," here he lifted his cap reverently, "is with God! We, you and I, and all, must so bear ourselves that she shall not have died in vain." To Sailor Willy's tear-blurred eyes, as he looked upward, it seemed as if the great white gull which perched as he spoke on the yard of the flagstaff over his head was in some way an embodiment of the spirit of the lost girl, and, like the lightning phantasmagoria of a dream, there flitted across his mind many an old legend and eerie belief gained among the wolds and barrows of his Yorkshire home.

There was not much more to be said between the men, for they understood each other, and men of their class are not prone to speak more than is required. They walked northwards, and for a long time they stood together on the edge of the cliff, now and again gazing seawards, and ever and anon to where below their feet and falling tide was fretting and churning amongst the boulders at the entrance of the Watter's Mou'.

Neil was unconsciously watching his companion's face and following his thoughts, and presently said, as though in answer to something that had gone before: "Then ye think she'll drift in here, if onywhere?" Willy started as though he had been struck, for there seemed a positive brutality in the way of putting his own secret belief. He faced Neil quickly, but there was nothing in his face of any brutal thought. On the contrary, the lines of his face were so softened that all his likeness to his sister stood out so markedly as to make the heart of her lover ache with a fresh pang—a new sense, not of loss, but of what he had lost. Neil was surprised at the manner of his look, and his mind working back gave him the clue. All at once he broke out:

"O Willy mon, we'll never see her again! Never! never! till the sea gies up its dead, what can we dae, mon? what can we dae? what can we dae?"

Again there was a new wrench to Sailor Willy's heart. Here were almost Maggie's very words of the night before, spoken in the same despairing tone, in the same spot, and by one who was not only her well-beloved brother, but who was, as he stood in this abandonment of his grief, almost her living image. However, he did not know what to say, and he could do nothing but only bear in stolid patient misery the woes that came upon him. He did all that could be done—nothing—but stood in silent sympathy and waited for the storm in the remorseful young man's soul to pass. After a few minutes Neil recovered somewhat, and, pulling himself together, said to Willy with what bravery he could:

"A'll gang look after father. A've left him ower lang as't is!" The purpose of Maggie's death was beginning to bear fruit already.

He went across the field straight towards where his father's cottage stood under the brow of the slope towards the Water of Cruden. Sailor

Willy watched him go with sadness, for anything that had been close to Maggie was dear to him, and Neil's presence had been in some degree an alleviation of his pain.

During the hours that followed he had one gleam of pleasure—something that moved him strangely in the midst of his pain. Early in the morning the news of Maggie's loss had been taken to the Castle, and all its household had turned out to aid vigorously in the search. In his talk with the lieutenant and his men, and from the frequent conversation of the villagers, the Earl had gathered pretty well the whole truth of what had occurred. Maggie had been a favourite with the ladies of the Castle, and it was as much on her account as his own that the Mastership of the Harbour had been settled prospectively on MacWhirter. That this arrangement was to be upset since the man had turned smuggler was taken for granted by all, and already rumour and surmise were busy in selecting a successor to the promise. The Earl listened but said nothing. Later on in the day, however, he strolled up the cliff where Willy paced on guard, and spoke with him. He had a sincere regard and liking for the fine young fellow, and when he saw his silent misery his heart went out to him. He tried to comfort him with hopes, but, finding that there was no response in Willy's mind, confined himself to praise of Maggie. Willy listened eagerly as he spoke of her devotion, her bravery, her noble spirit, that took her out on such a mission; and the words fell like drops of balm on the seared heart of her lover. But the bitterness of his loss was too much that he should be altogether patient, and he said presently:

"And all in vain! All in vain! she lost, and her father ruined, his character gone as well as all his means of livelihood—and all in vain! God might be juster than to let such a death as hers be in vain!"

"No, not in vain!" he answered solemnly, "such a deed as hers is never wrought in vain. God sees and hears, and His hand is strong and sure. Many a man in Buchan for many a year to come will lead an honester life for what she has done; and many a woman will try to learn her lesson in patience and self-devotion. God does not in vain put such thoughts into the minds of His people, or into their hearts the noble bravery to carry them out."

Sailor Willy groaned. "Don't think me ungrateful, my lord," he said, "for your kind words—but I'm half wild with trouble, and my heart is sore. Maybe it is as you say—and yet—and yet the poor lass went out to save her father and here he is, ruined in means, in character, in prospects—for who will employ him now just when he most wants it. Everything is gone—and she gone too that could have helped and comforted him!"

As he spoke there shot through the mind of his comforter a thought followed by a purpose not unworthy of that ancestor, whose heroism and self-devotion won an earldom with an ox-yoke as its crest, and the circuit of a hawk's flight as its dower. There was a new tone in the Earl's voice as he spoke:

"You mean about the harbour-mastership! Don't let that distress you, my poor lad. MacWhirter has lapsed a bit, but he has always borne an excellent character, and from all I hear he was sorely tempted. And, after all, he hasn't done—at least completed—any offence. Oh!" and here he spoke solemnly, "poor Maggie's warning did come in time. Her work was not in vain, though God help us all! she and those that loved her paid a heavy price for it. But even if MacWhirter had committed the offence, and it lay in my power, I should try to prove that her noble devotion was not without its purpose—or its reward. It is true that I might not altogether trust MacWhirter until, at least, such time as by good service he had re-established his character. But I would and shall trust the father of Maggie MacWhirter, that gave her life for him; and well I know that there isn't an honest man or woman in Buchan that won't say the same. He shall be the harbourmaster if he will. We shall find in time that he has reared again the love and respect of all men. That will be Maggie's monument; and a noble one too in the eyes of God and of men!"

He grasped Willy's hand in his own strong one, and the hearts of both men, the gentle and the simple, went out each to the other, and became bound together as men's hearts do when touched with flame of any kind.

When he was alone Willy felt somehow more easy in his mind. The bitterest spirit of all is woe—the futility of Maggie's sacrifice—was gone, exorcised by the hopeful words and kind act of the Earl, and the resilience of his manhood began to act.

And now there came another distraction to his thoughts—an ominous weather change. It had grown colder as the day went on, but now the heat began to be oppressive, and there was a deadly stillness in the air; it was manifest that another storm was at hand. The sacrifice of the night had not fully appeased the storm-gods. Somewhere up in that Northern Unknown, where the Fates weave their web of destiny, a tempest was brewing which would soon boil over. Darker and darker grew the sky, and more still and silent and oppressive grew the air, till the cry of a sea-bird or the beating of the waves upon the rocks came as distinct and separate things, as though having no counterpart in the active world. Towards sunset the very electricity in the air made all animate nature so nervous that men and women could not sit quiet, but moved restlessly. Susceptible women longed to scream out and vent their feelings, as did the cattle in the meadows with their clamorous lowing, or the birds wheeling restlessly aloft with articulate cries. Willy Barrow stuck steadfastly to his post. He had some feeling—some presentiment that there would soon be a happening—what, he knew not; but, as all his thoughts were of Maggie, it must surely be of her. It might have been that the thunderous disturbance wrought on a system overtaxed almost beyond human endurance, for it was two whole nights since he had slept. Or it may have been that the recoil from despair was acting on his strong nature in the way that drives men at times to desperate deeds, when they rush into the thick of battle, and, fighting, die. Or it may simply have been that the seaman in him spoke through all the ways and offices of instinct and habit, and that with the foreknowledge of coming stress woke the power that was to combat with it. For great natures of the fighting kind move with their surroundings, and the spirit of the sailor grew with the storm pressure whose might he should have to brave.

Down came the storm in one wild, frenzied burst. All at once the waters seemed to rise, throwing great sheets of foam from the summit of the lifting waves. The wind whistled high and low, and screamed as it swept through the rigging of the flagstaff. Flashes of lightning and rolling thunderclaps seemed to come together, so swift their succession. The rain fell in torrents, so that within a few moments the whole earth seemed one filmy sheet, shining in the lightning flashes that rent the black clouds, and burn and rill and runlet roared with rushing water. All through the hamlet men and women, even the hardiest, fled to shelter—all save the one who paced the rocks above the Watter's Mou', peering as he had done for many an hour down into the depths below him in the pauses of his seaward glance. Something seemed to tell him that Maggie was coming closer to him. He could feel her presence in the air and the sea; and the memory of that long, passionate kiss, which had made her his, came back, not as a vivid recollection, but as something of the living present. To and fro he paced between the flagstaff and the edge of the rocks; but each turn he kept further and further from the flagstaff, as though some fatal fascination was holding him to the Watter's Mou'. He saw the great waves come into the cove tumbling and roaring; dipping deep under the lee of the Ship's Starn in wide patches of black, which in the dark silence of their onward sweep stood out in strong contrast to the white turmoil of the churning waters under his feet. Every now and again a wave greater than all its fellows—what fishermen call the "sailor's wave"—would ride in with all the majesty of resistless power, shutting out for a moment the jagged whiteness of the submerged rocks, and sweeping up the cove as though the bringer of some royal message from the sea.

As one of these great waves rushed in, Willy's heart beat loudly, and for a second he looked around as though for some voice, from whence he knew not, which was calling to him. Then he looked down and saw, far below him, tossed high upon the summit of the wave, a mass that in the gloom of the evening and the storm looker like a tangle of wreckage—spar and sail and rope—twirling in the rushing water round a dead woman, whose white face was set in an aureole of floating hair. Without a word, but with the bound of a panther, Willy Barrow sprang out on the projecting point of rock, and plunged down into the rushing wave whence he could meet that precious wreckage and grasp it tight.

DOWN IN THE VILLAGE THE men were talking in groups as the chance of the storm had driven them to shelter. In the rocket-house opposite the Salmon Fisher's store had gathered a big cluster, and they were talking eagerly of all that had gone by. Presently one of them said:

"Men, oughtn't some o' us to gang abeen the rocks and bide a wee wi' Sailor Willy? The puir lad is nigh daft wi' his loss, an 'a wee bit companionship wouldna be bad for him." To which a sturdy youth answered as he stepped out:

"A'l go bide wi' him. It must be main lonely for him in the guard-house the nicht. An' when he's relieved, as A hear he is to be, by Michael Watson ower frae Whinnyfold, A'll gang wi' him or tak him hame wi' me. Mither'll be recht glad to thole for him!" and drawing his oilskin closer round his neck he went out in the storm. As he walked up the path to the cliff the storm seemed to fade away—the clouds broke, and through the wet mist came gleams of fading twilight; and when he looked eastwards from the cliff the angry sea was all that was of storm, for in the sky was every promise of fine weather to come. He went straight to the guard-house and tried to open the door, but it was locked; then he went to the side and looked in. There was just sufficient light to see that the place was empty. So he went along the cliff looking for Willy. It was now light enough to see all round, for the blackness of the sky overhead had passed, the heavy clouds being swept away by the driving wind; but nowhere could he see any trace of the man he sought. He went all along the cliff up the Watter's Mou', till, following the downward trend of the rock, and splashing a way through the marsh—now like a quagmire, so saturated was it with the heavy rainfall—he came to the shallows opposite the Barley Mill. Here he met a man from The Bullers, who had come along by the Castle, and him he asked if he had seen Willy Barrow on his way. The decidedly negative answer "A've seen nane. It's nae a night for ony to be oot than can bide wi'in!" made him think that all might not be well with Sailor Willy, and so he went back again on his search, peering into every hole and cranny as he went. At the flagstaff he met some of his companions, who, since the storm had passed, had come to look for weather signs and to see what the sudden tempest might have brought about. When they heard that there was no sign of the coastguard they separated, searching for him, and shouting lest he might have fallen anywhere and hear their voices.

All that night they searched, for each minute made it more apparent that all was not well with him; but they found no sign. The waves still beat into the Watter's Mou' with violence, for though the storm had passed the sea was a wide-stretching mass of angry waters, and curling white crowned every wave. But with the outgoing tide the rocky bed of the cove broke up the waves, and they roared sullenly as they washed up the estuary.

In the grey of the morning a fisher-boy rushed up to a knot of men who were clustered round the guard-house and called to them:

"There's somethin' wollopin' aboot i' the shallows be the Barley Mill! Come an' get it oot! It looks like some ane!" So there was a rush made to the place. When they got to the islands of sea-grass the ebbing tide had done its work, and stranded the "something" which had rolled amid the shallows.

There, on the very spot whence the boat had set sail on its warning errand, lay its wreckage, and tangled in it the body of the noble girl who had steered it—her brown hair floating wide and twined round the neck of Sailor Willy, who held her tight in his dead arms.

The requiem of the twain was the roar of the breaking waves and the screams of the white birds that circled round the Watter's Mou'.

End

# Bengal Roses

## Chapter I

THE MAIL HAD BROUGHT FROM Nice a cardboard box of flowers. The study was hot and close, despite the open windows, so when I opened it the scent of the roses filled the air with a new fragrance. I took out the spray on the top, a magnificent cluster of great pink Bengal roses; but the day of glory of this kind is a short one, and the journey was long; the mere motion of lifting the spray finished the work of destruction. I held in my hand only a bare stalk, whilst the moss green carpet was scattered with the great petals of the flowers. From the open box still came the sweet, simple fragrance of some more hardy Vulcan roses, and that cool, earthy smell which clings around damp moss.

And then a flood of memory rushed over me, aided by that best of mnemonics, a once-known perfume. I lit a cigar, and as I sat in my easy chair, with the roses beside me, the light of the July evening paled and paled, till I sat alone in the darkness. Twenty years of hopes, struggles and success were obliterated, and I lived again an old chapter of my boy's life, which contained the fragments of a romance. All came back so vividly that time and space were annihilated. I did not merely remember; once more the things were! Ah, me! that chapter of boyish love and jealousy, which has neither youth nor age! Once again I remembered how these things worked into other lives, and then I lived the past again.

A SWEET OLD GARDEN OF a country rectory, large and full of queer nooks and shady places. Great lime trees on one side, where in summer the bees kept up a perpetual hum, and under whose shelter the moss grew deep and green. Just without the shadow, so that there was shelter from wind, but no lack of sun, a great trellis, covered with a luxuriant growth of Bengal roses. Hard by, some prim old trees of yew and juniper and arbor vitae. But of all these the rose trellis was, of old, the most sweet, and is now most full of memories.

Beside it some former incumbent had placed an old Greek marble seat, a segment of a circle adorned with flutings and finished with tigers' heads and claws. This had been brought from Greece long, long ago by a wealthy patron and given to the rector as a tribute to his archaeological worth. Time had wrought its changes, and the damp and the shade had filled the hollows and crevices of the carved marble with delicate green. This was always a favorite haunt of mine, and here I mainly learned my lessons and also studied such romances as were available. Being a delicate child, I had been sent to live with the rector, so that I might get plenty of exercise and fresh air and country living. Mr. Petersen was an old man, and, although never a brilliant scholar, was an excellent teacher for such a lad as I was. Mrs. Petersen was nearly as old as her husband, and, as their circumstances were not good, I have no doubt that, though the money that my parents paid was hardly earned, it was a welcome addition to the housekeeping. There was but one servant in the house; the gardener attended to the cows and pigs and my pony, these being the only animals kept. After a while I grew quite strong and hardy, and by myself took long walks and rides all around the country. It was my habit to study the county map which hung in the hall, and to so arrange my rambles that by degrees I came to have a local topographical knowledge certainly not possessed by my tutor, whose age and circumstances and whose habits of a quiet, retired life debarred him from such exercise. I had no companion of my own age, except when at home in London, for at Westoby Puerorum the children were few, and of such a kind that I had but little in common with them. We met at Sunday school, and as I did not care for their horseplay and got disgusted with their perpetual lying, they voted me a muff, and left me alone—after I had proved in one or two pitched battles that at any rate I was not a coward.

I was about 12 years old when there came an addition to our circle in the shape of a grand-daughter of Mrs. Petersen by her first marriage, an orphan, with neither home nor friends. Before she came there were anxious discussions between the old people as to the probable result of her coming. It was evident there was some old cause for anxiety, and once I heard a remark which puzzled me. It was made by Mrs. Petersen:—

"It is so good of you, Edward, and, my dear. I see through all your sweet forbearance; but it is not right that you should be troubled with folk that don't belong to you. Arabella always took her own way in spite of me—and of her poor father—and maybe her daughter will want to do the same. We have lived too peacefully, you and I, dear, all these years to be willing to let any disturbance come through someone we never saw," and the old lady wiped away a quiet tear.

"Nay, my dear," said the rector, "I might well say, as Ruth said to Naomi, 'Thy people shall be my people.' And, my dear, your God and mine is hers also, and we are all children of his family. Let the little girl come. I doubt not that he will watch over her and mould all things to good purpose." And so it was that Bella Devanti came to us.

I do not think that anyone was so pleased at the idea of her coming as I was. The old people at concern for the future, and the maid, who saw in prospect more waiting and more cooking and more washing and another bed to make, grumbled to the gardener, who, though he had no prospect of added work, grumbled sympathetically. For me there was no concern. In those days I suppose I took it for granted, as other boys do, then beds are made and victuals cooked and clothes washed by some dispensation of providence specially arranged for the benefit of boys. The young bird when it opens its mouth where the provender abided by the parents' instinct takes little thought of whence or how it comes. The thinking belongs to a later period, when there are other little beaks open and other tiny voices that clamor at need.

When Arabella Devanti arrived I proceeded with the simple, selfish, directness of a schoolboy to fall in love with her, despite the great gulf of five years fixed between us. In this I was not alone, for the feeling was shared in common but the whole household. Even the maid and the gardener gave in, and, as is the wont of such, changed the form or cause of their grumbling, for of course of grumbling was perennial. When Maria, that was the maid, found that Miss Devanti insistent on making her own bed and looking after herself, as she alleged that she had always done, and began straightway to take apart in the labor of the household, she grew almost rebellious. Finally a compromise was arrange, to the effect that Bella was to be allowed to help in the cooking if she left the rougher domestic work to Maria. Her pretty little foreign ways became a new pleasure in the household, and there was, I am bound to say, a marked improvement in the cuisine. She used to do things with eggs that I dream of yet.

Bella and I became at once great friends. She helped me with my lessons, and taught me music and drawing; and I taught her to ride my pony, and to play cricket, and le-gras, and other games of an old-fashioned kind, which were a tradition in the rectory. We used to sit everyday, when the weather was fine on the old marble seat; and the Bengal roses, all summer long, used to keep shedding their great petals over the green moss beneath. There I learned my lessons; Bella was a good mistress, for she would not allow any trifling or inattention. I began to feel, after a while, that her sway was a strong one, and that if I wanted her to do anything I must begin by being master of my work.

Quite three years passed in this way, and I was now a good sized lump of a boy, and began to fancy myself a man. In school this feeling generally finds an outlet in a plentitude of hats, and a choice of neckties; but in our rustic life there was no such outlet, and even the increase of my passion for Bella did not move me to try to add to my attractions in her eyes. She was always most kind to me, and there was between us a genuine affection. She used to tell me all her little secrets, and I to tell her mine. Still, I never felt quite satisfied. There was not that complete abandonment or effacement of herself—that losing her own individuality in that of the other—which the masculine lover, even from his cradle, seems to demand. There always was for her, even in those day dreams which she shared with me, to be some order of things other than present, something to come yet of quite a different kind to that which existed. Indeed, some unknown individual was to make his appearance was to charm us both by his worth and beauty and the gallantry of his bearing. With a seeming generosity she always insisted on giving me a portion of the pleasure of his society, and on my angry remonstrance and disclaimer to share at all in his hateful presence she would laugh softly through her blushes, and then, after a while, tried to soothe me by some added deference to my wishes—my wishes regarding something else. As a matter fact I grew intensely jealous, and the keen eyes of jealousy found food everywhere and in everything. Although I loved Bella more than ever, I began to have moments of what I believed to be hate for her also.

It was at this time that we had a break in the monotony of our lives at Westoby Puerorum. Our squire had in his youth been a pupil of Mr. Petersen. Indeed, it was after the young squire went to college that the old squire presented him to the living; and whenever the young squire—now the squire himself, and no longer young—came to Westoby Grange he always managed to pay a visit to his old tutor. This necessitated something of a drive, for the Grange was in Westoby Magnus, and was distant some eight miles. He had been away for a long time, for his winters were spent abroad, and he had several other estates, so that his summers were divided. He chiefly lived at a place nearly two-hundred miles away, where the ground was high and the air more bracing. This time he had only a small party at the Grange, and when he rode over to see Mr. Petersen, he took with him a young gentleman to whom at first I took a liking. It was only when I found that Bella had taken a liking to him also that I began to recognise in him certain evil qualities. He seemed as frank as a boy for all that he was a captain in a crack cavalry regiment. He was sitting on the marble seat between Bella and me before either of us seemed to realise the fact that he was only a stranger after all. Even after I had begun to realise his bad qualities—and perhaps to invent some for him also—I could not but like him. He was such a handsome fellow, so bright and cheery, and with such a winning manner, that I could not help it; but I could not forgive Bella for liking him also, and the more jealous I grew up him the more unreasonably angry I became with her. He did not remain very long, for the quire's visit was but a flying one; but before he went he promised to ride over from Cotterham, where he was quartered, and to bring me some flies of his own tying, which he found most effective in the waters of our county. When he had gone, Bella and I sat under the Bengal roses and talked of him in the shade from the afternoon sun. It angered me whenever Bella found new points to admire in him, and so after a while I began to turn the conversation. It was now getting on for sunset, and it was our habit to take the clouds round the setting sun as a garden wherein to found our romances. This evening, with some instinct or intention, I grew more definite that ever in my description of the hero who was to come, making him in every essential the exact opposite to Captain Chudleigh, even to the extent of making him a great noble instead of a "honourable" and a younger son, which the captain was. Bella would not give her own views as to what the hero should be like, but she differed with me point by point as we went along. This made me very angry, and in my boyish petulance I stood up and said to her passionately:

"I believe you're in love with him, Bella! Take him if you want to! I don't care!" I was striding off when she rose up and ordered me so imperiously to come back that, without thinking of any opposition to her wishes, I returned to the seat. She had sat down again; her dark eyes were blazing. She held her hands for a moment clasped over her heart, and then after a pause said to me:—

"Robert"—this was cutting, for hitherto she had never called me anything but "Bobby"—"Robert, you have no right to say such a thing to me—to anybody. You are born a gentleman, and nothing could justify such an affront. I take it now that you do not know better, and that you were angry, though what cause of anger there is I fail to see. But such a thing must never occur again! You are getting old enough to think for yourself." I was crushed. "Getting old enough!"—"getting!" I who had for years been nurturing a passion for a grown-up woman! It left me speechless.

I sat silent a while, and felt myself grown red and white by turns; and then a gush of some feeling came over me, and despite all I could do the tears came to my eyes and ran through the fingers which I held before my face. In an instant Bella changed, and spoke to me lovingly, entreating pardon, and trying, as she spoke, to take away my hands. I repulsed her, and would have risen and run away, but that she held me tight. I suppose the difference in our ages became then more marked than it had ever been, for, with sudden impulse, I threw myself on my knees on the grass beside her, and, hiding my head in her lap, had my cry out, whilst she tenderly stroked my hair, silent all the time, with the instinct of a true woman.

We seemed better friends than ever after that night. I could not but feel that there had come some sort of chasm between us: but the recognition of such a thing was the first step to its bridging, and although I said no more of any feeling which might between her and Captain Chudleigh I tacitly recognised such a thing as possible and respected it.

Less than a week elapsed before Captain Chudleigh paid his promised visit, and when he came Bella was the one who seemed to avoid him, whilst he and I grew great friends. We all three sat under the roses after luncheon—we called it lunch to strangers, but it was in reality our dinner—and were together all the time except for half an hour when I was rummaging in the attic for an old book of etching by Piranesi which Bella thought she had seen there some months before. I did not find it, however, and when I came back they were both silent, and he was just about taking his leave. They had quite forgotten about the book. I offered to ride a part of the way the Captain Chudleigh, and he acquiesced heartily, although I thought I saw him make a queer kind of sace to Bella when he thought I was not looking. He was silent for a while after we had started, but presently he grew quite gay and alughed and sang and made jokes to me as we rode along. When it was time for me to return he promised that he would ride over again some day soon. When I got back I found Bella still sitting under the roses, and so abstracted that she started when I spoke to her.

Some days afterwards I got a line from Cotterham, saying that Captain Chudleigh would on the following day ride over to lunch with the squire; and that he would, if he might, look into the rectory on his way back, when perhaps Miss Devanti and I would give him a cup of tea under the roses. He came, and we had tea on the marble seat, Mrs. Petersen not being very well had lain down, and the rector was writing his sermon for the next day. It was a very pleasant afternoon, and we all enjoyed ourselves. When the sun was setting Bella sent me to look if Captain Chudleigh's horse had been cared for, and I went willingly, for he rode beautiful horses. When I came back Bella and the captain say silent at either of the seat, he with a rose in his buttonhole which had not been there before. This gave me a new pang jealously, and I did not offer to ride part of his way, although I had been looking forward for the last twenty-four hours to the pleasure of so doing. Bella and I said but little to each other than evening.

The next day I went out for a long walk, taking my lunch with me, as I usually did on such occasions. This expedition had been planned nearly a week before, for I was to explore an old ruin which I had never visited on the high road I went to strike across the country; but in leaping my first ditch I turned my ankle, and had to abandon my expedition, for that day at all events. However, I ate my lunch, and when I felt sufficiently recovered began my journey home. It was very tiring and my ankle pained me much, so that when I got into our own grounds I was thoroughly fagged out. The afternoon sun was beating strongly down, and the shade of the trellised roses, with the cool, green moss, looked so inviting that I lay down and forthwith fell asleep.

I waked to hear voices on the other side of the thick trellis—Bella's voice and Captain Chudleigh's! They were whispering; but, low as their voices were, I could hear distinctly, and what I heard made my heart beat and my ears tingle. He was telling Bella of his love for her, and she murmured an answer that satisfied him, and then I heard their kiss. Boy as I was I knew that I had no right to be there, and so I crawled away out of earshot, being careful to keep the trellis between us, and reached my own room without anyone seeing me. I lay down on my bed, with my heart and my temples throbbing, and felt anew all the pangs of jealousy with despair added. I waited there till the evening fell, and then, when I knew I would meet no one, left the house and came round to the front door, making what noise I reasonably could, and limped in to where the family were at supper.

They were all concerned when they heard my accident, which I took care not to say had taken place early in the day. Fortunately the pain and fatigue accounted for my pale face and nervous manner. Bella wanted herself to bathe my ankle, but I insisted that Maria should do it. She was looking so radiantly happy that I could bear the sight of her.

All the next day Bella was very sweet, and we sat on the marble seat, I with my ankle bandaged on a chair in front of me. As the day wore on I expected that Bella would make some confidence, and I was by that time prepared—after some upbraiding—to give her my sympathy and approval. Self-love demanded that the occasion should not pass unnoticed, But the confidence never came, and I grew resolved that if she chose to keep her secret she might, and that I also would keep mine. The only satisfaction I had—and when I look back on it I think it was a pretty mean one—was that I would not let her do the smallest service for my lame ankle. On this point I was as doggedly resolved as I could be about anything.

Bella's secrecy seemed to me not a negative but positive thing. I almost began to think that she had told me a falsehood, and to imagine all sorts of things. Being ever on the watch I did detect now and then some small acts of secretiveness rendered necessary by her possession of so big a secret. For instance towards the end of the week there came a letter which made her blush and her breast heave, but she never said a word of it. Of course, I pretended not to notice. That night I lay awake thinking of it, and as I lay awake I heard a very low whistle. I rose softly and looked out of the window. I heard a stir in Bella's room, which was next to mine, and in a few minutes I saw her step out of the porch—the door was never locked or bolted at the rectory—and steal softly in the direction of the rose trellis. This struck me as so strange that, in spite of the sense of the meanness of the act, I determined to see what it all meant. My jealously had already told me, but I wanted to be sure, I stole softly to the back of the trellis. There was a yellow moon, and the shadows were black so I came close unnoticed. There I heard the voice I expected and feared to hear, and which if I had not heard what have disappointed me.

Captain Chudleigh's voice was resonant and resolute, and there was something in it of a triumph, but Bella's voice was faint and tremulous, nevertheless it was sweet, sweeter than ever, with a thrill in it which I had never heard before, and which made me as I listened grow cold with despair, although my heart flamed anew with jealously. I heard Captain Chudleigh say:—

"I have got it—the bishop's secretary got it for me—and now we can be married where and when we will!" There was no answer; but she evidently drew close to him, for I heard the sound of a kiss—a long one.

Then she said:—

"Oh! Reggy, is it necessary that we keep it a secret? It will pain my grandfather and grandmother so much, they have been so good to me!"

His answer was given with decision.

"My dear Bella, it is necessary. My father would noy allow our marriage if he knew of it in time. You see, neither of my two brothers has any family, and the governor says that as I have no fortune I must marry money, and as I must succeed I must marry rank."

Bell said, shyly:

"Then, Reggy, we had better say goodbye. Here! Now! If all our parents are against us, where can our happiness lie?"

Reggy evidently drew her to him as he whispered, tenderly:

"But we love each other, Bella: and the governor will forgive us when we are married," and there was much more to the same effect. Then Captain Chudleigh took out a paper and read it to her in the moonlight. I can see that his arm was round her as they stood in the moonlight. I can see that his arm was round her as they stood in the moonlight, hidden from the house by the yew tree behind the marble seat. When they showed signs of going I lay down close, close behind the trellis, for I was afraid to stir lest they should see me. After some efforts and many goodbyes tore herself away, but not before Reginald Chudleigh had secured her promise that she would meet him at Mirkenfield church at seven in the morning on the second day following.

When Bella had stolen back to her room her lover stood looking after her, and I heard him mutter a low curse—an angry, dissatisfied curse on himself—and then as he turned away I heard him say it:—

"Poor little girl! Poor little girl! It is too devilish bad! So sweet and trustful! If I didn't love her so; or if I had more money!" And then I lost sight of him as he passed into the shadowy darkness of the trees.

After a while I, too, stole back to my bed. My mind was in a turmoil, but through all its murkiness I remember a fixed resolution in my heart—that I, too, would be at Mirkenfield, for I felt that some wrong wasn't intended to Bella. I knew the place, for I had two or three times been over there. It was a tiny village, which time and desertion from economic causes had made tinier still. The church was an old one almost in ruins, which was left always open since no one ever went into it between Sunday and Sunday.

## Chapter II

THE NEXT DAY WHEN WE sat together on the old marble seat Bella was very tender with me. I was full of emotion myself, for, now I was sure that she loved another—vanity is so great in boys that I still held myself to be a rival—I could find it in my heart to be very tender to her. Once or twice I mentioned the name of the Mirkenfield's, but when I saw that she held her peace, though the quick blush betrayed her somewhat, I said no more, but waived.

As she said goodnight that evening Bella's voice and manner were full of tenderness, and as she lay in her room I heard her more than once sob. That night was like a never-ending nightmare to me, and I sometimes wondered whether it was not all a dream.

It was a nearly ten miles to Mirkenfield, so at the earliest glint of dawn I rose, under the impression that I had no slept, and stole downstairs. I heard the clock strike four as I stepped out of the porch, keeping out of sight of Bella's window. As I had not heard Bella stir I took it that she was still asleep. I went into th fields, for I did not want anyone to see me, and at length struck the road beyond the nine clump. There, before me on the road, I saw hurrying along none other than Bella! I slipped into the wood again, and ran and walked as quickly as I could so that I might get well ahead without her seeing me. As I knew the shortcuts I easily effected this object, and within some two and a half hours arrived within sight of Mirkenfield. Then I slipped into the fields and woods again, and came round to the back of the church. Keeping round the corner I saw two men waiting, carefully hidden behind a great clump of yew trees from the sight of any casual stranger passing on the road. One of them was Captain Chudleigh, and the other was the groom whom I had seen with him when he wrote over to Westoby Grange.

Captain Chudleigh had only just arrived, and was making inquiries from the groom. From their secretive manner, however, and the mysterious way they looked round them, I came to the conclusion that there was some mischief on foot, and so I stole softly behind the yew trees and listened. I heard the master say:—

"Is he here?"

"Yes, sir: in the vestry. I was afraid he might be seen and it would not do as he is a stranger."

"Has he all the properties which requires?"

"Yes, sir; his surplice and bands and the bogus registry books, and all. He is fly one, sir, up to every move on the board. But beg perdon, sir. He says he must have the cash beforehand. He didn't want no credit to the spondoolicks down. Them was his very words."

"Here it is. You share it, I suppose?" and he threw disdainfully to the groom a bag which chinked as the latter caught it.

"There," he said, "take it and be sure you clear out as quick as you can. Remember it is penal servitude for the pair of you if it should come out afterwards."

"All right, sir. No chance of anything going wrong. No one ever goes into the old church, and it being a church—she—the lady won't have no suspicion. My eye, sir, but he's a clever one at fixing things."

"Take care it is all right. Be here to witness as the clock strikes. In the meantime look after the horses while I go up the road to meet her." Then he murmured again as he had done that night:

"All right! Indeed. All wrong! And a nice pack scoundrels we are, with me the biggest of them!"

I began to realize to the full the cruel wrong that was intended, and my mind was made up what I should do. I stoke away from the yews, and when I was out of the earshot ran up to the parson's house, which was across the graveyard from the church. I rang the bell softly and waited with my heart in my mouth. The door was opened by the parson's *locum tenens*, a tall, powerful, fresh-coloured young man, with a frank eye and a strong, resolute jaw.

I gasped out, "May I see you at once, and privately?" He eyed me for a moment and with a look which began with a smile and ended with a frown, and said quickly:

"Come in here, my boy!" and threw open the study door, which he shut carefully behind him. "Now," he said, "tell me frankly what it is and without fear."

I told him who I was and then what I knew and suspected. He interrupted me but once, when he said, angrily:

"The scoundrels, and in the very church, too. Well, we shall see!"

When I had finished he said:

"You have done very wisely in coming to me, and at once. Come with me now, and do not say anything unless I ask you. This is a case when we must both be silent and discrete—for the present at all events." He hurried across the churchyard, walking on the grass so that his footsteps would not sound. I followed him. He opened the vestry door quickly and we went in. As the door opened a man turned round to us, a clean-shaven man, who had on a surplice and bands, and whose face had an evil, crafty look. He grew very pale when he came in, and glanced around hurriedly as for a way of escape. The parson strode forward, and with a wrestler's grip, caught him by the throat, and motioning me to open the door took him and pushed him before him across the churchyard and into his own study. At first the man tried to struggle; but he very soon gave up the idea as he felt how powerless he was in the grasp of the athletic young parson, and he was evidently afraid to cry out. When we were in the study his captor made him sit down, and then said:—

"Now tell me all about it."

The fellow threw himself upon his knees and began a confession of how he had been employed to take part in a mock marriage. As he was speaking, the clock on the mantel chimed the quarter to seven, so the parson stopped him:—

"There is no time to lose. I shall tie you up and leave you here for a while. If you try to struggle or cry out I shall at once take you myself to the nearest police-station, and give you in charge. In the meantime I shall see how matters go, and then decide how I shall deal with you."

He then got some cord and tied up the fellow most scientifically, gagging him with a gag extemporized from a handkerchief. He then put on his surplice; and, coming out, locked the study door behind him. He called to his housekeeper, and told her to come quietly into the church as the clock struck the hour, and to bring the gardener with her. Then, telling me to come with him, he went back across the churchyard. He told me to remain in the vestry, but to look at the service through the door held partially open, and to remain unseen as long as I could.

Presently, I saw Bella and Captain Chudleigh come into the church, followed a little after by the groom, who sat in a corner behind a pillar. Then, but a minute later, there came, unobserved by Bella or Captain Chudleigh, an old man and woman, who I surmised to be the housekeeper and gardner. When the groom saw them he sheared off a little, so as to keep the pillar between them and himself. The parson stepped out from the vestry. When the groom saw him he started and grew very pale. He half rose as if to move off, but the parson, who had to pass close to him, said:—

"You are a witness, I suppose. Come up close!" And thence forward he kept an eye on him to see that he did not run away. When the bridal pair stood before the Communion rails the parson said:—

"You have a license from the Bishop, I understand; show it to me." Captain Chudleigh took it from his pocket and handed it to him. He read it through carefully and then asked him:—

"Are you the Hon. Captain Reginald Chudleigh, bachelor, mentioned in this document?"

"I am."

Then turning to Bella he asked:

"Are you the Arabella Devanti, spinster, mentioned herein?"

"I am."

Then he proceeded with the marriage service. As there was no one to give away the bride he performed that function himself. As Chudleigh answered "I will" his voice faltered and he grew very, very pale, but Bella's voice was low and clear and fraught with love as she made her acceptance.

When the service was over the parson said a few brief words, hoping that the marriage performed that day might lead to peace here and hereafter, and exhorted the married pair that they should trust each other and be ever true. He finished with a solemn warning that they had that day undertaken a new life, and that whatever wrongs and faults had been should be now forgotten, except to afford them a light and warning against evils to come. Whilst this short homily was being delivered, Captain Chudleigh looked ill at ease and impatient, and now and again bit his lips; but he controlled himself, and was silent.

Then they came into the vestry, and I hid behind a surplice hanging on the wall. On the table were the great volumes of the registry which the parson had taken from the chest, and in the one of the marriages the young parson proceeded to write the new marriage. He had beckoned the two old people to come along with the groom, and said, as he asked them to sign:

"Witnesses are necessary by law, so I have asked these two who were present to add their names." So they both signed, Captain Chudleigh again repressing his impatience. Then the groom and the old people went out, and Captain Chudleigh, who had begun to have an anxious look on his face, turning to Bella, said:

"Will you wait a moment in the church, my dear, whilst I say a word to the clergyman?"

Bella smiled at him lovingly, and saying as she shook her finger at him archly, "Don't be long," went out and waited in the church Soon as she was gone Captain Chudleigh closed the vestry door, and, coming close to the clergyman, said to him in a low voice:—

"Is it all right?"

"Yes; it is all right!" answered the other, with an exceedingly firm, not to say aggressive, manner.

"All is arranged?"

"All as it should be."

"Then my man will pay you the sum agreed on. He had the money. The books, are they all right?"

"Quite right!"

Captain Chudleigh began to move to the door, but he looked ill at ease, and his manner was a hanging dog manner. As he put his hand on the latch to open it the parson spoke:

"Captain Chudleigh!"

He turned and raised his eyebrows interrogatively.

"Captain Chudleigh, are you satisfied that you are duly and solemnly married?"

Chudleigh let go the latch and came close as he asked, angrily, in a low voice:

"What the devil do you mean?"

"I mean this," said the other, unconsciously throwing himself into a fighting attitude, for his college days were too recent to be easily forgotten, "that you came here with the intention of committing a foul and dastard wrong to a sweet and innocent woman, and of committing it by the help of the machinery of the Church and the law, and in the very shadow of God's own House. But God be praised! Your wickedness was known in time, and you are now surely and securely married as can be by the Church's law and the law of the land. Oh, man, have you no shame—no remorse? You are young! You cannot be all hard and bad! It is not too late! You have a sweet and good wife, though in not confiding in her relatives she had run a fearful risk, and for her sake I shall be silent so far as I can. But go down on your knees and thank the Almighty that He has vouchsafed in His mercy to save you from the actual commission of such a grievous sin—though the moral guilt be heavy on you all the same."

For half a minute Captain Chudleigh hung his head, and a dark scowl spread over his face; but then the man in him asserted itself, and with the fierce stamp of his foot, as if he was crushing something evil, he said:

"You are right! I am a black-hearted scoundrel, and unfit to tie the shoe of that sweet woman. But, thank God! It has not been too late. Let me tell you—though I can't expect you to believe me—that I was as miserable over this dastard act as a man could be, and to the last day of my life, I shall thank you for having saved her—and me!"

"Do not thank me," said the young clergyman, moved. "Thank Almighty God, and hereafter in your life show by your deeds that you are grateful for so great a mercy. And thank also one other, only for whose quick thought and energy this evil would have been wrought."

Chudleigh turned quickly. "Tell me who it is, so that I may give him thanks."

"You can thank him when he's a man. He is only a boy now."

"Bobby? God bless him."

"And now, Captain Chudleigh, join your wife; and take my advice—go straight with her to her uncle, and tell him of the marriage. I shall deal with those scoundrels of yours so that they may not try to blackmail you. Your conduct—your later conduct—has made one willing to help you. Send the groom to me presently; and, let me advise you, get rid of him as soon as you can. He is a dangerous man."

But Chudleigh would not go at once.

"No!" said he, "I have a duty to my wife; and it had better begin now. I shall have no secrets from her! Let me tell her all, and then, if she will forgive me, we can begin life afresh."

So the parson took me into the graveyard, and we stayed there nearly half an hour, till Bella came and called me in. Her eyes were swollen with crying; but despite it, she looked happy, and Chudleigh's face was also not without it traces of deep emotion. Bella thanked the parson, and held his hand whilst she did so; and then she took me in her arms and kissed me, but said never a word: she knew what I understood. Then the Captain came and held out his hand, and said with a tremor in his voice:

"Won't you shake hands, Bobby? Bella has forgiven me, or I would not dark to ask!" So we shook hands.

Then Bella and her husband drove back to Westoby Puerorum and I walked back as quickly as I could; but they had gone before I arrived, and Mr. and Mrs. Petersen were beginning to realise what had happened.

I suppose the young parson took strong measures with the rascals and frightened them effectually, for they went away and were never troublesome.

And now Bella is a countess, and her husband and her children adore her. And on the anniversary of her wedding day she and her husband always send me a bunch of roses from wherever they may be. If there are no roses then they send someother flower that has memories—perhaps lest any of us should forget.

# A Yellow Duster

When my old friend Stanhope came unexpectedly, late in life, into a huge fortune he went traveling round the world for a whole year with his wife before settling down. We had been friends in college days, but I had seen little of him during his busy professional life. Now, however, in our declining years, chance threw us together again, and our old intimacy became renewed. I often stayed with him, both at Stanhope Towers and in his beautiful house in St. James's-square; and I noticed that wherever he was, certain of his curios went with him. He had always been a collector in a small way, and I have no doubt that in his hard-working time, though he had not the means to gratify his exquisite taste, the little he could do served as a relief to the worry and tedium of daily toil. His great-uncle, from whom he inherited, had a wonderful collection of interesting things; and Stanhope kept them much in the same way as he had found them—not grouped or classified in anyway, but placed in juxtaposition as taste or pleasure prompted. There was one glass-covered table which stood always in the small drawing room, or rather sitting room, which Mr. and Mrs. Stanhope held as their own particular sanctum. In it was a small but very wonderful collection of precious and beautiful things; an enormous gold scarib with graven pictures on its natural panels, such a scarib as is not to be found even amongst the wonderful collection at Leyden; a carved star ruby from Persia, a New Zealand chieftain's head wrought in greenstone, a jade amulet from Central India, an enamelled watch with an exquisitely-painted miniature of Madame du Barri, a perfect Queen Anne farthing laid in a contemporary pounce-box of gold and enamel, a Borgia ring, a coiled serpent with emerald eyes, a miniature of Peg Woffington by Gainsborough, in a quaint frame of aqua marines, a tiny Elzivir Bible in cover of lapis lazuli mounted in red gold, a chain of wrought iron as delicate as hair, and many other such things, which were not only rare and costly as well as beautiful, but each of which seemed to have some personal association.

And yet in the very middle of the case was placed a common cotton duster, carefully folded. It was not only coarse and common in its texture, but it was of such crude and vulgar colours that it looked startlingly out of place in such a congeries of beautiful treasures. It was so manifestly a personal relic that for a long time I felt some diffidence in alluding to it; though I always looked at that particular table, for as Mrs. Stanhope was good enough to share her husband's liking for me, I was always treated as one of themselves and admitted to their special sitting-room.

One day when Stanhope and I were bending over the case, I remarked:—

"I see one treasure there which must be supreme, for it has not the same intrinsic claim as the others!" He smiled as he said:—

"Oh, that! You are right; that is one of the best treasures I have got. Only for it all the rest might be of no avail!"

This piqued my curiosity, so I said:—

"May an old friend hear the story? Of course, it is evident by its being there that it is not a subject to be shunned."

"Right again!" he answered, and opening the case he took out the duster and held it in his hand lovingly. I could see that it was not even clean; it was one that had manifestly done service.

"You ask the missis," he said: "and if she doesn't mind I'll tell you with pleasure."

At tea that afternoon, when we were alone, I asked Mrs. Stanhope if I might hear the story. Her reply was quick and hearty:—

"Indeed you may! Moreover, I hope I may hear it, too!"

"Do you mean to tell me," I said, "that you don't know why it is there?" She smiled as she replied:—

"I have often wondered; but Frank never told me, and I never asked. It is a long, long time since he kept it. It used to be in the safe of his study till he came into Stanhope Towers; and then he put it where it is now. He keeps the key of the table himself, and no one touches the things in it but him. You noticed, I suppose, that everything in it is fastened down for travelling?"

When I told Stanhope that his wife permitted him to tell me the story, I added her own hope that she, too, might hear it. He said:

"Very well! Tonight after dinner—we are alone this evening—we will come in here and I shall tell you."

When we were alone in the room and the coffee cups had been removed he began:

"Of all the possessions I have, which come under the designation of real or personal estate, that old, dirty, flaring, common duster is the most precious. It is, and has been, a secret pleasure to me for all these years to surround it with the most pretty and costly of my treasures; for so it has a symbolical effect to me. I was once near a grave misunderstanding with my wife—indeed it had begun. This was not long into the second year of our marriage, when the bloom of young wedlock had worn off, and we had begun to settle down to the grim realities of working life. You know my wife is a good many years younger than I am, and when we married I had just about come to that time of life when a man begins to distrust himself as important in the eyes of a beautiful young woman. Lily was always so sweet to me, however, that out of her very sweetness I began to distrust her somewhat. It seemed almost unreasonable that she should be always willing to yield her wishes to mine. At first this distrust was on a very shadowy and unreal basis; but as we grew into the realities of life on small means, it was not always possible for her to forego her wishes in the same way. I had my work to do; and she had her own life to lead, and her own plans to make. I daresay I was pretty unreasonable at times. A man gets worried about his work, and if he tries to keep the worry to himself he sometimes overlooks the fact that his wife, not knowing the facts, cannot understand the almost vital importance of small arrangements which he has to make. So she unconsciously thwarts him."

Here Mrs. Stanhope came over and sat on a stool beside him, and put her hand in his. He stroked it gently and went on:—

"I was especially anxious not to worry her about this time, for there was a hope that our wishes for a child were to be realised, and in my very anxiety to save her from trouble I created the very thing I dreaded. Some little question arose between us; a matter in itself of so small importance that I have quite forgotten it, though the issues then bearing on it were big enough to be remembered. For the purpose of my work things had to be settled in my way, but I could not explain to her without letting her share the worry, and, in addition, I feared that as we were at two, my having held back anything from her might be construed into a want of confidence. Thus it was that her opposition to me became far graver than the occasion itself warranted; and in my blind helplessness, with no one to confide in, I began to fancy that the reason of her opposition was that she did not love me. Let me tell you, old friend—you cannot know, since you were never married—that when once you raise this spirit it is hard to exorcise it. It grows, and grows, and grows, like the genius in the 'Arabian Nights,' until it fills the universe. With this fatal suspicion in my mind every little act of petulance or self-will, everything done or undone, said or unsaid, became 'proof as strong as Holy Writ' that she did not love me; until I grew morbid on the subject. Like the people of old, I wanted a sign.

"One day the strain of silence became too great for me to bear. I broke my resolution of reticence, and taxed her that she did not love me. At first he laughed; for she felt, as she told me afterwards, that the idea was ridiculous. Anyhow, I did not wait to understand, or to weigh her feeling. Her laughter maddened me, and I spoke out some bitter things. 'Oh, yes, my dear, I did!' (This in response to a pressure from the hand that held his, and a warning finger of the other raised.) She tried to bear with me bravely for a while; but at length her feelings mastered her, and the tears rose in her eyes and trickled down her cheeks. But even then I was obdurate. The suspicion of weeks, and all the bitterness of it which had kept me awake so many nights, could not be allayed in a moment. I began to doubt even her very tears. They might, I thought, have come from annoyance at having to explain, from chagrin, from vexation, from anything except the real cause, true womanly and wifely feeling. Again I wanted a sign. And I got it."

His wife's hand closed harder on his; I could see the answering pressure of his hand as he went on:

"She had been dusting the little knick-knacks in the drawing room, using for the purpose a duster of a peculiarly aggressive pattern. It was one of a set put aside for this special purpose, and therefore chosen of a colour not to be confused with the rest of the domestic appliances. She still held this in her hand; and whilst I stood looking at her with something like rage in my heart, and with my brain a seething mass of doubt as to her half-hysterical sobbing, she raised the duster unconsciously to her face and began to wipe her tears away with it.

"That settled me! Here was a sign that not even a jealous idiot could mistake! Had the thing been less gaudily hideous, had it even been clean, I might still have wallowed in my doubt; but now the conviction of the genuineness of her grief swept me like a great burst of sunshine through fog, and cleared it away forever. I took her in my arms and tried to comfort her; and from that hour to this there has never been—I thank God for it with all my heart—a doubt between us. Nothing but love and trust and affection! I noticed where she placed the duster, and in the night I came and took it and put it safely away. Do you wonder now, old friend, why I value that rag; why it has a sacred value in my eyes?"

By this time Mrs. Stanhope was shading her face, and I could see the tears roll down her cheeks. "Frank, dear," she said, "let me have your key a moment?" He handed the bunch to her without a word. She selected the key, opened the table top, and took out the duster, which she kissed. Then turning to her husband, as she dried her eyes, she said, "Frank, dear, this is the second time you have made me cry in my long, happy life; but, ho, how different!" Stanhope spoke: "Lily, dear, the first time you used that duster I noticed the glaring contrast of its colour to your black hair, and now it holds its own against the coming grey," and he took her in his arms and kissed her. She turned to me and said: "I think the story was worth the telling—and the hearing—don't you? I have allowed this poor, dear old rag to remain in its place of honour all these years because my husband wished it so; but now it shall hold its place in my heart as well as his. God does not always speak in thunder; there are softer notes in the expression of His love and tenderness. Oh, Frank!"

What more she said I know not; for by this time I had stolen quietly away, leaving them alone together.

# A Young Widow

When I had dusted the little boy down and he had grown calm after his fright, I lectured him on the danger of coasting down steep hills, until at all events he had acquired some mastery of the bicycle. He seemed duly penitent, and acknowledged in his boyish way that if I had not ridden after him and steered him he might have been killed. He was still tearful when he stammered out:

"I wish my mother could have thanked you!"

"Nevermind, my boy," I said; "you don't say anything; unless you tell your father."

"Can't," he said, as his tears burst out afresh: "Father's dead years ago." I said no more, but left him at the house which he pointed out as that in which he lived. He told me that his name was Bobbie Harcourt, and he had hoped he would see me again. "Why don't you call?" he added, as he ran up the steps.

As I rode home I thought to myself that the mother of such a pretty boy must be a sweet creature. A widow, too. I noted mentally. Young widowhood is always more or less a pleasing thought to a bachelor, especially when, like myself, he is beginning to notice his hair thinning on the top. I told Bobbie where I lived, so I was not altogether surprised when next day I got a letter in a lady's hand signed "Ada Harcourt," thanking me for what she deemed the great service I had rendered for her and all her family. That letter, even after I answered it, somehow impressed me, and every morning for a week, as I shaved myself and noticed the thin place "on top," my thoughts reverted to it. I always ended by taking it from my pocket and spreading it on the dressing table in front of me.

Then I took my courage in both hands and called at Woodbine Villa. The short time which elapsed between my knock, which began boldly and ended timidly, and the opening of the door was such as I am told drowning men experience—filled with a countless multitude of embrassing memories. The trim maid who opened the door looked a little surprised when I asked if Mrs. Harcourt was at home; but with an apologetic, "Pardon me a moment, sir," darted away, leaving the door open. She came downstairs again more slowly, and, in a somewhat embarrassed, giggling way, asked me to please come in. "My mistress, sir," she said, "will be down in a few minutes, if you will kindly wait!"

I entered the pleasant drawing room and tried, in the helpless way of embarrassed visitors, to gain some knowledge of my hosts by their surroundings.

Everything was pretty; but the faces of all the pictures of photographs were strange, so that it was as with recognition of an old friend that I came across a photograph of Bobbie, evidently done some two or three years before.

I was ill at ease, for manifestly my coming had in some way disturbed the household. Overhead there was rushing about to and fro, and the sound of drawers opening and shutting, and of doors banging. I thought I could hear somewhere afar off the voice of my friend Bobbie, but in a different and lighter vein than when I had listened to his tearful promises of amendment. Then I became gravely anxious; a full sense of impropriety in calling pressed upon me, for light steps drew near the door. Then there entered the room the most beautiful young woman I thought I had ever seen.

Her youth, her dancing eyes, her pink cheeks suffused with blushes, and the full lips showing scarlet against her white teenth, seemed to shine through the deep widow's weeds which she wore as a ray of sunshine gleams through a fog. Indeed, the smile was multiplied as the gleam of golden hair seemed to make the "weeded" cap a solemn mockery. She advanced impulsively and shook me warmly by the hand, as with very genuine feeling she thanked me for my heroic rescue of her, "dear Bobbie." At first she seemed somewhat surprised at my appearance, and, seeing with a woman's instinct that I noticed it, said frankly:

"How young you are! Why, from what Bobbie told me, I thought you were an old—a much older man." The thin space seemed to become conscious, as though a wave of either heat or cold had passed over it, and as I somehow seemed to recognize in the fair widow an "understanding," soul, I bent my head some that she could see the telltale places I remarked:

"To children we grown-ups seem often older than even we are!"

In a demure way, and in a veiled, not to say smothered, voice she answered: "Ah, yes, that is so. To us who have known sorrow time passes more quickly than to their light-hearted innocence! Alas! Alas!" She stopped suddenly, and, putting her deeply edged handkerchief to her face, gasped out: "Pardon me, I shall return in a moment," and left the room hurriedly. I felt more than uncomfortable. I had evidently touched on some tender chord of memory, though what I could not guess. All I could do was to wait till she returned and then take myself off as soon as possible.

There was some talking and whispering on the stairs outside. I could not hear the words spoken, for the door was shut, but suddenly it opened, and Bobbie, red-faced and awkward, shot into the room. He was a very different boy now. There were no tears, no sadness, no contrition. He was a veritable mass of fun, full of laughter and schoolboy mirth. As he shook hands with me he said:

"I hope mother has thanked you properly!" and turned away and stamped with some kind of surprised feeling. The ways of boys are hard to understand. When Mrs. Harcourt returned, which she did very shortly, now quite composed, and looking more beautiful and more charming than ever, Bobbie slipped away. There was somehow a greater constraint about his mother. Some impalpable veil seemed to be between us: she was as if more distant from me. I recognized its import, and shortly made my adieux. As she bade me goodbye she said that we might perhaps never meet again, as she was shortly going to take the boy abroad: but that she rejoiced that it had been her privilege to meet face to face his brave preserver. She used more of such phrases, which for days after seemed to hang in my memory like sweet music. The maid, when she let me out, seemed sympathetic and deferential, but there was in her manner, a concealed levity which somehow grated on me.

For the next fortnight I tried to keep Mrs. Harcourt out of my thoughts, with the usual result. You can't serve ejectments on thoughts! They are tenants at will, their own will, and only effect struggling with them is that they banish everything else, and keep the whole field to themselves. Working or playing, walking or sleeping, walking, riding or sitting still, the sweet, beautiful eyes of Mrs. Harcourt were ever upon me, and her voice seemed to sound in my ears.

I found that my bicycle carried me, seemingly of its own will, past her door on every occasion when I had to use a lamp. Seeing at last her intention of foregin travel had not been carried out, I ventured one day, in an agony of perturbation to call again.

When I was opposite the house I thought I saw in the window the back of Ada's head—I had come to think of her as "Ada" now, I was, therefore, somewhat surprised when, after some delay, the maid, with a demure face, told me that Mrs. Harcourt was not at home. I felt almost inclined to argue the matter with the maid, who was now giggling as on the former occasion when suddenly Bobbie came running out of the back hall and called to me:

"Oh, Mr. Denison, won't you come in? Ma is here and will be delighted to see you!" He threw open the door of the drawing room, which was the first room on the ground floor, and ushered me in, turning round and grinning at me as he said:

"Ma, here is Mr. Denison come to see you. Excuse me coming in!" With that he went out, shutting the door behind him.

I think she was as much startled and amazed as I was, as she stood facing me with her cheeks flaming red. She had discarded her widows' weeds, and was now in a simple gray frock, with pink bows at neck and waist, which made her look years younger than even she had done before; her beautiful golden hair was uncovered. As I advanced, which I did with warmth, for it seemed to me somehow that discarding of the widow's dress opened up new possibilities to herself, she bowed somewhat coldly. She did not, however, refuse to shake hands, though she did so timidly. I felt awkward and ill at ease; things were not somehow going as smoothly as I wished, and the very passion that filled me made its repression a difficulty. I couldn't remember a single thing either of us said at that interview; I only recollect taking up my hat and moving off with mingled chagrin and diffidence. When I was near the door she came impulsively after me, and taking me by the hand, said:

"This is goodbye, indeed, as I shall not be able to see you again. You will understand, will you not?" Her words puzzled me; but she had made a request, and such, though it entailed denial of my own wishes, could only be answered in one way. I put my hand to my heart and bowed.

As I walked away, all the world seemed a blank space, and myself a helpless atom whirling in it alone.

That night I thought of nothing but Mrs. Harcourt, and with the gray of the dawn in my mind was made up. I would see her again, for I feared she would leave without even knowing my feelings toward her. I got up and wrote her a letter, saying that I would do myself the honor of calling that afternoon, and that I trusted she would see me, as I had something very important to say. When I retired to bed after posting the letter I fell asleep and and went on dreaming of her, and my dreams were heavenly.

When I knocked at the door in the afternoon the maid looked all demure, and showed me, without a word, into the drawing room.

Almost immediately following her exit Mrs. Harcourt came in. My heart rejoiced when I saw that she was dressed as on the previous day. She shook hands with me and gravely sat down. When I had sat alos, she said:

"You wanted to say something to me?"

"Yes," I answered quickly, for the ferver in me was beginning to speak. "I wanted to tell you that—" With a gesture she stopped me:

"One moment! Before you say anything, let me tell you something. I have a shameful confession to make. In a foolish moment I thought to play a joke, never thinking that it might reflect on my dear dead mother. Bobbie is not my son; he is only my brother, who has been in my care since my mother died, years ago. When he told me of the brave way you saved him, and when the kind letter you sent in answer to mine showed me you had mistaken our relationship, Bobbie and I laughed over it together, and I said what a lark it would be to pretend, if the occasion served, to be his mother. Then you called, and the spirit of mischief moved me to a most unseemly joke. I dressed up in mother's clothes, and tried to pass myself off as Bobbie's mother. When I had seen you and recognized your kindness, I seemed in all ways a brute; but all I could do was to try that it might go on no more. Oh, if you only knew!"

She put her pretty hands before her face, and I saw the tears drop through them. That pained me, but it gave me heart. Coming close to her, I took her hands and pulled them away, and looked in her brave eyes as I said:

"Oh, let me speak! I must! I must! I came here today to ask you to—. Won't you let Bobbie be my brother too?"

And he is.

# The Bridal of Death

I f any evidence had been wanted of how absolutely one and all of us had come to believe in the spiritual existence of the Egyptian Queen, it would have been found in the change which n a few minutes had been effected in us by the statement of voluntary negation made, we all believed, through Margaret. Despite the coming of the fearful ordeal, the sense of which it was impossible to forget, we looked and acted as though a great relief had come to us. We had indeed lived in such a state of terrorism during the days when Mr. Trelawny was lying in a trance that the feeling had bitten deeply into us. No one knows till he has experienced it, what it is to be in constant dreadof some unknown danger which may come at anytime and in any form.

The change was manifested in different ways, according to each nature. Margaret was sad. Doctor Winchester was in high spirits, and keenly observant; the process of thought which had served as an antidote to fear, being now relieved from this duty, added to his intellectual enthusiasm. Mr. Corbeck seemed to be in a retrospective rather than a speculative mood. I was myself rather inclined to be gay; the relief from certain anxiety regarding Margaret was sufficient for me for the time.

As to Mr. Trelawny he seemed less changed than any. Perhaps this was only natural, as he had had in his mind the intention for so many years of doing that in which we were tonight engaged, that any event connected with it could only seem to him as an episode, a step to the end. His was that commanding nature which looks so to the end of an undertaking that all else is of secondary importance. Even now, though his terrible sternness relaxed under the relief from the strain, he never flagged nor faltered for a moment in his purpose. He asked us men to come with him; and going to the hall we presently managed to lower into the cave an oak table, fairly long and not too wide, which stood against the wall in the hall. This we placed under the strong cluster of electric lights in the middle of the cave. Margaret looked on for a while; then all at once her face blanched, and in an agitated voice she said:

"What are you going to do, Father?"

"To unroll the mummy of the cat! Queen Tera will not need her Familiar tonight. If she should want him, it might be dangerous to us; so we shall make him safe. You are not alarmed, dear?"

"Oh no!" she answered quickly. "But I was thinking of my Silvio, and how I should feel if he had been the mummy that was to be unswathed!"

Mr. Trelawny got knives and scissors ready, and placed the cat on the table. It was a grim beginning to our work; and it made my heart sink when I thought of what might happen in that lonely house in the mid-gloom of the night. The sense of loneliness and isolation from the world was increased by the moaning of the wind which had now risen ominously, and by the beating of waves on the rocks below. But we had too grave a task before us to be swayed by external manifestations: the unrolling of the mummy began.

There was an incredible number of bandages; and the tearing sound—they being stuck fast to each other by bitumen and gums and spices—and the little cloud of red pungent dust that arose, pressed on the senses of all of us. As the last wrappings came away, we saw the animal seated before us. He was all hunkered up; his hair and teeth and claws were complete. The eyes were closed, but the eyelids had not the fierce look which I expected. The whiskers had been pressed down on the side of the face by the bandaging; but when the pressure ws taken away they stood out, just as they would have done in life. He was a magnificent creature, a tiger-cat of great size. But as we looked at him, our first glance of admiration changed to one of fear, and a shudder ran through each one of us; for here was a confirmation of the fears which we had endured.

His mouth and his claws were smeared with the dry, red stains of recent blood!

Doctor Winchester was the first to recover; blood in itself had small disturbing quality for him. He had taken out his magnifying-glass and was examining the stains on the cat's mouth. Mr. Trelawny breathed loudly, as though a strain had been taken from him.

"It is as I expected," he said. "This promises well for what is to follow."

By this time Doctor Winchester was looking at the red stained paws. "As I expected!" he said. "He has seven claws, too!" Opening his pocket-book, he took out the piece of blotting-paper marked by Silvio's claws, on which was also marked in pencil a diagram of the cuts made on Mr. Trelawny's wrist. He placed the paper under the mummy cat's paw. The marks fitted exactly.

When we had carefully examined the cat, finding, however, nothing strange about it but its wonderful preservation, Mr. Trelawny lifted it from the table. Margaret started forward, crying out:

"Take care, Father! Take care! He may injure you!"

"Not now, my dear!" he answered as he moved towards the stairway. Her face fell. "Where are you going?" she asked in a faint voice.

"To the kitchen," he answered. "Fire will take away all danger for the future; even an astral body cannot materialise from ashes!" He signed to us to follow him. Margaret turned away with a sob. I went to her; but she motioned me back and whispered:

"No, no! Go with the others. Father may want you. Oh! it seems like murder! The poor Queen's pet. . . !" The tears were dropping from under the fingers that covered her eyes.

In the kitchen was a fire of wood ready laid. To this Mr. Trelawny applied a match; in a few seconds the kindling had caught and the flames leaped. When the fire was solidly ablaze, he threw the body of the cat into it. For a few seconds it lay a dark mass amidst the flames, and the room was rank with the smell of burning hair. Then the dry body caught fire too. The inflammable substances used in embalming became new fuel, and the flames roared. A few minutes of fierce conflagration; and then we breathed freely. Queen Tera's Familiar was no more!

When we went back to the cave we found Margaret sitting in the dark. She had switched off the electric light, and only a faint glow of the evening light came through the narrow openings. Her father went quickly over to her and put his arms round her in a loving protective way. She laid her head on his shoulder for a minute and seemed comforted. Presently she called to me:

"Malcolm, turn up the light!" I carried out her orders, and could see that, though she had been crying, her eyes were now dry. Her father saw it too and looked glad. He said to us in a grave tone:

"Now we had better prepare for our great work. It will not do to leave anything to the last!" Margaret must have had a suspicion of what was coming, for it was with a sinking voice that she asked:

"What are you going to do now?" Mr. Trelawny too must have had a suspicion of her feelings, for he answered in a low tone:

"To unroll the mummy of Queen Tera!" She came close to him and said pleadingly in a whisper:

"Father, you are not going to unswathe her! All you men. . . ! And in the glare of light!"

"But why not, my dear?"

"Just think, Father, a woman! All alone! In such a way! In such a place! Oh! it's cruel, cruel!" She was manifestly much overcome. Her cheeks were flaming red, and her eyes were full of indignant tears. Her father saw her distress; and, sympathising with it, began to comfort her. I was moving off; but he signed to me to stay. I took it that after the usual manner of men he wanted help on such an occasion, and man-like wished to throw on someone else the task of dealing with a woman in indignant distress. However, he began to appeal first to her reason:

"Not a woman, dear; a mummy! She has been dead nearly five thousand years!"

"What does that matter? Sex is not a matter of years! A woman is a woman, if she had been dead five thousand centuries! And you expect her to arise out of that long sleep! It could not be real death, if she is to rise out of it! You have led me to believe that she will come alive when the Coffer is opened!"

"I did, my dear; and I believe it! But if it isn't death that has been the matter with her all these years, it is something uncommonly like it. Then again, just think; it was men who embalmed her. They didn't have women's rights or lady doctors in ancient Egypt, my dear! And besides," he went on more freely, seeing that she was accepting his argument, if not yielding to it, "we men are accustomed to such things. Corbeck and I have unrolled a hundred mummies; and there were as many women as men amongst them. Doctor Winchester in his work has had to deal with women as well of men, till custome has made him think nothing of sex. Even Ross has in his work as a barrister. . ." He stopped suddenly.

"You were going to help too!" she said to me, with an indignant look.

I said nothing; I thought silence was best. Mr. Trelawny went on hurriedly; I could see that he was glad of interruption, for the part of his argument concerning a barrister's work was becoming decidedly weak:

"My child, you will be with us yourself. Would we do anything which would hurt or offend you? Come now! be reasonable! We are not at a pleasure party. We are all grave men, entering gravely on an experiment which may unfold the wisdom of old times, and enlarge human knowledge indefinitely; which may put the minds of men on new tracks of thought and research. An experiment," as he went on his voice deepened, "which may be fraught with death to anyone of us—to us all! We know from what has been, that there are, or may be, vast and unknown dangers ahead of us, of which none in the house today may ever see the end. Take it, my child, that we are not acting lightly; but with all the gravity of deeply earnest men! Besides, my dear, whatever feelings you or any of us may have on the subject, it is necessary for the success of the experiment to unswathe her. I think that under any circumstances it would be necessary to remove the wrappings before she became again a live human being instead of a spiritualised corpse with an astral body. Were her original intention carried out, and did she come to new life within her mummy wrappings, it might be to exchange a coffin for a grave! She would die the death of the buried alive! But now, when she has voluntarily abandoned for the time her astral power, there can be no doubt on the subject."

Margaret's face cleared. "All right, Father!" she said as she kissed him. "But oh! it seems a horrible indignity to a Queen, and a woman."

I was moving away to the staircase when she called me:

"Where are you going?" I came back and took her hand and stroked it as I answered:

"I shall come back when the unrolling is over!" She looked at me long, and a faint suggestion of a smile came over her face as she said:

"Perhaps you had better stay, too! It may be useful to you in your work as a barrister!" She smiled out as she met my eyes: but in an instant she changed. Her face grew grave, and deadly white. In a far away voice she said:

"Father is right! It is a terrible occasion; we need all to be serious over it. But all the same—nay, for that very reason you had better stay, Malcolm! You may be glad, later on, that you were present tonight!"

My heart sank down, down, at her words; but I thought it better to say nothing. Fear was stalking openly enough amongst us already!

By this time Mr. Trelawny, assisted by Mr. Corbeck and Doctor Winchester, had raised the lid of the ironstone sarcophagus which contained the mummy of the Queen. It was a large one; but it was none too big. The mummy was both long and broad and high; and was of such weight that it was no easy task, even for the four of us, to lift it out. Under Mr. Trelawny's direction we laid it out on the table prepared for it.

Then, and then only, did the full horror of the whole thing burst upon me! There, in the full glare of the light, the whole material and sordid side of death seemed staringly real. The outer wrappings, torn and loosened by rude touch, and with the colour either darkened by dust or worn light by friction, seemed creased as by rough treatment; the jagged edges of the wrapping-cloths looked fringed; the painting was patchy, and the varnish chipped. The coverings were evidently many, for the bulk was great. But through all, showed that unhidable human figure, which seems to look more horrible when partially concealed than at any other time. What was before us was Death, and nothing else. All the romance and sentiment of fancy had disappeared. The two elder men, enthusiasts who had often done such work, were not disconcerted; and Doctor Winchester seemed to hold himself in a business-like attitude, as if before the operating-table. But I felt low-spirited, and miserable, and ashamed; and besides I was pained and alarmed by Margaret's ghastly pallor.

Then the work began. The unrolling of the mummy cat had prepared me somewhat for it; but this was so much larger, and so infinitely more elaborate, that it seemed a different thing. Moreover, in addition to the ever present sense of death and humanity, there was a feeling of something finer in all this. The cat had been embalmed with coarser materials; here, all, when once the outer coverings were removed, was more delicately done. It seemed as if only the finest gums and spices had been used in this embalming. But there were the same surroundings, the same attendant red dust and pungent presence of bitumen; there was the same sound of rending which marked the tearing away of the bandages. There were an enormous number of these, and their bulk when opened was great. As the men unrolled them, I grew more and more excited. I did not take a part in it myself; Margaret had looked at me gratefully as I drew back. We clasped hands, and held each other hard. As the unrolling went on, the wrappings became finer, and the smell less laden with bitumen, but more pungent. We all, I think, began to feel it as though it caught or touched us in some special way. This, however, did not interfere with the work; it went on uninterruptedly. Some of the inner wrappings bore symbols or pictures. These were done sometimes wholly in pale green colour, sometimes in many colours; but always with a prevalence of green. Now and again Mr. Trelawny or Mr. Corbeck would point out some special drawing before laying the bandage on the pile behind them, which kept growing to a monstrous height.

At last we knew that the wrappings were coming to an end. Already the proportions were reduced to those of a normal figure of the manifest height of the Queen, who was more than average height. And as the end drew nearer, so Margaret's pallor grew; and her heart beat more and more wildly, till her breast heaved in a way that frightened me.

Just as her father was taking away the last of the bandages, he happened to look up and caught the pained and anxious look of her pale face. He paused, and taking her concern to be as to the outrage on modesty, said in a comforting way:

"Do not be uneasy, dear! See! there is nothing to harm you. The Queen has on a robe.—Ay, and a royal robe, too!"

The wrapping was a wide piece the whole length of the body. It being removed, a profusely full robe of white linen had appeared, covering the body from the throat to the feet.

And such linen! We all bent over to look at it.

Margaret lost her concern, in her woman's interest in fine stuff. Then the rest of us looked with admiration; for surely such linen was never seen by the eyes of our age. It was as fine as the finest silk. But never was spun or woven silk which lay in such gracious folds, constrict though they were by the close wrappings of the mummy cloth, and fixed into hardness by the passing of thousands of years.

Round the neck it was delicately embroidered in pure gold with tiny sprays of sycamore; and round the feet, similarly worked, was an endless line of lotus plants of unequal height, and with all the graceful abandon of natural growth.

Across the body, but manifestly not surrounding it, was a girdle of jewels. A wondrous girdle, which shone and glowed with all the forms and phases and colours of the sky!

The buckle was a great yellow stone, round of outline, deep and curved, as if a yielding globe had been pressed down. It shone and glowed, as though a veritable sun lay within; the rays of its light seemed to strike out and illumine all round. Flanking it were two great moonstones of lesser size, whose glowing, beside the glory of the sunstone, was like the silvery sheen of moonlight.

And then on either side, linked by golden clasps of exquisite shape, was a line of flaming jewels, of which the colours seemed to glow. Each of these stones seemed to hold a living star, which twinkled in every phase of changing light.

Margaret raised her hands in ecstasy. She bent over to examine more closely; but suddenly drew back and stood fully erect at her grand height. She seemed to speak with the conviction of absolute knowledge as she said:

"That is no cerement! It was no meant for the clothing of death! It is a marriage robe!"

Mr. Trelawny leaned over and touched the linen robe. He lifted a fold at the neck, and I knew from the quick intake of his breath that something had surprised him. He lifted yet a little more; and then he, too, stood back and pointed, saying:

"Margaret is right! That dress is not intended to be worn by the dead! See! her figure is not robed in it. It is but laid upon her." He lifted the zone of jewels and handed it to Margaret. Then with both hands he raised the ample robe, and laid it across the arms which she extended in a natural impulse. Things of such beauty were too precious to be handled with any but the greatest care.

We all stood awed at the beauty of the figure which, save for the face cloth, now lay completely nude before us. Mr. Trelawny bent over, and with hands that trembled slightly, raised this linen cloth which was of the same fineness as the robe. As he stood back and the whole glorious beauty of the Queen was revealed, I felt a rush of shame sweep over me. It was not right that we should be there, gazing with irreverent eyes on such unclad beauty: it was indecent; it was almost sacrilegious! And yet the white wonder of that beautiful form was something to dream of. It was not like death at all; it was like a statue carven in ivory by the hand of a Praxiteles. There was nothing of that horrible shrinkage which death seems to effect in a moment. There was none of the wrinkled toughness which seems to be a leading characteristic of most mummies. There was not the shrunken attenuation of a body dried in the sand, as I had seen before in museums. All the pores of the body seemed to have been preserved in some wonderful way. The flesh was full and round, as in a living person; and the skin was as smooth as satin. The colour seemed extraordinary. It was like ivory, new ivory; except where the right arm, with shattered, bloodstained wrist and missing hand had lain bare to exposure in the sarcophagus for so many tens of centuries.

With a womanly impulse; with a mouth that drooped with pity, with eyes that flashed with anger, and cheeks that flamed, Margaret threw over the body the beautiful robe which lay across her arm. Only the face was then to be seen. This was more startling even than the body, for it seemed not dead, but alive. The eyelids were closed; but the long, black, curling lashes lay over on the cheeks. The nostrils, set in grave pride, seemed to have the repose which, when it is seen in life, is greater than the repose of death. The full, red lips, though the mouth was not open, showed the tiniest white line of pearly teeth within. Her hair, glorious in quantity and glossy black as the raven's wing, was piled in great masses over the white forehead, on which a few curling tresses strayed like tendrils. I was amazed at the likeness to Margaret, though

I had had my mind prepared for this by Mr. Corbeck's quotation of her father's statement. This woman—I could not think of her as a mummy or a corpse—was the image of Margaret as my eyes had first lit on her. The likeness was increased by the jewelled ornament which she wore in her hair, the "Disk and Plumes," such as Margaret, too, had worn. It, too, was a glorious jewel; one noble pearl of moonlight lustre, flanked by carven pieces of moonstone.

Mr. Trelawny was overcome as he looked. He quite broke down; and when Margaret flew to him and held him close in her arms and comforted him, I heard him murmur brokenly:

"It looks as if you were dead, my child!"

There was a long silence. I could hear without the roar of the wind, which was now risen to a tempest, and the furius dashing of the waves far below. Mr. Trelawny's voice broke the spell:

"Later on we must try and find out the process of embalming. It is not like any that I know. There does not seem to have been any opening cut for the withdrawing of the viscera and organs, which apparently remain intact within the body. Then, again, there is no moisture in the flesh; but its place is supplied with something else, as though wax or stearine had been conveyed into the veins by some subtle process. I wonder could it be possible that at that time they could have used paraffin. It might have been, by some process that we know not, pumped into the veins, where it hardened!"

Margaret, having thrown a white sheet over the Queen's body, asked us to bring it to her own room, where we laid it on her bed. Then she sent us away, saying:

"Leave her alone with me. There are still many hours to pass, and I do not like to leave her lying there, all stark in the glare of light. This may be the Bridal she prepared for—the Bridal of Death; and at least she shall wear her pretty robes."

When presently she brought me back to her room, the dead Queen was dressed in the robe of fine linen with the embroidery of gold; and all her beautiful jewels were in place. Candles were lit around her, and white flowers lay upon her breast.

Hand in hand we stood looking at her for a while. Then with a sigh, Margaret covered her with one of her own snowy sheets. She turned away; and after softly closing the door of the room, went back with me to the others who had now come into the dining room. Here we all began to talk over the things that had been, and that were to be.

Now and again I could feel that one or other of us was forcing conversation, as if we were not sure of ourselves. The long wait was beginning to tell on our nerves. It was apparent to me that Mr. Trelawny had suffered in that strange trance more than we suspected, or than he cared to show. True, his will and his determination were as strong as ever; but the purely physical side of him had been weakened somewhat. It was indeed only natural that it should be. No man can go through a period of four days of absolute negation of life without being weakened by it somehow.

As the hours crept by, the time passed more and more slowly. The other men seemed to get unconsciously a little drowsy. I wondered if in the case of Mr. Trelawny and Mr. Corbeck, who had already been under the hypnotic influence of the Queen, the same dormance was manifesting itself. Doctor Winchester had periods of distraction which grew longer and more frequent as the time wore on.

As to Margaret, the suspense told on her exceedingly, as might have been expected in the case of a woman. She grew paler and paler still; till at last about midnight, I began to be seriously alarmed about her. I got her to come into the library with me, and tried to make her lie down on a sofa for a little while. As Mr. Trelawny had decided that the experiment was to be made exactly at the seventh hour after sunset, it would be as nearly as possible three o'clock in the morning when the great trial should be made. Even allowing a whole hour for the final preparations, we had still two hours of waiting to go through, and I promised faithfully to watch her and to awake her at anytime she might name. She would not hear of it, however. She thanked me sweetly and smiled at me as she did so; but she assured me that she was not sleepy, and that she was quite able to bear up. That it was only the suspense and excitement of waiting that made her pale. I agreed perforce; but I kept her talking of many things in the library for more than an hour; so that at last, when she insisted on going back to her father's room I felt that I had at least done something to help her pass the time.

We found the three men sitting patiently in silence. With manlike fortitude they were content to be still when they felt they had done all in their power.

And so we waited.

The striking of two o'clock seemed to freshen us all up. Whatever shadows had been settling over us during the long hours preceding seemed to lift at once, and we all went about our separate duties alert and with alacrity. We looked first to the windows to see that they were closed; for now the storm raged so fiercely that we feared it might upset our plans which, after all, were based on perfect stillness. Then we got ready our respirators to put them on when the time should be close at hand. We had from the first arranged to use them, for we did not know whether some noxious fume might not come from the Magic Coffer when it should be opened. Somehow it never seemed to occur to any of us that there was any doubt as to its opening.

Then, under Margaret's guidance, we carried the body of Queen Tera, still clad in her Bridal robes, from her room into the cavern.

It was a strange sight, and a strange experience. The group of grave silent men carrying away from the lighted candles and the white flowers the white still figure, which looked like an ivory statue when through our moving the robe fell back.

We laid her in the sarcophagus, and placed the severed hand in its true position on her breast. Under it was laid the Jewel of Seven Stars, which Mr. Trelawny had taken from the safe. It seemed to flash and blaze as he put it in its place. The glare of the electric lights shone cold on the great sarcophagus fixed ready for the final experiment—the Great Experiment, consequent on the researches during a lifetime of these two travelled scholars. Again, the startling likeness between Margaret and the mummy, intensified by her own extraordinary pallor, heightened the strangeness of it all.

When all was finally fixed, three-quarters of an hour had gone; for we were deliberate in all our doings. Margaret beckoned me, and I went with her to her room. There she did a thing which moved me strangely, and brought home to me keenly the desperate nature of the enterprise on which we were embarked. One by one, she blew out the candles carefully, and placed them back in their usual places. When she had finished she said to me:

"They are done with! Whatever comes—Life or Death—there will be no purpose in their using now!"

We returned to the cavern with a strange thrill as of finality. There was to be no going back now!

We put on our respirators, and took our places as had been arranged. I was to stand by the taps of the electric lights, ready to turn them off or on as Mr. Trelawny should direct. His last caution to me to carry out his instructions exactly was almost like a menace; for he warned me that death to any or all of us might come from any error or neglect on my part. Margaret and Doctor Winchester were to stand between the sarcophagus and the wall, so that they would not be between the mummy and the Magic Coffer. They were to note accurately all that should happen with regard to the Queen.

Mr. Trelawny and Mr. Corbeck were to see the lamps lighted: and then to take their places, the former at the foot, the latter at the head, of the sarcophagus.

When the hands of the clock were close to the hour, they stood ready with their lit tapers, like gunners in old days with their linstocks.

For the few minutes that followed, the passing of time was a slow horror. Mr. Trelawny stood with his watch in his hand, ready to give the signal.

The time approached with inconceivable slowness; but at last came the whirring of wheels which warns that the hour is at hand. The striking of the silver bell of the clock seemed to smite on our hearts like the knell of doom. One! Two! Three!

The wicks of the lamps caught, and I turned out the electric light. In the dimness of the struggling lamps, and after the bright glow of the electric light, the room and all within it took weird shape, and everything seemed in an instant to change. We waited, with our hearts beating. I know mine did; and I fancied I could hear the pulsation of the others. Without, the storm raged; the shutters of the narrow windows shook and strained and rattled, as though something was striving for entrance.

The seconds seemed to pass with leaden wings; it was as though all the world were standing still. The figures of the others stood out dimly, Margaret's white dress alone showing clearly in the gloom. The thick respirators, which we all wore, added to the strange appearance. The thin light of the lamps, as the two men bent over the Coffer, showed Mr. Trelawny's square jaw and strong mouth, and the brown, wrinkled face of Mr. Corbeck. Their eyes seemed to glare in the light. Across the room Doctor Winchester's eyes twinkled like stars, and Margaret's blazed like black suns.

Would the lamps never burn up!

It was only a few seconds in all till they did blaze up. A slow, steady light, growing more and more bright; and changing in colour from blue to crystal white. So they stayed for a couple of minutes, without any change in the Coffer being noticeable. At last there began to appear all over it a delicate glow. This grew and grew, till it became like a blazing jewel; and then like a living thing, whose essence was light.

Mr. Trelawny and Mr. Corbeck moved silently to their places beside the sarcophagus.

We waited and waited, our hearts seeming to stand still.

All at once there was a sound like a tiny muffled explosion, and the cover of the Coffer lifted right up on a level plane a few inches; there was no mistaking anything now, for the whole cavern was full of light. Then the cover, staying fast at one side, rose slowly up on the other, as though yielding to some pressure of balance. I could not see what was within, for the risen cover stood between. The Coffer still continued to glow; from it began to steal a faint greenish vapour which floated in the direction of the sarcophagus as though impelled or drawn towards it. I could not smell it fully on account of the respirator; but, even through that, I was conscious of a strange, pungent odour. The vapour got somewhat denser after a few seconds, and began to pass directly into the open sarcophagus. It was evident now that the mummied body had some attraction for it; and also that it had some effect on the body, for the sarcophagus slowly became illumined as though the body had begun to glow. I could not see within from where I stood, but I gathered from the faces of all the four watchers that something strange was happening.

I longed to run over and take a look for myself; but I remembered Mr. Trelawny's solemn warning, and remained at my post.

The storm still thundered round the house, and I could feel the rock on which it was built tremble under the furious onslaught of the waves. The shutters strained as though the screaming wind without would in very anger have forced an entrance. In that dread hour of expectancy, when the forces of Life and Death were struggling for the mastery, imagination was awake. I almost fancied that the storm was a living thing, and animated with the wrath of the quick!

All at once the eager faces round the sarcophagus were bent forward. The look of speechless wonder in the eyes, lit by that supernatural glow from within the sarcophagus, had a more than mortal brilliance.

My own eyes were nearly blinded by the awful, paralysing light, so that I could hardly trust them. I saw something white rising up from the open sarcophagus. Something which appeared to my tortured eyes to be filmy, like a white mist. In the heart of this mist, which was cloudy and opaque like an opal, was something like a hand holding a fiery jewel flaming with many lights. As the fierce glow of the Coffer met this new living light, the green vapour floating between them seemed like a cascade of brilliant points—a miracle of light!

But at that very moment there came a change. The fierce storm, battling with the shutters of the narrow openings, won victory. With the sound of a pistol shot, one of the heavy shutters broke its fastening and was hurled on its hinges back against the wall. In rushed a fierce blast which blew the flames of the lamps to and fro, and drifted the green vapour from its course.

On the very instant came a change in the outcome from the Coffer. There was a moment's quick flame and a muffled explosion; and black smoke began to pour out. This got thicker and thicker with frightful rapidity, in volumes of ever-increasing density; till the whole cavern began to get obscure, and its outlines were lost. The screaming wind tore in and whirled it about. At a sign from Mr. Trelawny Mr. Corbeck went and closed the shutter and jammed it fast with a wedge.

I should have liked to help; but I had to wait directions from Mr. Trelawny, who inflexibly held his post at the head of the sarcophagus. I signed to him with my hand, but he motioned me back. Gradually the figures of all close to the sarcophagus became indistinct in the smoke which rolled round them in thick billowy clouds. Finally, I lost sight of them altogether. I had a terrible desire to rush over so as to be near Margaret; but again I restrained myself. If the Stygian gloom continued, light would be a necessity of safety; and I was the guardian of the light! My anguish of anxiety as I stood to my post was almost unendurable.

The Coffer was now but a dull colour; and the lamps were growing dim, as though they were being overpowered by the thick smoke. Absolute darkness would soon be upon us.

I waited and waited, expecting every instant to hear the command to turn up the light; but none came. I waited still, and looked with harrowing intensity at the rolling billows of smoke still pouring out of the casket whose glow was fading. The lamps sank down, and went out; one by one.

Finally, there was but one lamp alight, and that was dimly blue and flickering. I kept my eyes fixed towards Margaret, in the hope that I might see her in some lifting of the gloom; it was for her now that all my anxiety was claimed. I could just see her white frock beyond the dim outline of the sarcophagus.

Deeper and deeper grew the black mist, and its pungency began to assail my nostrils as well as my eyes. Now the volume of smoke coming from the Coffer seemed to lessen, and the smoke itself to be less dense. Across the room I saw a movement of something white where the sarcophagus was. There were several such movements. I could just catch the quick glint of white through the dense smoke in the fading light; for now even the last lamp began to flicker with the quick leaps before extinction.

Then the last glow disappeared. I felt that the time had come to speak; so I pulled off my respirator and called out:

"Shall I turn on the light?" There was no answer. Before the thick smoke choked me, I called again, but more loudly:

"Mr. Trelawny, shall I turn on the light? Answer me! If you do not forbid me, I shall turn it on!"

As there was no reply, I turned the tap. To my horror there was no response; something had gone wrong with the electric light! I moved, intending to run up the staircase to seek the cause, but I could now see nothing, all was pitch dark.

I groped my way across the room to where I thought Margaret was. As I went I stumbled across a body. I could feel by her dress that it was a woman. My heart sank; Margaret was unconscious, or perhaps dead. I lifted the body in my arms, and went straight forward till I touched a wall. Following it round I came to the stairway, and hurried up the steps with what haste I could make, hampered as I was with my dear burden. It may have been that hope lightened my task; but as I went the weight that I bore seemed to grow less as I ascended from the cavern.

I laid the body in the hall, and groped my way to Margaret's room, where I knew there were matches, and the candies which she had placed beside the Queen. I struck a match; and oh! it was good to see the light. I lit two candies, and taking one in each hand, hurried back to the hall where I had left, as I had supposed, Margaret.

Her body was not there. But on the spot where I had laid her was Queen Tera's Bridal robe, and surrounding it the girdle of wondrous gems. Where the heart had been, lay the Jewel of Seven Stars.

Sick at heart, and with a terror which has no name, I went down into the cavern. My two candles were like mere points of light in the black, impenetrable smoke. I put up again to my mouth the respirator which hung round my neck, and went to look for my companions.

I found them all where they had stood. They had sunk down on the floor, and were gazing upward with fixed eyes of unspeakable terror. Margaret had put her hands before her face, but the glassy stare of her eyes through her fingers was more terrible than an open glare.

I pulled back the shutters of all the windows to let in what air I could. The storm was dying away as quickly as it had risen, and now it only came in desultory puffs. It might well be quiescent; its work was done!

I did what I could for my companions; but there was nothing that could avail. There, in that lonely house, far away from aid of man, naught could avail.

It was merciful that I was spared the pain of hoping.

# A Star Trap

W hen I was apprenticed to theatrical carpentering my master was
John Haliday, who was Master Machinist—we called men in
his post 'Master Carpenter' in those days—of the old Victoria Theatre,
Hulme. It wasn't called Hulme; but that name will do. It would only stir
up painful memories if I were to give the real name. I daresay some of
you—not the Ladies (this with a gallant bow all round)—will remember
the case of a Harlequin as was killed in an accident in the pantomime.
We needn't mention names; Mortimer will do for a name to call him by—
Henry Mortimer. The cause of it was never found out. But I knew it;
and I've kept silence for so long that I may speak now without hurting
anyone. They're all dead long ago that was interested in the death of
Henry Mortimer or the man who wrought that death."

"Any of you who know of the case will remember what a handsome,
dapper, well-built man Mortimer was. To my own mind he was the
handsomest man I ever saw."

The Tragedian's low, grumbling whisper, "That's a large
order," sounded a warning note. Hempitch, however, did not seem to
hear it, but went on:

"Of course, I was only a boy then, and I hadn't seen any of you
gentlemen—Yer very good health, Mr. Wellesley Dovercourt, sir, and
cettera. I needn't tell you, Ladies, how well a harlequin's dress sets off a
nice slim figure. No wonder that in these days of suffragettes, women
wants to be harlequins as well as columbines. Though I hope they won't
make the columbine a man's part!"

"Mortimer was the nimblest chap at the traps I ever see. He was so
sure of hisself that he would have extra weight put on so that when the
counter weights fell he'd shoot up five or six feet higher than anyone
else could even try to. Moreover, he had a way of drawing up his legs
when in the air—the way a frog does when he is swimming—that made
his jump look ever so much higher."

"I think the girls were all in love with him, the way they used to stand
in the wings when the time was comin' for his entrance. That wouldn't
have mattered much, for girls are always falling in love with some man or
other, but it made trouble, as it always does when the married ones take
the same start. There were several of these that were always after him,

more shame for them, with husbands of their own. That was dangerous enough, and hard to stand for a man who might mean to be decent in anyway. But the real trial—and the real trouble, too—was none other than the young wife of my own master, and she was more than flesh and blood could stand. She had come into the panto, the season before, as a high-kicker—and she could! She could kick higher than girls that was more than a foot taller than her; for she was a wee bit of a thing and as pretty as pie; a gold-haired, blue-eyed, slim thing with much the figure of a boy, except for. . . and they saved her from any mistaken idea of that kind. Jack Haliday went crazy over her, and when the notice was up, and there was no young spark with plenty of oof coming along to do the proper thing by her, she married him. It was, when they was joined, what you Ladies call a marriage of convenience; but after a bit they two got on very well, and we all thought she was beginning to like the old man—for Jack was old enough to be her father, with a bit to spare. In the summer, when the house was closed, he took her to the Isle of Man; and when they came back he made no secret of it that he'd had the happiest time of his life. She looked quite happy, too, and treated him affectionate; and we all began to think that that marriage had not been a failure at any rate."

"Things began to change, however, when the panto, rehearsals began next year. Old Jack began to look unhappy, and didn't take no interest in his work. Loo—that was Mrs. Haliday's name—didn't seem over fond of him now, and was generally impatient when he was by. Nobody said anything about this, however, to us men; but the married women smiled and nodded their heads and whispered that perhaps there were reasons. One day on the stage, when the harlequinade rehearsal was beginning, someone mentioned as how perhaps Mrs. Haliday wouldn't be dancing that year, and they smiled as if they was all in the secret. Then Mrs. Jack ups and gives them Johnny-up-the-orchard for not minding their own business and telling a pack of lies, and such like as you Ladies like to express in your own ways when you get your back hair down. The rest of us tried to soothe her all we could, and she went off home."

"It wasn't long after that that she and Henry Mortimer left together after rehearsal was over, he saying he'd leave her at home. She didn't make no objections—I told you he was a very handsome man."

"Well, from that on she never seemed to take her eyes from him during every rehearsal, right up to the night of the last rehearsal, which, of course, was full dress—'Everybody and Everything.'"

"Jack Haliday never seemed to notice anything that was going on, like the rest of them did. True, his time was taken up with his own work, for I'm telling you that a Master Machinist hasn't got no loose time on his hands at the first dress rehearsal of a panto. And, of course, none of the company ever said a word or gave a look that would call his attention to it. Men and women are queer beings. They will be blind and deaf whilst danger is being run; and it's only after the scandal is beyond repair that they begin to talk—just the very time when most of all they should be silent."

"I saw all that went on, but I didn't understand it. I liked Mortimer myself and admired him—like I did Mrs. Haliday, too—and I thought he was a very fine fellow. I was only a boy, you know, and Haliday's apprentice, so naturally I wasn't looking for any trouble I could help, even if I'd seen it coming. It was when I looked back afterwards at the whole thing that I began to comprehend; so you will all understand now, I hope, that what I tell you is the result of much knowledge of what I saw and heard and was told of afterwards—all morticed and clamped up by thinking."

"The panto, had been on about three weeks when one Saturday, between the shows, I heard two of our company talking. Both of them was among the extra girls that both sang and danced and had to make theirselves useful. I don't think either of them was better than she should be; they went out to too many champagne suppers with young men that had money to burn. That part doesn't matter in this affair—except that they was naturally enough jealous of women who was married—which was what they was aiming at—and what lived straighter than they did. Women of that kind like to see a good woman tumble down; it seems to make them all more even. Now real bad girls what have gone under altogether will try to save a decent one from following their road. That is, so long as they're young; for a bad one what is long in the tooth is the limit. They'll help anyone down hill—so long as they get anything out of it."

"Well—no offence, you Ladies, as has growed up!—these two girls was enjoyin' themselves over Mrs. Haliday and the mash she had set up on Mortimer. They didn't see that I was sitting on a stage box behind a built-out piece of the Prologue of the panto, which was set ready for night. They were both in love with Mortimer, who wouldn't look at either of them, so they was miaw'n cruel, like cats on the tiles. Says one":

"'The Old Man seems worse than blind; he won't see.'"

"'Don't you be too sure of that,' says the other. 'He don't mean to take no chances. I think you must be blind, too, Kissie.' That was her name—on the bills anyhow, Kissie Mountpelier. 'Don't he make a point of taking her home hisself every night after the play. You should know, for you're in the hall yourself waiting for your young man till he comes from his club.'"

"'Wot-ho, you bally geeser,' says the other—which her language was mostly coarse—'don't you know there's two ends to everything? The Old Man looks to one end only!' Then they began to snigger and whisper; and presently the other one says":

"'Then he thinks harm can be only done when work is over!'"

"'Jest so,' she answers. 'Her and him knows that the old man has to be down long before the risin' of the rag; but she doesn't come in till the Vision of Venus dance after half time; and he not till the harlequinade!'"

"Then I quit. I didn't want to hear anymore of that sort."

"All that week things went on as usual. Poor old Haliday wasn't well. He looked worried and had a devil of a temper. I had reason to know that, for what worried him was his work. He was always a hard worker, and the panto. season was a terror with him. He didn't ever seem to mind anything else outside his work. I thought at the time that that was how those two chattering girls made up their slanderous story; for, after all, a slander, no matter how false it may be, must have some sort of beginning. Something that seems, if there isn't something that is! But no matter how busy he might be, old Jack always made time to leave the wife at home."

"As the week went on he got more and more pale; and I began to think he was in for some sickness. He generally remained in the theatre between the shows on Saturday; that is, he didn't go home, but took a high tea in the coffee shop close to the theatre, so as to be handy in case there might be a hitch anywhere in the preparation for night. On that Saturday he went out as usual when the first scene was set, and the men were getting ready the packs for the rest of the scenes. By and bye there was some trouble—the usual Saturday kind—and I went off to tell him. When I went into the coffee shop I couldn't see him. I thought it best not to ask or to seem to take any notice, so I came back to the theatre, and heard that the trouble had settled itself as usual, by the men who had been quarrelling going off to have another drink. I hustled up those who remained, and we got things smoothed out in time for them all to have their tea. Then I had my own. I was just then beginning to feel the responsibility of my business, so I wasn't long over my food, but came back to look things over and see that all was right, especially the trap, for that was a thing Jack Haliday was most particular about. He would overlook a fault for anything else; but if it was along of a trap, the man had to go. He always told the men that that wasn't ordinary work; it was life or death."

"I had just got through my inspection when I saw old Jack coming in from the hall. There was no one about at that hour, and the stage was dark. But dark as it was I could see that the old man was ghastly pale. I didn't speak, for I wasn't near enough, and as he was moving very silently behind the scenes I thought that perhaps he wouldn't like anyone to notice that he had been away. I thought the best thing I could do would be to clear out of the way, so I went back and had another cup of tea."

"I came away a little before the men, who had nothing to think of except to be in their places when Haliday's whistle sounded. I went to report myself to my master, who was in his own little glass-partitioned den at the back of the carpenter's shop. He was there bent over his own bench, and was filing away at something so intently that he did not seem to hear me; so I cleared out. I tell you, Ladies and Gents, that from an apprentice point of view it is not wise to be too obtrusive when your master is attending to some private matter of his own!"

"When the 'get-ready' time came and the lights went up, there was Haliday as usual at his post. He looked very white and ill—so ill that the stage manager, when he came in, said to him that if he liked to go home and rest he would see that all his work would be attended to. He thanked him, and said that he thought he would be able to stay. 'I do feel a little weak and ill, sir,' he said. 'I felt just now for a few moments as if I was going to faint. But that's gone by already, and I'm sure I shall be able to get through the work before us all right.'"

"Then the doors was opened, and the Saturday night audience came rushing and tumbling in. The Victoria was a great Saturday night house. No matter what other nights might be, that was sure to be good. They used to say in the perfesh that the Victoria lived on it, and that the management was on holiday for the rest of the week. The actors knew it, and no matter how slack they might be from Monday to Friday they was all taut and trim then. There was no walking through and no fluffing on Saturday nights—or else they'd have had the bird."

"Mortimer was one of the most particular of the lot in this way. He never was slack at anytime—indeed, slackness is not a harlequin's fault, for if there's slackness there's no harlequin, that's all. But Mortimer always put on an extra bit on the Saturday night. When he jumped up through the star trap he always went then a couple of feet higher. To do this we had always to put on a lot more weight. This he always saw to himself; for, mind you, it's no joke being driven up through the trap as if you was shot out of a gun. The points of the star had to be kept free, and the hinges at their bases must be well oiled, or else there can be a disaster at anytime. Moreover, 'tis the duty of someone appointed for the purpose to see that all is clear upon the stage. I remember hearing that once at New York, many years ago now, a harlequin was killed by a 'grip'—as the Yankees call a carpenter—what outsiders here call a scene-shifter—walking over the trap just as the stroke had been given to let go the counter-weights. It wasn't much satisfaction to the widow to know that the 'grip' was killed too."

"That night Mrs. Haliday looked prettier than ever, and kicked even higher than I had ever seen her do. Then, when she got dressed for home, she came as usual and stood in the wings for the beginning of the harlequinade. Old Jack came across the stage and stood beside her; I saw him from the back follow up the sliding ground-row that closed in on the Realms of Delight. I couldn't help noticing that he still looked ghastly pale. He kept turning his eyes on the star trap. Seeing this, I naturally looked at it too, for I feared lest something might have gone wrong. I had seen that it was in good order, and that the joints were properly oiled when the stage was set for the evening show, and as it wasn't used all night for anything else I was reassured. Indeed, I thought I could see it shine a bit as the limelight caught the brass hinges. There was a spot light just above it on the bridge, which was intended to make a good show of harlequin and his big jump. The people used to howl with delight as he came rushing up through the trap and when in the air drew up his legs and spread them wide for an instant and then straightened them again as he came down—only bending his knees just as he touched the stage."

"When the signal was given the counter-weight worked properly. I knew, for the sound of it at that part was all right."

"But something was wrong. The trap didn't work smooth, and open at once as the harlequin's head touched it. There was a shock and a tearing sound, and the pieces of the star seemed torn about, and some of them were thrown about the stage. And in the middle of them came the coloured and spangled figure that we knew."

"But somehow it didn't come up in the usual way. It was erect enough, but there was not the usual elasticity. The legs never moved; and when it went up a fair height—though nothing like usual—it seemed to topple over and fall on the stage on its side. The audience shrieked, and the people in the wings—actors and staff all the same—closed in, some of them in their stage clothes, others dressed for going home. But the man in the spangles lay quite still."

"The loudest shriek of all was from Mrs. Haliday; and she was the first to reach the spot where he—it—lay. Old Jack was close behind her, and caught her as she fell. I had just time to see that, for I made it my business to look after the pieces of the trap; there was plenty of people to look after the corpse. And the pit was by now crossing the orchestra and climbing up on the stage."

"I managed to get the bits together before the rush came. I noticed that there were deep scratches on some of them, but I didn't have time for more than a glance. I put a stage box over the hole lest anyone should put a foot through it. Such would mean a broken leg at least; and if one fell through, it might mean worse. Amongst other things I found a queer-looking piece of flat steel with some bent points on it. I knew it didn't belong to the trap; but it came from somewhere, so I put it in my pocket."

"By this time there was a crowd where Mortimer's body lay. That he was stone dead nobody could doubt. The very attitude was enough. He was all straggled about in queer positions; one of the legs was doubled under him with the toes sticking out in the wrong way. But let that suffice! It doesn't do to go into details of a dead body. . . I wish someone would give me a drop of punch."

"There was another crowd round Mrs. Haliday, who was lying a little on one side nearer the wings where her husband had carried her and laid her down. She, too, looked like a corpse; for she was as white as one and as still, and looked as cold. Old Jack was kneeling beside her, chafing her hands. He was evidently frightened about her, for he, too, was deathly white. However, he kept his head, and called his men round him. He left his wife in care of Mrs. Homcroft, the Wardrobe Mistress, who had by this time hurried down. She was a capable woman, and knew how to act promptly. She got one of the men to lift Mrs. Haliday and carry her up to the wardrobe. I heard afterwards that when she got her there she turned out all the rest of them that followed up—the women as well as the men—and looked after her herself."

"I put the pieces of the broken trap on the top of the stage box, and told one of our chaps to mind them, and see that no one touched them, as they might be wanted. By this time the police who had been on duty in front had come round, and as they had at once telephoned to headquarters, more police kept coming in all the time. One of them took charge of the place where the broken trap was; and when he heard who put the box and the broken pieces there, sent for me. More of them took the body away to the property room, which was a large room with benches in it, and which could be locked up. Two of them stood at the door, and wouldn't let anyone go in without permission."

"The man who was in charge of the trap asked me if I had seen the accident. When I said I had, he asked me to describe it. I don't think he had much opinion of my powers of description, for he soon dropped that part of his questioning. Then he asked me to point out where I found the bits of the broken trap. I simply said":

"'Lord bless you, sir, I couldn't tell. They was scattered all over the place. I had to pick them up between people's feet as they were rushing in from all sides.'"

"'All right, my boy,' he said, in quite a kindly way, for a policeman, 'I don't think they'll want to worry you. There are lots of men and women, I am told, who were standing by and saw the whole thing. They will be all subpoenaed.' I was a small-made lad in those days—I ain't a giant now'—and I suppose he thought it was no use having children for witnesses when they had plenty of grown-ups. Then he said something about me and an idiot asylum that was not kind—no, nor wise either, for I dried up and did not say another word."

"Gradually the public was got rid of. Some strolled off by degrees, going off to have a glass before the pubs closed, and talk it all over. The rest us and the police ballooned out. Then, when the police had taken charge of everything and put in men to stay all night, the coroner's officer came and took off the body to the city mortuary, where the police doctor made a post mortem. I was allowed to go home. I did so— and gladly—when I had seen the place settling down. Mr. Haliday took his wife home in a four-wheeler. It was perhaps just as well, for Mrs. Homcroft and someother kindly souls had poured so much whisky and brandy and rum and gin and beer and peppermint into her that I don't believe she could have walked if she had tried."

"When I was undressing myself something scratched my leg as I was taking off my trousers. I found it was the piece of flat steel which I had picked up on the stage. It was in the shape of a star fish, but the spikes of it were short. Some of the points were turned down, the rest were pulled out straight again. I stood with it in my hand wondering where it had come from and what it was for, but I couldn't remember anything in the whole theatre that it could have belonged to. I looked at it closely again, and saw that the edges were all filed and quite bright. But that did not help me, so I put it on the table and thought I would take it with me in the morning; perhaps one of the chaps might know. I turned out the gas and went to bed—and to sleep."

"I must have begun to dream at once, and it was, naturally enough, all about the terrible thing that had occurred. But, like all dreams, it was a bit mixed. They were all mixed. Mortimer with his spangles flying up the trap, it breaking, and the pieces scattering round. Old Jack Haliday looking on at one side of the stage with his wife beside him—he as pale as death, and she looking prettier than ever. And then Mortimer coming down all crooked and falling on the stage, Mrs. Haliday shrieking, and her and Jack running forward, and me picking up the pieces of the broken trap from between people's legs, and finding the steel star with the bent points."

"I woke in a cold sweat, saying to myself as I sat up in bed in the dark":
"'That's it!'"

"And then my head began to reel about so that I lay down again and began to think it all over. And it all seemed clear enough then. It was Mr. Haliday who made that star and put it over the star trap where the points joined! That was what Jack Haliday was filing at when I saw him at his bench; and he had done it because Mortimer and his wife had been making love to each other. Those girls were right, after all. Of course, the steel points had prevented the trap opening, and when Mortimer was driven up against it his neck was broken."

"But then came the horrible thought that if Jack did it, it was murder, and he would be hung. And, after all, it was his wife that the harlequin had made love to—and old Jack loved her very much indeed himself and had been good to her—and she was his wife. And that bit of steel would hang him if it should be known. But no one but me—and whoever made it, and put it on the trap—even knew of its existence—and Mr. Haliday was my master—and the man was dead—and he was a villain!"

"I was living then at Quarry Place; and in the old quarry was a pond so deep that the boys used to say that far down the water was boiling hot, it was so near Hell."

"I softly opened the window, and, there in the dark, threw the bit of steel as far as I could into the quarry."

"No one ever knew, for I have never spoken a word of it till this very minute. I was not called at the inquest. Everyone was in a hurry; the coroner and the jury and the police. Our governor was in a hurry too, because we wanted to go on as usual at night; and too much talk of the tragedy would hurt business. So nothing was known; and all went on as usual. Except that after that Mrs. Haliday didn't stand in the wings during the harlequinade, and she was as loving to her old husband as a woman can be. It was him she used to watch now; and always with a sort of respectful adoration. She knew, though no one else did, except her husband—and me."

WHEN HE FINISHED THERE WAS a big spell of silence. The company had all been listening intently, so that there was no change except the cessation of Hempitch's voice. The eyes of all were now fixed on Mr. Wellesley Dovercourt. It was the role of the Tragedian to deal with such an occasion. He was quite alive to the privileges of his status, and spoke at once:

"H'm! Very excellent indeed! You will have to join the ranks of our profession, Mr. Master Machinist—the lower ranks, of course. A very thrilling narrative yours, and distinctly true. There may be some errors of detail, such as that Mrs. Haliday never flirted again. I . . . I knew John Hallday under, of course, his real name. But I shall preserve the secret you so judiciously suppressed. A very worthy person. He was stage carpenter at the Duke's Theatre, Bolton, where I first dared histrionic triumphs in the year—ah H'm! I saw quite a good deal of Mrs. Haliday at that time. And you are wrong about her. Quite wrong! She was a most attractive little woman—very!"

The Wardrobe Mistress here whispered to the Second Old Woman:

"Well, ma'am, they all seem agoin' of it tonight. I think they must have ketched the infection from Mr. Bloze. There isn't a bally word of truth in all Hempitch has said. I was there when the accident occurred—for it was an accident when Jim Bungnose, the clown, was killed. For he was a clown, not a 'arlequin; an' there wasn't no lovemakin' with Mrs. 'Aliday. God 'elp the woman as would try to make love to Jim; which she was the Strong Woman in a Circus, and could put up her dooks like a man. Moreover, there wasn't no Mrs. 'Aliday. The carpenter at Grimsby, where it is he means, was Tom Elrington, as he was my first 'usband. And as to Mr. Dovercourt rememberin'! He's a cure, he is; an' the Limit!"

THE EFFECT OF THE MASTER Machinist's story was so depressing that the M.C. tried to hurry things on; any change of sentiment would, he thought, be and advantage. So he bustled along:

"Now, Mr. Turner Smith, you are the next on the roster. It is a pity we have not an easel and a canvas and paint box here, or even some cartridge pager and charcoal, so that you might give us a touch of your art—what I may call a plastic diversion of the current of narrative genius which has been enlivening the snowy waste around us." The artistic audience applauded this flight of metaphor—all except the young man from Oxford, who contented himself by saying loudly, "Pip-pip!" He had heard something like it before at the Union. The Scene Painter saw coming danger, for the Tragedian had put down his pipe and was clearing his throat; so he at once began.

# The Way of Peace

I knew both Michael Hennessey and his wife Katty, though under the local pronunciation of the surname—Hinnessey. I had often gone into the little farmhouse to smoke a pipe with the old man, and to have, before I came away, a glass of milk from the old woman's clean, cool dairy. I had always understood that they were looked upon as a model couple; and it was within my knowledge that a little more than a year ago they had celebrated their golden wedding. But when old Lord Killendell—"The Lard" as they called him locally—suggested that I should ask old Michael how it was that they had lived such a happy life, there was something in his tone and the quiet laugh which followed it, which made me take the advice to heart. More especially when Lady Killendell, who had always been most kind to me, added with an approving smile—

"Do! You are a young man and a bachelor; you will learn something which may be of some service to you later on in your life."

The next time I was near Hennessey's farm the advice occurred to me, and I went in. The two old folk were alone in the house. Their work for the day—the strenuous work—was done, and they were beginning the long evening of rest, which is the farmer's reward for patient toil. We three sat round the hearth enjoying the glowing fire, and the aromatic smell of the burning turf, which is the only fuel used in that part of Ireland

I gradually led conversation round to the point of happy marriages by way of the Golden Wedding, which was not yet so far off as to have lost interest to the old folk.

"They tell me," I said presently, "that you two are the happiest couple in the Country. I hope that is so? You look it anyway; and everytime I have seen you the idea has been with me."

"That's true, God be thanked!" said Michael, after a pause.

"Amin!" joined in Katty, as she crossed herself.

"I wish you'd tell me how you do it?" I asked. Michael smiled this time, and his wife laughed.

"Why do ye want to know, acushla?" she said in reply. This put me in a little personal difficulty. As a matter of fact, I was engaged to be married, but I had been enjoined not to say anything about it—as yet. So I had to put my request on general grounds, which is never so appealing as when such information is asked for personal reasons.

"Well, you see, Mrs. Hennessey," I said, stumbling along as well as I could, "a man would always like to know a secret like that. It is one which might—at sometime in his life—be—be useful to him. He—"

"Begob it might, yer 'ann'r," broke in Michael. "Divil recave me if a young man beginnin' life wid a knowledge like that mightn't have all the young women iv a township follyin' round afther him like a flock iv geese afther a ghander." He was interrupted in turn by Katty—

"Ay, or th' ould wans too!" Then she turned to me—

"An' so ye're goin' to be married, yer 'ann'r. More power to ye; an' as many childher as there's days in the month."

"Hold hard there, ma'am!" I retorted. "That would be an embarras de richesse." She winced at the foreign phrase, so I translated it—"too much of a good thing—as the French say. But why do you think I'm going to be married?"

"Ah, go on out iv that wid ye! For what would a young man like yer 'ann'r want to know how marrid people does get on wid wan another, unless he's ceasin' to be a bhoy himself!" (In Ireland a man is a "bhoy" so long as he remains a bachelor. I have myself known a "bhoy" over ninety.) Her inductive ratiocination was too much for me; I remained silent.

"Begob, surr, Katty was wan too many for ye there!" chuckled the old man.

"Quite right, Michael, so she was!" I said. "But now that she has found me out, mayn't I have the price of the discovery? Won't you tell me how you have lived together so happily for so many years?"

"Ay, surr, there hasn't been a harrd wurrd betune us since the day afther we was married."

"The day after you were married?" I commented. "I wonder you didn't begin on the wedding-day itself!"

"Now that's all right, surr, an' mayhap so we would if we was beginnin' life out iv a book. Mayhap it was that we found out the way for ourselves, bekase we wasn't lookin' for it on any particular road. I'm thinkin' that that's the usual way for threasures bein' found 'Tisn't always—aye or mostly—the people that goes about shtickin' rods into places or knockin' chunks wid hammers from off iv other people's property that finds hidden money. Sure 'tis thim that goes about mindin' their own business that comes across it whin they're laste expectin' it." This was a long speech for Michael; and Katty, with her instinctive wish to please, expressed herself in subtle flattery given in an overt aside—

"Mind ye, the wisdom iv him. It does come bubblin' up, like a spring out iv a big book full iv writin' what no man can undhershtand!" Then I joined in myself—

"That is a good idea, Michael. The knowledge that can make two people happy is indeed a treasure. Won't you tell me how to find it? The finding, of course, a man must do for himself. But where there is a road, it is wise to know something about it before you start on a journey."

"Thrue for ye, surr. But I'm misdoubtin' meself if there's a road at all—a high-road iv coorse, I mane. But mind ye, 'tisn't on the high-roads that happiness walks. 'Tis the boreens in a man's own houldin'—nigh to his own home—an' his own heart!" This time Katty's comment was made directly to her husband—

"Begob, Mike, but it's a pote ye're becomin' in yer ould age. Boreens in yer heart! indade! An' here have I been thrampin' for half a century up an' down our own boreen; an' sorra wance have I seen happiness walkin' there more than on the mail-road itself."

This new philosophy was taking us away from the subject, so I led them back to it—"

"Well, even if there isn't a high-road—a road for all—won't you tell me what road you and Katty took? Then I may be able—some day—to find a road like it." The old man winked at me and chuckled; taking the pipe from his lips he jerked the mouth-piece backward over his shoulder.

"Ask her, surr. 'Tis she that can tell you— av the places."

"Won't you tell me, Katty?" I asked.

"Wid all the plisure in life, yer 'ann'r. 'Tis not much to tell for sure— an' mayhap not worth the tellin'; but av ye wish ye shall hear.

"As that ould man there says, it began the mornin' afther he was married on to me. Mind ye, at the beginnin'—I don't want ye to decave yerself about that bekase that's part iv the shtory—we was mighty fond of aich other. My! but he was the fine bhoy! Tall an' big an' shtrong an' mastherful; an' 'tis the proud girrl I was whin he ixprissed himself to me. I was that proud that I kem home leppin' so that me mother noticed it an' said: 'Katty, has that impident villin Mike Hinnessey been tellin' ye that ye're a good-lookin' girleen?'—for mind ye I wasn't thin grown up but only a shtep afther a skeuneuch. 'H'm'!' sez I. ''Tis more than that; he has asked me no less than to be married on to me.' That fetched her up, I can tell ye. 'Glory be,' sez she. 'What is the childher comin' to at all at all? You to be marrid that has no more to yer feet nor yer back than a flapper duck on the bog; an' him that can't bring a thing to the fair that he can't carry. Him that has but only yistherday left his father's cabin an' got one for himself; widout a shtick in it but the thruckle he lies on, an' the creel he ates aff.'" Instinctively I looked round the fine farm-kitchen in which we sat, with its good, solid, oak furniture, its plentitude of glass and crockery all daintily clean and bright. Michael noticed my look and said, gravely nodding his head as he spoke—

"That's all her doin', surr. That's Katty's!"

"Don't mind him, surr! 'Tis the kind good heart iv him that says it. But it's not my doin'. That's Michael's own work. Surely I only was careful wid the money that he arn'd!" Here I harked back to the main subject with a hint—

"And you said to your mother—?"

"Well, yer 'ann'r, I shtood right up to her—wasn't Michael worth it?—an' sez I: 'Michael is the bist man nor iver I see; an' I'm for him an' for no one else. He's poor I know, an' so am I. But plaze God he'll not be poor always; an' I'll wait for him if 'tis all me life!' Well, me mother was a good woman, an' she seen the tears in me eyes an' knew I was in arnest. She kem an' put her arms round me an' sez she: 'That's right, me child. That's the way to love; an' it's worth all the rist iv the wurrld. He's a good bhoy is Michael; an' 'tis right sure I am that he loves ye. An' whin the both iv ye think the time has come 'tis not me nor yer poor dead father that'll shtand betune ye.' I knew—faix only too well—what a harrd time me poor mother had, for the times was bad. That was the year of the potato-rot, an' throughout the counthry min an' weemin— an' worse still, the poor childhers—was dyin' be shcores. An' Michael knew too; an' ere long he sez to me: 'Katty, come wid me soon. Sure, acushla, if 'tis nothin' else 'twill be wan mouth less for yer poor mother to feed.' When Michael shpoke like that I wasn't the wan to say him nay."

Both were silent and I waited a while, till, seeing that they considered the tale as told, I ventured to recall them once again—

"But you haven't told me about the road yet."

"Oh, that, surr," said Katty with a laugh—"that was simple enough— may I tell him, Michael?"

"Go an, woman! Go an!" he answered with a growl.

"As Michael tould ye, surr, it began the day afther our weddin'. Ye know, surr, people like us didn't go off on honeymoons in thim days—not like they do now, poor or rich. Whin a woman kem into her husband's home she took life as 'twas to be foreninst her. I cooked Michael's supper an' me own on our weddin' night, just as I've done iver since. I knew that the fair at Killen was on the nixt day an' that Michael was lookin' to goin' to it; an' I made up me mind that he'd not go that day. So in the mornin' whin I done me hair—for a coorse I got up first to get the breakfast—I hid the rack. . ."

"The rack? Pardon my interrupting, but I don't understand." She was not offended but proceeded to explain—

"The rack-comb, surr. The thing ye brush yer hair wid. Wid poor folk it's all the brush-an'-comb they have. It was not thin like it is now whin ivery wan in a house has their own. Why, me son from Ameriky when he kem to shtay wid us had what he called a 'dressin'-bag' wid brushes an' combs enough to clane the heads iv all the parish. But in thim times if the house had wan that was all that was needed. When I looked back Michael was up an' was shavin' himself.

"'Gettin' ready for the fair?' sez I to him.

"'Yiz!' sez he, not sayin' much for the lip iv him was that twitched up to get smooth for the razor.

"'Ye're not!' sez I.

"'I am!' sez he.

"'Ye're not!' sez I again.

"I don't suppose ye undhershtand, surr, the feelin' iv a young wife when she knows that her man is her own. I had only been marrid on the yisiherday, an' whin I knew how Michael loved me I thought I was him as well as meself too. When a woman is marrid she thinks—an' never more than the day afther—that what she wishes is fixed an' done. She manes so well be her man—an' for all her life, mind ye—that she has no thought that everything isn't right. She has to larn! She has to larn; an' the sooner that she larns the betther for herself an' ivery wan else! Whin Michael had wiped his razor he put his hand on the windy-sill to take up the rack where it always lay. Not findin' it, he sez to me—

"'Katty, where's the rack?'

"'I won't tell ye,' sez I. I was up in meself afther me wan day iv a wife.

"'I want the rack, Katty,' he sez quite quiet.

"'Ye'll not get it,' sez I. . . 'Ye're not goin' to the fair today!'

"'I'm goin' to the fair today, an' ivery day I like!' he sez quieter nor iver, 'an' I want the rack.'

"'Ye'll not get it,' sez I. Wid that he took me face in his hands an' kissed me on the mouth. An' thin whin I let him go afther I had giv it back, he fetched me a shlap on the side iv me head that made me think that the house was full iv bells all clatterin' away at wanst, as sez he—

"'Katty, bring me the rack!'

She stopped and sat down, resuming her knitting as though she had said all she intended.

"And then?" I ventured to hint. She looked up at me and then over at Michael and said—

"Well, I wint acoorse an' brung him the rack. An' from that day to this we niver had a harrd wurrd wan for th'other." Michael chuckled.

"That's the road, surr. Some wan must be masther iv th' house. That time it had got to be me. An' I was—an' I am!" Here he stood up and bent over and kissed the old lady heartily. "An', surr, take it to mind that there's been no happier woman in Ireland—no, nor out of it—nor Katty."

It didn't seem quite a sufficient charting of the Road, so I ventured to appeal to Mrs. Hennessey again:—

"Did he go to the fair?" She had evidently been thinking, for she began almost at my first word. Since then, in trying to find a motive for her interruption, I have concluded that she thought her words might put Michael in a bad light; as one who was more or less of a bully.

"He combed his hair an' his moustache, an' he put on his coat wid the tails, an' shtuck his pipe in the front iv his caubeen, an' tuk his blackthorn. Thin he kissed me an' wint out. I looked out iv the door afther him, an' saw him turn the comer; an' then I kem in an' began to tidy up the house.

"Thin the door darkened, an' in kem Michael. He flung his caubeen an' his blackthorn in the corner, an' tuk me in his arrms, an' sez he—

"'Katty, alana-ma-chree, I'm not goin' to the fair this day. Bekase ye don't wish it, me darlin', not bekase ye merely want to kape me from it. Shure I love you alone, an' I wouldn't do nothin' to hurt ye. But always remimber that I'm a man an' used to man's ways; an' a man doesn't like bein' ordhered about be any wan—even be a wife that he loves an' that loves him.'" Her eyes were soft and shiny, and she looked affectionately at the sturdy old man. Then she turned to me and went on—

"An' that's the sort iv man that I've kep the peace wid for all these years. An' isn't he worth it? An' doesn't he desarve it—a man like that? I tell ye, surr, that's the way to thrate a woman; an' that's the way that a woman ought to be thrated. Sure, afther all, they're but childher iv a bigger kind. An' what's the way to thrate childher? 'Tisn't all done be shmiles an' pettin', an' be bread an' sugar. They want to get the hard hand now and again, an' they does the same whin they're grown into min and weemin. 'Tis the hand iv the mother that's the most tindher. Thin, whin that's not enough, the father has to give thim a clip on the ear if it's a girrl, or a cut wid a switch if it's a bhoy.

"An', mind ye, that's the aisiest punishment they iver gits. Whin they don't larn things from them 'tis harder they git it whin they come to larn from the warld!"

# The Burial of the Rats

L eaving Paris by the Orleans road, cross the Enceinte, and, turning to the right, you find yourself in a somewhat wild and not at all savoury district. Right and left, before and behind, on every side rise great heaps of dust and waste accumulated by the process of time.

Paris has its night as well as its day life, and the sojourner who enters his hotel in the Rue de Rivoli or the Rue St. Honore late at night or leaves it early in the morning, can guess, in coming near Montrouge—if he has not done so already—the purpose of those great waggons that look like boilers on wheels which he finds halting everywhere as he passes.

Every city has its peculiar institutions created out of its own needs; and one of the most notable institutions of Paris is its rag-picking population. In the early morning—and Parisian life commences at an early hour—may be seen in most streets standing on the pathway opposite every court and alley and between every few houses, as still in some American cities, even in parts of New York, large wooden boxes into which the domestics or tenement-holders empty the accumulated dust of the past day. Round these boxes gather and pass on, when the work is done, to fresh fields of labour and pastures new, squalid, hungry-looking men and women, the implements of whose craft consist of a coarse bag or basket slung over the shoulder and a little rake with which they turn over and probe and examine in the minutest manner the dustbins. They pick up and deposit in their baskets, by aid of their rakes, whatever they may find, with the same facility as a Chinaman uses his chopsticks.

Paris is a city of centralisation—and centralisation and classification are closely allied. In the early times, when centralisation is becoming a fact, its forerunner is classification. All things which are similar or analogous become grouped together, and from the grouping of groups rises one whole or central point. We see radiating many long arms with innumerable tentaculae, and in the centre rises a gigantic head with a comprehensive brain and keen eyes to look on every side and ears sensitive to hear—and a voracious mouth to swallow.

Other cities resemble all the birds and beasts and fishes whose appetites and digestions are normal. Paris alone is the analogical apotheosis of the octopus. Product of centralisation carried to an ad absurdum, it fairly represents the devil fish; and in no respects is the resemblance more curious than in the similarity of the digestive apparatus.

Those intelligent tourists who, having surrendered their individuality into the hands of Messrs. Cook or Gaze, "do" Paris in three days, are often puzzled to know how it is that the dinner which in London would cost about six shillings, can be had for three francs in a cafe in the Palais Royal. They need have no more wonder if they will but consider the classification which is a theoretic speciality of Parisian life, and adopt all round the fact from which the chiffonier has his genesis.

The Paris of 1850 was not like the Paris of today, and those who see the Paris of Napoleon and Baron Haussmann can hardly realise the existence of the state of things forty-five years ago.

Amongst other things, however, which have not changed are those districts where the waste is gathered. Dust is dust all the world over, in every age, and the family likeness of dust heaps is perfect. The traveller, therefore, who visits the environs of Montrouge can go back in fancy without difficulty to the year 1850.

In this year I was making a prolonged stay in Paris. I was very much in love with a young lady who, though she returned my passion, so far yielded to the wishes of her parents that she had promised not to see me or to correspond with me for a year. I, too, had been compelled to accede to these conditions under a vague hope of parental approval. During the term of probation I had promised to remain out of the country and not to write to my dear one until the expiration of the year.

Naturally the time went heavily with me. There was no one of my own family or circle who could tell me of Alice, and none of her own folk had, I am sorry to say, sufficient generosity to send me even an occasional word of comfort regarding her health and well-being. I spent six months wandering about Europe, but as I could find no satisfactory distraction in travel, I determined to come to Paris, where, at least, I would be within easy hail of London in case any good fortune should call me thither before the appointed time. That "hope deferred maketh the heart sick" was never better exemplified than in my case, for in addition to the perpetual longing to see the face I loved there was always with me a harrowing anxiety lest some accident should prevent me showing Alice in due time that I had, throughout the long period of probation, been faithful to her trust and my own love. Thus, every adventure which I undertook had a fierce pleasure of its own, for it was fraught with possible consequences greater than it would have ordinarily borne.

Like all travellers I exhausted the places of most interest in the first month of my stay, and was driven in the second month to look for amusement whithersoever I might. Having made sundry journeys to the better-known suburbs, I began to see that there was a terra incognita, in so far as the guide book was concerned, in the social wilderness lying between these attractive points. Accordingly I began to systematise my researches, and each day took up the thread of my exploration at the place where I had on the previous day dropped it.

In process of time my wanderings led me near Montrouge, and I saw that hereabouts lay the Ultima Thule of social exploration—a country as little known as that round the source of the White Nile. And so I determined to investigate philosophically the chiffonier—his habitat, his life, and his means of life.

The job was an unsavoury one, difficult of accomplishment, and with little hope of adequate reward. However, despite reason, obstinacy prevailed, and I entered into my new investigation with a keener energy than I could have summoned to aid me in any investigation leading to any end, valuable or worthy.

One day, late in a fine afternoon, toward the end of September, I entered the holy of holies of the city of dust. The place was evidently the recognised abode of a number of chiffoniers, for some sort of arrangement was manifested in the formation of the dust heaps near the road. I passed amongst these heaps, which stood like orderly sentries, determined to penetrate further and trace dust to its ultimate location.

As I passed along I saw behind the dust heaps a few forms that flitted to and fro, evidently watching with interest the advent of any stranger to such a place. The district was like a small Switzerland, and as I went forward my tortuous course shut out the path behind me.

Presently I got into what seemed a small city or community of chiffoniers. There were a number of shanties or huts, such as may be met with in the remote parts of the Bog of Allan—rude places with wattled walls, plastered with mud and roofs of rude thatch made from stable refuse—such places as one would not like to enter for any consideration, and which even in water-colour could only look picturesque if judiciously treated. In the midst of these huts was one of the strangest adaptations—I cannot say habitations—I had ever seen. An immense old wardrobe, the colossal remnant of some boudoir of Charles VII or Henry II, had been converted into a dwelling-house. The double doors lay open, so that the entire menage was open to public

　　　　　　　　　　　　　　　　　　　　　　　　　　　　BRAM STOKER

view. In the open half of the wardrobe was a common sitting-room of some four feet by six, in which sat, smoking their pipes round a charcoal brazier, no fewer than six old soldiers of the First Republic, with their uniforms torn and worn threadbare. Evidently they were of the mauvais sujet class; their blear eyes and limp jaws told plainly of a common love of absinthe; and their eyes had that haggard, worn look which stamps the drunkard at his worst, and that look of slumbering ferocity which follows hard in the wake of drink. The other side stood as of old, with its shelves intact, save that they were cut to half their depth, and in each shelf of which there were six, was a bed made with rags and straw. The half-dozen of worthies who inhabited this structure looked at me curiously as I passed; and when I looked back after going a little way I saw their heads together in a whispered conference. I did not like the look of this at all, for the place was very lonely, and the men looked very, very villainous. However, I did not see any cause for fear, and went on my way, penetrating further and further into the Sahara. The way was tortuous to a degree, and from going round in a series of semi-circles, as one goes in skating with the Dutch roll, I got rather confused with regard to the points of the compass.

When I had penetrated a little way I saw, as I turned the corner of a half-made heap, sitting on a heap of straw an old soldier with threadbare coat.

"Hallo!" said I to myself; "the First Republic is well represented here in its soldiery."

As I passed him the old man never even looked up at me, but gazed on the ground with stolid persistency. Again I remarked to myself: "See what a life of rude warfare can do! This old man's curiosity is a thing of the past."

When I had gone a few steps, however, I looked back suddenly, and saw that curiosity was not dead, for the veteran had raised his head and was regarding me with a very queer expression. He seemed to me to look very like one of the six worthies in the press. When he saw me looking he dropped his head; and without thinking further of him I went on my way, satisfied that there was a strange likeness between these old warriors.

Presently I met another old soldier in a similar manner. He, too, did not notice me whilst I was passing.

By this time it was getting late in the afternoon, and I began to think of retracing my steps. Accordingly I turned to go back, but could

see a number of tracks leading between different mounds and could not
ascertain which of them I should take. In my perplexity I wanted to see
someone of whom to ask the way, but could see no one. I determined to
go on a few mounds further and so try to see someone—not a veteran.

I gained my object, for after going a couple of hundred yards I saw
before me a single shanty such as I had seen before—with, however,
the difference that this was not one for living in, but merely a roof with
three walls open in front. From the evidences which the neighbourhood
exhibited I took it to be a place for sorting. Within it was an old woman
wrinkled and bent with age; I approached her to ask the way.

She rose as I came close and I asked her my way. She immediately
commenced a conversation; and it occurred to me that here in the very
centre of the Kingdom of Dust was the place to gather details of the
history of Parisian rag-picking—particularly as I could do so from the
lips of one who looked like the oldest inhabitant.

I began my inquiries, and the old woman gave me most interesting
answers—she had been one of the ceteuces who sat daily before the
guillotine and had taken an active part among the women who signalised
themselves by their violence in the revolution. While we were talking
she said suddenly: "But m'sieur must be tired standing," and dusted a
rickety old stool for me to sit down. I hardly liked to do so for many
reasons; but the poor old woman was so civil that I did not like to run
the risk of hurting her by refusing, and moreover the conversation of
one who had been at the taking of the Bastille was so interesting that I
sat down and so our conversation went on.

While we were talking an old man—older and more bent and wrinkled
even than the woman—appeared from behind the shanty. "Here is
Pierre," said she. "M'sieur can hear stories now if he wishes, for Pierre
was in everything, from the Bastille to Waterloo." The old man took
another stool at my request and we plunged into a sea of revolutionary
reminiscences. This old man, albeit clothed like a scare-crow, was like
anyone of the six veterans.

I was now sitting in the centre of the low hut with the woman on
my left hand and the man on my right, each of them being somewhat
in front of me. The place was full of all sorts of curious objects of lumber,
and of many things that I wished far away. In one corner was a heap
of rags which seemed to move from the number of vermin it contained,
and in the other a heap of bones whose odour was something shocking.
Every now and then, glancing at the heaps, I could see the gleaming

eyes of some of the rats which infested the place. These loathsome objects were bad enough, but what looked even more dreadful was an old butcher's axe with an iron handle stained with clots of blood leaning up against the wall on the right hand side. Still these things did not give me much concern. The talk of the two old people was so fascinating that I stayed on and on, till the evening came and the dust heaps threw dark shadows over the vales between them.

After a time I began to grow uneasy, I could not tell how or why, but somehow I did not feel satisfied. Uneasiness is an instinct and means warning. The psychic faculties are often the sentries of the intellect; and when they sound alarm the reason begins to act, although perhaps not consciously.

This was so with me. I began to bethink me where I was and by what surrounded, and to wonder how I should fare in case I should be attacked; and then the thought suddenly burst upon me, although without any overt cause, that I was in danger. Prudence whispered: "Be still and make no sign," and so I was still and made no sign, for I knew that four cunning eyes were on me. "Four eyes—if not more." My God, what a horrible thought! The whole shanty might be surrounded on three sides with villains! I might be in the midst of a band of such desperadoes as only half a century of periodic revolution can produce.

With a sense of danger my intellect and observation quickened, and I grew more watchful than was my wont. I noticed that the old woman's eyes were constantly wandering toward my hands. I looked at them too, and saw the cause—my rings. On my left little finger I had a large signet and on the right a good diamond.

I thought that if there was any danger my first care was to avert suspicion. Accordingly I began to work the conversation round to rag-picking—to the drains—of the things found there; and so by easy stages to jewels. Then, seizing a favourable opportunity, I asked the old woman if she knew anything of such things. She answered that she did, a little. I held out my right hand, and, showing her the diamond, asked her what she thought of that. She answered that her eyes were bad, and stooped over my hand. I said as nonchalantly as I could: "Pardon me! You will see better thus!" and taking it off handed it to her. An unholy light came into her withered old face, as she touched it. She stole one glance at me swift and keen as a flash of lightning.

She bent over the ring for a moment, her face quite concealed as though examining it. The old man looked straight out of the front of the shanty before him, at the same time fumbling in his pockets and producing a screw of tobacco in a paper and a pipe, which he proceeded to fill. I took advantage of the pause and the momentary rest from the searching eyes on my face to look carefully round the place, now dim and shadowy in the gloaming. There still lay all the heaps of varied reeking foulness; there the terrible blood-stained axe leaning against the wall in the right hand corner, and everywhere, despite the gloom, the baleful glitter of the eyes of the rats. I could see them even through some of the chinks of the boards at the back low down close to the ground. But stay! these latter eyes seemed more than usually large and bright and baleful!

For an instant my heart stood still, and I felt in that whirling condition of mind in which one feels a sort of spiritual drunkenness, and as though the body is only maintained erect in that there is no time for it to fall before recovery. Then, in another second, I was calm-coldly calm, with all my energies in full vigour, with a self-control which I felt to be perfect and with all my feeling and instincts alert.

Now I knew the full extent of my danger: I was watched and surrounded by desperate people! I could not even guess at how many of them were lying there on the ground behind the shanty, waiting for the moment to strike. I knew that I was big and strong, and they knew it, too. They knew also, as I did, that I was an Englishman and would make a fight for it; and so we waited. I had, I felt, gained an advantage in the last few seconds, for I knew my danger and understood the situation. Now, I thought, is the test of my courage—the enduring test: the fighting test may come later!

The old woman raised her head and said to me in a satisfied kind of way:

"A very fine ring, indeed—a beautiful ring! Oh, me! I once had such rings, plenty of them, and bracelets and earrings! Oh! for in those fine days I led the town a dance! But they've forgotten me now! They've forgotten me! They? Why they never heard of me! Perhaps their grandfathers remember me, some of them!" and she laughed a harsh, croaking laugh. And then I am bound to say that she astonished me, for she handed me back the ring with a certain suggestion of old-fashioned grace which was not without its pathos.

The old man eyed her with a sort of sudden ferocity, half rising from his stool, and said to me suddenly and hoarsely:

"Let me see!"

I was about to hand the ring when the old woman said:

"No! no, do not give it to Pierre! Pierre is eccentric. He loses things; and such a pretty ring!"

"Cat!" said the old man, savagely. Suddenly the old woman said, rather more loudly than was necessary:

"Wait! I shall tell you something about a ring." There was something in the sound of her voice that jarred upon me. Perhaps it was my hypersensitiveness, wrought up as I was to such a pitch of nervous excitement, but I seemed to think that she was not addressing me. As I stole a glance round the place I saw the eyes of the rats in the bone heaps, but missed the eyes along the back. But even as I looked I saw them again appear. The old woman's "Wait!" had given me a respite from attack, and the men had sunk back to their reclining posture.

"I once lost a ring—a beautiful diamond hoop that had belonged to a queen, and which was given to me by a farmer of the taxes, who afterwards cut his throat because I sent him away. I thought it must have been stolen, and taxed my people; but I could get no trace. The police came and suggested that it had found its way to the drain. We descended—I in my fine clothes, for I would not trust them with my beautiful ring! I know more of the drains since then, and of rats, too! but I shall never forget the horror of that place—alive with blazing eyes, a wall of them just outside the light of our torches. Well, we got beneath my house. We searched the outlet of the drain, and there in the filth found my ring, and we came out.

"But we found something else also before we came! As we were coming toward the opening a lot of sewer rats—human ones this time—came toward us. They told the police that one of their number had gone into the drain, but had not returned. He had gone in only shortly before we had, and, if lost, could hardly be far off. They asked help to seek him, so we turned back. They tried to prevent me going, but I insisted. It was a new excitement, and had I not recovered my ring? Not far did we go till we came on something. There was but little water, and the bottom of the drain was raised with brick, rubbish, and much matter of the kind. He had made a fight for it, even when his torch had gone out. But they were too many for him! They had not been long about it! The bones were still warm; but they were picked clean. They had even eaten their own dead ones and there were bones of rats as well as of the man. They took it cool enough those other— the human ones—and joked of their comrade when they found him dead, though they would have helped him living. Bah! what matters it—life or death?"

"And had you no fear?" I asked her.

"Fear!" she said with a laugh. "Me have fear? Ask Pierre! But I was younger then, and, as I came through that horrible drain with its wall of greedy eyes, always moving with the circle of the light from the torches, I did not feel easy. I kept on before the men, though! It is a way I have! I never let the men get it before me. All I want is a chance and a means! And they ate him up—took every trace away except the bones; and no one knew it, nor no sound of him was ever heard!" Here she broke into a chuckling fit of the ghastliest merriment which it was ever my lot to hear and see. A great poetess describes her heroine singing: "Oh! to see or hear her singing! Scarce I know which is the divinest."

And I can apply the same idea to the old crone—in all save the divinity, for I scarce could tell which was the most hellish—the harsh, malicious, satisfied, cruel laugh, or the leering grin, and the horrible square opening of the mouth like a tragic mask, and the yellow gleam of the few discoloured teeth in the shapeless gums. In that laugh and with that grin and the chuckling satisfaction I knew as well as if it had been spoken to me in words of thunder that my murder was settled, and the murderers only bided the proper time for its accomplishment. I could read between the lines of her gruesome story the commands to her accomplices. "Wait," she seemed to say, "bide your time. I shall strike the first blow. Find the weapon for me, and I shall make the opportunity! He shall not escape! Keep him quiet, and then no one will be wiser. There will be no outcry, and the rats will do their work!"

It was growing darker and darker; the night was coming. I stole a glance round the shanty, still all the same! The bloody axe in the corner, the heaps of filth, and the eyes on the bone heaps and in the crannies of the floor.

Pierre had been still ostensibly filling his pipe; he now struck a light and began to puff away at it. The old woman said:

"Dear heart, how dark it is! Pierre, like a good lad, light the lamp!"

Pierre got up and with the lighted match in his hand touched the wick of a lamp which hung at one side of the entrance to the shanty, and which had a reflector that threw the light all over the place. It was evidently that which was used for their sorting at night.

"Not that, stupid! Not that! The lantern!" she called out to him.

He immediately blew it out, saying: "All right, mother, I'll find it," and he hustled about the left corner of the room—the old woman saying through the darkness:

"The lantern! the lantern! Oh! That is the light that is most useful to us poor folks. The lantern was the friend of the revolution! It is the friend of the chiffonier! It helps us when all else fails."

Hardly had she said the word when there was a kind of creaking of the whole place, and something was steadily dragged over the roof.

Again I seemed to read between the lines of her words. I knew the lesson of the lantern.

"One of you get on the roof with a noose and strangle him as he passes out if we fail within."

As I looked out of the opening I saw the loop of a rope outlined black against the lurid sky. I was now, indeed, beset!

Pierre was not long in finding the lantern. I kept my eyes fixed through the darkness on the old woman. Pierre struck his light, and by its flash I saw the old woman raise from the ground beside her where it had mysteriously appeared, and then hide in the folds of her gown, a long sharp knife or dagger. It seemed to be like a butcher's sharpening iron fined to a keen point.

The lantern was lit.

"Bring it here, Pierre," she said. "Place it in the doorway where we can see it. See how nice it is! It shuts out the darkness from us; it is just right!"

Just right for her and her purposes! It threw all its light on my face, leaving in gloom the faces of both Pierre and the woman, who sat outside of me on each side.

I felt that the time of action was approaching; but I knew now that the first signal and movement would come from the woman, and so watched her.

I was all unarmed, but I had made up my mind what to do. At the first movement I would seize the butcher's axe in the right-hand corner and fight my way out. At least, I would die hard. I stole a glance round to fix its exact locality so that I could not fail to seize it at the first effort, for then, if ever, time and accuracy would be precious.

Good God! It was gone! All the horror of the situation burst upon me; but the bitterest thought of all was that if the issue of the terrible position should be against me Alice would infallibly suffer. Either she would believe me false—and any lover, or anyone who has ever been one, can imagine the bitterness of the thought—or else she would go on loving long after I had been lost to her and to the world, so that her life would be broken and embittered, shattered with disappointment and despair. The very magnitude of the pain braced me up and nerved me to bear the dread scrutiny of the plotters.

I think I did not betray myself. The old woman was watching me as a cat does a mouse; she had her right hand hidden in the folds of her gown, clutching, I knew, that long, cruel-looking dagger. Had she seen any disappointment in my face she would, I felt, have known that the moment had come, and would have sprung on me like a tigress, certain of taking me unprepared.

I looked out into the night, and there I saw new cause for danger. Before and around the hut were at a little distance some shadowy forms; they were quite still, but I knew that they were all alert and on guard. Small chance for me now in that direction.

Again I stole a glance round the place. In moments of great excitement and of great danger, which is excitement, the mind works very quickly, and the keenness of the faculties which depend on the mind grows in proportion. I now felt this. In an instant I took in the whole situation. I saw that the axe had been taken through a small hole made in one of the rotten boards. How rotten they must be to allow of such a thing being done without a particle of noise.

The hut was a regular murder-trap, and was guarded all around. A garroter lay on the roof ready to entangle me with his noose if I should escape the dagger of the old hag. In front the way was guarded by I know not how many watchers. And at the back was a row of desperate men—I had seen their eyes still through the crack in the boards of the floor, when last I looked—as they lay prone waiting for the signal to start erect. If it was to be ever, now for it!

As nonchalantly as I could I turned slightly on my stool so as to get my right leg well under me. Then with a sudden jump, turning my head, and guarding it with my hands, and with the fighting instinct of the knights of old, I breathed my lady's name, and hurled myself against the back wall of the hut.

Watchful as they were, the suddenness of my movement surprised both Pierre and the old woman. As I crashed through the rotten timbers I saw the old woman rise with a leap like a tiger and heard her low gasp of baffled rage. My feet lit on something that moved, and as I jumped away I knew that I had stepped on the back of one of the row of men lying on their faces outside the hut. I was torn with nails and splinters, but otherwise unhurt. Breathless I rushed up the mound in front of me, hearing as I went the dull crash of the shanty as it collapsed into a mass.

It was a nightmare climb. The mound, though but low, was awfully steep, and with each step I took the mass of dust and cinders tore down with me and gave way under my feet. The dust rose and choked me; it was sickening, foetid, awful; but my climb was, I felt, for life or death, and I struggled on. The seconds seemed hours; but the few moments I had in starting, combined with my youth and strength, gave me a great advantage, and, though several forms struggled after me in deadly silence which was more dreadful than any sound, I easily reached the top. Since then I have climbed the cone of Vesuvius, and as I struggled up that dreary steep amid the sulphurous fumes the memory of that awful night at Montrouge came back to me so vividly that I almost grew faint.

The mound was one of the tallest in the region of dust, and as I struggled to the top, panting for breath and with my heart beating like a sledge-hammer, I saw away to my left the dull red gleam of the sky, and nearer still the flashing of lights. Thank God! I knew where I was now and where lay the road to Paris!

For two or three seconds I paused and looked back. My pursuers were still well behind me, but struggling up resolutely, and in deadly silence. Beyond, the shanty was a wreck—a mass of timber and moving forms. I could see it well, for flames were already bursting out; the rags and straw had evidently caught fire from the lantern. Still silence there! Not a sound! These old wretches could die game, anyhow.

I had no time for more than a passing glance, for as I cast an eye round the mound preparatory to making my descent I saw several dark forms rushing round on either side to cut me off on my way. It was now a race for life. They were trying to head me on my way to Paris, and with the instinct of the moment I dashed down to the right-hand side. I was just in time, for, though I came as it seemed to me down the steep in a few steps, the wary old men who were watching me turned back, and one, as I rushed by into the opening between the two mounds in front, almost struck me a blow with that terrible butcher's axe. There could surely not be two such weapons about!

Then began a really horrible chase. I easily ran ahead of the old men, and even when some younger ones and a few women joined in the hunt I easily distanced them. But I did not know the way, and I could not even guide myself by the light in the sky, for I was running away from it. I had heard that, unless of conscious purpose, hunted men turn always to the left, and so I found it now; and so, I suppose, knew also my pursuers, who were more animals than men, and with cunning or instinct had found out such secrets for themselves: for on finishing a quick spurt, after which I intended to take a moment's breathing space, I suddenly saw ahead of me two or three forms swiftly passing behind a mound to the right.

I was in the spider's web now indeed! But with the thought of this new danger came the resource of the hunted, and so I darted down the next turning to the right. I continued in this direction for some hundred yards, and then, making a turn to the left again, felt certain that I had, at any rate, avoided the danger of being surrounded.

But not of pursuit, for on came the rabble after me, steady, dogged, relentless, and still in grim silence.

In the greater darkness the mounds seemed now to be somewhat smaller than before, although—for the night was closing—they looked bigger in proportion. I was now well ahead of my pursuers, so I made a dart up the mound in front.

Oh joy of joys! I was close to the edge of this inferno of dust heaps. Away behind me the red light of Paris in the sky, and towering up behind rose the heights of Montmartre—a dim light, with here and there brilliant points like stars.

Restored to vigour in a moment, I ran over the few remaining mounds of decreasing size, and found myself on the level land beyond. Even then, however, the prospect was not inviting. All before me was dark and dismal, and I had evidently come on one of those dank, low-lying waste places which are found here and there in the neighbourhood of great cities. Places of waste and desolation, where the space is required for the ultimate agglomeration of all that is noxious, and the ground is so poor as to create no desire of occupancy even in the lowest squatter. With eyes accustomed to the gloom of the evening, and away now from the shadows of those dreadful dust heaps, I could see much more easily than I could a little while ago. It might have been, of course, that the glare in the sky of the lights of Paris, though the city was some miles away, was reflected here. Howsoever it was, I saw well enough to take bearings for certainly some little distance around me.

In front was a bleak, flat waste that seemed almost dead level, with here and there the dark shimmering of stagnant pools. Seemingly far off on the right, amid a small cluster of scattered lights, rose a dark mass of Fort Montrouge, and away to the left in the dim distance, pointed with stray gleams from cottage windows, the lights in the sky showed the locality of Bicetre. A moment's thought decided me to take to the right and try to reach Montrouge. There at least would be some sort of safety, and I might possibly long before come on some of the cross roads which I knew. Somewhere, not far off, must lie the strategic road made to connect the outlying chain of forts circling the city.

Then I looked back. Coming over the mounds, and outlined black against the glare of the Parisian horizon, I saw several moving figures, and still a way to the right several more deploying out between me and my destination. They evidently meant to cut me off in this direction, and so my choice became constricted; it lay now between going straight ahead or turning to the left. Stooping to the ground, so as to get the advantage of the horizon as a line of sight, I looked carefully in this direction, but could detect no sign of my enemies. I argued that as they had not guarded or were not trying to guard that point, there was evidently danger to me there already. So I made up my mind to go straight on before me.

It was not an inviting prospect, and as I went on the reality grew worse. The ground became soft and oozy, and now and again gave way beneath me in a sickening kind of way. I seemed somehow to be going down, for I saw round me places seemingly more elevated than where I was, and this in a place which from a little way back seemed dead level. I looked around, but could see none of my pursuers. This was strange, for all along these birds of the night had followed me through the darkness as well as though it was broad daylight. How I blamed myself for coming out in my light-coloured tourist suit of tweed. The silence, and my not being able to see my enemies, whilst I felt that they were watching me, grew appalling, and in the hope of someone not of this ghastly crew hearing me I raised my voice and shouted several times. There was not the slightest response; not even an echo rewarded my efforts. For a while I stood stock still and kept my eyes in one direction. On one of the rising places around me I saw something dark move along, then another, and another. This was to my left, and seemingly moving to head me off.

I thought that again I might with my skill as a runner elude my enemies at this game, and so with all my speed darted forward.

Splash!

My feet had given way in a mass of slimy rubbish, and I had fallen headlong into a reeking, stagnant pool. The water and the mud in which my arms sank up to the elbows was filthy and nauseous beyond description, and in the suddenness of my fall I had actually swallowed some of the filthy stuff, which nearly choked me, and made me gasp for breath. Never shall I forget the moments during which I stood trying to recover myself almost fainting from the foetid odour of the filthy pool, whose white mist rose ghostlike around. Worst of all, with the acute despair of the hunted animal when he sees the pursuing pack closing on him, I saw before my eyes whilst I stood helpless the dark forms of my pursuers moving swiftly to surround me.

It is curious how our minds work on odd matters even when the energies of thought are seemingly concentrated on some terrible and pressing need. I was in momentary peril of my life: my safety depended on my action, and my choice of alternatives coming now with almost every step I took, and yet I could not but think of the strange dogged persistency of these old men. Their silent resolution, their steadfast, grim, persistency even in such a cause commanded, as well as fear, even a measure of respect. What must they have been in the vigour of their youth. I could understand now that whirlwind rush on the bridge of Arcola, that scornful exclamation of the Old Guard at Waterloo! Unconscious cerebration has its own pleasures, even at such moments; but fortunately it does not in anyway clash with the thought from which action springs.

I realised at a glance that so far I was defeated in my object, my enemies as yet had won. They had succeeded in surrounding me on three sides, and were bent on driving me off to the left-hand, where there was already some danger for me, for they had left no guard. I accepted the alternative—it was a case of Hobson's choice and run. I had to keep the lower ground, for my pursuers were on the higher places. However, though the ooze and broken ground impeded me my youth and training made me able to hold my ground, and by keeping a diagonal line I not only kept them from gaining on me but even began to distance them. This gave me new heart and strength, and by this time habitual training was beginning to tell and my second wind had come. Before me the ground rose slightly. I rushed up the slope and found before me a waste of watery slime, with a low dyke or bank looking black and grim beyond. I felt that if I could but reach that dyke in safety I could there, with solid ground under my feet and some kind of path to guide me, find with comparative ease a way out of my troubles. After a glance right and left and seeing no one near, I kept my eyes for a few minutes to their rightful work of aiding my feet whilst I crossed the swamp. It was rough, hard work, but there was little danger, merely toil; and a short time took me to the dyke. I rushed up the slope exulting; but here again I met a new shock. On either side of me rose a number of crouching figures. From right and left they rushed at me. Each body held a rope.

The cordon was nearly complete. I could pass on neither side, and the end was near.

There was only one chance, and I took it. I hurled myself across the dyke, and escaping out of the very clutches of my foes threw myself into the stream.

At any other time I should have thought that water foul and filthy, but now it was as welcome as the most crystal stream to the parched traveller. It was a highway of safety!

My pursuers rushed after me. Had only one of them held the rope it would have been all up with me, for he could have entangled me before I had time to swim a stroke; but the many hands holding it embarrassed and delayed them, and when the rope struck the water I heard the splash well behind me. A few minutes' hard swimming took me across the stream. Refreshed with the immersion and encouraged by the escape, I climbed the dyke in comparative gaiety of spirits.

From the top I looked back. Through the darkness I saw my assailants scattering up and down along the dyke. The pursuit was evidently not ended, and again I had to choose my course. Beyond the dyke where I stood was a wild, swampy space very similar to that which I had crossed. I determined to shun such a place, and thought for a moment whether I would take up or down the dyke. I thought I heard a sound—the muffled sound of oars, so I listened, and then shouted.

No response; but the sound ceased. My enemies had evidently got a boat of some kind. As they were on the up side of me I took the down path and began to run. As I passed to the left of where I had entered the water I heard several splashes, soft and stealthy, like the sound a rat makes as he plunges into the stream, but vastly greater; and as I looked I saw the dark sheen of the water broken by the ripples of several advancing heads. Some of my enemies were swimming the stream also.

And now behind me, up the stream, the silence was broken by the quick rattle and creak of oars; my enemies were in hot pursuit. I put my best leg foremost and ran on. After a break of a couple of minutes I looked back, and by a gleam of light through the ragged clouds I saw several dark forms climbing the bank behind me. The wind had now begun to rise, and the water beside me was ruffled and beginning to break in tiny waves on the bank. I had to keep my eyes pretty well on the ground before me, lest I should stumble, for I knew that to stumble was death. After a few minutes I looked back behind me. On the dyke were only a few dark figures, but crossing the waste, swampy ground were many more. What new danger this portended I did not know—could only guess. Then as I ran it seemed to me that my track kept ever sloping away to the right. I looked up ahead and saw that the river was much wider than before, and that the dyke on which I stood fell quite away, and beyond it was another stream on whose near bank I saw some of the dark forms now across the marsh. I was on an island of some kind.

My situation was now indeed terrible, for my enemies had hemmed me in on every side. Behind came the quickening roll of the oars, as though my pursuers knew that the end was close. Around me on every side was desolation; there was not a roof or light, as far as I could see. Far off to the right rose some dark mass, but what it was I knew not. For a moment I paused to think what I should do, not for more, for my pursuers were drawing closer. Then my mind was made up. I slipped down the bank and took to the water. I struck out straight ahead, so as to gain the current by clearing the backwater of the island for such I presume it was, when I had passed into the stream. I waited till a cloud came driving across the moon and leaving all in darkness. Then I took off my hat and laid it softly on the water floating with the stream, and a second after dived to the right and struck out under water with all my might. I was, I suppose, half a minute under water, and when I rose came up as softly as I could, and turning, looked back. There went my light brown hat floating merrily away. Close behind it came a rickety old boat, driven furiously by a pair of oars. The moon was still partly obscured by the drifting clouds, but in the partial light I could see a man in the bows holding aloft ready to strike what appeared to me to be that same dreadful pole-axe which I had before escaped. As I looked the boat drew closer, closer, and the man struck savagely. The hat disappeared. The man fell forward, almost out of the boat. His comrades dragged him in but without the axe, and then as I turned with all my energies bent on reaching the further bank, I heard the fierce whirr of the muttered "Sacre!" which marked the anger of my baffled pursuers.

That was the first sound I had heard from human lips during all this dreadful chase, and full as it was of menace and danger to me it was a welcome sound for it broke that awful silence which shrouded and appalled me. It was as though an overt sign that my opponents were men and not ghosts, and that with them I had, at least, the chance of a man, though but one against many.

But now that the spell of silence was broken the sounds came thick and fast. From boat to shore and back from shore to boat came quick question and answer, all in the fiercest whispers. I looked back—a fatal thing to do—for in the instant someone caught sight of my face, which showed white on the dark water, and shouted. Hands pointed to me, and in a moment or two the boat was under weigh, and following hard after me. I had but a little way to go, but quicker and quicker came the boat after me. A few more strokes and I would be on the shore, but I felt the oncoming of the boat, and expected each second to feel the crash of an oar or other weapon on my head. Had I not seen that dreadful axe disappear in the water I do not think that I could have won the shore. I heard the muttered curses of those not rowing and the laboured breath of the rowers. With one supreme effort for life or liberty I touched the bank and sprang up it. There was not a single second to spare, for hard behind me the boat grounded and several dark forms sprang after me. I gained the top of the dyke, and keeping to the left ran on again. The boat put off and followed down the stream. Seeing this I feared danger in this direction, and quickly turning, ran down the dyke on the other side, and after passing a short stretch of marshy ground gained a wild, open flat country and sped on.

Still behind me came on my relentless pursuers. Far away, below me, I saw the same dark mass as before, but now grown closer and greater. My heart gave a great thrill of delight, for I knew that it must be the fortress of Bicetre, and with new courage I ran on. I had heard that between each and all of the protecting forts of Paris there are strategic ways, deep sunk roads, where soldiers marching should be sheltered from an enemy. I knew that if I could gain this road I would be safe, but in the darkness I could not see any sign of it, so, in blind hope of striking it, I ran on.

Presently I came to the edge of a deep cut, and found that down below me ran a road guarded on each side by a ditch of water fenced on either side by a straight, high wall.

Getting fainter and dizzier, I ran on; the ground got more broken—more and more still, till I staggered and fell, and rose again, and ran on in the blind anguish of the hunted. Again the thought of Alice nerved me. I would not be lost and wreck her life: I would fight and struggle for life to the bitter end. With a great effort I caught the top of the wall. As, scrambling like a catamount, I drew myself up, I actually felt a hand touch the sole of my foot. I was now on a sort of causeway, and before me I saw a dim light. Blind and dizzy, I ran on, staggered, and fell, rising, covered with dust and blood.

"Halt la!"

The words sounded like a voice from heaven. A blaze of light seemed to enwrap me, and I shouted with joy.

"Qui va la?" The rattle of musketry, the flash of steel before my eyes. Instinctively I stopped, though close behind me came a rush of my pursuers.

Another word or two, and out from a gateway poured, as it seemed to me, a tide of red and blue, as the guard turned out. All around seemed blazing with light, and the flash of steel, the clink and rattle of arms, and the loud, harsh voices of command. As I fell forward, utterly exhausted, a soldier caught me. I looked back in dreadful expectation, and saw the mass of dark forms disappearing into the night. Then I must have fainted. When I recovered my senses I was in the guard room. They gave me brandy, and after awhile I was able to tell them something of what had passed. Then a commissary of police appeared, apparently out of the empty air, as is the way of the Parisian police officer. He listened attentively, and then had a moment's consultation with the officer in command. Apparently they were agreed, for they asked me if I were ready now to come with them.

"Where to?" I asked, rising to go.

"Back to the dust heaps. We shall, perhaps, catch them yet!"

"I shall try!" said I.

He eyed me for a moment keenly, and said suddenly:

"Would you like to wait awhile or till tomorrow, young Englishman?" This touched me to the quick, as, perhaps, he intended, and I jumped to my feet.

"Come now!" I said; "now! now! An Englishman is always ready for his duty!"

The commissary was a good fellow, as well as a shrewd one; he slapped my shoulder kindly. "Brave garcon!" he said. "Forgive me, but I knew what would do you most good. The guard is ready. Come!"

And so, passing right through the guard room, and through a long vaulted passage, we were out into the night. A few of the men in front had powerful lanterns. Through courtyards and down a sloping way we passed out through a low archway to a sunken road, the same that I had seen in my flight. The order was given to get at the double, and with a quick, springing stride, half run, half walk, the soldiers went swiftly along. I felt my strength renewed again—such is the difference between hunter and hunted. A very short distance took us to a low-lying pontoon bridge across the stream, and evidently very little higher up than I had struck it. Some effort had evidently been made to damage it, for the ropes had all been cut, and one of the chains had been broken. I heard the officer say to the commissary:

"We are just in time! A few more minutes, and they would have destroyed the bridge. Forward, quicker still!" and on we went. Again we reached a pontoon on the winding stream; as we came up we heard the hollow boom of the metal drums as the efforts to destroy the bridge was again renewed. A word of command was given, and several men raised their rifles.

"Fire!" A volley rang out. There was a muffled cry, and the dark forms dispersed. But the evil was done, and we saw the far end of the pontoon swing into the stream. This was a serious delay, and it was nearly an hour before we had renewed ropes and secured the bridge sufficiently to allow us to cross.

We renewed the chase. Quicker, quicker we went towards the dust heaps.

After a time we came to a place that I knew. There were the remains of a fire—a few smouldering wood ashes still cast a red glow, but the bulk of the ashes were cold. I knew the site of the hut and the hill behind it up which I had rushed, and in the flickering glow the eyes of the rats still shone with a sort of phosphorescence. The commissary spoke a word to the officer, and he cried:

"Halt!"

The soldiers were ordered to spread around and watch, and then we commenced to examine the ruins. The commissary himself began to lift away the charred boards and rubbish. These the soldiers took and piled together. Presently he started back, then bent down and rising beckoned me.

"See!" he said.

It was a gruesome sight. There lay a skeleton face downwards, a woman by the lines—an old woman by the coarse fibre of the bone. Between the ribs rose a long spike-like dagger made from a butcher's sharpening knife, its keen point buried in the spine.

"You will observe," said the commissary to the officer and to me as he took out his note book, "that the woman must have fallen on her dagger. The rats are many here—see their eyes glistening among that heap of bones—and you will also notice"—I shuddered as he placed his hand on the skeleton—"that but little time was lost by them, for the bones are scarcely cold!"

There was no other sign of anyone near, living or dead; and so deploying again into line the soldiers passed on. Presently we came to the hut made of the old wardrobe. We approached. In five of the six compartments was an old man sleeping—sleeping so soundly that even the glare of the lanterns did not wake them. Old and grim and grizzled they looked, with their gaunt, wrinkled, bronzed faces and their white moustaches.

The officer called out harshly and loudly a word of command, and in an instant each one of them was on his feet before us and standing at "attention!"

"What do you here?"

"We sleep," was the answer.

"Where are the other chiffoniers?" asked the commissary.

"Gone to work."

"And you?"

"We are on guard!"

"Peste!" laughed the officer grimly, as he looked at the old men one after the other in the face and added with cool deliberate cruelty, "Asleep on duty! Is this the manner of the Old Guard? No wonder, then, a Waterloo!"

By the gleam of the lantern I saw the grim old faces grow deadly pale, and almost shuddered at the look in the eyes of the old men as the laugh of the soldiers echoed the grim pleasantry of the officer.

I felt in that moment that I was in some measure avenged.

For a moment they looked as if they would throw themselves on the taunter, but years of their life had schooled them and they remained still.

"You are but five," said the commissary; "where is the sixth?" The answer came with a grim chuckle.

"He is there!" and the speaker pointed to the bottom of the wardrobe. "He died last night. You won't find much of him. The burial of the rats is quick!"

The commissary stooped and looked in. Then he turned to the officer and said calmly:

"We may as well go back. No trace here now; nothing to prove that man was the one wounded by your soldiers' bullets! Probably they murdered him to cover up the trace. See!" again he stooped and placed his hands on the skeleton. "The rats work quickly and they are many. These bones are warm!"

I shuddered, and so did many more of those around me.

"Form!" said the officer, and so in marching order, with the lanterns swinging in front and the manacled veterans in the midst, with steady tramp we took ourselves out of the dust heaps and turned backward to the fortress of Bicetre.

MY YEAR OF PROBATION HAS long since ended, and Alice is my wife. But when I look back upon that trying twelvemonth one of the most vivid incidents that memory recalls is that associated with my visit to the City of Dust.

End

# A Dream of Red Hands

The first opinion given to me regarding Jacob Settle was a simple descriptive statement. "He's a down-in-the-mouth chap": but I found that it embodied the thoughts and ideas of all his fellow-workmen. There was in the phrase a certain easy tolerance, an absence of positive feeling of any kind, rather than any complete opinion, which marked pretty accurately the man's place in public esteem. Still, there was some dissimilarity between this and his appearance which unconsciously set me thinking, and by degrees, as I saw more of the place and the workmen, I came to have a special interest in him. He was, I found, forever doing kindnesses, not involving money expenses beyond his humble means, but in the manifold ways of forethought and forbearance and self-repression which are of the truer charities of life. Women and children trusted him implicitly, though, strangely enough, he rather shunned them, except when anyone was sick, and then he made his appearance to help if he could, timidly and awkwardly. He led a very solitary life, keeping house by himself in a tiny cottage, or rather hut, of one room, far on the edge of the moorland. His existence seemed so sad and solitary that I wished to cheer it up, and for the purpose took the occasion when we had both been sitting up with a child, injured by me through accident, to offer to lend him books. He gladly accepted, and as we parted in the grey of the dawn I felt that something of mutual confidence had been established between us.

The books were always most carefully and punctually returned, and in time Jacob Settle and I became quite friends. Once or twice as I crossed the moorland on Sundays I looked in on him; but on such occasions he was shy and ill at ease so that I felt diffident about calling to see him. He would never under any circumstances come into my own lodgings.

One Sunday afternoon, I was coming back from a long walk beyond the moor, and as I passed Settle's cottage stopped at the door to say "how do you do?" to him. As the door was shut, I thought that he was out, and merely knocked for form's sake, or through habit, not expecting to get any answer. To my surprise, I heard a feeble voice from within, though what was said I could not hear. I entered at once, and found Jacob lying half-dressed upon his bed. He was as pale as death, and the sweat was simply rolling off his face. His hands were unconsciously gripping the bed-clothes as a drowning man holds on to whatever he may grasp. As I came in he half arose, with a wild, hunted look in his eyes, which were wide open and staring, as though something of horror had come before him; but when he recognised me he sank back on the couch with a smothered sob of relief and closed his eyes. I stood by him for a while, quiet a minute or two, while he gasped. Then he opened his eyes and looked at me, but with such a despairing, woeful expression that, as I am a living man, I would have rather seen that frozen look of horror. I sat down beside him and asked after his health. For a while he would not answer me except to say that he was not ill; but then, after scrutinising me closely, he half arose on his elbow and said—

"I thank you kindly, sir, but I'm simply telling you the truth. I am not ill, as men call it, though God knows whether there be not worse sicknesses than doctors know of. I'll tell you, as you are so kind, but I trust that you won't even mention such a think to a living soul, for it might work me more and greater woe. I am suffering from a bad dream."

"A bad dream!" I said, hoping to cheer him; "but dreams pass away with the light—even with waking." There I stopped, for before he spoke I saw the answer in his desolate look round the little place.

"No! no! that's all well for people that live in comfort and with those they love around them. It is a thousand times worse for those who live alone and have to do so. What cheer is there for me, waking here in the silence of the night, with the wide moor around me full of voices and full of faces that make my waking a worse dream than my sleep? Ah, young sir, you have no past that can send its legions to people the darkness and the empty space, and I pray the good God that you may never have! As he spoke, there was such an almost irresistible gravity of conviction in his manner that I abandoned my remonstrance about his solitary life. I felt that I was in the presence of some secret influence which I could not fathom. To my relief, for I knew not what to say, he went on—

"Two nights past have I dreamed it. It was hard enough the first night, but I came through it. Last night the expectation was in itself almost worse than the dream—until the dream came, and then it swept away every remembrance of lesser pain. I stayed awake till just before the dawn, and then it came again, and ever since I have been in such an agony as I am sure the dying feel, and with it all the dread of tonight." Before he had got to the end of the sentence my mind was made up, and I felt that I could speak to him more cheerfully.

"Try and get to sleep early tonight—in fact, before the evening has passed away. The sleep will refresh you, and I promise you there will not be any bad dreams after tonight." He shook his head hopelessly, so I sat a little longer and then left him.

When I got home I made my arrangements for the night, for I had made up my mind to share Jacob Settle's lonely vigil in his cottage on the moor. I judged that if he got to sleep before sunset he would wake well before midnight, and so, just as the bells of the city were striking eleven, I stood opposite his door armed with a bag, in which were my supper, and extra large flask, a couple of candles, and a book. The moonlight was bright, and flooded the whole moor, till it was almost as light as day; but ever and anon black clouds drove across the sky, and made a darkness which by comparison seemed almost tangible. I opened the door softly, and entered without waking Jacob, who lay asleep with his white face upward. He was still, and again bathed it sweat. I tried to imagine what visions were passing before those closed eyes which could bring with them the misery and woe which were stamped on the face, but fancy failed me, and I waited for the awakening. It came suddenly, and in a fashion which touched me to the quick, for the hollow groan that broke from the man's white lips as he half arose and sank back was manifestly the realisation or completion of some train of thought which had gone before.

"If this be dreaming," said I to myself, "then it must be based on some very terrible reality. What can have been that unhappy fact that he spoke of?"

While I thus spoke, he realised that I was with him. It struck me as strange that he had no period of that doubt as to whether dream or reality surrounded him which commonly marks an expected environment of waking men. With a positive cry of joy, he seized my hand and held it in his two wet, trembling hands, as a frightened child clings on to someone whom it loves. I tried to soothe him—

"There, there! it is all right. I have come to stay with you tonight, and together we will try to fight this evil dream." He let go my hand suddenly, and sank back on his bed and covered his eyes with his hands.

"Fight it?—the evil dream! Ah! no sir no! No mortal power can fight that dream, for it comes form God—and is burned in here"; and he beat upon his forehead. Then he went on—

It is the same dream, ever the same, and yet it grows in its power to torture me everytime it comes."

"What is the dream?" I asked, thinking that the speaking of it might give him some relief, but he shrank away from me, and after a long pause said—

"No, I had better not tell it. It may not come again."

There was manifestly something to conceal from me—something that lay behind the dream, so I answered—

"All right. I hope you have seen the last of it. But if it should come again, you will tell me, will you not? I ask, not out of curiosity, but because I think it may relieve you to speak." He answered with what I thought was almost an undue amount of solemnity—

"If it comes again, I shall tell you all."

Then I tried to get his mind away from the subject to more mundane things, so I produced supper, and made him share it with me, including the contents of the flask. After a little he braced up, and when I lit my cigar, having given him another, we smoked a full hour, and talked of many things. Little by little the comfort of his body stole over his mind, and I could see sleep laying her gentle hands on his eyelids. He felt it, too, and told me that now he felt all right, and I might safely leave him; but I told him that, right or wrong, I was going to see in the daylight. So I lit my other candle, and began to read as he fell asleep.

By degrees I got interested in my book, so interested that presently I was startled by its dropping out of my hands. I looked and saw that Jacob was still asleep, and I was rejoiced to see that there was on his face a look of unwonted happiness, while his lips seemed to move with unspoken words. Then I turned to my work again, and again woke, but this time to feel chilled to my very marrow by hearing the voice from the bed beside me—

"Not with those red hands! Never! never!" On looking at him, I found that he was still asleep. He woke, however, in an instant, and did not seem surprised to see me; there was again that strange apathy as to his surroundings. Then I said:

"Settle, tell me your dream. You may speak freely, for I shall hold your confidence sacred. While we both live I shall never mention what you may choose to tell me,"

"I said I would; but I had better tell you first what goes before the dream, that you may understand. I was a schoolmaster when I was a very young man; it was only a parish school in a little village in the West Country. No need to mention any names. Better not. I was engaged to be married to a young girl whom I loved and almost reverenced. It was the old story. While we were waiting for the time when we could afford to set up house together, another man came along. He was nearly as young as I was, and handsome, and a gentleman, with all a gentleman's attractive ways for a woman of our class. He would go fishing, and she would meet him while I was at my work in school. I reasoned with her and implored her to give him up. I offered to get married at once and go away and begin the world in a strange country; but she would not listen to anything I could say, and I could see that she was infatuated with him. Then I took it on myself to meet the man and ask him to deal well with the girl, for I thought he might mean honestly by her, so that there might be no talk or chance of talk on the part of others. I went where I should meet him with none by, and we met!" Here Jacob Settle had to pause, for something seemed to rise in his throat, and he almost gasped for breath. Then went on—

"Sir, as God is above us, there was no selfish thought in my heart that day, I loved my pretty Mabel too well to be content with a part of her love, and I had thought of my own unhappiness too often not to have come to realise that, whatever might come to her, my hope was gone. He was insolent to me—you, sir, who are a gentleman, cannot know, perhaps, how galling can be the insolence of one who is above you in station—but I bore with that. I implored him to deal well with the girl, for what might be only a pastime of an idle hour with him might be the breaking of her heart. For I never had a thought of her truth, or that the worst of harm could come to her—it was only the unhappiness to her heart I feared. But when I asked him when he intended to marry her his laughter galled me so that I lost my temper and told him that I would not stand by and see her life made unhappy. Then he grew angry too, and in his anger said such cruel things of her that then and there I swore he should not live to do her harm. God knows how it came about, for in such moments of passion it is hard to remember the steps from a word to a blow, but I found myself standing over his dead body, with my hands crimson with the blood that welled from his torn throat. We were alone and he was a stranger, with none of his kin to seek for him and murder does not always out—not all at once. His bones may be whitening still, for all I know, in the pool of the river where I left him. No one suspected his absence, or why it was, except my poor Mabel, and she dared not speak. But it was all in vain, for when I came back again after an absence of months—for I could not live in the place—I learned that her shame had come and that she had died in it. Hitherto

I had been borne up by the thought that my ill deed had saved her future, but now, when I learned that I had been too late, and that my poor love was smirched with that man's sin, I fled away with the sense of my useless guilt upon me more heavily than I could bear. Ah! Sir, you that have not done such a sin don't know what it is to carry it with you. You may think that custom makes it easy to you, but it is not so. It grows and grows with every hour, till it becomes intolerable, and with it growing, too, the feeling that you must forever stand outside Heaven. You don't know what that means, and I pray God that you never may. Ordinary men, to whom all things are possible, don't often, if ever, think of Heaven. It is a name, and nothing more, and they are content to wait and let things be, but to those who are doomed to be shut out forever you cannot think what it means, you cannot guess or measure the terrible endless longing to see the gates opened, and to be able to join the white figures within.

"And this brings me to my dream. It seemed that the portal was before me, with great gates of massive steel with bars of the thickness of a mast, rising to the very clouds, and so close that between them was just a glimpse of a crystal grotto, on whose shinning walls were figured many white-clad forms with faces radiant with joy. When I stood before the gate my heart and my soul were so full of rapture and longing that I forgot. And there stood at the gate two mighty angels with sweeping wings, and, oh! so stern of countenance. They held each in one hand a flaming sword, and in the other the latchet, which moved to and fro at their lightest touch. Nearer were figures all draped in black, with heads covered so that only the eyes were seen, and they handed to each who came white garments such as the angels wear. A low murmur came that told that all should put on their own robes, and without soil, or the angels would not pass them in, but would smite them down with the flaming swords. I was eager to don my own garment, and hurriedly threw it over me and stepped swiftly to the gate; but it moved not, and the angels, loosing the latchet, pointed to my dress, I looked down, and was aghast, for the whole robe was smeared with blood. My hands were red; they glittered with the blood that dripped form them as on that day by the river bank. And then the angels raised their flaming swords to smite me down, and the horror was complete—I awoke. Again, and again, and again, that awful dream comes to me. I never learn form the experience, I never remember, but at the beginning the hope if ever there to make the end more appalling; and I know that the dream does not come out of the common darkness where the dreams abide, but that it is sent from God as a punishment! Never, never shall I be able to pass the gate, for the soil on the angel garments must ever come from these bloody hands!"

I listened as in a spell as Jacob Settle spoke. There was something so far away in the tone of his voice—something so dreamy and mystic in the eyes that looked as if through me at some spirit beyond—something so lofty in his very diction and in such marked contrast to his workworn clothes and his poor surroundings that I wondered if the whole thing were not a dream.

We were both silent for a long time. I kept looking at the man before me in growing wonderment. Now that his confession had been made, his soul, which had been crushed to the very earth, seemed to leap back again to uprightness with some resilient force. I suppose I ought to have been horrified with his story, but, strange to say, I was not. It certainly is not pleasant to be made the recipient of the confidence of a murderer, but this poor fellow seemed to have had, not only so much provocation, but so much self-denying purpose in his deed of blood that I did not feel called upon to pass judgment upon him. My purpose was to comfort, so I spoke out with what calmness I could, for my heart was beating fast and heavily—

"You need not despair, Jacob Settle. God is very good, and his mercy is great. Live on and work on in the hope that some day you may feel that you have atoned for the past." Here I paused, for I could see that sleep, natural sleep this time, was creeping upon him. "Go to sleep," I said; "I shall watch with you here, and we shall have no more evil dreams tonight."

He made an effort to pull himself together, and answered—

"I don't know how to thank you for your goodness to me this night, but I think you had best leave me now. I'll try and sleep this out; I feel a weight off my mind since I have told you all. If there's anything of the man left in me, I must try and fight out life alone."

"I'll go tonight, as you wish it," I said; "but take my advice, and do not live in such a solitary way. Go among men and women; live among them. Share their joys and sorrows, and it will help you to forget. This solitude will make you melancholy mad."

"I will!" he answered, half unconsciously, for sleep was overmastering him.

I turned to go, and he looked after me. When I had touched the latch I dropped it, and, coming back to the bed, held out my hand. He grasped it with both his as he rose to a sitting posture, and I said my goodnight, trying to cheer him—

"Heart, man, heart! There is work in the world for you to do, Jacob Settle. You can wear those white robes yet and pass through that gate of steel!"

Then I left him.

A week after I found his cottage deserted, and on asking at the works was told that he had "gone north," no one exactly knew whither.

Two years afterwards, I was staying for a few days with my friend Dr. Munro in Glasgow. He was a busy man, and could not spare much time for going about with me, so I spent my days in excursions to the Trossachs and Loch Katrine and down the Clyde. On the second last evening of my stay I came back somewhat later than I had arranged, but found that my host was late too. The maid told me that he had been sent for to the hospital—a case of accident at the gas-works, and the dinner was postponed an hour; so telling her I would stroll down to find her master and walk back with him, I went out. At the hospital I found him washing his hands preparatory to starting for home. Casually, I asked him what his case was.

"Oh, the usual thing! A rotten rope and men's lives of no account. Two men were working in a gasometer, when the rope that held their scaffolding broke. It must have occurred just before the dinner hour, for no one noticed their absence till the men had returned. There was about seven feet of water in the gasometer, so they had a hard fight for it, poor fellows. However, one of them was alive, just alive, but we have had a hard job to pull him through. It seems that he owes his life to his mate, for I have never heard of greater heroism. They swam together while their strength lasted, but at the end they were so done up that even the lights above, and the men slung with ropes, coming down to help them, could not keep them up. But one of them stood on the bottom and held up his comrade over his head, and those few breaths made all the difference between life and death. They were a shocking sight when they were taken out, for that water is like a purple dye with the gas and the tar. The man upstairs looked as if he had been washed in blood. Ugh!"

"And the other?"

"Oh, he's worse still. But he must have been a very noble fellow. That struggle under the water must have been fearful; one can see that by the way the blood has been drawn from the extremities. It makes the idea of the Stigmata possible to look at him. Resolution like this could, you would think, do anything in the world. Ay! it might almost unbar the gates of Heaven. Look here, old man, it is not a very pleasant sight, especially just before dinner, but you are a writer, and this is an odd case. Here is something you would not like to miss, for in all human probability you will never see anything like it again." While he was speaking he had brought me into the mortuary of the hospital.

On the bier lay a body covered with a white sheet, which was wrapped close round it.

"Looks like a chrysalis, don't it? I say, Jack, if there be anything in the old myth that a soul is typified by a butterfly, well, then the one that this chrysalis sent forth was a very noble specimen and took all the sunlight on its wings. See here!" He uncovered the face. Horrible, indeed, it looked, as though stained with blood. But I knew him at once, Jacob Settle! My friend pulled the winding sheet further down.

The hands were crossed on the purple breast as they had been reverently placed by some tenderhearted person. As I saw them my heart throbbed with a great exultation, for the memory of his harrowing dream rushed across my mind. There was no stain now on those poor, brave hands, for they were blanched white as snow.

And somehow as I looked I felt that the evil dream was all over. That noble soul had won a way through the gate at last. The white robe had now no stain from the hands that had put it on.

End

# GREATER LOVE

We was just standin' here at about eleven in the evenin', an' the moon was beginnin' to rise. We could see the little patch of light growin' bigger an' bigger, just as it is now, an' we knew that before many moments the light would be up over the sea. My back was to the sea, an' Bill was leanin' agin' the handrail, just like you now.

It ain't much, sir, after all; leastwise to you; but it was, aye, an' it is, a deal to me, for it has all my life in it, such as it is. There's a deal of poetry an' story-tellin' in books; but, Lor' bless ye, if ye could see the heart right through of even such men as me, you'd have no need o' books when you wanted poetry and romance. I often think that them chaps in them don't feel a bit more nor we do when things is happenin'; it's only when they're written down that they become heroes an' martyrs, an' suchlike. Why, Bill was as big a hero as any of them. I often wished as how I could write, that I might tell all about him.

Howsumdever, if I can't write, I can talk, an' if you're not in a hurry, an'll wait till I tell you all, I'll be proud. It does me good to talk about Bill.

Well, when I turned round an' faced Bill I see his eyes with the light in 'em, an' they was glistenin'. Bill gives a big gulp, an' says to me:

"Joe, the world's a big place, big enough for you an' me to live in without quarrelin'. An', mayhap, the same God us made one woman would make another, an' we might both live an' be happy. You an' me has been comrades for long, an' God knows that, next to Mary, I'd be sad to see you die, so whatever comes, we won't quarrel or think hard of one another, sure we won't, Joe."

He put out his hand, an' I took it sudden. We held hands for a long time. I thought he was in low spirits, and I wished to cheer him, so I says:

"Why, Bill, who talks o' dyin' that's as hearty as we?"

He shook his head sadly, an' says he:

"Joe, I don't vally my life at a pin's head, an' I ain't afraid to die. For her sake or for yours—aye, even for her pleasure—I'd—No matter. Just see if I turn coward if I ever get the chance to do her a service."

Well, we stood there for a long time. Neither of us said a word, for I didn't like to speak, although I would several times have liked to ask him a question. An' then I gave up wishin' to speak, an' began to think, like him.

I thought of all the time Bill an' me had been friends an' comrades, an' how fond we were both of Mary, an' she of us. Ye see, when we was all children, the little thing took such a fancy for both of us that we couldn't help likin' her for it, and so we became, in course of time, like big brothers to her. She would come down on the shore with Bill an' me an' sit quiet all the day an' never say a word or do anything to annoy us or put us out. Sometimes we'd go out sailin', an' then she would come an' sit beside whoever was steerin' till he'd ask her to come up an' sit on his knee. Then she'd put up her little arms round his neck an' kiss him, an' would stay as quiet as a mouse till she'd have to change her place. That was the way, sir, that we both came to be so fond of her.

An', sure enough, when she began to grow up, Bill an' me wanted none other but her. An' the more she grew, the prouder we were of her, till at last we found out that we were both of us in love with her. But we never told her so, or let her see it; an' she had grown up so amongst us that she never suspected it. She said so long after.

Then Bill an' me held a kind of council about what was to be done, an' so we came to be talkin' on the bridge that night. Mary was growin' into a young woman, an' we feared that somether chap might take her fancy, if one of us didn't get her at once. Bill was very serious, far more serious than me, for I had somehow got the idea into my head as how Mary cared for me, an' as long as I felt that I couldn't feel either unhappy or downhearted.

All at once Bill's face grew brighter, an' there was a soft look in his eyes.

"Joe," he says, "whatever happens, Mary must never hang her head. The lass is tender-hearted, and she likes both of us, we know; an' as she can only love one of us, it might pain her to think that when she was marryin' one man she was leavin' a hole in the life of his comrade. So she must never know as how we both love her, if we can prevent it."

When we got that far, I began to grow uneasy. I began to distrust Bill—God forgive me for it—an' to think that maybe he was fixin' some plan for to cut me out. I must have been jealous, that was it. But I was punished for my distrust when he went on:

"Joe, old lad, we both love her an' we love each other; an' God knows I'd go away, an' willin', an' leave her to you, but who knows that mayhap she'd like me better of the two. Women is queer creatures in lettin' a fellow see their hearts till they see his first."

Then he stayed quiet, an' so I says to him:

"How are we to manage to do that, Bill? If we tell her, won't she know that we both love her? An' you said you wouldn't like her to do that."

"That's just what I was thinkin' of," he says. "An' I see how we may do it. One of us must go to her an' find out if she loves him, an' if she does, the other will say nothin'."

I felt feared, so I asked him:

"Who is to go, Bill?"

He came over an' took me by the shoulder, an' says he:

"Joe, so far as I can see, the lass cares for you the most; you must go first an' find out."

I tried not to appear joyful, an' I says:

"Bill, that isn't fair; whoever goes first has the best chance. Why won't you go, or why not draw lots?" I've had a many hard tussles in my time, both with men an' things, but I never had such a struggle as I had to say them words.

"Joe," says Bill, "you must do all you can to win her yourself, an' don't let any thoughts of me hinder you. I'll be best pleased by seein' her an' you happy, if so be she loves you." Then he stood up from leaning on the rail, an' says he:

"Joe, give me your hand before we go, an' mind, I charge you on your honor as a man, never while I'm livin', to let Mary know as how I loved her, in case she chooses you." So I promised. I felt Bill's hand grip like a vice, an' then we turned an' walked away home an' never spoke another word that night, either of us.

I didn't sleep much that night, and when it began to get to mornin' I got up an' went down to the sea an' had a swim, an' that freshened me up somewhat. I wasn't much of a swimmer myself, but I could manage to keep myself up pretty well. That was the point where I envied Bill most of all. He was the finest swimmer I ever see. He did a many things well, an' no lad in this county could come near him in anything he chose to do; but in swimmin' none could come anigh him at all. An' many's the time it stood to others as well as himself.

Well, when I had had my bathe, I went up toward Mary's home, an' found myself goin' in to ask her straight off to marry me. Then I began to think it was too early for Mary to be up; so I stole away on tiptoe, an' walked round the house. Then I thought I'd go an' look up Bill, an' came anigh his house. But when I came to the door, as I didn't like to knock, I thought I'd speer in, an' see if he was asleep. So I stole to the window an' looked in.

I never shall forget to my dyin' day what I saw then. I wasn't a bad fellow, thank God, at anytime, but I couldn't be a bad fellow or do anything I thought very wrong after that. There was Bill, just as I had left him the night before. He had never changed his clothes, an' the candle was flickerin' down in the socket, unheeded. He was kneelin' down by the bed, with his arms stretched out before him, an' his face down on the quilt. That was thirty-seven year ago, but it seems like yesterday. I thought at first he was sleepin', but I saw from a movement he made that he was awake. So I stole away, guiltylike, an' went down an' stood beside the sea. I took off my hat, an' let the wind blow about my forehead, for somehow it felt burnin', an' I looked out over the sea for long. Somehow my heart beat like as if it was lead, an' I felt half choked. I dunno how long I would have stayed there only for Bill. He came behind me, and put his hand on my shoulder and said, sudden:

"Why, Joe, what are you doin' here?"

I turned, startled, an' saw that he was smilin'. I was so thunderstruck at seein' the change, that for a moment I said nothin'. He says to me again:

"Joe, I thought you'd have more to do than think of eatin' this mornin', an' it's bad to court on an empty stomach! So come up to my place; I've got breakfast for the both of us."

I couldn't realize that this hearty chap was the man I saw prayin' after the long night. I looked at him keenly, but could see no sign of his actin' a part in his face. He was gayer an' livelier than ever, an' in such good spirits that he made me gay, too. I couldn't forget how I'd seen him a short while since; but I laid the thought by, an' didn't let it trouble me. I went up to his place. It was clean an' tidy as ever, an' the breakfast was ready. He made me eat some, an' when I was done, he brushed me up an' tidied me, an' says he:

"Go in an' win, old lad. God bless ye!" I went away toward Mary's house; but before I lost sight of Bill, I turned, an' he waved his hand to me with a kind smile an' went in an' shut the door.

I went on toward Mary's; but the farther I went the slower I got. An' when I got to the garden gate I stopped altogether. I stayed moonin' about there for a while, till at last Mary sees me an' comes out. I don't know how to tell you what took place then. I ain't more bashfuller than a man of my years ought to be, but somehow it comes rough on a man to tell this kind of thing. Oh, no; it ain't that I don't remember it all; for I do, well. But, ye see—ye won't laugh at me? I know'd ye wouldn't;

I ax yer pardon. Well, to prove it to ye, I'll say what I never said yet to mortal, except Mary—an' that only once.

Mary comes out to me, runnin' like a little girl, with her face all dimplin' over with pleasure, an' she says:

"Why, Joe, what brings you here at this hour? Come in, Joe! Mother, here's Joe! Have you had your breakfast, Joe? Come in!"

I felt that I would never have courage to speak out before her mother if I went into the cottage, so I stayed beside the gate an' let her talk on. As I looked at her then, I could hardly believe what I was come for; it seemed like doin' something wrong to try to change her from what she was. She looked so lovely an' so bright that it seemed a pity ever to wish her to be aught else—even my own wife. An', beside, the thought came an' hit me hard, that mayhap she wouldn't have me, after all. I tried to think on that; but, Lor' bless ye, I couldn't. It seemed somethin' so terrible that I couldn't think it. However, I stood still, sayin' nothin', till she began to notice. I wasn't used to be sheepish before Mary or anyone else; so when she had done her talkin' she looked at me sudden, an' then her eyes fell, an', after a moment, she blushed up to the roots of her hair an' says:

"Joe, what's the matter with you? You don't look as usual."

I blurted out all in a moment:

"No, Mary; nor I ain't the same as usual, for I'm in trouble."

She came close to me before I could say anymore—she wasn't lookin' down or blushin' then—an' she says:

"Oh, Joe, I'm sorry for that." An' she put her arm on my shoulder. Then she went on, in a kind o' tender voice:

"Did you tell Bill?"

"Yes," I says.

"And what did he say?"

"He told me to come to you!"

"To me, Joe?" she says, an' looked puzzled.

"Yes," I says, in despair like. "I'm in trouble, Mary, for I want you to marry me."

"Oh, Joe!" she says, an' drew away a little. Then she says to me, with a queer look on her face:

"Joe, run an' tell Bill I want to see him—to come as soon as he can."

Well, them words went through me like so many knives, an' if ever I could have hated Bill, it would have been then. What could she want Bill for, I thinks to myself, but to find out if he loves her, too—an' to have him? I thinks how mad a woman would be to have me when she could get a man like Bill. I was afraid to say anything, so I set off smart for him, for I feared I wouldn't be able to tell him if I didn't go at once. I tried not to think while I was goin' down the road; but I couldn't get her words out of my head. They seemed to keep time with my feet, an' I heard them over an' over again:

"Tell—Bill—I—want—to—see—him! Tell—Bill—I—want—to—see—him!"

At last I got to the house, an' found Bill inside, mendin' a net that hung agin' the wall. He turned round quickly when I came in, an' his heart began to beat so hard that I could see it thumpin' inside his guernsey. He saw I wasn't lookin' pleased, so he came near an' put his two hands on my shoulders an' looked me in the face.

"What cheer, Joe?" he says, an' I could see that he was tryin' to control himself. When I told him the message, he began tremblin' all over, an' got as white as a sheet. Then he says to me in a thick kind o' voice:

"Joe, how did she look when she said it?"

I tried to tell him, an' asked him to hurry on.

"In a minute," says he, an' went into the other room.

When he came back I turned round, expectin' to see him got up a bit; but there he was just as he went in, in his old workin' clothes. But he was quiet lookin', an' had a smile on his face.

"Bill, old lad," I says, "aren't ye goin' to tidy up a bit? Mayhap Mary'd like to see ye neat."

"No," he says; "I'll go as I am. If it be as it may be, she won't like me none the worse for comin' quick; an' if it don't be—Come on, Joe, an' don't keep her waitin'."

Well, we walked up the road without sayin' a word. When we came in sight of Mary's cottage it seemed darker to me than it had been.

Mary came out of the gate to meet us, an' when she spoke to Bill I dropped behind. They two went into the arbor that we had built for her. They sat talkin' for a few minutes—I could see them through the hedge—an' at last I saw Bill bend down his head an' kiss her. She put her arms round his neck an' kissed him. An' at that the whole of the light seemed to go out of the sky, an' I wished I was dead.

I would have gone away, but I could hardly stir. I leaned up against the hedge, an' didn't mind anymore till I heard Bill's voice callin' me. I came in at the gate, puttin' on as good a face as I could, an' came into the arbor.

Bill an' Mary was standin' up, an' Bill's face looked beamin', while Mary's was red as a rose.

Bill beckoned me over, an' when I came near, he says:

"Well, Mary, shall I tell him now?"

"Yes, Bill," she says, in a kind of a whisper; so he says to me:

"Joe, I give her to you! She wouldn't let none do it but me; for she says she loves me like as a brother. Take her, Joe, an' love her well, an' God bless ye both!"

He put her in my arms, an' she clung to me.

I was bewildered, an' could hardly see; but when I came to look about there was Mary in my arms, with her face buried in my breast, an' her arms round my neck.

Bill was makin' down the road, upright an' steady as ever. Even then, for a moment, I couldn't think of Mary, for my thoughts went back to when I saw Bill kneelin' beside his bed, with his arms stretched out, an' I felt—if you'll believe me—more sorrow than joy. I know now that Bill had wrestled with the devil that night, an' threw him, if ever a man did. Poor Bill! Poor Bill!

I suppose I needn't tell you what Mary an' me said? It wouldn't sound much, at any rate, altho' it pleased us. When I felt that she loved me I forgot even Bill, an' we was happier than tongue could tell.

Well, the time went on for a month or two, an' we was thinkin' of gettin' married soon. I was gettin' my cottage ready an' spendin' some of the money I had saved to make it bright for Mary. Bill worked with me early an' late, but it wasn't only his time that he gave to me. He would often go into the town to buy the things I wanted, an' I'm sure he never got them for what he told me. I said nothin', for I knew that it would only hurt him, an' it was little enough that I could do for Bill to let him help if he chose. I used to watch him to see if he wasn't unhappy, but I never seed a sign of sorrow on him. He always looked happy an' bright, an' he worked harder than ever, an' was kinder to all around him. I knew he didn't forget—for how could he forget Mary?—an' I feared at times lest he might fret in secret. But I never seed him grieve. I could hardly imagine, when I would think on it, how Mary came to take me or love me when Bill was nigh her.

Well, the time wasn't long goin' by, for we was happy, an' had all our lives before us, an', at length, the day came round before we was to be married. It was Easter Sunday we was to be married on, an' all the people as knew Mary an' me—an' that was all the village—was goin' to have a grand holiday. We was to go an' have a feast out on the island, an' we was gettin' the boats cleaned an' nice an' smart for the occasion. In coorse, everybody had to bring their own inners; but we was to join them all together an' make a grand feast. We had got a cask o' beer, an' we was to have great doin's an' a dance on the grass. There's the finest sod for dancin' in the countryside out yonder on the island, an' we'd got Mike Wheeler to bring his fiddle, with an extra set of strings. We weren't to come home till evenin' when the tide turned, an' then we would have a race home.

Well, Bill an' me, we both took tea at Mary's house that evenin', an' when we came home Bill asked me to go into his house for awhile an' have a quiet talk. We lit our pipes, drew up our chairs, an' sat down by the fire an' puffed away, without sayin' a word for sometime, an' then Bill says to me:

"Well, Joe, there won't be a man in the church tomorrow that won't envy you—except myself."

I thought of him kneelin' down by the bedside that mornin' when he says that, so I thought to tell him. I put down my pipe an' came an' put my arms on his shoulder, as I used to do when we was boys together, an' told him all I knew. He just shook hands with me, an' says he:

"Joe, it was a hard fight, but, thank God, I won. I've crushed out all the old love now. Why, lad, tomorrow she'll be your wife, an' I'll care for her no more than any other woman—as a sweetheart, I mean, for I'm a brother to her now as long as we live—an' to you, Joe. It ain't that I think less of her, for I'd walk into the fire for her this minute, but—I can't explain it, Joe. You know what I mean."

"Bill," I says, "you've been a true friend to me an' Mary, an' I hope we'll always be able to show how much we both love you. May God judge me hard when I die if ever I have a hard thought of you as long as I live!"

We said no more after that. I went out, but came back in a minute to tell Bill to be sure to come an' wake me if he was up first; but when I was passin' the window I see him hangin' a coat up over it. It wasn't that he thought I'd spy on him again that he did that. I saw that in his face; but he feared I might see him again somehow, and that it might pain me.

Well, I woke in the mornin' as soon as it was daylight, an' went down an' had a swim, an' then came home an' brushed my new clothes an' laid out the shirt that Mary had worked for me herself, an' washed as white as snow. Then Bill came down to me. He was to take his breakfast with me that mornin', an' he came all dressed for the weddin' in a new suit of clothes. He was a real handsome, fine fellow at anytime, but he looked like a gentleman that mornin'. Then I thought that Mary must have done right to choose a laborin' man like me rather than a chap like Bill, that was above all of us, except in his heart.

We went off to the church an' waited till Mary an' her mother came. All the people was there outside the porch, an' some of the gentlefolks was inside. The squire's family was in their pew, for, ye see, Mary was a favorite with them all, an' they came early to church to see her married. I felt very solemn then, but I could hardly feel as how Mary was goin' to marry me. There she was, as lovely as an angel, an' blushin' like a rose. I said my "I will" in a low voice, for it seemed awkward to me to say it loud; but Mary said hers out in a clear, sweet voice, an' then the parson blessed us, an' spoke to us so solemn that we both cried, an' Mary nestled up close to me. When it came to kiss the bride, Bill was first, an' claimed the kiss, so the other lads had to give up. Bill bent down an' took her pretty face between his two hands an' kissed her on the forehead.

Agin the weddin' was over, it was time for service, so we all went to our seats—an' I never felt solemner in my life than I did then; nor did Mary, either.

When the service was over we all came out; an' the people stood by on both sides to let Mary an' me walk down the churchyard together an' go first out of the gate.

We all went down to the beach, where the boats was ready on the shore. Some of them was freshly painted, an' a couple had bright ribbons tied about them. Bill's boat was the one that Mary an' me was to go in, an' Bill himself was to pull stroke oar in her. He had got for a crew three of the young fellows we knew best, an' who was the cracks at rowin', an' we was determined to race all the other boats to the island. The lads had all run on before us, an' when we came down to the beach the boats was all ready, an' the baskets with the dinner put in them, so we all got on board, an' off we started.

Mary an' me, we held the rudder together, an' Bill an' his lads bent to their oars, an' away we flew, an' in a quarter of an hour came to the island, leading the others by a hundred yards. We all got out, an' the lads carried up the baskets to the slope up yonder, where you see the moonlight shine on the island, where there was a fine, level place on the edge of the cliff.

The grass there was short an' as smooth as a table; an' when you stood on the edge of the cliff the water was straight below you, for the rock went sheer some forty feet. Mary an' me stood there on the edge while the lads an' the girls got ready the feast, for they wouldn't let us put hand to anything; an' we looked at the water hurryin' by under us. The tide had turned, an' the water was runnin' like a mill race down away past the island, an' runnin' straight away for the head off there as far as you can see. The currents is very contrary here, so you'd better not get caught in them when you're sailin' or swimmin'.

We all sat down, an' if we didn't enjoy our dinner, all of us, it was a queer thing; an' after dinner was over the girls insisted on havin' a dance. We got the things all cleared off an' danced away for sometime, an' then someone proposed blind man's buff. One young fellow was blinded, an' we all stood round; an' then the fun began. The young chap—Mark Somers by name—used to make wild rushes to try an' get someone, an' then the girls yelled out, an' they all scurried away as quick as they could, an' the fun grew greater an' greater. At last he made a dive over to the place where Mary was standin' near the brink of the cliff. We all yelled to her to take care where she was goin'; but I suppose she thought it was merely our fun, for she laughed an' screamed out like the others—an' stepped backward. Before anyone could stop her, she went over the edge of the cliff an' disappeared. I was sittin' up on a rock, an' when I saw her fall over the edge I gave a cry that you might have heard a mile away an' jumped down an' ran across the grass.

But a better man than me was there before me. Bill had pulled off his jacket an' kicked off his shoes, an' was at the edge before me. Before he jumped, he cried out:

"Joe, run for the boats, quick! I'll keep her up till you come. I can swim stronger nor you."

I didn't wait a second, but ran down to where the boats was drawn up on the beach. Some of the chaps came with me as hard as they could run, an' we shoved down the nearest boat. But in spite of all our efforts—an' we was so mad with excitement that not one of us but had the strength of ten—it took us a couple of minutes to get out fair on the water.

Well, when we was fair started I pulled so hard that I broke my oar, an' we had to stop to get another; an' then we had to row all the way round the spur of the rocks out there before we could even see whereabout Mary an' Bill should be. The men an' women on the rocks screamed out to us an' pointed in their direction, an' the boat flew along at every stroke. But the current was mortal strong, an' they had been for nigh five minutes in the water before we caught sight of them. An' it seemed to me to be years before we came anigh them at all. Mary was weighed down with her clothes, an' Bill with his; an', in spite of what a swimmer I knew Bill was, I feared lest we should come too late.

At last we began to close on them. I could see over my shoulder as we rowed. I could only see Mary's face, but that was beacon enough for me. I called to one of the men to slip into my place an' row, an' he did, an' I got out into the bows. There was Mary with her face all white an' her eyes closed, as if she was dead; her hair was all draggin' in the water, an' as the current rolled her along, her dress moved as if it was some strange fish under the water. I could see othin' of Bill; but I hadn't need to think, for I knew that where Mary was there was Bill somewhere anigh to her. When we came nearer I saw where Bill was.

Look here, he was down under the water, an' with his last breath he was keepin' her afloat till we came. I saw his two hands rise up out of the water, holdin' her up by the hair; but that was all. Many's the time since then that, in spite of all I loved Mary, I was tempted to be cross with her—for we laborin' men is only rough folk, after all, an' we have a deal o' hardship to bear at times. But whenever I was tempted to say a hard word, or even to think hard of her, them two hands of Bill's seemed to rise up between me an' her, and I could no more think or say a hard word than I could stand quiet an' see another man strike her. An' I wouldn't be like for to do that!

Well, we took them into the boat an' came home. Mary recovered, for she had only had the shock of her fall; but when we took in Bill, it was only—

He kept his word that he spoke to me that night; he gave up his life for hers! You'll see that on his tomb in the churchyard that we all put up to him:

> "Greater Love Hath No Man Than This:
> That a Man Shall Give Up His Life For His Friend."

There's no more left like Bill. An' Mary thinks it, too, as well as me.

# A Note About the Author

Bram Stoker (1847–1912) was an Irish novelist. Born in Dublin, Stoker suffered from an unknown illness as a young boy before entering school at the age of seven. He would later remark that the time he spent bedridden enabled him to cultivate his imagination, contributing to his later success as a writer. He attended Trinity College, Dublin from 1864, graduating with a BA before returning to obtain an MA in 1875. After university, he worked as a theatre critic, writing a positive review of acclaimed Victorian actor Henry Irving's production of *Hamlet* that would spark a lifelong friendship and working relationship between them. In 1878, Stoker married Florence Balcombe before moving to London, where he would work for the next 27 years as business manager of Irving's influential Lyceum Theatre. Between his work in London and travels abroad with Irving, Stoker befriended such artists as Oscar Wilde, Walt Whitman, Hall Caine, James Abbott McNeill Whistler, and Sir Arthur Conan Doyle. In 1895, having published several works of fiction and nonfiction, Stoker began writing his masterpiece *Dracula* (1897) while vacationing at the Kilmarnock Arms Hotel in Cruden Bay, Scotland. Stoker continued to write fiction for the rest of his life, achieving moderate success as a novelist. Known more for his association with London theatre during his life, his reputation as an artist has grown since his death, aided in part by film and television adaptations of *Dracula*, the enduring popularity of the horror genre, and abundant interest in his work from readers and scholars around the world.

# A Note from the Publisher

Spanning many genres, from non-fiction essays to literature classics to children's books and lyric poetry, Mint Edition books showcase the master works of our time in a modern new package. The text is freshly typeset, is clean and easy to read, and features a new note about the author in each volume. Many books also include exclusive new introductory material. Every book boasts a striking new cover, which makes it as appropriate for collecting as it is for gift giving. Mint Edition books are only printed when a reader orders them, so natural resources are not wasted. We're proud that our books are never manufactured in excess and exist only in the exact quantity they need to be read and enjoyed. To learn more and view our library, go to minteditionbooks.com

# bookfinity & ◳ MINT EDITIONS

Enjoy more of your favorite classics with Bookfinity,
a new search and discovery experience for readers.
With Bookfinity, you can discover more vintage
literature for your collection, find your Reader Type,
track books you've read or want to read,
and add reviews to your favorite books.
Visit www.bookfinity.com, and click on
Take the Quiz to get started.

Don't forget to follow us
@bookfinityofficial and @mint_editions